D1412548

Reading Irish-American Fiction

READING IRISH-AMERICAN FICTION

THE HYPHENATED SELF

MARGARET HALLISSY

palgrave
macmillan

READING IRISH-AMERICAN FICTION
© Margaret Hallissy, 2006.

First published in 2006 by
PALGRAVE MACMILLAN™
175 Fifth Avenue, New York, N.Y. 10010 and
Houndmills, Basingstoke, Hampshire, England RG21 6XS
Companies and representatives throughout the world.

PALGRAVE MACMILLAN is the global academic imprint of the Palgrave Macmillan division of St. Martin's Press, LLC and of Palgrave Macmillan Ltd. Macmillan® is a registered trademark in the United States, United Kingdom and other countries. Palgrave is a registered trademark in the European Union and other countries.

ISBN 1–4039–7090–4

Library of Congress Cataloging-in-Publication Data

Hallissy, Margaret.
    Reading Irish-American fiction : the hyphenated self / by Margaret Hallissy.
        p. cm.
    Includes bibliographical references and index.
    ISBN 1–4039–7090–4 (alk paper)
        1. American fiction—Irish-American authors—History and criticism.
    2. Irish-Americans—Intellectual life. 3. Irish-Americans in literature.
    I. Title.

PS153.178H35 2006
813.009'89165—dc22   2005051333

A catalogue record for this book is available from the British Library.

Design by Newgen Imaging Systems (P) Ltd., Chennai, India.

First edition: March 2006

10 9 8 7 6 5 4 3 2 1

Printed in the United States of America.

For Grace and Raymond Duggan
on the other side

Contents

ACKNOWLEDGMENTS

This book would not have been possible without the institutional support of the C.W. Post Campus of Long Island University. In addition to providing research time and sabbatical leave, the university's flexible course-scheduling policy allows for a faculty member's research interests to be incorporated into the curriculum in timely fashion. The dean of the College of Arts and Sciences, Dr. Katherine Hill-Miller, has provided encouragement and advice at crucial points in the development of the manuscript. The Chair of the English Department, Dr. Edmund Miller, has been as ever a supportive colleague. He has scheduled Irish- and Irish-American fiction courses to help me develop my thinking on the material in this book, and he is always available with a fund of information. Dr. Joan Digby, director of the Honors Program, has enabled me to present Irish- and Irish-American writers to the university's most talented students in the form of courses, tutorials, and theses. Dr. Kay Sato, director of the Hutton House Lecture Series, supported my research by adding my lectures to her offerings. The writer of a book like this benefits greatly from students' insights, and so I thank my students in my Irish- and Irish-American fiction courses for the comments and questions that teach the teacher.

My husband Jerry and my daughter Megan have indulged my obsession with things Irish by undertaking journeys to Ireland that have been far more successful than those of the American characters in these novels. My daughters Maria Casey and Jennifer Hallissy have provided cheerleading, computer troubleshooting, and editorial advice. My friend Dr. Jean E. Fisher has been exactly the sort of reader I envision for this book. Intelligent, enthusiastic, and a fellow Irish-American, she has kindly read all five novels and the manuscript in draft, providing helpful insights. To all, many thanks.

Preface

Connections and Separations

There are few real Irish people in the United States. They know little about authentic Irish culture, and care less. The Irish American is a victim of cultural disintegration, as much so as the Mayan Indian. We have to go back to the beginning, to learn again what it means to be Irish.

—Brian Heron

I am Irish and Irish Americans always irritate me. They pretend to be Irish when in fact they are Americans through and through.

—Bob Geldof

The tricksy tiny hyphen . . . is used quite distinctly to connect (or separate) individual words.

—Lynne Truss

When I was growing up in the 1950s, in New York's borough of Queens, in St. Patrick's parish (the church's administrative grid still serving then as our global positioning system), the question of national origins often came up. At such times, my mother, Grace Duggan, would assert that we were "Irish-*American*"—the stress in her voice, accompanied by a nod of her head and a just-perceptible squaring of her shoulders, falling decisively on the latter element of the term. In that little apartment, the only sign of the "Irish" in Irish-American was a shillelagh, said to have been brought from Ireland by my father Raymond's father Frank. Aside from the shillelagh, nothing in the apartment attested to the Irish background of its three inhabitants. Catholicism was everywhere—prayer cards, rosaries, crucifixes, a holy water font at the front door—but Irishness, nowhere. No books about Ireland were read, no Irish music was played, nothing remotely Celtic decorated the walls, or, in the form of jewelry or clothing, ourselves. Neither of my parents had been to Ireland or expressed any desire to do so; neither had any specifically Irish interests or were affiliated with any Irish groups; neither celebrated St. Patrick's Day in any way other than watching the parade on television, which was almost unavoidable if television was to be watched at all, given the few channels available in those days.

Despite or perhaps because of being unacknowledged, however, Irishness permeated every aspect of our lives: in the perceived necessity immediately to identify by nationality anyone not clearly Irish; in the tendency to separate ourselves, psychologically if not physically, from other ethnic groups; in the distrust of those others, whose ways were not our ways; in the belief that Irish Catholics, and only Irish Catholics, were proper neighbors or friends or schoolmates or professional advisors, or, most emphatically, prospective mates. It is no coincidence that the derogatory adjective *parochial* derives from the same linguistic roots as the noun *parish* (the Greek root, *paroikos*, is most relevant, as it means "near the house"). In all possible ways we young Irish-American Catholics were encouraged to stay home, to remain within the parish. In subtle and not-so-subtle ways, we were taught, not to hate, but to be wary of those outside the parish; even, in the case of the other dominant Catholic ethnic group of the time and place, the Italians, to distrust some of those within it.

Much of this keeping-ourselves-to-ourselves behavior was designed to preserve our Catholic faith from what we believed were imminent onslaughts of proselytizers and unbelievers, and was acknowledged as such. But the matter of preserving our Irishness was more ambiguously presented. Many of the sisters who taught in St. Patrick's School must have been of Irish background, since many Irish women were members of the religious orders that staffed the Catholic schools at the time. But their ethnicity was concealed behind their religious names, elegant and Latinate: Sister Maria Incarnata, Sister Mary Immaculata. In school, St. Patrick's Day was celebrated enthusiastically, as one would expect; we children were invited to hearken back to the days of the Kerry dancers and to cut out construction-paper shamrocks. This flurry of Hibernian activity, which of course included all the students, might have occurred merely because our school was named after the saint; I do not recall any sense that I, personally, had any more special connection to the songs, the dances, the shamrocks than my Italian- and German-American classmates. At home, being Irish was conveyed to me indirectly, in a variety of baffling customs, and in unusual turns of phrase in speech. Only much later and after both my parents were dead was I able to identify some of these as distinctly Irish, taught to my Irish-*American* parents by their Irish parents, and conveyed without explanation to American me. Irishness was not so much discussed as assumed to be the norm from which others deviated.

But the lives of some of those others, especially our Italian neighbors, seemed better to me than ours was. A major area of conflict in my household centered around food. Unlike our Italian neighbors, whose food rituals (at least as seen from the outside) seemed gregarious and celebratory, my family seemed to experience the preparation and consumption of food as a painful duty best done in private. Since my mother was in charge of food purchases and preparation, her idiosyncrasies shaped our diet. A pudgy adolescent, I found baffling my mother's continual urging that I eat even more than my already hearty appetite demanded. As her authority on nutritional matters, she quoted the words of her own mother, Margaret Flynn Dunn: " 'Eat enough for tomorrow.' " I did not take my late grandmother's words as seriously as my mother wished, however. With what I saw as irrefutable logic, I would explain how, if I ate enough today for tomorrow, and then enough tomorrow for that day's tomorrow, I'd become even plumper than I was. My mother would turn from me in silent fury. Despite my attempts to show her the error of her ways, she persisted in other food habits that irritated me: saving tiny portions of leftovers, to be joylessly ingested long after they had lost any possible gustatory appeal; insisting that every such scrap be consumed, past the point of satiety. "We have to finish this up," she would sigh. I had no patience with this penitential approach to cuisine. Why could we not do as our neighbors did, gather happily around a table groaning with Italian food, not only delicious but enthusiastically prepared?

Years later, reading Frank McCourt's *Angela's Ashes*, like many another Irish-American, I suspect, I had an epiphany worthy of a character in the fiction of James Joyce. Mine was a food epiphany. The triggering episode was the one in which the child Frank gives the lone raisin in his raisin bun to his even hungrier classmate Paddy Clohessy:

> I wanted the raisin for myself but I saw Paddy Clohessy standing in the corner with no shoes and the room was freezing and he was shivering . . . so I walked over and gave Paddy the raisin because I didn't know what else to do and all the boys yelled that I was a fool and a feckin' eejit and I'd regret the day and after I handed the raisin to Paddy I longed for it but it was too late now. . . .[1]

At last, thanks to Frank McCourt, I understood what anxiety lay behind my mother's saving bits and scraps of food almost as small as this raisin. While she had been born in New York in 1905, her mother was born in County Waterford in 1869, only fifteen years or so, depending on what date one accepts for its ending, after the Great Famine. My great-grandparents, therefore, were Famine survivors; and their daughter Margaret, my grandmother, was eventually left a widow, raising nine children on her own in

New York. That unknown, long-dead woman, my grandmother, she who thought one must eat enough for tomorrow, must have followed her own advice; judging from the size of the wedding ring Michael Dunn gave her in 1892, she was a large woman. Yet she must surely have remembered her own mother's all-too-realistic fears of starvation, must have often worried about feeding her own children, and must have passed that anxiety about food along to my mother. I, however, was not worried about the reliability of the food supply in Queens; fearing no famine, I saw no need to stockpile body fat for future use. After reading McCourt's memoir, I did understand; but how could I, as an American child, have understood my grandmother's words without also understanding the historical connection between the Irish and hunger? Did my mother understand that she hoarded scraps of food at least in part because of the Great Hunger in Ireland? Did the nuns who taught me, Irish as at least some of them must have been, know about the Famine but not teach us about it? Perhaps there was a conscious conspiracy to keep silence; perhaps it was just that the connection with Ireland had become too tenuous by then, too much a matter of songs and shamrocks.

Despite the paucity of our knowledge, the history of the Irish shaped our lives. Irish poverty was the basis of one of my mother's favorite expressions: "making the poor mouth." P. W. Joyce defines this phrase as meaning "making out or pretending that you are poor."[2] In my mother's usage, this phrase heaped scorn on those who complained about money, even if indeed they were poor. Such behavior—not *being* poor, a common condition in our modest neighborhood, but *complaining* about being poor—was disgraceful. Personal finances were the second most private area of life (the first being, naturally, sex, which would not be discussed at all, ever). So "making the poor mouth" implied the confluence of several disgraceful situations: an inadequate breadwinner; an inability of other family members to live on the breadwinner's income, whatever it might be; speaking of the unspeakable; implying in the very act of discussing the matter that the listener was about to be hit up for a loan to compensate for the poor-mouther's improvidence. I had never heard this expression from anyone except my mother until, on my first day on Irish soil, I heard it used, in the same scornful tone my mother had used, by a tour bus driver in the Aran Islands refusing an Irish customer's request for what Americans call a senior citizen's discount. "Ah, would you listen to her makin' the poor mouth, now?" the bus driver lamented to all who had ears to hear. He won his point; the woman paid full fare; and I learned that my mother, who left her own neighborhood only with the greatest reluctance, was using an Irish phrase, probably her own mother's. The contempt implied in the phrase for those so lacking in self-respect as to seek sympathy—or worse, charity—for what was to her mother's generation a universal condition explained my mother's frugality: saving scraps of food, eating enough for tomorrow, were precautions taken so that the day would never come when she (or I) would make the poor mouth. The Irish had long been poor, and dignity demanded that one suffer in silence.

Another, related expression, and one that she actually said in Irish, also had to do with money. She pronounced the term as "fla-*hoo*-la," and, judging from the context clues, it meant carelessness about money, throwing money around in a showy, extravagant fashion. Her tone of voice was scornful, suggesting that it described just the kind of behavior *now* that would cause the perpetrator to be making the poor mouth *later*. Upon researching the meaning of this word, I find that, according to P.W. Joyce, it is spelled *flahoolagh*, and means "plentiful" (with an analogy to the generosity of the Irish chieftains);[3] and according to Loreto Todd, it is spelled *flaithiúil*, and means "generous."[4] Assuming that Joyce and Todd know the Irish language better than a second-generation Irish-American who had never been to Ireland, my mother's personal adaptation of the word's meaning was probably an expression of the belief that she, the youngest of a widow's nine children, would never be in a position in which spending money freely would be anything other than foolishness.

While my mother worried about finances, my father, more lighthearted by nature, specialized in entertainment. My father's role in preserving what little Irish culture made it across the Atlantic to my home in Long Island City was in the realm of song and story. Privately, my father would sing Irish songs (or their American knockoffs). He sang, not well but enthusiastically, such Irish weepies as "Mother Machree" and "Galway Bay." Yet he never expressed, to me at least, any desire to visit the land that inspired these songs; the nostalgia in the songs seemed to be enough of Ireland for him. He also liked to tell jokes in a faked brogue. His favorite, oft-repeated, was of the genre that appears in one novel discussed in this book: a "Paddy" story. An Irish woman asks her husband for money to buy a new pram, the old one having broken under the strain of transporting twelve children. To which her husband replies (imagine a New Yorker's version of Irish speech here): "Ah, here it is, but this time, would you get one that will *last*!" Such paternal Hibernicisms would stop at the doorway of our apartment. Stereotypical Irish behavior in the outside world was foreign to him. Not a teetotaler, my father was nevertheless an abstemious drinker (one and no more), and was no frequenter of bars, Irish or otherwise. Gregarious, cheerful, fond of children, music, and repartee, he could easily have been cast as a typical Irishman in a film, as long as the part did not require a pub scene.

My parents probably did not consider their behaviors Irish, and I certainly did not at the time. Indeed they seemed to downplay any characteristics other than their surname that might publicly identify them as Irish. My parents' ambivalent relationship to their ethnicity was, I learned later, characteristic of the second generation to which they belonged. For that generation was undertaking two simultaneous and contradictory tasks: they were attempting to blend in; and they were attempting to remain separate. No wonder their behavior seems odd. They avoided visible indications of their Irishness; but they nurtured a sense of separateness in their private associations nonetheless. In their little apartment in Long Island City, they kept themselves to themselves, associating only with family and with a select few of the ever-changing roster of the other tenants in the building. There my mother and father died, at the ages of ninety and one hundred respectively. It is fitting and proper that the last sounds they heard in this life were the sounds of Irish speech: that of their caregivers. I like to think that they felt themselves home again, hearing voices so much like those of their mothers, Margaret Dunn and Delia Duggan.

Since my parents died, I have seen what my father often sang about but never saw: the sun going down on Galway Bay. But I have also come back again in that I have chosen to focus on the kind of literature that speaks to me because it speaks of people like me: Irish-Americans. This book retraces the steps of my own literary journey for readers who are interested in exploring the Irish-American past through fiction as I did. The book reads these five novels in such a way as to, in Brian Heron's phrase, "go back to the beginning, to learn again what it means to be Irish."[5] The book sketches in the Irish background, presenting what American readers need to know about Irish history, mythology, and customs to appreciate these American novels. I have organized the chapters not by chronology—all the novels were published from 1989 to 1999—but in pedagogical fashion, from simple to complex. I am not suggesting that some of these novels are less sophisticated than others, but rather that some require more detailed Irish background than others, and those that do are discussed later, in the hopes that the material presented in earlier chapters will also prove enlightening with regard to them. If readers follow the order of novels suggested here, my hope is that they will find themselves, at the end of the process, less the "victim of cultural disintegration," in Heron's words,[6] than they were when they started. The sources listed in the bibliography will enable readers, if they so desire, to expand their knowledge further.

In my research, I have come to see that, while no one family, surely not my own, can be seen as typical of a vast historical movement, each Irish-American's family story is connected to the larger story of the Irish in Ireland and America. I have also come to realize that the type of investigation I have undertaken can most comfortably be done by a third-generation Irish-American like myself. Not only have people like me reaped the benefits of the educational and financial opportunities for which our grandparents emigrated, but we are in a position to claim both sides of the hyphen as our own: Irish and American. The emigrant generation's story was about survival in a new land; the second generation's story was about assimilation, making that land accept them as "real" Americans. The third generation, secure in its American identity, can explore the part of themselves that is Irish. One way of doing that is by reading fiction which explores the meaning of the hyphenated self.

To understand these novels, it is first necessary to focus on the characters who emigrated and to place them in historical context. At this point, readers of literature depend on the work of historians; first among them with regard to the history of Irish emigration is Kerby A. Miller, whose *Emigrants and Exiles: Ireland and the Irish Exodus to North America* (1985) is the definitive study to date. The following overview draws on the work of Miller and others, the intent being to link the individual stories of the emigrants in the novels to the larger framework of Irish history. Since the motives for emigration changed over time, the fictional emigrants are discussed in chronological order. Like their historical counterparts, the emigrants in these novels left Ireland for economic, political, and sociocultural reasons. The strength of each of these motivating factors varies depending on the individual and the time period in which he or she emigrated. Why they left the land of their birth is a crucial question, in that the answer affects not only their own characterization, but the image of Ireland and the Irish that they transmitted to their American children and grandchildren.

The great-great-grandparents of Patricia Dolan, the protagonist of Katherine Weber's *The Music Lesson*, left Ireland during and shortly after the Great Famine (1845–49). While neither the first famine nor the last, the Great Famine is the watershed event of Irish history: everything that happened in Ireland is dated as before, during, or after. The basic facts are stark and grim: following a blight on the 1845 potato crop, with successive blights over the following five years, "half the population disappeared—just like that. Into graves or off across the ocean."[7] Kerby Miller cites a more conservative but still disastrous figure of 2.5 million (out of an original 8.5 million) for population loss from 1845 to 1855, which not only constituted a "demographic catastrophe" at the time, but set a pattern of population decline in Ireland that has not yet been reversed.[8] It is a truism of Famine studies that, for many years, the collective memory of its horrors was suppressed. In the recent past, and in particular since the 150th anniversary of the Famine in 1995, this alleged cultural amnesia has been largely eradicated; research on and artistic response to the Famine has become intense. In the northeast United States alone, Famine memorial parks have been opened to the public in Boston in 1998, in New York in 2002, and in Philadelphia in 2003. Fiction exploring the continuing impact of the

Famine on contemporary Irish and Irish-Americans such as Seán Kenny's *The Hungry Earth* (1997) and Lisa Carey's *In the Country of the Young* (2002) have reached an expanding readership. New insights into the Famine have been provided by historians like Christine Kinealy, Robert Scally, and Cormac Ó Gráda. For the reader of fiction, the best point at which to begin study of the Famine is Cecil Woodham-Smith's *The Great Hunger: Ireland 1845–1849*, published in 1962. Later historians have examined every aspect of Woodham-Smith's work, confirming some insights and questioning others; but this work remains the single work to which all refer, the one that must be read by anyone who hopes to understand the tragic story that can only be sketched here.

Michael Dolan, Patricia's great-great-grandfather on her father's side, emigrated from Skibbereen in 1848, and her mother's ancestors from Cork in 1851. Skibbereen is well known to readers of Woodham-Smith as the scene of some of the most extreme sufferings caused by the Famine. In an 1846 letter imploring the Duke of Wellington to help the starving population, Nicholas Cummins, the magistrate of Cork, described a scene that he observed in Skibbereen:

> . . . the scenes which presented themselves were such as no tongue or pen can convey the slightest idea of. In the first [cottage], six famished and ghastly skeletons, to all appearances dead, were huddled in a corner on some filthy straw, their sole covering what seemed a ragged horsecloth. . . . I approached with horror, and found by a low moaning they were alive—they were in fever, four children, a woman and what had once been a man. It is impossible to go through the detail. Suffice it to say, that in a few minutes I was surrounded by at least 200 such phantoms, such frightful specters as no words can describe, either from famine or from fever.[9]

Cummins's description of death by starvation or by the infections consequent upon severe malnutrition could be multiplied hundreds of times over in contemporary sources. The "phantoms" that Cummins described would never become any American's ancestors; only those who were well enough to get to a port city and able to pay passage from there could have any hope of emigrating. Even those relatively fortunate ones risked an equally harrowing death at sea; their story is told in Edward Laxton's *The Famine Ships: The Irish Exodus to America* (1997). Those who remained in Ireland and survived were scarred; they dealt with the psychological trauma of the Famine with suppression and silence.[10] This may have been their only way of coping with the intense emotions generated by the British response to the Famine while at the same time continuing to live under British rule.

At the time of the Famine, Ireland was part of the British Empire; the decision-making powers of government were based in London. Therefore, if help were to come for the stricken population, its source should have been the empire of which Ireland was a part. What happened instead is succinctly phrased in the often-quoted words of Irish patriot John Mitchel (1815–75): " 'The Almighty, indeed, sent the potato blight, but the English created the Famine.' "[11] Historians generally agree that the scientific cause of the destruction of the potato crop in 1845 and subsequent years was a fungus; but the moral responsibility for its becoming the Great Famine, one of the great demographic disasters in history, is the British government's. John Waters, writing in 1997, sums up a viewpoint shared by many: "When I speak about it in public, I make a point of saying, unequivocally, that the Famine was an act of genocide, driven by racism and justified by ideology."[12] Professional historians add volumes of nuances to generalizations like Waters's, but the real-life equivalents of Patricia Dolan's great-great-grandparents would have brought with them to America opinions similar to his and Mitchel's about the British government: that it could have saved them, should have saved them, but deliberately did not save them; that both its inadequate action and deliberate inaction were based on contempt for the Irish people; that the feeble best that can be said about the British government of the period was that its members were in thrall to *laissez-faire* economics, which required them to do nothing to affect market forces, while millions died.

Emotions generated by Famine suffering were carried across the ocean and passed down the generations, as was the rage against England, which was more acceptable to express in the United States than it was in Ireland. The result was an "anti-British feeling among some of the descendants in America of those forced to emigrate as a result of the Famine . . . often attributed to strong race memories."[13] Memories transmitted from survivors like Patricia Dolan's forebears would keep the Famine alive in the minds of future generations. Ancestral anger influences Patricia to involve herself in a plot against the British crown, despite the fact that she herself never experiences more than the vaguest anti-Irish sentiment. This apparent disconnect between one's own experience and historical memory is not surprising; as Caroline Ramsay notes, "the Famine endures in the Irish collective unconscious, the way the Holocaust in Germany resides within Jews who have never experienced anti-Semitism."[14]

By 1913, when Ellen and Vincent MacNamara in Mary Gordon's *The Other Side* leave Ireland, Ireland's people are no longer starving, but the legacy of the Famine persists. Irish emigration predated the Famine; but after the Famine, emigration became "a self-perpetuating phenomenon and an integral, automatically accepted feature of Irish life."[15] Despite improvements in Ireland, emigration continued, and continues still. Over 150,000 people emigrated from Ireland from 1911 to 1920, as did Ellen and

Vincent.[16] Like many of his historical counterparts, Vincent leaves for economic reasons, but not survival. He will not starve if he stays, but he leaves to avoid being a superfluous person in terms of the post-Famine landholding system in Ireland. The way land was owned after the Famine was an attempt to remedy at least one of the problems that contributed to it: partible inheritance. Before the Famine, when landowners died, the land was divided into smaller and smaller parcels, enabling more sons of each family to marry and form families of their own. Over generations, this process resulted in plots of land so small that only potatoes could be grown on them. As the potato was nutritious (one can, and many did, live on potatoes almost exclusively), and as the potato is one of the few crops readily grown on tiny plots, the result was an increasing marriage rate, an increasing population, and an increasing dependence on the potato. Thus it came to pass that, when the Famine struck in 1845, there were no readily available alternatives to the one crop that could support so many on so little land.

After the Famine, in an effort to promote more varied farming and thus prevent this overdependence on one crop in the future, changes were made in the landholding system. The custom of splitting the land among the men of a family was replaced by a primogenitive system in which the land was left to the oldest son. Younger sons and any daughters who did not marry another landowner were expected to make their living in some other way, with emigration being the main option.[17] This process was so effective that by 1914, one year after Vincent emigrated, "both land and livestock were increasingly concentrated among a small minority of farmers."[18] This allowed for raising more varied crops, but rendered enormous numbers of young people redundant. Many of those who emigrated at the same time as Vincent and Ellen did were, like Vincent, "non-inheriting sons," young and alone; on their journeys or when they arrived, they would find young Irishwomen like themselves, as the women of the time were emigrating too, and in similar numbers.[19] While young men like Vincent left Ireland to avoid uselessness, many were also attracted, as was Vincent, to a country in which the streets may not have been paved with gold as legend had it, but where steady, relatively well-paying, and even interesting work was available.[20] Most of these jobs were in cities. Unlike other emigrant groups, the Irish tended to stay in or near the cities where they first landed in America; one theory about the "marked preference" of the Irish in America for urban life[21] is that the Irish developed an aversion for life on the land, which had failed them in Ireland.

Unlike Vincent, with his rural background, other emigrants, like Ellen, town dwellers and the children of merchants or tradesmen, were less affected by the system of land tenure. Nevertheless, because the mass emigration that had begun before the Famine was massively increased by the Famine, all post-Famine generations came to see emigration as a way to flee personal and family problems that they identify, rightly or wrongly, as peculiarly Irish. Ellen leaves Ireland for reasons less concrete than economics (as the daughter of a prosperous publican or pub-keeper, she is relatively secure), but which nevertheless made Ireland highly aversive to her. Chief target of Ellen's anger is the Catholic church, the baleful influence of which, she believes, traps the Irish people in a peasant fatalism. Her story of the bees in church, which becomes a major element of her American family's perceptions of Ireland, is an illustration of her response to Ireland's dominant faith. Sixteen-year-old Ellen cannot express her thoughts as does historian Kerby Miller, but it is clear that what upsets her in the episode of the bees is, in Miller's words, the way a "traditional Irish Catholic worldview" tends to "deprecate innovation, initiative, and the assumption or attribution of personal responsibility."[22] The incident becomes for Ellen an archetype of Irish passivity. The place in which such a mentality prevails, she concludes, is a place from which she must escape.

Another reason for Ellen's departure, a reason she does not admit, is the fate of her mother, whose devastating mental illness is, in Ellen's view, caused by the conditions of life in Ireland. Writing in 1979 of the situation up to that date, Nancy Schefer-Hughes contrasts the "high morale and stunning accomplishments of the Irish abroad" with the "demoralization of the Irish at home," and cites as evidence of the latter the fact that Ireland had at the time "the highest hospitalization treatment rate for mental illness in the world."[23] Mental illness as severe as Ellen's mother's is of course not unique to Ireland; but what passed for treatment of it was shaped by pervasive elements of the culture. While mental illness of the degree of her mother's could probably not be successfully treated anywhere in the first decade of the twentieth century, in Ireland any kind of treatment was impeded by custom and tradition. Ellen's father's decision to isolate his wife, covering up the problem rather than seeking help for it, was shaped by the Irish taboo on "discussion with strangers of 'family' problems or difficulties,"[24] a prohibition that rules out even such limited professional help as was available. The same kind of fatalism that leaves bees unmolested in church also leaves the mentally ill untreated, especially if their illness does not threaten others. Because Ellen's mother is harmless, and because the custom was that a "strong kinship network," led, in her case, by her husband, would "protect and shield a villager from designation as insane,"[25] there is no need publicly to admit to the problem. While Ellen condemns her father, she too observes the same cultural prohibition against disclosure, concealing the problem for years from Vincent. The very behavior that so alienates Ellen from her father—isolating her mother in a house specially built for that purpose; hiring a single caregiver to keep her safe, but hidden, there—is kinder than the other alternative: an institution that would be unable to help her mother either, and that might have employed more radical, even cruel, treatments. Given the time, Ellen's father's response to the problem is humane; but Ellen, too young to understand how few her father's options were, leaves Ireland in 1913 with a mixture of fear of and contempt for her native land as a place where a beloved wife and mother can suffer such a fate.

Gordon may have picked 1913 as the date of Ellen's and Vincent's departure specifically to avoid a political theme, as the next decade was to bring momentous political changes to Ireland. The year 1916, the emigration year of James Blatchley's grandfather in Thomas Moran's *The World I Made for Her*, is a key date in Irish history. Sixty-six years had passed since the Famine, with the Irish still living under the jurisdiction of the government which, they believed, had watched them starve. During that period, the groundwork was laid for the events that commenced in 1916, on Easter Monday, when a small group of rebels seized control of Dublin's General Post Office. Its leaders issued the Declaration of the Republic, which reads in part:

> We declare the right of the people of Ireland to the ownership of Ireland and to the unfettered control of Irish destinies, to be sovereign and indefeasible. The long usurpation of that right by a foreign people and government has not extinguished that right, nor can it ever be extinguished except by the destruction of the Irish people.[26]

This document bears the same relationship to the Republic of Ireland that the Declaration of Independence does to the United States; but unlike the American Revolution, the Easter Rising did not in fact free Ireland from British rule. The rebels held their position for six days until British troops quelled the Rising and executed its leaders. While the Easter Rising seemed to end in failure (and it is likely that its leaders knew that it would), the rebellion itself and the martyrdom of its leaders were decisive factors in the eventual formation of the independent Republic five years later, with the signing of the Anglo-Irish Treaty over the winter of 1921–22.

While all the signers of the Declaration of the Republic were executed, many of their more than 1,600 followers survived to face two main choices: to stand and fight further, or to emigrate. The former course was taken by such famous figures of later Irish history as Éamon de Valera, who played a key role in the Rising (although he did not sign the Declaration) but was spared hanging because of his United States citizenship;[27] he later went on to carve out a long and significant (if at points controversial) political career, most notably as president of the Republic of Ireland. Another survivor was

Michael Collins, who as de Valera's representative, signed the Anglo-Irish Treaty of 1921–22 (and was assassinated in 1922 for doing so). Not all participants in the Rising stayed to fight another day as did these two: many historical analogues of James Blatchley's Irish grandparent, "Grandda Synge," in Thomas Moran's *The World I Made for Her*, emigrated in the wake of the Rising rather than "be hanged by the English." Nuala's remark—that Grandda Synge left Ireland " 'when the rats left the ship' "— suggests that an Irish person such as Nuala might believe that the surviving 1916 rebels should have stayed and fought further, as did de Valera and Collins. Blatchley's comment that his grandfather was "no rat, just a republican"[28] suggests that he, as an American, would attach much less emotion to his grandfather's flight, seeing it as an eminently sensible reason for an Irishman to emigrate to America.

Grandda Synge is the one emigrant character in these novels who leaves Ireland for political reasons; and by the twentieth century, fear of starvation is no longer a motive for emigration. The other twentieth-century emigrants in the fiction weigh the merits of the two countries, Ireland and America, and choose America for its greater economic and social opportunity. Some time in the first two decades of the twentieth century, Billy Lynch's Uncle Daniel, in Alice McDermott's *Charming Billy*, leaves Ireland; while his motives are not specified in the novel, they can be inferred by what he does when he gets to New York. Daniel builds his career as a motorman, one of those relatively low-paying but secure jobs that gave the Irish a foothold in the middle class. Job security makes it possible for him to rent a modest apartment, marry, and have a child. But Daniel's main interest in life is bringing other Irish emigrants to New York. He emulates his nineteenth-century emigrant forebears in assuming the responsibility of financing other emigrants. Thus not only does his emigration strengthen rather than loosen his ties to Ireland,[29] but his emigrants, his "Paddies," become, for him, more significant than his family. Historians debate whether the type of job in which Uncle Daniel spends his life trapped the Irish in the lower middle class;[30] but in the novel it is not Daniel's income but his propensity for spending it on assisting other emigrants that keeps his family's circumstances modest.

The novel's other emigrant, "Irish Mary," is a minor character, but significant in that she exemplifies characteristics of women emigrants of the twentieth century. Young women like Mary left Ireland for many of the same reasons that men did, but with some additional reasons specific to women. Many left to escape problems rooted in nineteenth-century Irish life: the low status of women in the family and in the larger society; poor economic and marital prospects; and limited freedom with regard to sexual and even marital choice.[31] In the 1980s as in the previous hundred years, as

Linda Dowling Almeida points out, emigrants were still "motivated by a desire to escape what they felt was a restrictive and suffocating culture and lifestyle in Ireland."[32] Among the many factors limiting Irish women in particular, restrictions on sexual behavior figure prominently. While there are good historical and sociological reasons for the strict sexual morality that developed in Ireland, the Catholic church remains the key source of harsh social sanctions and the great prohibitor of all but reproductive married sex. Except for Ellen in *The Other Side*, all of the twentieth-century women in these fictions add to their other reasons for emigrating a desire for the kind of sexual freedom that is only possible in a country where restrictions and sanctions do not apply, where, as one young woman who emigrated in the 1980s puts it, " 'nobody cares what you do.' "[33]

Sexual freedom comes with a price tag, however. Judging as with Uncle Daniel by her behavior once she arrives in New York, Irish Mary in *Charming Billy* emigrated to live independently, to improve herself, and to marry. She does improve herself economically and socially. After being a nanny for a wealthy Irish-American family, she attends, with their help, City College of New York—at the time a major facilitator of the very process of upward educational, and consequently social, mobility in which Mary takes part—and becomes a teacher. From nanny to teacher: this is just the sort of improvement for which women emigrated. On the other hand, she is not successful if her goal is to marry. In New York she is free to engage in a sexual relationship with Dennis; but in New York Dennis is also free not to marry her when she does. In Ireland at the time social pressure might have been brought to bear on Dennis to marry her; but in New York, it is not. Supported by her teaching job, Mary can live independently; but she never marries. The trade-offs involved in embracing American sexual freedom are also apparent in the story of Clíona and her daughter Grace in Lisa Carey's *The Mermaids Singing*. Clíona originally comes to Boston to study nursing. Her situation in Ireland was dictated by family customs. She was required to fill the role in the family played by her mother, who died when Clíona was thirteen; she had to wait for a younger sister to be old enough to take over the job before she could leave. Had she carried out her plan to earn a nursing credential in Boston, she would have raised her social status through her profession as does Irish Mary; but her pregnancy derails this plan and leaves her at the same point of entry into the job market at which many of her nineteenth-century predecessors were: domestic service.

Despite the failure of her original plan, Clíona's story is significant with respect to the history of Irish emigration in that she is on the cusp of a dramatic change: from travel by sea to travel by air. Air travel is not only a convenience but a new metaphor for the relationship between Ireland and America. When Clíona first arrives in Boston, she does so by boat as did her predecessors. The ocean voyage is easier than it was in the past, and this affects Clíona's level of commitment to her life in America. She is ambivalent about defining herself as an emigrant: on the one hand, she later claims never to have intended to stay in the United States; on the other hand, she gives her daughter what she regards as an American name, as if she and the girl intend to stay. Ambivalence is all the more sustainable in the age of air transportation; the journey across the ocean, once barely survivable, is now simple enough to be readily reversible. This means that travelers need no longer make the definitive choice between the two countries, and they can go home again.

By about 1960, when Clíona leaves Ireland, and about 1979, when she returns with her daughter Grace, a satisfactory life is possible there, even though Clíona has not fulfilled the dream for which she first emigrated. Older now, Clíona is more interested in financial security than she once was, and she finds it in Ireland. But by 1983, her daughter Grace feels "captured" in Ireland, constricted by a traditional lifestyle, "trapped in a life that had been mapped out by the previous generations on the island." Being an island wife is too limiting for her, so Grace seeks, and finally finds, " 'escape routes.' "[34] The two women's contrasting responses reflect their differing ages, but also reflect the fact that by the 1980s Ireland was more prosperous economically than it had been, but still too repressive for an American-born woman.

Nuala in Thomas Moran's *The World I Made for Her*, who emigrates in the late 1980s or early 1990s, responds to cultural repression as does Grace. As Nuala explains to Blatchley, " 'Living in Ireland is like living at the bottom of a damp, old well.' " To Nuala, the traditional culture reeks of " 'ancient decay,' " and it is only possible to live in the " 'open air' " on the American side of the Atlantic.[35] Nuala and Brigit, representatives of the "New Irish" of the 1980s and later,[36] leave Ireland to escape the restrictions on women which are still a feature of Irish society. In New York, where no one cares what they do, women like Nuala and Brigit can define themselves for themselves, achieving financial independence and personal autonomy. The underside of this autonomy is that they are just as free to make poor decisions as to make good ones. Their stories represent another change in the conditions of emigration in that both Nuala and Brigit come to the United States with a professional identity already established and work in New York in the same field as they would have in Ireland. This fact points to an improvement in access to professional training in Ireland and a leveling off of opportunity in both countries. The women are not dependent on any American, or America itself, for their educational or professional status; they emigrate with it rather than to find it. By the end of the twentieth century, the economic disparity between the two cultures that had motivated emigration from Famine times to the end of the twentieth century is narrowing, and the stories of Clíona, Grace, Nuala, and Brigit reflect that historical trend. On the other hand, the three younger women see Irish culture as antithetical to the needs of their sexual natures. But the contrast between the motives of the Famine generation—emigrate or die—and their motives is a measure of how far the Irish had come on both sides of the Atlantic.

Late-twentieth-century emigrants like these enjoy a major advantage in that their predecessors had already done the hard work of making a place for them in American society. The Famine and immediately post-Famine emigrant generation, landing on the shores of a country unprepared for their en masse arrival, settled mainly though not exclusively in the seaport cities where they disembarked; it is no accident that the American setting of all five novels is either New York or Boston. Conspicuous because of their accent and their (to proper WASPs) disorderly, often drunken behavior (their propensity for causing public disturbances giving the Paddy wagon its name), these new emigrants must have seemed almost impossible to assimilate. But these wild Irish were replaced in one generation by others who were tamer, who began to blend in with the receiving society, who aspired to become, above all else, respectable. The quest for respectability involved trade-offs and the interpretation of mixed messages. The second generation, many of whose fictional counterparts appear in these novels, reached maturity with fewer visible signs of ethnicity, as American more than Irish; yet at the same time they were expected not to abandon the very heritage that they seemed so intent upon downplaying.

This they did by creating a small world for themselves, a small Catholic world. Catholic institutions allowed them to do this, indeed were established for this purpose: to create environments in which Catholics would not have to compete with or be threatened by a dominant group, but would themselves be the dominant group. This effort was so successful that even now, as this book is written, Catholics, if they so choose, can spend virtually their whole lives inside the parish, being born, educated, working, even dying in church-affiliated institutions. But parochialism had its price. Staying within the parish meant restricting opportunities and narrowing choices. In educational matters, for example, limitations on choice were the norm in the Irish-American community well into the twentieth century. For a moment in history, Irish-American Catholics were told to, and many did, live in a smaller (and, they thought, safer) world of their own. But the larger world beckoned. The first Irish Catholic to be elected president, John F. Kennedy, went to Harvard: this sent a signal that it was time for at least some of the Irish to move out of the parish and into the mainstream.

The great achievements of the Irish in all areas of American life, culminating in the eyes of many with that 1960 election, have eclipsed the memory of poor hungry Paddy and Brigit, arriving in America a century earlier with nothing but the strength to do manual or domestic labor. Paddy's and Brigit's great-grandchildren face little discrimination in education, employment, or housing anymore; there is even a certain social cachet in being any sort of pure ethnic in an increasingly homogenized society. No longer worried about being treated badly in nonsectarian institutions, no longer as distrustful of the "others" as their parents and teachers raised them to be, Irish-Americans are increasingly found outside the parish, living their personal and professional lives outside the Irish neighborhood, outside the Catholic institutional system, often outside the religion itself. By the third generation or later, Irish-Americans typically feel little need to stress their American identity; born and raised in New York or Boston or Chicago, what else can they be but American? This leaves them free to explore the other side of the hyphen, the Irish side. The fear of not being accepted as true Americans has shifted to other, more recent newcomers, sadly for them. But for Irish-Americans, confidence in their American selves has allowed many to explore their Irish selves; this book is the product of one such exploration

A reader of the history of the Irish in America soon discovers that a basic question must be answered: What name should be used to describe Americans of Irish descent, and how is it to be rendered typographically? This is not trivial, as it makes a statement about identity. Brian Heron and Bob Geldof use the term "Irish American" (no hyphen) to indicate people of Irish background who were born in the United States; and they call those of Irish descent who live in Ireland "the Irish," or, in Heron's formulation, "real Irish people." The implication of Heron's phrasing is that only the Irish in Ireland are really Irish, which of course may well be so. Terms like "Irish American" point to the fact that the United States is different from, say, France or Spain, in that its citizens share geography but not ethnicity; such terms dissect the nation into its component parts, separating some of its citizens from others by the country of their ancestors. Without the hyphen, the term Irish American connotes an American who belongs to the subdivision Irish; American is the noun, Irish the adjective describing it. Another way of describing those people of Irish descent who live in the United States is the one chosen by historian Kevin Kenny as the title of his book, *The American Irish: A History.* The opposite of "Irish American," Kenny's term uses "American" as an adjective modifying "Irish," as if to suggest that "American Irish" is a subset of "Irish," as if further to suggest that the Irish who live in America are more similar to than different from the Irish who live in Ireland. A third possibility is to use the hyphenated term, Irish-American. In *Eats, Shoots & Leaves: The Zero Tolerance Approach to Punctuation*, Lynne Truss says that "the tricksy tiny hyphen . . . is used quite distinctly to connect (or separate) individual words."[37] Because these novels all examine the issue of how Irish identity is connected to or separated from American identity, the hyphenated term is the appropriate one for this book. The characters in these novels are Irish-Americans in the hyphenate sense, that is, as American people who are linked to, yet disconnected from, the Irish.

A major issue explored in all five works is the precise nature of both the conjunction and the disjunction between the two poles of the characters' identity. The central characters have been raised to think of themselves as Irish, which, compared to Americans of other ethnicities, they are; but their beliefs and assumptions are tested when they meet "real" Irish people. The Americans come to these encounters thinking that Irish people are similar to themselves, but find that in key ways they are not; and when the Americans journey to Ireland, which they believe they know, having "learned" about it from song and story, some of them find the experience profoundly disillusioning. Their psychological task is not only to come to a deeper understanding of a people and a place that they thought they already knew, but to incorporate that new understanding into their own sense of themselves.

In the interaction between the American characters and the Irish characters, in the journeys to Ireland that the American characters undertake, a cultural clash takes place that is the more shocking for being unexpected. After all, to the Americans, these Irish people are supposed to be, if not sisters and brothers, at least cousins; and the land from which they come is supposed to be, in some sense, home. The problem is, of course, that these fictional Americans of Irish descent do not in fact know Ireland or the Irish, but they think they do, and it is what they know that isn't so that makes their interactions with the Irish so unsatisfying for them (and, if Bob Geldof is right and if they were real people, irritating to the Irish as well). In each novel, American characters must learn to understand Irish characters who emerge as they are from the historical experience of the Irish. The goal of this book is to help the reader to do so as well. A dimension of the irony in all five novels is that the reader will then know more about Ireland and the Irish than the American characters do, and will therefore be able to perceive where the American characters are going astray in their relationships with the Irish characters. Often this occurs because what the Americans know is partial, superficial, fragmentary; they bring to their encounters with Ireland and the Irish bits and pieces of the kind of Irish lore that crossed the Atlantic, the stories the emigrants told, the songs they sang. Often, too, they rely on the kind of character types and stereotypes that are part, but only part, of the Irish experience in America and Ireland.

Introduction

Irish Types, American Patterns

Like historical people, the characters in these fictions exist at a point in time in the history of the Irish in America, and in some cases are typical of that history. That is not to say, however, that they are stereotypical. Anyone would recognize a stereotype like the Stage Irishman of nineteenth-century comedy: "He has an atrocious Irish brogue, perpetual jokes, blunders and bulls in speaking and never fails to utter, by way of Hibernian seasoning, some wild screech or oath of Gaelic origin at every third word: he has an unsurpassable gift of blarney and cadges for tips and free drinks. His hair is of a fiery red: he is rosy-cheeked, massive, and whiskey loving. . . ."[1] While none of the novels being discussed here employ such crude stereotypes as that of the Stage Irishman, the novels do draw on certain elements typical of the Irish in America; and the two concepts, type and stereotype, need to be differentiated.

In literary terms, a stereotyped character is "oversimplified," relying on "generalizations about racial, national, or sexual groups"; in his dictionary of literary terms, Edward Quinn gives an example with which he obviously expects the general reader to be familiar: "the rendering of Irish Americans as drunken and pugnacious in 19th-century political cartoons."[2] The practice of stereotyping is the basis of what literary critics call stock characters, character types that predictably recur in certain genres; use of such characters is a mainstay of formula fiction. When writers of serious fiction use stereotypes or stock characters, they often do so in such a way as to call into question the presumptions upon which the stereotypes are based, often by combining "stereotypical features" with "individualized features."[3] In serious fiction, when the stock situation does occur, it is handled in a more nuanced fashion than in formula fiction. For example, readers of Alice McDermott's *Charming Billy* know that in the nineteenth century the Irish were often stereotyped as drunks; yet readers must still be prepared to examine the way Billy is more than merely a stereotypical Irish drunk. Ironically, the Irish-American characters in the novels discussed here often do not examine their own stereotypes about the Irish as thoughtfully as readers are expected to do. Because the characters are more cut off from their heritage than they realize, they will not usually see where the stereotype is wrong, or at least where it does not apply to the individual before them. Knowing only the stereotype, they tend to miss any aspect of the Irish characters that deviates therefrom.

While characters in these fictions draw upon, but are never merely, literary stereotypes, they are sometimes typical in another sense in that people like them actually existed historically; the characters evolve from, and conform to, the history of the Irish on both sides of the Atlantic. Typical characters may be typical in several ways, and those ways may cut across categories; for example, a policeman is also somebody's son and a Catholic. At the same time, a fully developed character will probably also be untypical in some way. The interaction of the various categories and the extent to which a character deviates from or conforms to literary or historical type becomes part of the reader's understanding of that character.

As in other literary genres, stock character types often function in stock situations. But when they do, such situations must also be examined carefully to avoid stock responses. For example, one does not have to read far into Irish and Irish-American fiction before realizing that a stock situation in such fiction is the encounter between a priest and a layperson. The stock response would be to regard the scene as an example of the imposition of clerical authority on a free spirit, as an instance of the clergy's very real propensity to act as conduits of "institutional guilt."[4] After all, most readers know how the Irish were castigated as a "priestridden Godforsaken race" by Stephen Dedalus's father in James Joyce's *Portrait of the Artist as a Young Man*.[5] However, this response may not always be the author's intent. Each scene must be analyzed without prejudgment, especially if there are several such scenes in the same novel. Any discussion of typicality must be balanced by a realization that what might be interesting about these characters is precisely the way they deviate from type.

It is typical of these characters that they be Catholic, and that they have either a positive or negative (seldom a neutral) attitude toward the church. While the characters' Catholicism is often problematic for them, the novels are too subtle to be mere literary forms of Catholic-bashing. In the twenty-first century, everyone knows about the negative side of Catholicism, not only from writers like Joyce but from the daily press. But in the nineteenth century, the church in America was often seen more positively, as an asset to new emigrants from Ireland: it "bridged the chasm between rural Ireland

and urban America, providing psychological and spiritual comfort in a strange and hostile environment. Catholic parishes in American cities functioned as rural villages preserving a sense of community."[6] By the mid- to late-twentieth century, when most of these novels are set, the church had fulfilled this transitional role so well that its members no longer need the institutional support that their emigrant forebears did. Therefore, most of the modern characters have no more than a cultural attachment to the church. While a bishop might define few of these characters as "practicing" Catholics, fewer still would care about a bishop's definitions. What they choose for themselves amounts to a range of behaviors indicating varying degrees of commitment to Catholicism.

If Catholics are defined as those who engage in formal religious practices, they are a small minority in these novels. But they are cultural Catholics in that their milestones are marked by Catholic ritual; and at times some of them engage in Catholic practices. Dennis and Billy in *Charming Billy* go to mass; Dennis goes to confession; so does Grace in Lisa Carey's *The Mermaids Singing*. Patricia Dolan in Katherine Weber's *The Music Lesson* goes to mass only on the Catholic version of the high holy days, and then mainly for aesthetic reasons, "the smells, the odor of incense and true faith."[7] Vincent in Mary Gordon's *The Other Side* is a churchgoer, and Theresa in the same novel is what might be termed an evangelical Catholic. Gráinne in *The Mermaids Singing* moves toward Catholic practice in Ireland; but as a child in Boston, she knew the mass only as a show on cable television. As frequent as religious practice is the absence of it when such might be expected; no priest is called to Ellen's bedside in *The Other Side*, and though Blatchley is clearly dying in Thomas Moran's *The World I Made for Her*, neither of his Irish nurses see fit to enquire as to whether he is Catholic or not, that a priest might be called if he is. Other characters are ambivalent, or downright hostile. Grace in *The Mermaids Singing* and Cam, Dan, and Sharon in *The Other Side* do not conform to the church's teachings on extramarital sex, yet they cling to the church in other ways. Grace plans a Catholic funeral for herself, and through it, introduces her daughter to that hitherto suppressed aspect of her Irish heritage. Like Grace, Cam, Dan, and Sharon are alienated from the church more by the church's attitude toward them than by their own theological differences of opinion with the church; they act as if the church has rejected them for their sexual behavior more than they have rejected the church. For them, Catholicism has become more an ethnic marker and source of traditional customs than a set of beliefs or moral guidelines. Ellen in *The Other Side* has the most negative attitude to the church, implicating it in the problems for which she left Ireland, blaming it (as did James Joyce) for the problems of Ireland in general.

As basic as Catholicism is to most of these people, so also is their position within a family. Since the families are Irish-American, they are influenced, by way of conformity to or deviation from, the often unarticulated rules of family life brought to America by the emigrant generation. Thinking of themselves as American, however, they will often not fully understand how Irish expectations permeate their lives. Crucial to the characterization of many of the parents in these novels is the fact that they are closer to the Irish past than their children are, and thus the parents serve as conduits of that past to their American sons and daughters. Vincent in *The Other Side* and Pete Dolan in *The Music Lesson* clearly function in this role. In both of Alice McDermott's novels, fathers are shadowy figures and seem to play little role in the lives of their children. In *The Mermaids Singing*, a major element of the protagonist's psychological task is to discover her father, and to decide to what extent he, his country, and its traditions can compensate for the loss of her beloved mother and of her American self. Blatchley's English father has no role beyond conferring the surname that disguises his son's Irish identity from others and even from James himself.

Mothers are even more significant representatives of the Irish past than are fathers. A crucial element of several of the plots of these novels is the multilayered and interlacing relationship between emigrant women and their daughters and granddaughters, a relationship made more complicated by the country that the emigrant woman represents. In *The Mermaids Singing*, the young girl Gráinne's competing allegiances to Ireland and America are embodied, respectively, in her Irish grandmother and her emigrant mother. In *The Other Side*, Ellen MacNamara's flight from the fate of her own mother in Ireland becomes one element of the dominant personality that she herself becomes as a mother. Mothering, failures of mothering, loss of a mother, the inability to become a mother: all are key issues in these novels; and all are rendered more complex by the fact that a mother or grandmother is from another country.

As William Shannon notes, Irish mothers were known for their "willingness to sacrifice on behalf of the children,"[8] but expected compensatory sacrifices in return; so, apparently, did fathers. Charles Fanning points to a recurrent theme in both Irish and Irish-American fiction: "the dutiful self-immolation of children on behalf of their parents."[9] Strong social controls were imposed on young people to marry late or not at all.[10] Family patterns that may have made sense in Ireland persisted in the United States. For example, in rural Ireland after the Famine, sons were expected to refrain from marrying until they did in fact inherit the farm, and to live in their parents' house as their caretakers until the parents died. An unmarried man living this way was termed a "boy" regardless of age; and "boys" were expected to show the same devotion, particularly to their mothers, as their mothers had for them. For some, maturity, as defined by the death of the parents and inheritance of the farm, came too late, and "many of the inheritors remained permanently single."[11] While the rational element (inheriting the farm) dropped out of the equation in America, old patterns persisted; among Irish-Americans, "rates of permanent celibacy also remained unusually high,"[12] as if the same constraints on marriage applied in America as in Ireland. The inability of the "boy" to break away from his mother both physically and emotionally, especially by taking the decisive step of marrying in her lifetime, is a recurrent theme in both Irish and Irish-American fiction. Unmarried daughters also found their lives shaped by the same expectations.

While their home lives often follow poorly understood Irish family patterns, the occupations and consequent social status of the characters reflect the work history of the Irish in the United States. The world of work operated differently for the men of the emigrant generation than it did for the women. Male emigrants often entered the job market at its lowest level, doing hard physical labor like digging tunnels, building railroads, and laboring in the unskilled construction trades.[13] The Famine and immediately post-Famine generation of emigrant men lived like interchangeable and readily replaceable parts of the vast American industrial system, in "jobs that required physical strength and occupational flexibility."[14] This would change by the end of the nineteenth century, particularly in the New York area, in which most of the novels are set.[15] Like Vincent in *The Other Side*, whose first job in America is as an unskilled laborer digging a tunnel, but who works his way up into the skilled trades, by the beginning of the twentieth century many other American Irish moved into jobs requiring more skill and commanding better pay.[16] With the advent of unionization, these jobs began to provide a middle-class lifestyle and better educational opportunity for the next generation. This pattern too is visible in *The Other Side*. The founding parents of the family in America, Ellen and Vincent MacNamara, are early labor union organizers and in this they are typical of Irish-Americans of their generation.[17] Involvement in the labor movement was deplored by some conservative schools of Catholic thought, which considered them pro-Communist; Ellen's parish priest condemns her behavior and thus alienates her from the church irrevocably. But liberal Catholic opinion at the time supported unionization. Though not specifically theological in his motivation, Vincent reflects this latter body of opinion. Thus he is able to maintain his affiliation with the church while at the same time achieve better pay and some social mobility for himself and for later union members.

Another way in which the Irish moved up the social and economic ladder was by obtaining jobs in civil service or in stable private sector organizations. The well-known stereotype of the Irish policeman is based in reality.[18] Such jobs were physically dangerous but economically secure, providing an income that conferred at least lower-middle-class status and a base for further educational and social advancement in later generations.[19] In *The Music Lesson*, the Dolan family's work history is typical. Pete Dolan, the narrator's father, is a member of the Boston Police Department, as was his father before him. Progress in the Police Department is clearly indicated by rank, and Pete has risen in the force; he is a detective. Having the stability of a civil service job in the family, Pete's daughter, Patricia, can move into one of the learned professions, as an art historian. James Blatchley, the half-Irish protagonist in *The World I Made for Her*, is, in his career, a hybrid of Pete and Patricia; having completed most of the work for a doctorate in art history, he becomes a police officer in charge of investigating art forgeries for the New York Police Department. In addition to the protective services, the children of Irish emigrants often sought comparably secure jobs in utilities like Con Edison, as do Billy and Dennis in *Charming Billy*. But these two characters do so at a point in the history of the Irish in America at which such jobs would no longer be as desirable as they once were. When Dennis announces his intention of going to work for Con Edison, his mother protests: a job that is merely secure is not enough. At the end of World War II, Dennis is no longer confined to certain segments of the job market as the Irish once were; and so she sees his choice as evidence of lack of ambition.

Historians disagree as to whether the kind of jobs that disappoint Dennis's mother—secure, but relatively low-paid—helped or hindered Irish-Americans. Stephen Erie argues that "the relative security of blue-collar jobs in public works, police, and fire departments may have hindered the building of an Irish middle class by encouraging long tenure in poorly paid bureaucratic positions";[20] both McCaffrey[21] and Kenny[22] see some merit in Erie's argument. But McCaffrey cautions that if the Irish gravitated toward such jobs because they were "obsessed with security,"[23] they came by that obsession for historically valid reasons: "For people who suffered poverty in rural Ireland and urban America, security was a primary objective. Employment connected with politics was relatively stable and often supplemented by pensions, thus providing a base of confidence that eventually launched Irish America into the middle class."[24] Furthermore, McCaffrey argues, even if the Irish were to overcome their fear of advancement, discrimination would still have held them back.[25] Different opinions about how well the Irish did basically boil down to Bayor and Meagher's formulation:

> Were the Celts successful because most worked their way out of degrading poverty, or were they failures because too many of them seemed to get stuck

in the lower middle class too long? What held them back or thrust them forward? Were the values preached by the church a bulwark against demoralization or a barrier to capitalist risk taking and intellectual experimentation? Was carving a niche in public employment a useful strategy for a people with few skills, or was it a dead end that trapped the Irish in a morass of clerkships?[26]

All these historians are saying more formally what Dennis's mother said to him: "Cooper Union, City College. . . . A public speaking course then. The service, officer's training. Something else. Something more."[27] Her advice is right for Irish-Americans in general, but not for Dennis in particular. For him, the "something else"—what his mother knows but cannot define as the next step in educational and social mobility—would remain out of reach. Fueled by better education, much of it in the Catholic system, other Irish-Americans were beginning to move up within the middle class.[28] According to William Shannon, because the Irish valued "good talkers,"[29] Irish-Americans were drawn to professions requiring verbal proficiency, like teaching and the law. In *The Other Side*, the lawyer Jack Morrisey and his protégés Dan and Cam MacNamara all make their careers via their ability with the spoken word. With Dan and Cam's generation, moreover, the work histories of Irish-American men and women converge, with access to the same opportunities.

This, of course, had not always been the case. The women of the emigrant generation typically took jobs as domestic servants because their other options were also the "least-skilled, lowest-paying jobs"[30]—sewing in factories or at home, or taking in boarders. While domestic jobs were healthier, safer, and (with room and board factored in) better-paying than the men's manual labor, some at least must have hated domestic work. For Ellen MacNamara in *The Other Side*, her work as a lady's maid is degrading, especially since she is not a member of the social class in Ireland whose members typically took such jobs in the homes of others. For Clíona in *The Mermaids Singing*, housekeeping is, in her mind, only a way station on the road to training as a nurse; she becomes trapped in it when, unmarried, she becomes pregnant. By the 1940s, the nature of domestic work had changed for the Irish in America. In *Charming Billy*, Eva and Mary work as nannies for an affluent Irish-American family. Overseeing the seven children, especially in Long Island's desirable Hamptons, is not unduly onerous, and by this time nannying, especially in the summer, is more associated with youth than with social status or ethnicity. Nevertheless, the low esteem in which Dennis holds "Irish Mary" is at least in part attributable to her employment, however temporary, as a domestic; Claire Donavan, the American woman he eventually marries, has taken the next step up the social ladder and become an office worker.

In her work life, Claire is typical of her generation. While the first generation of Irish women dominated the domestic service job market, their "native-born" daughters would not follow them into the kitchens and laundries of the affluent but would "work as secretaries, stenographers, nurses or schoolteachers."[31] While such jobs would later come to be regarded as constituting an underpaid female ghetto, at the time they were a step up the middle-class ladder. Clíona in *The Mermaids Singing* wants to be a nurse; and Nuala and Brigit in *The World I Made for Her* are nurses, which allows them to immigrate legally and with professional status intact. While common in Irish-American life, teachers are few in this fiction. The upward educational and professional mobility of Irish women is exemplified by Sheila and Cam in *The Other Side*, the former a social worker, the latter a lawyer. Both professions require the kind of higher education previously available to Irish-American women, and to men as well, only if they joined religious orders.

For a time in the history of Irish-American Catholics, the priesthood provided security, social status, and a career path, and was a vehicle of "respectability and social mobility" not only for the priest himself but for his family.[32] By the late twentieth century, the exodus of young Catholics from the religious life, the failure of others to replace them, and the declining prestige of the priesthood is reflected in the marginalization of clergy in these fictions. Sheila's husband Steve Gallagher in *The Other Side* represents a stock Catholic type of the late twentieth century: the man who has left the priesthood to marry. Aside from Steve, the other priests who appear in the fiction are as different from each other as any other group of characters. According to William Shannon, priests historically were a more varied lot than one would imagine: they "did not compose a unified stereotype. . . . There were as many different kind of priests as there were Irishmen: brilliant intellectuals and orators, worldly types skillful at organization and maneuver, hardheaded parochialists devoted to the needs of their parish and not looking beyond their horizons, and rebellious zealots."[33] In the fiction, the reader must not be tempted to see the priest characters only through the lens of stereotype, but to look carefully for ways in which they diverge from type.

Some of the priest characters in the fiction typify ambiguities inherent in modern Catholic life. In *The Mermaids Singing*, the two priests are polar opposites. No story of American Catholic adolescence in the mid-twentieth century would be complete without the stock situation involving a young person going to confession, and none would be complete without a priest very much like the one to whom Grace makes her confession in *The Mermaids Singing*: the heavy-handed cleric devoted to inculcating sexual guilt. That priest is, however, counterbalanced by the priest Gráinne meets when she first arrives in Ireland. Though a rural parish priest, though named stereotypically, Father Paddy is a highly individualized rendering of a modern priest trained in pastoral psychology. More like a therapist than an agent of an angry God, as different as he can be from the judgmental cleric who so alienated her mother, Father Paddy responds sensitively to Gráinne's grief, thus making her feel welcome not only in Ireland but in the church. The two Irish priests in *The Other Side* serve a similar function, representing opposing views on the morality of emigration. All four of these fictional priests illustrate the variety of types one might expect to encounter in modern Catholicism.

The visit of a priest to a Catholic home (or the glaring absence of such a visit when one would ordinarily be expected) is a significant event in the family's life, and another kind of stock situation in the fiction. After Billy Lynch's funeral in *Charming Billy*, the priest who visits Maeve brings a message of forgiveness and healing. Including himself in the group of those who must absolve themselves of guilt in Billy's death, he avoids pious platitudes in favor of a more therapeutically based form of counseling. Billy's death, he says, " 'wasn't a failure of our affections, it was a triumph of the disease.' "[34] Treating the mourners sympathetically, he offers in this vignette a fine example of pastoral care. On the other hand, the priest who visits the MacNamara home in *The Other Side* is the kind of priest who is a staple of modern Irish fiction, one who acts as an instrument of social control. When he castigates Ellen for what he sees as her sinfulness in supporting the labor movement, his attempt to play in America the more intrusive role the clergy played in Ireland backfires. Usually a priest, even in New York, would assume that his opinion would be respected in a Catholic home; however, Ellen not only scorns his ideas but also expels him from her house. So contemptuous is Ellen of the Irish church that she is having none of its counterpart in New York. So fully has Ellen rejected the church as a result of this encounter that the family does not call a priest to her deathbed. When the matter is not even discussed in this nominally Catholic household, it is a strong sign that Ellen's estrangement from the church is so definitive that her family respects it at a moment when they might have been likely to revert to traditional religious practices.

If priests are few in these novels, nuns are fewer, and they too are depicted in a variety of ways. In *The World I Made for Her*, the hospital in Greenwich Village in New York seems modeled on St. Vincent's Hospital, a Catholic institution founded by an American order, the Sisters of Charity. Despite their major achievement in founding this great institution and the high level of education that enabled them to do so, the sisters are trivialized in being represented only by one "resident nun" whose idea of medical care is blessing Blatchley with water from "a holy shrine of miracles in

Mexico."[35] Nuala and Brigit owe their careers to the training provided by an order of Dublin nuns, yet they too mock the sisters there; Brigit is particularly contemptuous, questioning "why they were so cold and agitated if they were so happily married to Jesus."[36] Cynical Brigit may have been right, since many nuns, apparently not so happy, left the convent as did Sheila in *The Other Side.* Having left her order to marry Father Steve Gallagher, however, she spends the rest of her life seeking, in Irish-American culture, the coherent sense of herself that she had found in the religious life.

The changes in the lives of those nuns who remain in the convent are exemplified by Sisters Otile and Roberta in *The Other Side.* Sister Otile runs the innovative nursing home in which Vincent recovers from his injury. Superior of her dwindling religious order, she is the model of the modern nun. More a social worker than a religious, she runs a multigenerational home for society's throwaways. Her renovation of Maryhurst, the mansion donated to her order by a wealthy Catholic family, is a clear metaphor for the transformation of traditional religious life. Whatever the loss aesthetically, Otile (or O.T., as she prefers to be called) renovates the house entirely to focus it on the secular world and its needs. Otile herself seems more secular than Cam. Otile advises Cam to leave her husband and move in with her lover, all the while puffing on a cigarette, her opinions and behavior suggesting that more than the house has been renovated. While Otile seems to be the kind of person who could run any organization, her fellow religious, Sister Roberta—she likes to be called "Bobbi"—seems, despite her "Sister Power sweatshirt,"[37] to be childlike, emotionally fragile, and dependent on Vincent, who should by rights be dependent on her. Such are the strengths and weaknesses of the religious life as Mary Gordon sees them at the end of the twentieth century.

Sheila and Steve's abrupt departure from religious life is triggered by a photographer's capturing the two of them, still under vows, outside a motel room. That sex should be what even they regard as their downfall is no surprise. The famous sexual reticence of the Irish predated the Famine, but deepened with it as the Irish were "forced . . . to ponder the consequences of too many people on too little land."[38] The Irish heritage of hunger and deprivation, combined with their allegiance to the strictest norms of Catholic morality, combine to produce, even in America, a habit of celibacy. The custom of late marriage, or no marriage, produced a character type called the "old boys" or "old girls," those who live in their parents' home and, to all appearances, remain virginal beyond the usual time and sometimes for their whole lives. These include Dan Lynch in *Charming Billy* and Jack Morrisey in *The Other Side.* Even some of those who are married practice a form of celibacy. The sexless marriage of Bob Ulichni and Cam MacNamara in *The Other Side* is a case in point, an unfortunate result of their inability to deal with their infertility within the small Catholic world in which they operated as young people. Magdalene, Cam's mother, is a natural celibate, averse to sex after the disaster of the brief marriage that produced Cam. Her closest relationship, the more appealing to her because of its nonsexual nature, is with her business partner, a gay man.

In contrast to the sexually abstinent is the type of character who uses the bedroom as an arena in which to battle the church. Grace in *The Mermaids Singing* is the clearest example of this. Although she does love her husband Seamus O'Flaherty, she chooses a non-monogamous lifestyle to take a stand against the restricted life of the married (and Catholic) woman in rural Ireland; through an active sex life, she asserts her American (and pagan) identity. Cam in *The Other Side* is different from Grace, in that Cam does not engage in an affair simply to defy the church's rules against it; she loves Ira Silverman, and experiences sexual fulfillment with him for the first time. But Cam's relationship with Ira is affected by her problematic relationship with the church. Like Clíona in *The Mermaids Singing*, Cam sees her Jewish lover as the sine qua non of sensuality at least in part because he is Jewish; neither Irish nor Catholic, he is not staggering under the weight of cultural and theological taboos. Cam feels guilty for her affair with Ira because of Bob, but not because of the church. Her cousin Dan, on the other hand, embraces a lifestyle totally focused on guilt. Both he and Sharon Breen are so guilt-ridden for having broken up their respective first marriages that they cannot marry each other; instead they live joylessly in a quasi-penitential state.

As Lawrence McCaffrey observes, "Irish Catholics are as famous for their excessive drinking as for their sexual inhibitions."[39] The link between the two issues is another dimension of the Irish stereotype. For single men in Ireland, the pub provides an escape from frustrated sexuality; for married men, it offers escape from family life. The issue of whether all this pub-going produces more alcoholics among the Irish people, or among the American Irish, is a vexed one. But what is clear, according to Richard Stivers's *A Hair of the Dog*, is that for Irish men, drinking, especially in the social context of pub-going, was "an aspect of male identity," and for Irish-American men, "a symbol of Irish identity."[40] Inevitably, some hard drinkers will become alcoholics, as does Billy Lynch in *Charming Billy*. While his death from alcoholism is the central fact of the plot, he is not the only drinker in the novel. Dan Lynch justifies and romanticizes Billy's actions, suggesting that he is justifying his own; and Maeve's father's alcoholism makes Billy's familiar and acceptable to her. In *The Other Side*, Magdalene adjusts her life to her dual needs, for sympathy and for alcohol; paradoxically, she makes a relative success of it. Though alcoholism is destructive, alcoholics often are, as Billy is, charming. This may be so because of the traditional association of drinking with more pleasant elements of Irishness; as Stivers says, "the more one drank, the more Irish one became."[41]

Maintaining one's Irishness in the face of pressure to assimilate is an issue that confronts different generations in ways other than drinking, of course. In general, the farther from the emigrant generation a character is, the less Irish and the more American he or she is. The first generation's concern with becoming respectable, thus acceptable to the larger society, often translated into the suppression of ethnic-specific behaviors, not only in themselves but also in their children. If the emigrants were of the Famine or immediately post-Famine generation, it is no surprise that they would want to suppress memories that were mainly of suffering. Such escape, however, involved "the sundering of ties between their ethnic identity and their past. For the Irish, 'becoming American' was in this sense a matter of being cut adrift; Ireland became a distant, soft, romantic place, while the often grim realities of the Irish-American past receded gently into the mist."[42] For subsequent generations, career progress led to increased affluence, which led to further trade-offs for Irish-Americans: separation from their urban base; de-emphasis of Catholicism as a defining fact of their lives; and blending into suburban neighborhoods that were organized along economic lines rather than by either ethnicity or religion.[43] The change was drastic, but in many ways positive: "Nineteenth-century Irish-Americans were by and large poor, alienated and often despised; late twentieth-century Irish-Americans are about as well-off, educated and Americanized as anybody else."[44] As the American Irish became more educated and moved into professions, they tended to identify with people like themselves socioeconomically, only some of whom would be Irish Catholics. Without purposeful efforts to maintain the "bonds of ethnic community [which] were inevitably sundered by suburbanization,"[45] by the second or third generation Irish-Americans had assimilated so well that the situation to which Bob Geldof succinctly points was in fact the case; they became "Americans through and through."[46] In the fiction, it is at this point or later that, with the limited and fragmented understanding of the Irish past that they have, they meet the Irish characters: people they think they know, but do not. Most of the American characters stand firmly on their own side of an ocean of misunderstanding.

Some characters try to bridge this divide. What might be called the "hyphen" characters are specific to this type of fiction. Like the hyphen itself, which simultaneously links and separates, these characters connect the Irish to Irish-Americans, and the past to the present, while at the same time reminding the American characters of the gaps between them and the Irish. Often, but not always, they are members of the emigrant generation.

A key component of the hyphen character is the act of storytelling. The teller of tales carries traditions from one side of the ocean to another, in the process binding the American character to Ireland, but at the same time serving as a reminder that, for the American, this is second-hand experience. In *The World I Made for Her*, Nuala tells stories to Blatchley in an effort to ease his passage; in *The Mermaids Singing*, Clíona, Seamus, and Liam tell stories to Gráinne, in their effort to ease her very different transition from Boston to Ireland. In *The Music Lesson*, Pete Dolan tells his daughter Patricia his version of the history of Ireland; such stories as Pete's make her more sympathetic to the (mostly untrue) tales told to her by Mickey O'Driscoll. *Charming Billy* can be read as all story, as a communal attempt by all the mourners at Billy's funeral to tell his story rightly. But, since various mourners, particularly Dan Lynch and Rosemary, have different ways of telling the story, and since the narrator, Dan's daughter, was not present at the key events, the truth of the matter is forever ambiguous. In *The Other Side*, Ellen's and Vincent's similar, yet different, emigration stories provide their descendants with different estimations of the value of what has been left behind.

Two characters in these novels serve as special kinds of hyphen characters. Uncle Daniel in *Charming Billy* is a reminder of the system Kerby Miller calls "chain migration,"[47] by means of which one emigrant established him or herself in the United States and then financed the passage of others. The importance of this custom in facilitating mass emigration cannot be overestimated. Different yet still significant is the effort of Sheila in *The Other Side* to in effect "re-Irish" her family via strenuous Hibernian activities in New York. Her efforts, however, are undercut by the fact that she is not only not an emigrant, she has never even been a tourist; the world she makes for herself is in its way as much in her own mind as is Blatchley's in *The World I Made for Her*. While there is a comic element to both Uncle Daniel and Sheila, their efforts highlight the important issue of whether, and if so how, ties with Ireland are to be maintained; and what constitutes a genuine relationship between Americans and their Irish heritage.

Ultimately, however, the Irish-American characters in the fiction are tested in their grasp of their own heritage when they meet, and try to understand, individual Irish people. In *The World I Made For Her*, Blatchley must learn to know the woman he loves despite seeing her through a haze of nostalgia for an idealized country and past. Because in *The Mermaids Singing*, Gráinne must live in Ireland with an Irish family she has never known before, her experience is the most intense. Her father, her grandmother, cousins, a probable future lover: all are Irish, and all are mysterious to her; her task is not only to learn *about* them but also to learn that she *is* them. In contrast, in *The Music Lesson*, Patricia Dolan ultimately comes to grief because the Irish are not mysterious enough to her. Because she has listened to her father's stories, she thinks she knows the Irish, and thus her lover Mickey O'Driscoll, better than she does. In *Charming Billy*, Eva and Mary are the only people from Ireland that Billy will ever meet. In the case of Eva, his imaginative casting of her in a tragic role ignores the banality of much of Irish life. In *The Other Side*, Vincent and Ellen bring with them across the ocean conflicting stories of the Irish past. In the case of Ellen especially, her mad mother seems to represent all that is stagnant and dead, all that should rightly be left behind as the family moves into its future. All these characters experience tension between the two poles of their identity.

But before analyzing each of these novels in detail, two of the most significant "hyphen" elements, conduits of Irish heritage to Irish-Americans, must be considered: song and story. Both bear tradition, but in such biased and fragmentary ways that in all five novels Americans often think that they know more than they do about the country about which songs are sung and stories are told.

Chapter 1

What Americans Know and How They Know It: Song

In Benedict Kiely's short story "Homes on the Mountain," the narrator is one of a pair of twelve-year-old boys given to reading, but not singing, Irish songs from "a series called Irish Fireside Songs. The collective title appealed by its warm cosiness. The little books were classified into Sentimental, Patriot's Treasury, Humorous and Convivial, and Smiles and Tears. Erin, we knew from Tom Moore and from excruciating music lessons at school, went wandering around with a tear and a smile blended in her eye."[1] Music forms the backdrop for the narrator's thinking about the two mountain homes of the story's title. One is newly built, the retirement fantasy of a returned Yank. This character type, which recurs in Irish fiction, is an Irishman who emigrated, made his fortune in America, then returned to Ireland. The other house is the cottage of two bachelor brothers, John and Thady O'Neill, who seldom leave their own property, much less Ireland itself.

As the story progresses, it becomes obvious that the O'Neill homestead undercuts the image of Ireland presented to the narrator via the songbooks, an image that, presumably, is also a component of the dream of Ireland that makes Yanks return:

> Once it must have been a fine, long, two-storeyed, thatched farmhouse, standing at an angle of forty-five degrees to the roadway and build backwards into the slope of the hill. But the roof and the upper storey had sagged and, topped by the growth of years of rank decayed grass, the remnants of the thatched roof looked, in the Christmas dusk, like a rubbish heap a maniacal mass-murderer might pick as a burial mound for his victims.[2]

The house itself, however, is the least of the O'Neill brothers' failures. On his way to visit them, the young narrator hears his father's story of John, who courted Bessy from Cornevara for sixty years but never married her; and Thady, whose equal passion for women and salmon absorbed his days. Now, living in a decaying farmhouse " 'like pigs in a sty,' "[3] John and Thady signify the decline and fall of everything Irish, "the descent from Elysium of the Emerald Isle."[4] By making this journey to the house of the O'Neills, the narrator learns that this house, and the failed lives within it, are as much a part of Ireland's reality as the sentimental songs or the dreams of returned Americans.

The twelve-year-old who narrates this story is Irish and lives in Ireland. Yet he forms his ideas about his country from the lyrics of Thomas Moore, the nineteenth-century Irish poet (one of which, "Erin the Tear and the Smile in Thine Eyes,"[5] uses the imagery that the narrator remembers). There is another minor character in the story, a young man who is a "born American." This young man is visiting Ireland; but "never once in the course of his visit was able to see the Emerald Isle clearly."[6] He fails to see Ireland clearly mainly because he is drunk, but also because he is American, and so cannot be expected to see clearly. Unlike the drunken American, the Irish-born narrator can learn to see for himself the difference between the Emerald Isle of song and story and the Ireland of reality. His father's story is one of the vehicles of his new understanding; the other is direct experience, the visit to the O'Neills's house.

But what of the Irish-American characters in the works of fiction considered here? While they might see a postcard or two, or read a few of the simpler poems of William Butler Yeats, most of what they know, or think they know, about Ireland comes to them only via song and story, not through study of Irish history, not personal experience of the Irish or Ireland. Like the "born American" visitor in the Kiely story, but even if sober as he is not, such characters do not understand what they see. This is why the visits these characters make to Ireland and the contacts that they have with Irish people are often so unsatisfactory: the Americans operate within a false context, and on the basis of unreliable sources. They "know" Ireland from music, especially from the emigrant ballads and the American imitations thereof. They "know" the Irish past, and their own family's place in it, from storytellers, often family members, who tell the stories. But the American listener rarely takes the trouble to correct or refine what he hears in the songs or stories; metaphorically, he or she cannot visit the house of the O'Neill brothers. This leaves the listener character in the same position as the narrator was at the beginning of Benedict Kiely's story, with misguided perceptions shaped by song lyrics.

Kiely's young narrator has learned much of what he thinks he knows about his country from the songs of Thomas Moore. Moore's *Irish Melodies*, published in ten volumes from 1808 to 1834, put words to traditional Irish music in such an effective way that his themes and images permeated Irish music and even literature ever after,[7] and therefore popular perceptions (even in Ireland) of the Irish. According to Robert Welch, Moore "was preoccupied with what he saw as the close relationship between Irish music . . . and the national identity"; he defined his task as conveying in music "the essential goodness of long-suffering Eire."[8] Though Moore did not write ballads himself, his *Irish Melodies* influenced the ballad tradition, which would in turn be imitated by the commercial lyricists who followed in Moore's and the balladeers' wake. Moreover, Moore's lyrics gave the Irish a way of thinking about themselves (and gave Americans a way of thinking about them). In his introduction to *A Centenary Selection of Moore's Melodies*, Seamus Heaney describes how his "own sense of an Irish past was woven from the iconography of AOH [Ancient Order of Hibernians] banners and phantoms out of Moore's Melodies."[9] Moore's influence on the image of Ireland in the popular mind, on both sides of the Atlantic, can hardly be overestimated.

Moore's themes are conveniently summarized by William H.A. Williams in *'Twas Only an Irishman's Dream: The Image of Ireland and the Irish in American Popular Song Lyrics, 1800–1920*.[10] Moore, according to Williams, focuses on the heroic past, both historical and mythological, especially such events as those that support the cause of Irish nationalism. Songs of grief for lost heroes and "laments over Ireland's ancient wrongs"[11] keep the memory of past oppression alive. The personification of Ireland as a beautiful woman is linked to "the Irish sense of place and the beauty of the Irish countryside," both of which are believed to have a positive effect on the character of the Irish people.[12] Williams's analysis of the vocabulary of Moore's *Irish Melodies* reminds the reader how many of the themes not only of Irish music but also Irish literature have their origins in Moore: the "powerful sense of nostalgia" for the past; the motif of exile, of "wanderers longing for home"; the sense of connection between the living and the dead, which requires "continual remembering of the dead, a keeping faith with their memory"; and finally, the " 'sunshine and shadow' " or " 'smiles' and 'tears' " motif.[13] Williams believes that Moore virtually invented the iconography of Irishness to use in his songs: to him can be attributed the association of "the color green, the shamrock, and the harp" with Ireland.[14] So it is that "when British and American songwriters turned to Ireland, Moore's sentiments of longing, nostalgia, and the dream of the lost home would gather about their visions of Erin like the mists of twilight."[15] Moore's works were popular, sold well, and reached a wide audience, in the process becoming a vastly influential source of beliefs. Moore was still alive during the years of the Great Famine and the ensuing mass emigration (he died in

1852), but he did not himself write emigrant ballads; instead, he provided balladeers with ready-made themes and images.

Most important of these with regard to the ballad tradition are the exile motif, and the idealization of the country and its people. In Moore's "Tho' the Last Glimpse of Erin with Sorrow I See," the emigrant imagines Ireland as home all the more because he is "in exile" on a foreign shore.[16] In "As Slow Our Ship," the emigrant takes his last look at his native land.[17] In these as in other Moore lyrics, what the emigrant loses is not only incomparable natural beauty but also irreplaceable relationships. Nowhere are friends as true (see "When Cold in the Earth"[18]) or women as faithful (see "We May Roam Through This World" or "Lesbia Hath A Beaming Eye"[19]). Those who leave must indeed be forced to do so, as who would voluntarily leave this earthly paradise? To Moore, Ireland is no ordinary land but rather identical with the ancient kingdom of Innisfail, its "radiant green" so bright as to appear to be emanating from "emerald mines" ("Song of Innisfail"[20]). Because of Moore's great popularity, his hyperidealization of Ireland found its way into the emigrant ballads, thence to their commercial successors, thence to the myth of the "Emerald Isle," to be neatly packed in the cultural baggage of the Irish-American characters in these fictions.

Both the emigrant ballads of the Famine era and the later commercial versions partake of the general characteristics of the ballad tradition, which June Skinner Sawyers summarizes in *Celtic Music: A Complete Guide*. According to Sawyers, the ballad "represent[s] the essence of simplicity." Its focus on storytelling; its clear, memorable imagery; its repetitiveness; and its emotionalism all render the ballad accessible and appealing to a wide audience.[21] The emigrant ballads tell the story of the Irish journey to America, focusing particularly on the mass exodus resulting from the Great Famine of 1845–49. Overall, they are very similar to each other. Sawyers describes them as "sad laments steeped in nostalgia, and self pity, and singing the praises—literally—of their native soil while bitterly condemning the land of the stranger."[22] The emigrant ballads follow a consistent narrative arc: they summarize the causes, the process, and the effects of emigration; and they analyze the relationship of the Irish people with their enemies, the English, and their allies, the Americans.

While emigrant ballads are only one of the many forms of Irish music, they are the music that Americans know best. Written in English rather than Irish, performed year after year on St. Patrick's Day, and embodying a simple, palatable view of Ireland and the Irish, emigrant ballads provide Irish-Americans with a facile, unchallenging set of beliefs and an easy nostalgia for a place they may have never visited, and about which they may have little genuine curiosity. As a source for the mythology of emigration (as opposed to its history, a much more complex matter), the ballads present a consistent view of both Ireland and the Irish people, a view that informs the beliefs of the Irish-American characters in these novels. While there are thousands of ballads in various folklore collections, analysis of the ballads included in just one, *Irish Emigrant Ballads and Songs*, edited by Robert L. Wright, provides an outline of the ballad tradition and the key elements of its vocabulary, both of which are influenced by Moore's *Irish Melodies*.

The ballads praise Ireland's natural beauty and its people's dignity, both seen through the rosy lens of memory. Despite their love for Mother Ireland, her children are forced into exile by political, economic, and social problems. On the other side of a vast ocean, America beckons as a solution to all problems. But no matter how successful emigrants become, they never forget their native land. Their loyalty to Ireland manifests itself in several forms: financial support sent to the family; emigration assistance; the desire to return someday, even if only in spirit; a persistent nostalgia. These themes are repeated constantly in the ballads in the Wright collection.

Memories of the "green land," "beautiful Erin," the "shamrock shore"[23] are conflated with memories of childhood innocence.[24] The ballads portray childhood as carefree and guileless, "light-hearted."[25] In ballads, emigrants tend to have grown up in Ireland's rural areas, in an idealized pastoral setting like a "dear little cabin at the foot of the mountain";[26] rarely does a Dubliner long for the scenes of childhood. The beauties of Ireland's countryside, which are considerable, become part of all that has been lost. Invariably, description of the Irish landscape focuses on positive features: "salubrious and cheering" hills, "dark heathy mountains," "sweet lovely valleys," the "beautiful banks of the Shannon," and other "limpid and whisp'ring streamlets."[27] There, innocent "lambkins sport and play," but harmful beasts such as bears, snakes, and toads are conveniently absent.[28] The childhood home is a tiny "cot," "cottage," or "cabin,"[29] usually situated on or at the foot of a hill or a mountain.[30] Daytimes are spent tending cows, pigs, and potatoes; evenings involve sitting "around the fire on a cold winters [*sic*] night."[31] The greenness of the landscape is, not unexpectedly, an almost universal feature.

In this natural setting, peasants, usually represented by the emigrant's parents, live, poor but happy. As if simultaneously to assuage and to exacerbate the emigrant's guilt, parents are usually depicted as "aged,"[32] unable themselves to emigrate, yet wholeheartedly in support of emigration, despite the likelihood that they will never see their children again.[33] When the parents are dead, emigrant guilt focuses on a desire to visit their graves.[34] Also seen through the lens of nostalgia is the girl the emigrant has left behind. Since in the ballads (though not in historical reality) the vast majority of the emigrant narrators are male, the abandoned loves are women, descriptions of whom form a composite ideal Irishwoman of the time.

She is of course "pretty," a "dark-haired blue-eyed girl" with "teeth . . . like ivory . . . cheeks like the blooming rose."[35] Her character is no less sterling: she is "sincere, and virtuous as the dove," "faithful and kind," "sweet," "free from worldly pride," "proper, neat, and handsome"; one practical balladeer notes that his love is hardworking.[36] Most ballad emigrants depart promising that, no matter how tempting the American lassies, they will return to their loves, or send for them; one, rather lamely, promises only to think of his Irish girl.[37]

This earthly paradise was destroyed by the Great Famine:

> In our humble cabin midst wild scenes of nature,
> Where the breeze from the mountains the wild flowers wave,
> The pigs we had reared, and the patch of potatoes
> They were all the riches we ever did crave;
> The black famine came our crops they were blithed.
> The poor starving family none could employ—
> The rent was demanded our prayers were slighted
> And turned out of home was the poor Irish boy.[38]

In ballad lore, the Famine's worst ravages were caused by, or at least not assuaged by, the English. The last four lines of the above-quoted stanza summarize the fate of the Irish peasant. The potato crop failed; England provided inadequate help; the English absentee landlord demanded his rent nevertheless; the family was evicted; emigration was the only solution.

In addition to English malice, neglect, and/or incompetence during the Famine, the land ownership system prevailing in Ireland at the time contributed to the suffering of the Irish people. The soil of Ireland is described in the ballads as "bleak" and "barren";[39] even in good times a landholding cannot be infinitely subdivided to support all the sons of a large family:

> My father was a farming man, used to industry,
> He had two sons to manhood grown, and lovely daughters three.
> Our acres few that would not do, so some of us must roam,
> With sisters two I bade adieu to Erin's lovely home.[40]

Even in relatively favorable pre- or at least non-Famine circumstances, "roaming" or "wandering"[41] was a necessary outlet for the surplus progeny of farm families. Often the peasant family did not own the land that had supported it, perhaps for generations. In the ballads, the rapacious landlord and his henchmen (soldiers, sheriffs, bailiffs, police, tax-collectors)[42] provide the objective correlative for the feelings of persecution that caused many emigrants to define themselves as exiles. What historian Kerby Miller has masterfully demonstrated in *Emigrants and Exiles*[43] is borne out both in the ballad tradition and in its predecessor, Moore's *Melodies*: Irish emigrants had a sense not of voluntary emigration but of being "forced to some foreign, foreign clime," "banished," driven into "exile," by "troubles at home," chief among which was the wholesale evictions of peasants who failed to pay the "heavy tithes and taxes" levied upon them.[44] These historical episodes generated their own subtype of the emigrant ballad: the eviction ballad.

The typical eviction ballad tells the tale of a family that had lived on the land for a long time, eking out a modest living there; with the Famine, poverty becomes starvation; the cruel landlord not only evicts the starving family (often in the dead of winter), but also "tumbles," tears down, their cottage so that they might not return. A landscape of "houses levelled to the ground"[45] replaces the pastoral childhood Eden. The aged parents die of the Famine or of broken hearts; the surviving adult child tries to find work that is not tied to the land. But non-farm jobs are scarce, and when available at all, "the wages they are small"; often no employment at all is available, so a working man cannot support his family.[46] Thus, the emigrant is forced by "cruel fate . . . to emigrate," doomed to being "exiled all over the earth."[47] One balladeer sums it up succinctly:

> Why do Erin's sons and daughters
> Stray to a foreign land?
> That is well known to every one—
> Bad landlords and dear land. . . .[48]

While historically as well as in the ballad tradition, economic motives led to emigration, in the ballads, political oppression is also a motivating factor. Balladeers cite feelings of being "repressed" by the "tyrant" England, which refused to grant "equal rights" to Ireland.[49] Because they require more detailed knowledge of Irish history, the political ballads appeal to a more specialized audience; as such, they are less influential on the American characters in the fiction. But the simple imagery of slavery in the ballads[50] could resonate with Americans, given their own nation's history. A sense of servitude in Ireland made the lure of freedom in America all the greater, but did not blind the emigrants to the pain of parting, and of the difficult journey that lay before them.

The time of parting from loved ones became ritualized in the tradition of the "American wake," a ceremony of mourning for the emigrant who would in effect be dead to those he left behind (a custom that is discussed in more detail in relationship to Mary Gordon's *The Other Side*). One ballad describes the related custom of "convoying" or accompanying the emigrant as far as possible on the journey to the ship, in this case as far as the railroad:

> At every station on the line
> > From Templemore to-day,
> The roads were *black* with anxious groups
> > All crowding to *convey.*
> Their friends and neighbours to the train,
> > They strove to cheer them, too,
> But when the bell rung out farewell
> > Their cries would pierce you through.[51]

As Miller notes, the custom of the convoy, while intended to " 'cheer' the emigrants," actually served to "prolong the agony."[52]

The first glimpse of the ship is the emigrant's last chance to change his mind. That moment, the last glimpse of Ireland from the departing ship, is heart-wrenching.[53] Boarding the ship was, of course, only the beginning. While one emigrant ballad in Wright's collection reports a "pleasant passage," the balladeers usually focus on the terrors of the journey across the "raging main."[54] Fears of bad weather and outbreaks of fever aboard the ship[55] cause the emigrant's heart to "quail" at the sight of the "big steamships setting sail."[56] The danger of the trip is reflected in the many ballads in Wright's collection with titles like "The Melancholy Loss of . . . ," "The Sorrowful Lamentation on the Loss of . . . ," or "The Wreck of . . . ," followed by the name of a ship.[57] Moreover, the vast Atlantic signifies the tremendous psychological as well as physical impact of what was then likely to be an irrevocable decision.

On the other side of the ocean, America beckons as a land of hope and promise, where the wrongs of Ireland will be made right. Unlike enslaved Ireland, America is a new earthly paradise where there is "no tyranny . . . nor oppressing."[58] But political freedom is not enough; there must be economic opportunity too, or the grueling journey was in vain. As one balladeer put it of his native land, "If I'd a fair day's pay for a fair day's work I would not go away."[59] In America this goal can be achieved. Some balladeers, under the influence of the "streets paved with gold" myth, are wildly optimistic about a land in which "plenty doth abound" especially in the gold mines of California.[60] Most see the main advantage of America more reasonably, as "work and wages": employment is available at a fair rate of pay, which provides "food for all," not only potatoes either, but "beef and mutton."[61] The archvillain of the Irish countryside, the landlord, has no American counterpart; no "cruel task-masters" tyrannize over the worker, nor do "taxes and tithes . . . devour up [his] labour."[62] Similarly optimistic in the face of the discrimination against the Irish in some areas of employment (immortalized in the well-known ballad "No Irish Need Apply"[63]) is the notion that in America the Irish are not only tolerated but "cherished."[64]

In some ballads, hope is the dominant emotion. The emigrant will be welcomed by family and friends who have preceded him, some of whom can even provide practical assistance:

> Some thirty-second cousin,
> Or relation, I'll be bound,
> May find a poor neglected Pat,
> Can cultivate his ground . . .[65]

But in others, the downside of the emigrant experience manifests itself as a persistent nostalgia. Newcomers to America can no longer "hear a friendly voice / Or meet a loving smile," in a place where they are surrounded by "strange faces"; one ballad, striking an odd note given the usual urban destination of emigrants, even expresses fear of Indians.[66] Some ballads imagine emigrants as perpetually "troubled spirits," longing for home all their lives, going home only as spirits after death.[67] Special anxiety focuses on dying and being buried far from home.[68] Having lived his life among strangers, the emigrant fears that he will be lonely even in death, and worse, that he will not be properly mourned. One ballad concludes that not even monetary success is worth lying alone in one's grave.[69]

Nostalgia is also expressed in the desire to retain ties with Ireland, maintenance of which takes many forms. First among them is the desire to support the family back home and, if possible, to bring them over. The "American letter" from the emigrant to his family is a key motif in these ballads; in fact, many of the ballads are written in the form of such letters. One response, written from the viewpoint of the "poor old mother / Far across the sea," assumes that the "American letter" contains money; indeed that is its purpose.[70] Historians have documented the remarkable extent of the financial support provided by American emigrants to their families in Ireland,[71] and the ballads reflect such support.[72] When the emigrant is not portrayed as a pathetic orphan, the desire "to bring [his] parents out, if living still" is often mentioned.[73] So is the promise to reunite with the girl he left behind, as in this bouncy lyric: "I'm deep in love with Mollie Burke, as a jackass is in clover, / When I am settled, if she will come, I'll pay her passage over."[74]

The ballad in Wright's collection entitled "The Emigrant's Letter to his Mother" is a typical example of this subgenre. It is a versified imitation of an American letter containing the "American money" for the folks back home. Stock elements of the tradition appear: the emigrant's regret about leaving home; his close ties to the people left behind (in addition to his family, he asks for many of his friends by name and adds offhand words of consolation to his abandoned lady love); his success in America (he is "digging gold," presumably in California, which accounts for his ability to send the large sum he mentions, ten pounds); his confident air, contrasting with the "cries of woe" he reports hearing from new emigrants just off the boat. His requests of his Irish family are modest, token remembrances of his native land (a shirt, a pair of socks, a potato); but his promises to them are much more substantial: he intends to "pay [the] passage" of Kate and Fred (presumably siblings, who were often the beneficiaries of such largesse), and even his mother. He reminds the latter that when she comes she will need "a knife and fork the meat and bread to cut"; no longer will she depend on potatoes. Interestingly, the emigrant in "The Emigrant's Letter to his Mother" mentions his girl, Kate O'Brien, by name, but in rather dismissive tones. He abjures Kate to "stop her crying," because she is "making [him] a show"; he sends her "forty kisses," but not a promise of passage money. Clearly, unlike Mollie Burke, Kate O'Brien is being let down gently. The optimistic tone of "The Emigrant's Letter" clearly suggests that he is not pining for any aspect of Ireland, including her: he is sure that it is "much better to be in America."[75]

Despite the opportunity for success in America, despite the finality implied in the American wake tradition, some of the emigrant ballads are full of hope that the emigrants' separation from their loved ones in Ireland will be temporary.[76] They imagine themselves as returning Yanks, in a variety of modes. Some ballad narrators promise to come back to their true loves.[77] Some have a somber intent for their return trip, most typically to visit their parents' graves.[78] Another variant on the return theme is the emigrant's intention to do so unchanged in his essential nature, while at the same time metamorphosed into a rich American: "Perhaps in after years I'll come, unchanged to you again, / And if I win a golden store, I'll not forget you then. . . ."[79] One emigrant promises to "return / In grandeur like old ancient rome"; another, less grandiose, hopes merely to "become a money'd man in the land I'm going to."[80] Some believe in the so-called Fenian myth, according to which Ireland will be freed by an army of Irish-Americans "coming back in ships with vengeance on their lips"; others are "quite happy and contented" in America, noncommittal about coming back at all.[81]

June Skinner Sawyers sees the emigrant ballad as having a social function as well as a personal function. The ballad, says Sawyers, is a way of consistently stoking "that old Irish standby—guilt." Through the vehicle of the ballads, emigrants were continually reminded not only of their personal obligation to those left behind, but also their political debts to the nation as a whole: "Song after song told the emigrant in no uncertain terms that emigration from Ireland would never end and their sense of guilt for having left home would never go away until Ireland was an independent nation once again."[82] Kerby Miller explains the guilt content of the ballad in terms of what he calls the "exile convention."[83] If emigrants thought of themselves as having been forced to abandon their native land, some of their guilt could be assuaged. Furthermore, if they saw themselves as exiled by a cruel political oppressor, their return would be motivated not merely by a chance to show off American-made wealth, but also to "wreak vengeance on those deemed responsible for their country's sufferings and their own unhappy 'exile.' "[84] Later Irish fiction often depicts the returned Yank as an anomaly, neither here nor there, neither American nor Irish; but in the ballads, the returnee represents hope that the painful separation will one day end, and on this earth.

It would be pleasant to think that the emotions expressed in the emigrant ballads were indeed those felt by the emigrants themselves, but the question of authenticity in the emigrant ballads is a vexed one. Most of the ballads collected by Wright originally appeared in broadsides or chapbooks, placing their dates of composition in the nineteenth century.[85] Yet even with regard to songs written during the period of high emigration and written in Ireland, Miller says that "it is often quite difficult to distinguish 'genuine' folk compositions from commercial productions, so similar were their themes and so frequently did authors of both kinds of songs 'borrow' images and phrases from each other."[86] The situation with regard to the genuineness of the emotions expressed in the emigrant ballads becomes all the more complex because, in the late nineteenth and early twentieth century, the popularity of the more-or-less authentically Irish versions of the emigrant ballads encouraged numerous patently inauthentic Tin Pan Alley knockoffs, commercially produced lyrics that imitated these ballads and drew on the same emotions they did. These lyrics are one of many sources of the phony Hibernicism, the "sorry way in which Irish culture presents itself" in America, which Maureen Dezell wittily dubs "Eiresatz"; these songs are mocked by "fans of 'trad' music as 'Bing Crosby Irish.' "[87]

A typical such Eiresatz lyric is "Mother Machree," by Chauncey Olcott, Ernest Ball, and Reda Johnson Young, published in 1910.[88] Maureen Dezell calls this song "the mother of Irish-American sentimental mother songs, a secular hymn to self-sacrifice."[89] Mother's Irishness is announced by the Irish term of affection in the title and by Hibernicisms of dialect. The young Irishman's affection for his mother is exclusive and total. As in the emigrant ballads, in which, regardless of the emigrant's youth, the parents are always elderly, Mother Machree is all the more beloved for her gray hair and her wrinkles, caused by hard work and suffering. While the song never states that the singer is an emigrant who left his dear old mother behind in Ireland, this situation is suggested by the fact that the mother is remembered as part of the past rather than experienced in the singer's present life. The description of the mother's crucial role in his life draws upon conventional emigrant ballad imagery: she is compared to the candle set in a window to lead a traveler home. What Williams calls the "sunshine and shadow" ballad motif[90] is alluded to in the singer's memory of the mother's smiling eyes soothing his sorrow. Finally, the fact that the song could also be interpreted to mean that the mother is dead adds to its nostalgic tone, as does its lugubrious melody. The listener to a Tin Pan Alley song such as this is drawn into the atmosphere of the emigration ballad; the song's employment of typical themes and images connects it to a whole body of familiar material.

Another song, though neither authentically Irish nor even a Tin Pan Alley imitation, also became a vehicle of popular beliefs about Ireland and the Irish. "I'll Take You Home Again Kathleen" was written in 1875 by Thomas Westendorf, an Illinoisan who wrote the tune for his wife Jeanie, who was nostalgic for her home in Ogdensburg, New York. Despite the fact that Ireland is never mentioned in the lyric, the Irish name in the title and the fact that Westendorf, like the writers of "Mother Machree," drew on common emigrant ballad motifs caused Irish-Americans to regard the song as another authentic bearer of Irish tradition. The image of the ocean, and the nostalgia from which Kathleen suffers (she has grown pale, speaks sadly, has tears in her eyes), connect the song to the ballad tradition. Were she to return to Ireland, the bucolic scenes would cheer her and cause her to forget her grief. After all, although she married the singer and loves him dearly, her true home is Ireland (or Ogdensburg, New York). His promise, then, is to return her to that land and to all that she loves; if he does not, the implication is that she will dwindle and die.[91]

For all their sentimentality, oversimplification, and stereotyping, William H.A. Williams argues in 'Twas Only an Irishman's Dream that songs like "Kathleen," as well as those issuing forth from Tin Pan Alley, were an important tool of ethnic assimilation for the Irish. Williams sees the nineteenth-century Irish as being the first real " 'ethnic' group" in America, ethnicity in his definition being contingent upon their coming too quickly, in too great numbers, and with too many non-mainstream characteristics to be readily accepted by the larger society.[92] That such a radical "other" as the Irish were then would be stereotyped was inevitable; but such stereotyping, as it found its way into popular music, had, Williams thinks, positive as well as negative effects. On the one hand, popular songs on Irish themes spread oversimplified views of the Paddy; on the other hand, and somewhat paradoxically, such songs made Irishness itself more compatible with the American mainstream.[93] Because popular music relies on sales, it must, by definition, be acceptable to as many people as possible; this led, Williams says, to the suppression of the harshest and most offensive aspects of anti-Irish propaganda.[94] Thus, over the long run, popular music elevated the "*public* discourse about Irishness."[95]

In addition, and more relevant to their place in the fiction, Tin Pan Alley versions of emigrant ballads, as described by Williams, influenced the beliefs of Americans, especially Irish-Americans, about the country and its people. First, in the American-Irish songs, there is an all-pervasive sense of "romantic nostalgia" for the past,[96] even (perhaps especially) the painful parts. Second, a masochistic enjoyment of suffering is promulgated as an authentic component of the Irish character; Williams points to the authentic Irish emigrant ballad "Danny Boy" as the authoritative source for the pervasive " 'sunshine and shadow' motif" in Irish ballads.[97] Finally, the idealization of Ireland—its natural beauty, the charm and innocence of its people, especially its women—is combined with the exile motif, and both were reinforced by the facile rhyming of the " 'home/roam' theme."[98] All of these interrelated ideas were transmitted to the Irish-American public, as well as the larger American public, by the popular Tin Pan Alley songs of the late nineteenth and early twentieth centuries.[99]

It is no wonder that, for these Irish-American characters, even fragments of a remembered song bring the whole song flooding back into memory, and with it the traditional themes and imagery of all the other songs, all of Moore's *Melodies*, all the emigrant ballads, all the "Eiresatz" imitations.[100] When in McDermott's *Charming Billy* mourners sob to a graveside rendition of "Danny Boy," the song upon which Billy built his mournful life, when in Mary Gordon's *The Other Side* Ellen McNamara scorns the John McCormack songs that her husband Vincent loves, and hates her daughter Teresa for playing them, then the characters are responding not merely to the song itself but to all the history behind the song. Unlike the young Irish narrator in the Benedict Kiely story, however, the American characters cannot visit the O'Neill cottage, at least not at first; thus they have no norm against which to evaluate the picture of Ireland that these songs paint, or the validity of the feelings the songs engender. While some of them go to Ireland and visit the real country, others do not. Even when they do, so strong are the beliefs engendered by the music that they see the country in terms of the songs, not vice versa. Thus they are left with a highly sentimentalized version of Irishness, which they bring to their encounters with Irish people.

In these works of fiction, songs and stories are vehicles of "tradition-bearing," the preservation and transmission of tradition;[101] and listeners are tradition-receivers. Because the listener characters are American, they have little or no personal context in which to place the fragments of tradition transmitted to them; they know little else but these bits and pieces. In addition, the factor of repetition is crucial. Traditional music is considered such precisely because of its having been repeated over time. In this particular form of music, from Moore's *Melodies* to the emigrant ballads to the commercial imitations of both, the same imagery and themes appear. Because the songs are thought to be old and authentic (and some of them actually are), they seem to have authority. Song lyrics, whether old or new, Irish or otherwise, tend to feature simple messages expressed in clear and emotionally effective imagery. Because they are set to music, often repeated, and easily remembered, they engrave themselves on the mind with an effectiveness out of proportion to any truth they may contain.

When history is conveyed in an oral tale, the situation is even more complex. The crucial variable is the storyteller. Storytellers in these novels are usually either Irish people or members of the emigrant generation; therefore the storytellers assume a privileged position with respect to the material they narrate. Since no listener has any valid basis to question the storytellers' authority, the stories are accepted as authentic. Thus it happens that what the American characters think they know about Ireland from song and story is oversimplified, highly biased, but the more effective for all that.

Chapter 2

What Americans Know and How They Know It: Story

"The Irish don't really think about writing. It is just a natural extension of what we do all the time, which is talking." So says best-selling novelist Maeve Binchy.[1] A piece of evidence that Binchy is right about the importance of oral narrative to the Irish is the fact that in Irish schools, as part of their education in Irish language and culture, secondary-school students preparing for their "leaving certs," comprehensive exit exams, read a work whose English title is *An Old Woman's Reflections*. These are oral narratives collected from a story-teller named Peig Sayers (1873–1958), who lived on Great Blasket Island, off the Dingle Peninsula in southwestern Ireland. Sayers is presented to modern Irish students as an authentic representative of an ancient heritage, her tales as a true reflection of life as it was lived in a traditional culture now close to extinction. In his introduction to his English translation of Sayers's tales, Seamus Ennis describes such storytellers as Sayers as "caretakers of a peasant tradition, the carriers of an oral culture, that once covered the Atlantic fringe of Europe. They belong to antiquity, to a Europe that had no books, no radio, no cinema or television, a Europe whose only entertainment was the parish lore or the winter-night's tale told by a passing traveller."[2]

The frontispiece of Ennis's translation shows Sayers as an old woman, her head covered by a wool shawl, the shawl fastened by a crucifix, her hands clasped in a gesture of patience, perhaps prayer. She is the archetypal "tradition-bearer,"[3] one whose role is to preserve and transmit the past. Sayers's tales are full of humor and folk-wisdom, but the reason they are presented to Irish students as part of their official curriculum, and in the original Irish, is that the traditions they bear are considered important not only to be preserved, as in a museum, but also to shape young people's sense of their people's history and their own identity. The honor paid to Peig Sayers recognizes her preeminence in a traditional art form; the desire to preserve at least the knowledge if not practice of that art form is a tribute to its importance in Irish life.

Irish storytelling, however, is preserved in another way: in the fiction of the Irish-American experience. In this fiction, the storyteller character plays a specific role, that of a link between the Irish past and the American present. Usually such characters are the ones who have emigrated from Ireland, or at least are closer to the emigrant generation than are the listeners. This lends their tales a certain authenticity, and themselves a certain authority. Since the Irish-American characters are cut off from Irish traditions except as conveyed by these tradition-bearers, their stories have more weight. Much depends on how the storyteller character feels about his or her heritage. Such a character can either reinforce the "Eiresatz" view of Ireland;[4] debunk that view; or take any position in between. As the real thing, genuine Irish people, the storytellers are presumed not only to have authority, but also to share in the reflected glory of the tradition and the respect accruing to the storyteller.

The storyteller's role in Ireland is discussed in detail by Clodagh Brennan Harvey in *Contemporary Irish Traditional Narrative: The English Language Tradition*. Harvey traces the function of storytelling in the Irish past, its apparent decline with the modernization of even the more rural parts of Ireland, and its recent rejuvenation. With the upsurge of interest on both sides of the Atlantic in one of Ireland's traditional art forms, storytelling and its practitioners are once again being restored to their rightful place as tradition-bearers. While the story of storytelling is a complex matter involving such factors as Irish nationalism, the role of government-sponsored folklore collectors, and the survival of the Irish language, to understand the works of fiction discussed here, the crucial matter is not the content of the stories, or even their authenticity, but the process of storytelling, the rituals surrounding it, and the character of the storyteller.

According to Harvey, the custom of storytelling grew in Ireland, especially in the rural areas, in response to long winter nights and bad winter weather. Before the invention of the radio and the television, before the advent of all the social and technological changes that can collectively be called "modernization,"[5] nighttime entertainment consisted mainly of "the custom of nightly visiting, known as *ar cuirt* (literally, 'on a visit')";[6] the house being visited for the purpose of storytelling was termed a *ceili* house.[7] Harvey quotes a Kerryman's description of this custom as it was practiced up to the early twentieth century:

> When the long nights would come long ago, the people of this and another village would gather together every night sitting beside the fire . . . . Many a

device they would use to shorten the night. The man who had a long tale, or the man who had the shorter tales . . . used to be telling them. At that time people used to go earning their pay in County Limerick, County Tipperary, and County Cork, and many a tale they had when they would return, everyone with his own story, so that you would not notice the night passing.[8]

This Kerryman, Séan Ó Conaill, highlights three elements crucial to the history of the storytelling tradition and its significance in Irish-American fiction: the conditions under which storytelling took place; the kinds of stories that were told; and the distinction between the narrator and the non-narrator. The tales told while on a visit were oral; as Harvey points out, " 'orality' " and "folklore" are virtually synonymous.[9] As practiced in Ireland in the time Ó Conaill describes, tales were mainly told at all-male gatherings.[10] Complex cultural reasons (the custom of single-gender socializing) as well as simple practical ones (women's responsibility for the care of children) enforced different visiting patterns; Harvey believes that women probably had *ar cuirt* traditions of their own.[11] Georges Zimmerman cites a further complication in that, in the rural Irish towns in which these storytelling traditions developed, women who spent too much time outside their own homes were assumed to be negligent housekeepers; thus social sanctions inhibited women's participation in storytelling gatherings.[12]

While some aspects of women's role in the storytelling tradition are not clear,[13] what is known is that the gender of the storyteller was related to the type of tale told at these gatherings. Harvey explains the distinction between two Irish storytelling forms thus: the *scéalaíocht*, which Ó Conaill calls the "long tales," are ancient, highly stylized narratives of the gods and heroes of the Celtic past; and the *seanchas*, "shorter, more realistic forms (including local and family history, tales about encounters with various supernatural beings, and genealogical lore)."[14] Although it was usually considered inappropriate for women to narrate the *scéalaíocht*, tales of gods and heroes,[15] women could tell the "short tales," the *seanchas*. Taletellers were known as the *seanchaí* (Anglicized to such forms as "seanachie" or "shanachie"), and the title came to be associated with folk wisdom.[16] Women held an honored place in this branch of the tradition; Peig Sayers, is, as mentioned earlier, still studied in Irish schools; and folklorist Gordon MacLennan has collected the stories of another storyteller, Annie Bhán (1893–1963), a member of the same generation. Thus it is the "short-tale" tradition that allows for women narrators to claim the role of shanachie in Irish life; and it is this second form of story, especially the subtype concerned with family history, that is told in the American fiction discussed here. For one thing, the emphasis on the "short-tale" tradition is appropriate with regard to the mechanics of the fiction, the "long tales" being too long to be incorporated into a novel. For another, the kind of storytellers who would tell the "long tales" would be in short supply in Ireland itself, much less in America. But it is believable that ordinary Irish emigrants would be concerned about transmitting their family's story, or their own version of it, and that some of these would be the women, especially the older women, of a family.

Finally, Ó Conaill suggests that one element which distinguished story-tellers from their audiences was the element of travel: storytellers brought stories from some other place. Harvey elaborates on the relationship of the itinerant group known in Ireland as "the Travellers" to the storytelling tra-dition;[17] but Ó Conaill seems to mean not the Travellers as a distinct social group in Ireland, but rather a generic traveler, one who has been away and come back again with news for the stay-at-homes. Zimmerman regards both types of travelers as significant. But the element of travel is only one element of what makes storytellers define themselves as such and be accepted in that role.

In her analysis of storytelling in Ireland, Harvey discusses the difficulty of the researcher's identifying "who could rightly be considered a 'story-teller'. "[18] On the simplest level, because these tales are oral, the storyteller is the one who, in Ó Conaill's term, "had" the story, that is, had it in memory; that story is available only through that storyteller. Zimmerman describes how storytellers were actually considered owners of their particu-lar tales, to such an extent that no one but the original taleteller could appropriately tell a particular tale.[19] The social role of the storyteller is complex. In her fieldwork, Harvey followed in the wake of collectors dis-patched by the Irish Folklore Commission, a group established in 1935 to record and thus preserve this oral element of Irish culture. While recording and preserving, however, they also influenced the development of the tradition. Folklore Commission collectors were led to storytellers by mem-bers of the community. When the collectors did record their stories, they privileged both tellers and tales. The honor of having been "collected" by the Folklore Commission conferred official status, further enhancing both the storytellers' reputations in the community and their "self-concept of storyteller."[20]

To the non-folklorist, the Commission's effort to preserve, however praiseworthy its motive, would seem to have reshaped the very tradition it was trying to preserve. Recording an oral form seems to freeze a living tradition at a certain point in time; to privilege a single version of a story (the recorded one); and to anoint specific storytellers (the "collected" ones). The process of collecting in rural areas only also had the effect, according to historian Richard White, of singling out "rural people [as] the designated keepers of the national memory," as the "repository of true Irishness,"[21] as if to suggest that Dubliners, for example, were less Irish than their country cousins. On the national level, White sees the effort of the Irish Folklore Commission as at least partially a response to the political situation in the 1930s. With the Irish Republic only a decade old, its leaders were concerned with "constructing a 'true' Irish culture."[22] The Folklore Commission supported this effort by seeking out and preserving such tales as represented Irish culture as they imagined it. The perceived need to record may be an acknowledgment that the oral tradition was already moribund. As one Blasket Island storyteller explains his motives for recording his and his fellow islanders' lives, "I have written in detail about many events in our lives so that there might be some record of them somewhere, and I have tried to describe the character of the people around me, so that they may be remembered after they are gone, for the likes of us will not be seen again."[23] To this storyteller, writing down an oral form is an acknowledgment that his way of life is dying out.

But these late-twentieth-century novels show that Irish storytelling survives as an element of Irish-American fiction. In the works considered here, the storytelling tradition is used in a different way from the ballad tradition. Unlike the songs, whose themes and images are incorporated into the fiction, the content of the Irish stories is treated in various ways. In Irish-American fiction, the stories told are usually about the past. By story type, they may be either mythological (stories of Ireland's great heroes of myth and legend); folkloric (tales of the supernatural); macrohistorical (events of Irish history); or microhistorical (history of a family and its place within the history of Ireland). In the case of the mythological, folkloric, and macrohistorical stories, the content usually provides a backdrop against which is set the events of the present-time action of the fiction. In the case of the microhistorical tales, the telling of the family's story is a complex matter. In considering how storytelling works in these fictions, important, and intersecting, factors include the process of storytelling itself; the circumstances surrounding the telling of the tale; the character of the storyteller; the story's function in developing the storyteller's character; the character of the listener; the relationship of storyteller to listener; and the function of the story as bearer of tradition.

Storytelling works basically as a specialized form of dialogue. Like all dialogue in fiction, it is a mode of characterizing the speaker as well as an indicator of the nature of the relationship between speaker and listener. As with other kinds of dialogue, that which is said is said only because a particular listener is listening; and everything said subtly alters the relationship between speaker and listener. The speaker's motives are always relevant, as are the desired and actual response of the listener. Then there is the issue of truth and falsity. Stories can be true; not true; or a bit of each. Where the truth lies is often unclear to the listener, in that he or she was usually not present at the events being narrated (the presence of the listener at the events narrated in the story would render the story redundant). Several concepts derived from the folkloric analysis of Irish storytelling are useful in examining how storytelling works in this fiction.

Clodagh Harvey's definition of the storyteller, for example, is relevant when considering this type of character in fiction. The role of storyteller, according to Harvey, partly involves "self-concept" and partly involves the community's perceptions. To paraphrase Harvey's more complex definition, a storyteller is one who is regarded by others as telling stories within the traditional Irish framework.[24] In Ireland, the storyteller's position is one of prestige, power, and authority.[25] But in America, the storyteller cannot depend on tradition to validate his or her authority. So in the novels, the storytelling situation requires that the storyteller be sufficiently convincing to claim the authority inherent in the role. The listeners, the "non-narrators," may or may not accept him or her in that role, and may or may not be content not to tell their own stories. Seldom is the role of storyteller interchangeable within a given fictional work; storytellers do not usually become listeners at another point. Claiming the role is a power move; the storyteller asserts authority via the tale, presenting his or her experience in the past as more important, more valid, especially more authentically Irish than what the listener characters are experiencing in the present. This is why the family's emigrant is usually the storyteller. Emigrants are the ones who have earned the right to tell their stories. Because they have made the journey from Ireland to the United States, their memories are privileged, even their fables are privileged; theirs are the only stories worth telling.

Especially when it focuses on episodes of the family history in which the storyteller is also a participant, storytelling is fraught with all the traits of human memory and hidden motivation that make personal narrative unreliable. Two further concepts from folklore study are useful here. MacLennan distinguishes between two types of stories: the memorate and the fabulate. He defines the memorate as "a short, single-episode narrative recalling something that is claimed to have happened personally to someone"; while the fabulate is what results "when such a memory is transformed by the inventive fantasy of the people into something which transcends reality, but is still claimed to be true."[26] Both memorate and fabulate are the stories told by an individual, "storyteller X's story"; what X remembers is unique to X, and what X adds to the memorate to make it a fabulate is also unique to X. But the difference between memorate and fabulate is not the difference between fact and fiction; because of the vagaries of human memory, both are fictions, but in different ways.

In *Remembering Ahanagran: Storytelling in a Family's Past*, historian Richard White, reflecting on the past of his mother's Irish family, reflects on the unreliability of human memory as a guide to actual historical events. While history "values most what is least altered," memory "wants to rework not just the story but the very facts themselves."[27] To the professional historian, memories are notoriously fallible: "We alter stories. We drop some altogether, and we add others. Who is to know? We often do not know ourselves. We change; our stories change. But our stories make a claim on the past. This is how it happened, they say."[28] Conversely, once a tale is no longer told, the happenings it narrates fade; forgetting, or actively suppressing a tale, are both principles of selectivity.[29] Unlike the stories collected by folklorists, stories which are frozen in time once they are collected, personal stories based on memory are seldom recorded; thus they continue to develop within the oral traditions from which they emerged. Stories are conflated with other stories; they are subtly altered with each retelling (often depending upon who is listening); details are added, subtracted, emphasized, de-emphasized; tales are told so vividly that the teller as well as the listener can be convinced that things happened as described, whether they did or not. In other words, in MacLennan's terms, storytellers constantly transform memorates, which are already unreliable, into fabulates, which are unreliable too, but in a more imaginative way.[30] Since there is no definitive version of an oral tale, the meaning of each retelling of the tale is highly variable, depending on the situation and on the relationship between narrator and non-narrator at any given time.

In fiction, the relationship between the storyteller and the audience is crucial. These are not stories set down in a book for anyone to read, not stories told to strangers as in a dramatic performance, but stories told by one person to an other or others as part of a larger relationship. The storytelling situation in the fiction can serve a ritual function as it does in Ireland, that is, "bringing people together, cementing communal bonds and reinforcing a sense of group continuity."[31] But the storytelling situation can also have another function. In America, the storyteller cannot claim any sort of traditional authority. So the story can become, like any other piece of dialogue, a way of communicating the ideas of one character to another, usually in the hope of influencing the listener's behavior and/or beliefs. Consciously or unconsciously, the intent of the teller shapes the tale. Memory is selective; people remember what is meaningful to them and discard the rest. In a storytelling situation, which details are suppressed and which are stressed depends upon to whom the story is told at that point in the narrative. Much of the significance of X's story depends on whether Y and Z are listening and what X wants Y or Z to believe or do. In addition, because X's story must be told to others, the story becomes a dimension of the relationship between X and each of those others. Each episode involving tale telling, then, is a complicated transaction between teller and audience. Because narrator and non-narrator have a relationship that extends beyond the taletelling situation, the tale becomes a dimension of that relationship.

Finally, the Irish term *shanachie*, teller of the short tales, the *seanchas*, carries with it the connotation of the bearer of traditional wisdom. Zimmerman regards advanced age as a prerequisite to this role of "reservoir of wisdom."[32] In the novels, sometimes this is true and sometimes not. What is more crucial is that the storyteller claims to have a closer connection to the Irish past than the listener does, a connection which is important. Having heard the story, the listener characters must decide for themselves if that is so, if these words from the Irish past have any meaning in the American present. Harvey distinguishes between "narrators" and " 'nonnarrators,' "[33] the latter being members of the audience who never narrate but participate exclusively by listening. These people, termed " 'passive bearers' of tradition" by folklorists,[34] are far from passive in the American fiction. Their task is to evaluate the tradition, reject it totally, preserve it in whole or in part, perhaps even communicate it to others, becoming storytellers in their turn. If the process of storytelling is successful, the listeners accept the storyteller's view of Ireland, and incorporate his or her interpretations into their own view of the world. If the listener rejects or is indifferent to the story, then the opposite is true. But what is more typical than either complete acceptance or complete rejection is some middle ground between the two, in which the listener character accepts some of what the storyteller says and integrates it into his or her own view of Irishness and the Irish past.

Another angle from which to look at storytelling in the fiction is the issue of stories that are not told at all but should be, or stories which are told in such a way that distorted information is conveyed. The paradoxical secretiveness of a loquacious people means that stories that should be told are not. In such cases, the motives of the character who is withholding the story, or who is telling the story in a distorted way, are the most questionable. Sometimes a story is told about a historical event about which the reader may well know more than the listening character does. When the story is about some aspect of the Irish past that is recoverable in some other way than the oral tale, then the reader is invited to learn about it, form his or her own judgment about it, and analyze the interaction between storyteller and listener on the basis of that judgment. Has the storyteller altered the story in honest error? In an attempt to deceive or manipulate the listener? As a consequence of ignorance or other kinds of limitation? All these questions occur to the reader once the storytelling motif has been isolated. In all five of these Irish-American novels, story is used as a vehicle of tradition-bearing. That which is conveyed in story is often partial, at best; and it is the sorting out of the truth and falsity of the stories that carries the plot of each novel. Like song, story transmits bits and pieces of the Irish past to the Irish across the sea and down the generations; from these fragments, the Irish-American characters shape their responses to the Irish characters they meet, as well as to their own Irishness.

In Thomas Moran's *The World I Made for Her*, the protagonist, James Blatchley, creates from his hospital bed an imaginary Irish world composed of fragments of film and music. He imagines this world especially for Nuala, one of his nurses, who emigrated from Ireland. Influenced mainly by the John Wayne film *The Quiet Man*, Blatchley dreams of returning to a pastoral Ireland with Nuala, to live in rural simplicity. The stories Blatchley creates himself are like a film, starring himself as a returned Yank who, unlike the Wayne character in *The Quiet Man*, acclimates smoothly to the Irish way of life. Listening to Irish music in his hospital room provides a sound track for his imaginary film. However, Nuala, the female lead in his fantasy, has her own stories, and her own interpretation of the songs. The tension between Blatchley's image of Ireland and Nuala's is a key element of their growing love, a love culminating in their living out the story told in the traditional ballad "Carrickfergus."

In Lisa Carey's *The Mermaids Singing*, stories told and stories withheld form a series of links between three generations of women. Grace, born in America to an Irish emigrant mother, marries Seamus in Ireland; they have a daughter, Gráinne. Seamus tries to acculturate Grace to Ireland by telling her the mythological stories of the past. But when Grace takes their daughter and leaves Seamus, she also rejects Ireland and most of what it represents to her. Consequently, Grace withholds from Gráinne the true story of her father and her Irish heritage. But she does tell her daughter the story of Grace O'Malley, the pirate queen, because Grace O'Malley represents to Grace Malley the kind of woman she wants her daughter to be. When Grace dies and her mother Clíona comes to Boston to take Gráinne back to Ireland, the myths Clíona tells Gráinne have the same purpose as Seamus's to Grace: to cause Gráinne to accept not only being Irish but living in Ireland. Liam, Gráinne's young boyfriend, reinforces this process with his stories out of myth and folklore. Gráinne initially resists the stories, but gradually, as she begins to feel herself part of her Irish family, she not only accepts the loss of her mother and reconciles herself to a future in Ireland, but transforms her mother into a character in an Irish legend. When she imagines herself telling the story to a young cousin, the acculturation process is complete. Not only has Gráinne learned the story, she has herself become a shanachie.

In Katherine Weber's *The Music Lesson*, Pete Dolan is the storyteller character; he teaches his daughter Irish history as well as the family's place in it. But Pete's history course as taught to a child does not prepare her for meeting Mickey O'Driscoll, who inhabits an entirely different political reality, and who defines truth in terms of expediency. By what he says and what he does not say, Mickey tells a false tale. Mickey presents himself as her cousin and becomes her lover; but he is really a member of an Irish Republican terrorist organization who is using Patricia for political ends. When Patricia goes to Ireland for the first time to help Mickey perpetrate an art theft, she meets Nora O'Driscoll, who tells a story about a wooden settle, a piece of furniture upon which an "old granny peeling potatoes" could sit, the seat of which contains a hidden compartment in which fugitives could hide.[35] This story calls Patricia's attention to the difficulty (even for someone who thinks she already knows Ireland) of "looking beneath," of understanding Ireland. In this "land of eloquent storytellers who cannot distinguish truth from fiction,"[36] nothing is what it seems to be, Mickey above all. While Mickey is connected in Patricia's mind with Cúchulainn, the legendary Irish hero, he is also a terrorist who may be a threat to her as well as to his political enemies. Mickey's language, so charming at first, is offset by his silence; Mickey withholds the true story, at least from her, and so their relationship is at base as deceptive as the old granny's settle.

In Alice McDermott's *Charming Billy*, the whole novel is the attempt of the mourners at Billy's funeral to make sense of Billy's life and death by telling their own versions of his story. All attempt to answer the crucial question: Why did Billy drink himself to death? Was it in response to his loss of Eva, his "Irish girl," whom he regarded as the purpose and goal of his life? When Eva spends the money Billy sent her for her return passage to marry and buy a gas station, Billy's cousin Dennis makes up his own version of Eva's story; Dennis's untrue story makes Billy into a permanent mourner. Billy, some of his own mourners think, drank because, believing Eva dead, he imagined his life as a tragedy: an American Romeo outliving his Irish Juliet. Others think, however, that Billy's drinking antedated his loss of Eva, that he died of a disease that would have killed him even if he had married Eva. When Billy returns to Ireland to "take the pledge" to stop drinking, and to place flowers on Eva's grave, some storytellers believe that he met the now middle-aged Eva, alive and well in her gas station; this, they postulate, was the final factor leading to his decline. Crucial to the novel is the character of Eva. Is she like the Irish newcomers of the greenhorn stories? Is she like the sweet rustics of Uncle Daniel's "Paddy" stories, just waiting to be "brought over" by a willing American? Or is she a wily schemer ready to do a naive American out of his money and betray his fondest hopes? What are the mourners to make of Eva as representative of a mysterious people who may be nothing like the songs and stories about them? The novel is a story of competing storytellers, all of whom vie for the position of being the shanachie, the official teller of Billy's story.

In Mary Gordon's *The Other Side*, Ellen and Vincent MacNamara split the role of family elder and taleteller. The message they send to their progeny is an ambiguous one, as they tell conflicting emigration stories. Ellen's tale involves an infestation of bees in the parish church, a story that expresses the peasant fatalism which made Ireland intolerable to her. But that tale conceals a sadder tale, which Ellen does not tell: the story of her mother's madness following repeated miscarriages and stillbirths, and her father's taking a mistress in her mother's place. Vincent MacNamara's emigration story is also bifurcated, but in a different way. The macrohistorical reason why he left Ireland is one that affected all younger sons of his generation, who could not be supported by a landholding that is by custom, left to the oldest son only. But the triggering personal event was the hatred of that older brother, manifested in the brother's killing Vincent's pet lamb. When Ellen and Vincent each tell their own stories of their departure, they transmit conflicting views of Ireland that are passed down to the various members of the family they establish. Of the two, Vincent's memories of Ireland become softer and gentler with time; but Ellen's enduring hatred for all things Irish poisons every tale she tells. In addition to misrepresenting her own motives, Ellen is also capable of telling wholly false stories about Ireland, which she does to the wealthy and vapid Claire Fitzpatrick, for whom she works as a lady's maid when she first reaches America. Ellen's purpose in fabricating an Irish life seems to be to allow the hated Claire access only to a stereotype, a caricature of herself; revealing her real self to such a person as Ellen thinks Claire to be would be a violation of an already threatened privacy. When Cam and Dan, the only two members of the younger generation to visit Ireland, do so, they are faced with the task of reconciling the reality of Ireland to the diametrically opposed interpretations of it that have been conveyed to them by their grandparents.

At the most basic level, storytelling is about tradition. In *The Irish Storyteller*, Georges Zimmerman distinguishes a traditional society from a modern society on the basis of their attitudes toward change: a " 'traditional society' would tend to repeat what the ancients are said to have done," whereas " 'modern societies' feel compelled always to innovate."[37] The storytellers in these novels convey their sense of Ireland and the Irish to the American characters, who must then decide what to do with it. But to the Americans, these are always someone else's memories, not the "shared memories" that are part of a "national consciousness."[38] As members of a modern society, the American listeners must evaluate Irish tradition and relate it somehow to their own sense of themselves as hyphenated people.

Being an American, with ties to two countries, is no simple matter. In Sebastian Barry's novel *The Whereabouts of Eneas McNulty*, the eponymous hero, a wandering naif who somehow manages to avoid the great events of twentieth-century Irish history by being in the wrong place at the right time, thinks at one point that "he would like to be an American. It is a matter of hailing himself as such, he supposes, in his own mind."[39] But it is only Eneas's simplicity (and the fact that he never really tries to do it) that leads him to believe that making the transition from an Irishman to an American is easy, just a simple matter of "hailing" oneself as American. As Richard White sees it, "American is not something a person learns to be," but rather "an identity contested and fought over."[40] In the fiction, the process of becoming American involves coming to terms with the part of one's heritage that is *not* American: the other side of the hyphen. It is the task of the storyteller to convey that to the American characters; and it is the task of the listener to deal with it as he or she sees fit. As Richard White describes it, such a process simultaneously reaffirms both Irishness and American-ness: "celebrating where you came from is but another way of underlining who you are now: an American, a Yank."[41]

Learning about where they came from is, for the American characters, a function of song and story, both of which recreate Ireland and its people in another country. What White says of Irish stories is true of songs also, that they are a dimension of a particular sense of place. "The landscape," he observes, "was a set of stories as much as it was fences, fields, and buildings."[42] In Ireland, especially in rural areas, physical reminders of the past are everywhere, in the form of ancestral fields, ruined structures, ancient ring-forts. To such places do tales adhere. But the emigrant generation has left that place behind, and the younger American generation has never been there at all. In the United States, scant respect is shown for the artifacts of the past and, even if it were, it would not necessarily be the Irish emigrant's past that was respected. To the emigrants and more so to their progeny, the bits and pieces of Irish lore conveyed in song and story assume all the greater importance for being all there is, the only vehicle by which they can create Ireland in their imaginations. From these fragments, the characters try to put together a sense of what they think about the place, what connection they have or want to have to the ancestral homeland and to its people. If they do visit, the trip is an emotional journey as well, as they try to adjust the perception of their senses to the songs and stories they have heard.

But places are only the setting, the backdrop, for people. These fictions ask the reader to look beyond the stereotypes, but the stereotypes are always there, emerald green lenses through which the American characters see the Irish characters. If in these fictions Americans create in their minds an idealized vision of Ireland as the Emerald Isle of Moore's *Irish Melodies*, or as the Yeatsian Eden of Innisfree, that is a pleasant dream and no harm done. But if, under the influence of song and story and nothing else, they think of the ancestral homeland as populated exclusively by the sweet rural innocents of the emigrant ballads, or as the dwelling place of heroes, or as the isle of saints and scholars, they often come to grief.

Chapter 3

"Picture Postcard Ireland": Thomas Moran's *The World I Made for Her*

Chicken pox: the disease's name conjures up a childhood inconvenience; but when adults contract the disease, it can be life-threatening. Such is the case with James Synge Blatchley, a self-described "art cop," investigator of art thefts for the New York Police Department, mortally ill with what is usually a "kid's disease."[1] The novel centers on Blatchley's time in the Intensive Care Unit of a hospital in lower Manhattan. There, he is cared for by two nurses, young women from Ireland, with one of whom he falls in love, and with both of whom he becomes obsessed. Nuala and Brigit have crossed the ocean in search of a different life. Blatchley, grotesquely ill, confined to bed, intermittently in coma, escapes his failing body by crossing the ocean to Ireland in his mind, where he imagines an Irish world for Nuala. At first, because of his surname, Nuala and Brigit believe him to be an English-American; at first, he himself is unconcerned about his heritage. When Nuala and Brigit notice his middle name (his mother's maiden name) on his hospital record, they turn his attention to his Irish ancestry. His mother's people were from " 'south of Dublin', " his grandfather fled to the United States after being condemned to death for his part in one of the key events in Irish history, the 1916 Easter Rising.[2] Despite his strong connection to Ireland, and despite his being well traveled otherwise, Blatchley has never been what Brigit calls " 'back' " to his mother's country.[3] Now, because of his long and increasingly intimate relationship with both nurses, and his growing love for Nuala, Blatchley must go "back," in mind if not in body. James Synge Blatchley's last task on earth is to make sense of the part of his heritage that had hitherto been reduced to an easily ignored middle name. To do so, he goes back to an imaginary country, assembled from fragments of the Irish past. As he learns about Ireland through Nuala, he realizes that the country in his mind bears only a passing resemblance to the real country from which Nuala and Brigit emigrated; and its people, known only through media representations of them, bear little resemblance to Nuala and Brigit themselves. Despite this disillusionment, his passage into death is eased by his imagining the afterlife as a place very much like Ireland.

Catholic Girls and Pagan Goddesses: Stereotyping Irish Women

Blatchley begins to learn about the Irish not only from but also because of Nuala and Brigit, his two favorite nurses, who seem to him to represent Irish womanhood. First of all, they are nurses, and historically, nursing was an important profession for Irish women. While the generations of women emigrants who left Ireland in the wake of the Great Famine were likely to become domestics in America, later emigrants (or daughters of earlier emigrants) were likely to get an education; many became teachers or office workers, many others became nurses.[4] The apparent selflessness of the nursing profession fits nicely into the traditional beliefs about Irish women transmitted in song and story. As nurses, nurturers, they replace Blatchley's Irish mother in tending him in the infantile state to which illness has reduced him. This quasi-maternal function, along with their white garments, surrounds them with an aura of innocence, which fits his first impression of them as generic Irish lasses. But this is the late twentieth century in New York, and no one, not even an Irish woman, is as innocent as Blatchley imagines. Ironically, Nuala's and Brigit's professional status as nurses actually facilitates their deviation from Irish tradition. Their training in Ireland enables them to emigrate legally and with professional status intact; this gives them the ability to get a job and live on their own in anonymous New York, enjoying a degree of freedom, especially sexual freedom, not possible in Ireland. Each of them employs her freedom in a different way. As his knowledge of them increases, as he learns to respond to subtleties rather than stereotypes, Blatchley comes to see Nuala and Brigit in terms of three distinct but related constructs of Irish womanhood: woman as Catholic and virginal, woman as pagan and sexual, and woman as symbol of the land itself.

Nuala, especially in Brigit's satirical version of her, represents a simple, familiar version of Irish womanhood: the virginal Catholic saint. Catholic devotion to Jesus' mother Mary is a way of emphasizing the cultural importance of sexual purity as the most important, perhaps the only significant, womanly virtue. The Catholic church's restrictions on sexuality, traditionally regarded with the utmost seriousness in Ireland, are well known. But when Brigit canonizes her colleague as "Saint Nualala," her mocking elongation of her friend's name not only undercuts Nuala's qualifications for sainthood but mocks the very notion. If Nuala, unvirginal as she is, is a saint, sainthood, perhaps even virginity, are relative concepts rather than moral absolutes; Nuala is saintly only in contrast to Brigit. Blatchley thinks that Nuala accepts the role of foil to Brigit, and so believes herself to be "just another boring Catholic girl."[5] But Nuala is now a New Yorker, which is at least a challenge to and may even be a disqualification for conventional Catholic sanctity. One of the ways in which emigration is imagined in modern Irish novels, especially for women, and especially to big, anonymous cities like New York, is as an opportunity to live one's sexual life by one's own standards and not by those of Catholic Ireland. If Nuala is sexually saintly at all, it is only in comparison to Brigit. Nuala has had only a few lovers; with one of them, she was genuinely in love; at the time when the novel begins, she has been abstinent for a year. These qualifications place her, in Blatchley's mind at least, as close to the ideal of purity as is possible in late-twentieth-century Manhattan.

When Blatchley asks Brigit if she herself is a virgin, she replies, in a mock-Hiberno-English that she uses at no other time, " 'Is the pope Catholic? What else would a fine colleen like meself be. I'm saving up for marriage.' "[6] To Brigit, virginity is a relic of the Irish past. No emulator of the Virgin Mary, Brigit resembles instead an earlier, pre-Christian construct of Irish womanhood: that expressed in the mythological cycles out of the Celtic pagan past. Many of the women in these cycles, larger than human but not quite goddesses, were noted for their sexual voraciousness. For example, Maeve (or Medb), Queen of Connaught, a character in the eighth- to ninth-century epic *Táin Bó Cuailnge*, was said to be so insatiable that "she never had one man without another waiting in his shadow."[7] Celtic superwomen like Maeve wage war, mate with many men, are as powerful as or more powerful than their husbands, are even the source of any power those husbands may have. Since, as Charles Bowen explains, there was no tradition of an inherited kingship in Ireland, the "myth of the goddess' choice" developed to account for the selection of one man over another for the kingship.[8] Thus the woman whose choice of a man makes him a king is the goddess of sovereignty.[9] That chosen man must be "a flawless representative of [the] tribe,"[10] lest the tribe suffer from its leader's weakness. This symbolic connection between Brigit and the sovereignty goddess explains why Blatchley loves Nuala, not Brigit: in his current debilitated state, Blatchley cannot aspire to the favors of the sovereignty goddess. The symbolic connection between Brigit and Maeve also explains Brigit's sex life. As a modern-day Maeve, Brigit centers her life in New York around a bar, the name of which calls to mind the pagan underworld. At the Bells of Hell, many men are available to Brigit. Brigit is proud of living on the edge, which for her means alcohol and drugs in addition to sex.

Brigit's alcohol and drug use is another element of her connection with the Queen of Connaught and with the ancient Celtic past. Maeve's name means " 'the intoxicating, or intoxicated one.' "[11] Like her name, Maeve's behavior exhibits "the importance placed on the state of frenzy or ecstasy" in the Celtic culture.[12] When Brigit takes her drugs, particularly Ecstasy, this must be considered in the light of the ancient tradition that she represents, as well as of the Manhattan drug scene. In addition to Ecstasy and nightly pints of Guinness, Brigit uses a pain reliever pilfered from the hospital. Brigit's drug of choice, fentanyl, is a powerful narcotic analgesic intended to be used by cancer patients or those who, like Blatchley, are in chronic pain, as a remedy for "breakthrough pain," pain not alleviated by other opiates. It is not to be used with alcohol or other drugs, because both exaggerate its side effects; overdosing can be fatal.[13] Brigit, a nurse, knows all this when she injects fentanyl between her fingers with pediatric needles. But her death by fentanyl overdose is a logical extension of the way she lived, as did her ancient Celtic forebears, in a "state of frenzy or ecstasy."[14] For Brigit, life-threatening behaviors constitute, paradoxically, an affirmation of life. Her *carpe diem* philosophy bears little resemblance to Christian theology. In leaving Ireland, she leaves Catholicism also; in New York, she can live (and die) like the pagan she is.

If Nuala and Brigit represent two sides to the coin of Irish womanhood—Catholic "virgin" and pagan goddess—and Blatchley must choose (or be chosen by) only one, it must be Nuala. Not only is he not worthy of the sovereignty goddess, he must also love a woman who meets his need for the country itself, who indeed, symbolically, is the country. Imagining Ireland as a woman is a tradition dating back at least to Thomas Moore, who, in his *Irish Melodies*, "gave Ireland a feminine persona"; songwriters following in this tradition focused specifically on the countrywoman as the most authentic image of the land.[15] As George Russell (AE) points out in his 1899 work *Imaginations and Reveries*, an "ideal of Ireland," the perception of it as "a sacred land," was in people's minds even then; Russell mentions the poem "Dark Rosaleen" by James Clarence Mangan (1803–49) as an example of this phenomenon.[16] This poem, based on the seventeenth-century poem "Róisín Dubh" (ascribed to Owen Roe MacWard), compares the relationship between Ireland and its sons to that of a young girl and her lover. Rosaleen is a "virgin flower" who lives, innocently, "at home . . . in [her] emerald bowers," praying and thinking of her lover. Her sorrows are those of Ireland itself; her virginity must be defended against the rapist, England; and the lover's mission is to save Rosaleen by overthrowing English hegemony, thus restoring Ireland to her former glory, to "the golden throne" where she shall "reign, and reign alone." The lover's passion is intensely sexual, a "lightning in [his] blood," which is transmuted into the battle fury needed to save Rosaleen/Ireland:

> O! the Erne shall run red
>> With redundance of blood,
> The earth shall rock beneath our tread,
>> And flames wrap hill and wood,
> And gun-peal, and slogan cry,
>> Wake many a glen serene,
> Ere you shall fade, ere you shall die.[17]

Mangan's poetry, as Robert Welch points out, is characterized by "a patriotic zeal that almost approaches frenzy";[18] the metaphor of Ireland as a beloved woman allows for the transference of the passion that, in peacetime, a man might feel for a flesh-and-blood woman onto his beloved country, the most desirable woman of all.

So for Blatchley to imagine Ireland, he must love Nuala, as she, more closely than Brigit, conforms to his imaginary construct of the country itself, as rural Ireland. He cannot think of her as living the rest of her life, with him or without him, in New York, or even in Dublin. In order to fully represent Irishness, she must (at least in his fantasy) return to the country-side with which he identifies her. Blatchley's hopeless love for Nuala exists within the larger myth of the Emerald Isle itself, a "distant, soft, romantic place."[19] A world that never existed on either side of the Atlantic, this is an

> Ireland of imagination . . . transformed by commercial popular culture into a rural paradise peopled by handsome young men, beautiful colleens, cherished parents, glowing hearthsides, and friends and neighbors, all of whom were white and blue-eyed. The pipes and fiddles were always sounding and the dances were always about to begin. Sex was a hard-won kiss and love was eternal. A very different place, this imagined Ireland, from the gritty, crowded, multi-ethnic urban cities where most of Irish America lived. The Eden-like quality of this mythical Ireland of the popular song was reinforced by the fact that this was a "lost" land.[20]

Whenever Blatchley imagines Nuala in Ireland, the world he makes for her resembles the lost land of song and story. But Blatchley is no student of the songs of Moore or the poetry of Mangan, much less of the social commentary of George Russell. Like many Americans, Blatchley gets his beliefs from the popular media, from going to the movies and believing what he sees there; and it is from these images that he constructs his own version of the Emerald Isle.

Unreal Country: "The Quiet Man" and the Myth of the Emerald Isle

Had Blatchley never fallen ill, he would never have met Nuala and Brigit, and therefore would never have given the time and attention to Ireland and to things Irish that he does in his sickbed. If he had retained his health, he might well have been satisfied with the partial knowledge that most of the Irish-American characters in these fictions have: knowledge obtained by way of random fragments of the Irish experience. Because of his physical condition, however, Blatchley also cannot undertake a serious study of Irish history or literature. Thus Blatchley's impressions of Ireland and the Irish people are shaped by past experiences, especially his viewing of the 1952 John Wayne vehicle, *The Quiet Man*. He knows that the vision of Ireland he has gleaned from that film is inaccurate: "I'm sure my imagination is a generation or two out of date. Or it may have come completely out of books and movies, every Irish girl looking like Maureen O'Hara in *The Quiet Man*, every village so peaceful a mix of Catholic and Protestants."[21] He knows that the Ireland of this film is an unreal country, "a picture postcard sort of world, the stupidest illusion you can have."[22] But any works as popular as Wayne's films shape popular perceptions, especially in the absence of any nuanced thought; and so it is that *The Quiet Man* becomes a major component of James Blatchley's image of Ireland.

The film tells the story of a former boxer, Sean Thornton, known in the ring as "Trooper" Thorne. After accidentally killing an opponent, Thornton returns to his birthplace, an Irish town named Inisfree, presumably an allusion to the ideal place celebrated in Yeats's poem "The Lake Isle of Innisfree."[23] There he meets and falls in love with Mary Kate Danaher, played by Maureen O'Hara. Obstacles arise in the form of her loutish brother, Will, played by Victor McLaglen, who consents to the match but refuses to turn over the bride's dowry, her "fortune." Without her fortune, Mary Kate does not consider herself well and truly married, and thus for a time refuses to consummate the marriage. Thornton must settle conflicts on two related fronts: with his wife, an Irish shrew whose taming involves a degree of physical force that smacks of incipient spousal abuse; and with his brother-in-law, who must also be forced both to honor the dowry custom and to recognize the returned Yank as alpha male. What Thornton must come to understand is that Mary Kate's fortune represents not just the preservation of a quaint Irish custom but also "a sense of her own identity."[24] Thornton and Mary Kate are members of not one but two cultures. Each must come to terms with the other, and, to that end, each seeks counsel: he of Rev. Playfair, the Church of Ireland clergyman; she of Father Lonergan, the Roman Catholic priest. Thornton must also deal with an additional inner conflict with regard to engaging in battle with brother Will; Thornton left the ring, and the United States, because he killed. This being a comedy, the hero triumphs on all fronts. He and his bride live happily ever after amid bucolic Irish scenes, thus presumably healing the psychic wounds engendered by his traumatic experience in America (a topic that gets lost amid the other plot events).

What Blatchley remembers so clearly about *The Quiet Man* is not its confused values or wooden acting, but the fine photography of the Irish countryside, which builds on the very valid "association of Ireland with the beauties of nature" as celebrated in Irish songs like Thomas Moore's.[25] In the film, the camera pays homage to Ireland's natural and man-made beauties: its placid lakes; its stone bridges and walls; its rolling green fields; its Celtic crosses in windswept graveyards; its ruined castles; its country lanes down which a properly chaperoned courting couple might stroll; its thatched cottages right out of the emigrant ballads. Thornton's own birthplace is a "wee, humble cottage" at the foot of a suitably picturesque mountain. When Thornton repurchases and rehabilitates this cottage, he paints the door green, upon which Rev. Playfair's wife comments that "it looks the way all Irish cottages should look, and so seldom do. And only an American would have thought of emerald green." This single line of dialogue is the only hint that the makers of this film had their tongues in their cheeks at all; to Mrs. Playfair, only an American could be capable of such blatant "Eiresatz."[26]

While the natural landscape cannot be portrayed by the camera in any other way than accurately, the Irish characters in *The Quiet Man* could hardly be more stereotyped. The fact that the Irish actors are listed in the opening credits as a breed apart from the three American stars gives the viewer a clue as to how the Irish will be portrayed in the film. Even when factoring in the film's comic nature, it is hard to see any character as other than a caricature of Irishness. When Thornton arrives at the local railroad station, the railroad employees and the locals mime a gregarious, unsophisticated population whose hospitable reception of the returned Yank is mixed with awe. Thornton's late mother's sweetly Irish voice, speaking to him from the past, draws him back from the wicked United States to a bucolic scene of childhood innocence. When Thornton first glimpses Mary Kate Danaher, she is working as a shepherdess, thus neatly conjuring up pastoral images of the Irish past. The typical Irishness of Maureen O'Hara's beauty associates her character, as women often are in Irish poetry and song, "with the beauties of the Irish landscape."[27] When later she is revealed as hot-tempered and self-willed, that too is seen as part of her Irishness. The narrator, the Roman Catholic priest, Peter Lonergan, connives with the Church of Ireland rector, Rev. Mr. Playfair, in interfering in the lives of all and sundry; to judge from their chummy relationship, as Blatchley, idealist though he is, also notices, no sectarian strife ever existed in Ireland. An amiable carriage driver, Michaeleen Oge Flynn (played by Barry Fitzgerald), involves himself in the lovers' every doing, including acting as a chaperone to prevent prenuptial "pattyfingers." With his fellow pub-goers, Michaeleen is a merry drunk, neatly contrasting with the mean drunk, Will Danaher. The populace is given to bursting into songs like "The Wild Colonial Boy," "The Kerry Dancers," "Galway Bay," and Thomas Moore's "Believe Me If All Those Endearing Young Charms," further enhancing the Irishness of all proceedings. These singing Irish are, however, equally capable of metamorphosing into fighting Irish; the "match" between Thornton and Danaher is the high point of the film, with Mary Kate almost forgotten in this battle for male dominance. To be fair, the American character, Sean Thornton, is stereotyped as much as are the Irish. The title's characterization of him as the strong but silent type lends credence to the paucity of dialogue assigned to him; the "yup/nope" style of speaking characteristic of film cowboys serves Wayne well here, the taciturnity of the character compensating for Wayne's limited range of acting skills.

What is wrong with this picture of both the Irish and the American is, as Blatchley senses, that it presents a wildly oversimplified view of both cultures. Sean Thornton, though born in Ireland, is regarded by all as a Yank; yet it is unclear whether he, having returned, must acclimate to the villagers, or they to him. This is especially true with regard to his relationship with Mary Kate. The marriage choice, for one thing, is different in Ireland and America. At one point, her brother Will is refusing his consent; when Mary Kate obeys her brother, Thornton fumes at her, "It's what you say that counts, not him!" But, as the ubiquitous Michaeleen reminds him, "This is Ireland, not America," and Mary Kate cannot marry without her brother's consent. When Thornton denigrates Mary Kate's fortune as merely "furniture and stuff," the significance of the dowry to an Irish bride must be gently, if vaguely, explained, also by Michaeleen. Thornton's later behavior suggests that he never really wanted his Mary Kate to act like an American woman, and the taming-of-the-shrew theme ends with Thornton metamorphosed into a bossy patriarch, Mary Kate into a submissive wife.

Given this film's superficiality with regard to portrayal of Irish people and confusion over the very real differences between the American Irish and the Irish living in Ireland, it is small wonder that someone like Blatchley would develop no realistic vision but a collection of vague notions "a generation or two out of date" that become part of his "picture postcard sort of world."[28] Linda Dowling Almeida says that such films as *The Quiet Man* did, and still do, perpetuate "the image of Ireland as a pastoral ideal," a land "frozen in time," strictly a "tourist's Ireland." This image, Almeida says, was promoted by the travel industry on both sides of the Atlantic and was impossible even for people who actually traveled there to escape,[29] much less those who, like Blatchley, had only watched a film. Like Thornton, Blatchley had a Irish mother and a bad experience in the United States; he imagines being, like Thornton, a returned Yank. But it is to an unreal Ireland that Blatchley travels in his mind, and to which he brings his dream version of Nuala.

"Picture Postcard" or "Damp, Old Well": Two Views of Ireland

Rural Ireland is, to Blatchley, a utopian natural environment, especially as opposed to the dystopic artificial environment of the hospital, the ICU, and his own failing body. In his hospital bed, Blatchley makes a dream world out of the photographic images from *The Quiet Man*. His imaginings represent an experience somewhere between ordinary dreams, drug-induced hallucinations, and coma fantasies. Blatchley's dream world also features idealized landscapes of countries to which he has actually traveled; but because the world he makes for Nuala is also his version of the afterlife, it must be Ireland and no other country. His beloved Nuala is most closely associated with Ireland's natural beauty, its allegedly simple, pastoral people, rural childhood innocence. Even what to many is Ireland's least desirable feature, its climate, is to him part of Nuala's mystique: rain is "her natural element."[30] Postcard photos are never taken in the rain; so when Blatchley makes for Nuala a "world less sad" than the world of the ICU, the world he makes is highly idealized, a "picture postcard sort of world"[31] in which every day is sunny. But when Nuala is the storyteller, her stories correct Blatchley's highly edited version of the real country.

Blatchley's perfect land is like a film that can be rewound and replayed to allow him to take Nuala through various stages of her life. He begins by imagining her prenatal life; he supplies her with parents "in love with the sound of that ancient name"; he imagines her born peacefully, "with scarcely a tear or a wail just before one of those rare Irish dawns when the sun slipped up over the horizon undimmed by fog banks or clouds."[32]

This dream is all the better for the baby Nuala's inability to question, even in his imagination, the world he makes for her. Once Blatchley begins to imagine Nuala with a mind of her own, she is already beginning to step out of the postcard. Even within the most stereotypical Emerald Isle scenes of her childhood, he imagines Nuala as developing the skepticism about Ireland that will eventually contribute to her decision to emigrate. Blatchley imagines himself watching Nuala among other little girls, all of whom are making their First Communion against the backdrop of a pastoral landscape, featuring picturesque houses and other conventional elements of seaside charm. In one of the novel's few allusions to the predominant faith of Ireland, the beauty, and even the cost, of the girls' dresses is a testimony to the importance of the central ritual of Roman Catholic childhood. And the fact that First Communicants are, as custom dictates, prepubescent children further underlines what Blatchley perceives as Nuala's spiritual virginity, that quality which Brigit mocks by calling her "St. Nualala." Yet even in her youth and innocence, Nuala reminds him that his dream is not hers. Even in his dream, she tells Blatchley, " 'You've got it all wrong.' "[33]

As he dreams Nuala into maturity, Blatchley must come to terms with her sexuality, and does so in the most innocent (most Irish?) way possible: "I gave her a lovely loss of virginity in a hay barn with a boy who was also a virgin and was tender with her. It left her with a trust of and like for men."[34] At the same time as he imagines this Irish version of sex, he must also accept Nuala's sex life in New York. In that less innocent environment, he still finds a way to justify "her boys, the four or five" by making them men he can himself respect: "she didn't run off with bikers or junkies or misogynist stockbrokers or reptilian lawyers" or other unsavory types.[35] By the time of her most serious love affair, with Robbie, reality intrudes. By Nuala's account, Robbie was an intravenous drug user who contracted AIDS and died of it. Nuala, though uninfected physically, is infected psychologically, and comes to the point in her life at which she meets Blatchley as damaged in spirit as he is in body.

With Robbie dead, Blatchley rescripts Nuala's life with a healthy version of himself starring opposite Nuala. He will court Nuala just as a proper Irish girl should be courted (he has, after all, seen *The Quiet Man*, so knows how to avoid cultural misunderstandings about courtship). In his dream, he and Nuala go back to Ireland as a traditional courting couple. There, he, a more sensitive Yank than the John Wayne character, adapts himself easily to Irish ways. He changes his way of dressing, his way of eating, even their customary sleeping arrangements to please Nuala and to win her father's approval. He can easily imagine himself as belonging to Nuala's world, the world she would make for him if he were somehow to recover and if, an outcome only slightly less likely, he were to persuade her to return to Ireland with him.

The film still rolling in his mind, he imagines Nuala's later life as a married woman, living in a cottage that, except for its red door, is like the cottage refurbished by Sean Thornton in *The Quiet Man*:

> In the world I'd make for Nuala, she'd live in Ireland, I think, in a lovely little cottage with roses along the walk and geraniums in the windowpots. The cottage would be whitewashed inside and out, with ancient beams of wood so dark they were almost black. The front door would be painted a deep, rich red. Nuala's man would be up first, out feeding the Connemara pony that pulled their gig, and forking hay to the cattle. Nuala would still be in bed, stretching her limbs luxuriously under linen sheets. She'd think a little bit about New York and the one bad thing that happened, and she'd be glad to be in a place so safe.
>
> She'd get up and make strong tea, oatmeal with fresh cream, and toast. She'd eat with her man and smile at him across the little kitchen table that had belonged to her great-grandmother. She'd be wearing a cream cable-knit sweater and corduroy trousers tucked into Wellingtons. Her hair would be loose and wild as the gorse that sprawled all over the ridge behind the cottage.
>
> She's going to get pregnant one of these days soon.
>
> It's a picture postcard sort of world, the stupidest illusion you can have. Anyone who's ever traveled anyplace knows that for sure. Yet that's the best my mind can come up with just now. Maybe some depth and texture will come another time, and some sense of reality.
>
> Nuala will require this, I know. She won't live in dream-time.[36]

The details of Blatchley's dream of Ireland—the cottage with its roses and geraniums, its heavy wood beams and whitewashed walls; the Connemara pony and the gig it pulls; the hay forked to the cattle; the meal of tea, oatmeal with cream, and toast; the ancient table with its family history; Nuala's clothing, her sweater, her trousers, her Wellies—all seem straight out of an Irish Tourist Board brochure. Even as he creates this world, Blatchley knows that it is unreal. Nuala is a real woman, not a character in his personal drama. In this dream, he does not name himself as Nuala's companion, suggesting that he knows he will not be part of any world Nuala makes for herself.

Although James Blatchley is not aware of it, the pastoral world he has created for Nuala is one with important precedents in Irish culture, with special significance for Irish women. Éamon de Valera, who became *Taoseach* or prime minister in 1932, tried to inculcate an image of the country that reinforced the pastoral image. In his 1943 radio address on St. Patrick's Day, de Valera described a country that he believed was and in perpetuity ought to be

> "a land whose countryside would be bright with cosy homesteads, whose fields and villages would be joyous with the sound of industry, with the

romping of sturdy children, the contests of athletic youths and the laughter of comely maidens . . . in a word, the home of a people living the life that God desires that man should live."[37]

According to historian Charles Townshend, the "credibility of this image" was shaky even as de Valera spoke.[38] By the time women of Nuala's genera-tion were born, de Valera's image of Irishness as "encapsulated in a happy rural family life"[39] had long since palled. According to de Valera's theory, women in particular were expected to be "rooted to the national soil of Ireland."[40] In fact, more and more of them were, like the men, emigrating. Nevertheless, the old tradition lingered in the form of expectations of women's behavior. In an interview with Irish women living in England, Breda Gray records their frustration with their families' expectations that they should and will return to Ireland, their anger at having their lives out-side Ireland trivialized. One in particular, a young woman named Aine, laments her parents' assumption that Ireland is the place, the only place, "*where she rightly belongs.*"[41] As women, they are assumed to bear the bur-den of symbolically representing not only the country but also the quality of Irishness. Being a symbol seems to these women to require that they stay, or having left, return; and this regardless of their own inclinations in the matter. Ironically, all unaware of the historical context, Blatchley imagines Nuala much as the parents of Gray's interviewees do: denying the reality (and likely permanence) of her life outside Ireland; assuming that she will return to the only place "where she rightly belongs." However, like the women Gray interviewed, Nuala has her own story of Ireland, and of herself.

Contrasted with Blatchley's dreams of Nuala's childhood are Nuala's own stories, which express a more ambivalent view of growing up Irish. Only one of Nuala's stories imagines Ireland as pastoral paradise: the story of her grandfather, "an old man who loved her company and taught her what he knew," and his "old curragh, one of the last in Bantry." As a young girl of "eight or ten," Nuala habitually went fishing with her grandfather in a cur-ragh, the kind of small boat that figures so prominently in picture-postcard views of Ireland. While their catch was unimpressive, Nuala loved the way her grandfather taught her traditional ways. Particularly memorable was the spring during which they painted the boat in bright colors, which led to her naming the boat "Blue Johnny." Although her grandfather believed it was "bad luck to sail a boat named after yourself," he did sail it, to the delight of the " 'green girl' " Nuala was then. This is Nuala's favorite story; she tells it to Blatchley because she thinks he is " 'a man who'd understand' " and because it is " 'a pleasure . . . to tell the tales.' "[42] Like all storytellers in these fictions, Nuala preserves the past, represented by her grandfather and his Blue Johnny, and bears Irish traditions to her patient in New York. In this tale she memorializes the image of a pastoral land, home to a loving old man and his innocent young granddaughter. Her listener is perfectly receptive, the ideal audience for such a tale. Blatchley thinks of the story as "beautiful"; it provides him with "imaginary memories of a little redhead squealing with delight in her grandda's curragh,"[43] and reinforces his own view of "picture-postcard Ireland."

In other stories, however, Nuala presents a darker image. In Dublin, where she and Brigit attended nursing school, wild horses ran through the run-down tenements, places " 'where the government warehoused the unemployed, the unemployable, and the working poor, when the inner city slums crumbled beyond repair.' " The horses were wild, and ridden by " 'tenement boys' " of twelve to fourteen wilder than themselves, no rural lads posting through the countryside, but rather underage drug addicts and pushers " 'on heroin already; some sold it.' " While Nuala makes a better world for them in her own mind—she imagines them as " 'young Tartars on an Asian steppe, flying before the wind' "—she knows that their experience of life in Ireland differs from her own. Their version of English is unintelligible to her, and they know from her speech that "she wasn't one of their lot." These boys, members of the Dublin underclass, are of less value to the larger society than the horses upon which they ride; " 'animal-protection groups' " are concerned with cruelty to the horses, but not with the system that produces young drug-addicts and drug-dealers.[44] The antithesis of Nuala herself at the same age, at home in the country, her grandda's darling, these boys represent at least part of Ireland's urban present, and possibly its future. Blatchley's reaction to this story is more problematic. Heavily medicated, he drifts off to sleep. It is not clear whether these city boys are truly incorporated into his pastoral myth.

In another story, Nuala presents a negative view of even the rural areas. Her father worked at a big oil terminal near a town called Glengarriff, which, she says, even those most relentlessly upbeat sources of information, the tourist guidebooks, called " 'tawdry . . . Too many pubs and loose women, everything run-down and shabby.' " Though near to Bantry House, " 'what everyone said was the most beautiful property in all Ireland,' " the oil terminal where her father works is not only " 'ugly' " but also economically redundant. Her father is too, because when the terminal is closed, he remains " 'on the dole for the rest of his life,' " reduced to writing begging letters to his daughter in New York.[45] The economic problems of Nuala's parents, their dependency on American money[46] for their survival, highlights an unbeautiful aspect of the Emerald Isle: it is regarded by the young as a place from which they must escape. Like many other Irishwomen before her,[47] Nuala—although she " 'never would have chosen it' "—finds nursing a way out of the " 'damp, old well' " of Ireland into the

" 'open air' " of New York.[48] Nuala sees herself as unlike the other young Irish who remain in Ireland, young people who, she says, " 'give up at an early age.' " When Blatchley asks her to explain her perseverance, she cites two factors: her grandfather, and her education, the latter encouraged by her parents, who " 'saw the future and sent me to nursing school in Dublin to escape it.' "[49]

The death of Nuala's grandfather marks the passage of the old ways in Ireland. He dies, appropriately, just as she is about to leave for Dublin and her new life. His funeral is the last of a tradition that is itself dying, a " 'lovely, old-fashioned' " Irish sendoff, with " 'all the village walking behind the hearse drawn by two black ponies with stiff cockades rising between their ears . . . .And the rain it did rain down that day.' "[50] To bid farewell not only to her grandda but also to her childhood, Nuala takes a hatchet to Blue Johnny, sinking it. This rite of passage accomplished, she leaves for nursing school and her future. This is Nuala's emigration story: pushed out, like many of her generation, by economic factors, she leaves behind the world of rural childhood and with it Ireland's past; but she also leaves behind the tawdry urban slums and the dying coastal cities, which are Ireland's present and future. In so doing, she is one of a large cohort of young Irish who have made the same journey.

The "New Irish" and Their Music: Tradition and Innovation

Nuala's stories provide Blatchley with images out of which to construct a country; song lyric and poetry ease his journey to it. Considering Blatchley's condition and his interest in Ireland, it is fictionally probable that he would have Irish music playing in his hospital room as the backdrop to his imaginings. So important is music in this novel that it should be packaged with its own compact disc, in effect providing a sound track to the novel. Blatchley's discography includes many of the most important Irish musicians of the time in which the novel is set: Enya, Black 47, Dolores O'Riordan, Sinéad O'Connor, and Van Morrison and the Chieftains. Each of these musicians explores, in different ways, a key issue of the novel: the relationship between the Irish past and the Irish present. As was discussed earlier, traditional emigrant ballads dating from Famine times see Ireland through the dreamy haze of nostalgia. The music of Nuala and Brigit's generation, while it often incorporates traditional musical forms like the emigrant ballads (sometimes respectfully, sometimes ironically), also looks at the present and future of the Irish on both sides of the Atlantic with a realistic, even cynical, eye.

Blatchley listens to a variety of late-twentieth-century Irish music, but he finds traditional music, even in a language that he does not understand, most helpful in preparing him for his journey.

Nuala and Brigit, like some of the musicians popular with members of their generation, reflect new realities of the Irish emigration experience. Despite some similarities to the emigrants of the past who fled Ireland in search of a better life in America, their emigrant generation differs from previous ones. As life in Ireland improved and the disparity between the United States and Ireland decreased, emigration became an act of choice rather than desperation. In *Irish Immigrants in New York City, 1945–1995*, Linda Dowling Almeida compares these "New Irish" to their predecessors. In general, Almeida says, the relationship between emigrants from any nation and the host country is affected by emigrants' "sense of the two countries' relative status."[51] Those who emigrated in the 1980s or later, as Nuala and Brigit did, came to the United States with several advantages over earlier generations. Since 1922, if they were emigrating from the Republic of Ireland, they were leaving an independent nation; thus they brought with them a more positive legacy than did those who fled colonialism and oppression. Another advantage enjoyed by the New Irish was that, for over a hundred years, many other Irish had successfully negotiated the transition before them, clearing a path for them; no longer would the Irish have to struggle as mightily to overcome discrimination, nor would they be forced to accept society's most menial work. Economic problems in Ireland persisted and motivated many to emigrate; but as the twentieth century progressed, Ireland's economy improved. As the century ended, New Irish emigrants came from an Ireland to which some at least could imagine themselves returning. Thus some did not, says Almeida, "foresee themselves as Irish-Americans"; indeed, some saw the "trip to America [as] a commute rather than a final journey."[52] No longer did they need decisively and finally to reject an old culture and embrace a new one; a trans-Atlantic identity became an increasingly viable option. The music that Blatchley plays in his hospital room is one manifestation of a new phenomenon in the history of the Irish in America: a generation that can function within, and tolerate the tension between, two cultures.

Because they have their "green cards" and are living and working legally in New York, Nuala and Brigit are better off than the undocumented; in other ways, however, they are typical of New Irish in that they are living a different life in New York than they would have in Ireland. Almeida cites " 'restrictive lifestyle, culture' " as one of the main reasons for New Irish emigration, especially for women;[53] one of Breda Gray's interviewees, Pauline, confirms this motive for emigration, citing a desire " 'to live the life you want to live without, you know, your aunt sending the parish priest around.' "[54] It is obvious from Nuala and Brigit's behavior once in New York that they have broken free of all sexual prohibitions; but they have also, like Gray's interviewees, "resist[ed] the stereotypes and responsibilities which they associate with being Irish women."[55] Like others of their emigrant generation, they do not center their lives on the family; they emigrate together, but not with family, and not to family; they seem to feel no urgency about marrying and starting families of their own. Nuala's contact with her family involves mainly sending money home; Brigit seems unconnected to her family in Ireland. The two women neither share an apartment, nor do they live in an Irish neighborhood; according to Almeida, many New Irish are, like Nuala and Brigit, not content in the " 'ghettoes' of the outer boroughs," but prefer to "explore the unconventional lifestyle and freedom of the artistic and avant-garde in lower Manhattan."[56] The Irish bar that they frequent, the Bells of Hell, seems to be their only connection with the Irish community in New York; and, for Brigit at least, this is unfortunate. While they are legal emigrants, and thus can travel to Ireland at will, neither Nuala or Brigit expresses a desire to do so. Neither seems to be concerned with Catholic rituals or morality, even as components of their ethnicity. As New Irish, then, Nuala and Brigit regard being Irish differently from the way Blatchley does. While Nuala and Brigit are embarking on "a deliberate move away from the traditional,"[57] Blatchley is moving toward it. The two women have come to New York precisely to escape from the place with which they have, all unintentionally, caused Blatchley to become fascinated.

Despite their different agendas, however, all three can explore their own feelings about their Irishness and about each other via the music played in Blatchley's hospital room. The various groups and solo artists mentioned in the novel not only provide a brief summary of late-twentieth-century Irish music but also help to develop the novel's important themes, especially its examination of the traditional, rural past versus the urban and/or trans-Atlantic present. The music of Enya, which might well be considered "Eiresatz"[58] by some, hearkens back to an idealized version of Ireland. Whether her particular brand of music, called an "otherworldly . . . confection" by Geoff Wallis and Sue Wilson and as a progenitor of the "whole ethereal, wispy Celtic New Age scene" by June Skinner Sawyers,[59] is authentically Irish or not is a matter of debate among music critics. The music of the Cranberries, of which Dolores O'Riordan is a member, is likewise "Celtic-tinged," influenced by traditional Irish singing.[60] Allusions to the music of both Enya and the Cranberries develop the novel's theme of the Irish past. On the opposite end of the musical spectrum, but in different ways, are Sinéad O'Connor and Black 47. O'Connor's bad-girl image in music and in life redefines Irish womanhood, as Brigit is also trying to do, and in similar ways: by defying the religious and cultural forces that once determined Irish women's lives, O'Connor fashions herself as a modern incarnation of the pagan Celtic goddess. Black 47, a band named after the worst year of the Great Famine, has a political agenda; its logo is a shackled fist, upraised in a defiant gesture. The band's name as well as its repertory draw upon Ireland's long history of suffering and persecution. In addition, several of Black 47's songs allude to the dramatic change in lifestyle experienced by New Irish emigrants to New York. Sexual freedom may be liberating, but alcohol and drug use dooms others as it dooms Brigit, as songs like "Banks of the Hudson" and "New York, NY 10009," recorded on *Fire of Freedom*, acknowledge. The lyrics to these songs paint a picture of New York as at once a refuge from stultifying Irish life and at the same time a dangerous place, where a "Paddy" can be murdered by a drug dealer.

The artists to whom Blatchley listens put a name and face, then, on different ways of being Irish, both traditional and modern. The specific songs that most influence his thinking, however, are traditional ones, exploring traditional Irish themes. Blatchley seems most responsive to the types of songs recorded by the Chieftains, a group that June Skinner Sawyers calls "the most famous traditional-Irish-music band in the world. Period. No one comes close."[61] It is no surprise, then, that Blatchley would listen to their music, which interprets traditional Irish music for an international audience. The two songs that are most important in the novel focus on love, loss, and acceptance of loss, with the passage from suffering into acceptance often imagined as passing over a body of water. Blatchley, retreating into fantasy after a particularly unpleasant medical procedure, imagines Nuala singing a song that is entitled in Irish "*Siúil A Rúin*," in English "Go, my love."[62] In this lyric, the singer is about to lose a loved one, and attempting to let the loss happen as easily as possible. The singer would ease her own pain by easing the loved one's passage. The passage of the lover over a body of water is, as in the emigrant ballads, an indication of the dim hope for his return. The most the singer can do is let the lover go, with a prayer for a safe journey. Imagery from this song recurs in the novel's conclusion, when Nuala uses her nursing skills to give Blatchley a quiet, peaceful death.

In a key scene that also strongly prefigures the novel's conclusion, Nuala and Brigit are teasing Blatchley about his newfound fascination with things Irish, Nuala compares him to " 'one guy here last year who kept begging Brigit to sing Gaelic love songs to him.' " Brigit finds this earlier patient's naive assumption that Irish people speak Irish comical, " 'like I was Enya or something. Like a Dublin girl ever learns a line of Irish. Hicks like Nuala might know some Irish, but not us city girls.' "[63] Brigit is from Dublin, where Irish is more a school subject than a spoken language; Nuala is from Glengarriff in southwestern County Cork, close to if not actually within the

Irish-speaking area known as the *Gaeltacht*; thus Brigit thinks Nuala the more likely candidate for the position of Irish songstress. Playing with the idea of establishing his Irish credentials by means of the Irish language, Blatchley uses his alphabet board to spell out an Irish phrase, " 'TÁ MO CHLEAMHNAS DÉANTA.' " Skeptical Brigit protests that Blatchley " 'can't know Irish,' " and she asks him for more evidence. Blatchley cites a line from Yeats's "Song of Wandering Aengus": " 'It had become a glimmering girl.' "[64] Both he and Brigit have already dismissed Ireland's best-known poet; earlier, Brigit mocked Blatchley as " 'the type that goes moony over Yeats,' " but Blatchley thinks that it might be she, not he, who "reads too much Yeats." In any case, Yeats's brand of romanticism, "all that murmuring a little sadly how love fled and hid his head among a cloud of stars," seems, to Blatchley, outmoded: "The time for all that died long before we were born."[65] In this later scene, Brigit reiterates her opinion that " 'Yeats doesn't count,' " not just because he is out of date, as she and Blatchley agreed earlier, but because he wrote in English; only something " 'in Irish' " will do. Blatchley then has to admit, via the alphabet board, how slight his knowledge of Irish really is: " 'IRISH JUST CHIEFTAINS' SONG TITLE. DON'T KNOW ANY MORE.' "[66] Anyone who reads the album notes to Van Morrison's and the Chieftains's 1988 recording *Irish Heartbeat* could learn as much Irish as Blatchley knows.

Brigit and Nuala respond differently to Blatchley's linguistic trickery. Brigit, laughing, calls him a " 'rat-faced deceiver' "; but Nuala, translating the song title according to the album notes as "My Match it is Made," blushes, inadvertently acknowledging the song's deeper significance to her. Later, Nuala whispers to Blatchley, in Irish, a line from the same song. When Blatchley remembers to check the album notes to *Irish Heartbeat*, he finds the translation: " 'She's the wee lass that left my heart broken.' "[67] He in turn spells out to her, in Irish, the last lines of the song, which are, in English, " 'I heard the blackbird and the linnet say / That my love had crossed the ocean.' "[68] Nuala's response is significant in that it shows her ambivalence, simultaneously acknowledging and denying her growing attachment to Blatchley: " 'But mine's right here,' she lied. 'Not in this room, of course. Mine lives across the river in Brooklyn. Here there's only an ill fella too clever for his own good.' "[69]

The interweaving of the traditional song and the Yeats poem in this passage, while on the surface only a piece of flirtatious banter between Blatchley and Nuala, lends depth to the novel's exploration of the themes of love and loss. Analyzing the cultural significance of the Morrison/Chieftains recording, Kieran Keohane sees it as one of the many expressions of ambivalence central to the Irish identity: "We can't live away for love of home, but there's no life worth living at home."[70] Thus the themes of separation and loss that permeate Irish music. Because of their history of emigration across a vast sea, separation and loss are associated with a journey over water. In both "*Siúil A Rúin*" and "*Tá Mo Chleamhnas Déanta,*"[71] the separation of lovers is imagined in this way. In the former, the woman's lover has crossed over into France, leaving the singer bereft. In the latter, the singer, a man, is abandoned by a woman, who, the birds tell him, "had crossed the ocean." In both, the themes of loss of love and of crossing a body of water interweave. Nuala says her love too is across the water (from Manhattan, where the hospital is, one must cross the water, the East River, to get to Brooklyn); but her true love, with whom her match could be made, is Blatchley himself, if he can be kept from crossing the river of death. The imagery from this scene in the novel, both from Yeats and from the ballads, culminates in its conclusion, in which Nuala not only eases the passage but metaphorically accompanies Blatchley on his final journey.

Across the Water: The Final Journey

As the novel ends, it is clear that, despite the efforts of Nuala and Brigit and their colleagues at the ICU, Blatchley is going over to the other side. As his condition deteriorates, he starts to abandon his dream of happiness. Yet Blatchley's despairing realization that he has lost both Ireland and Nuala is belied by the loving death with which Nuala provides him. Brigit had promised that, when he was " 'really ready,' " she and Nuala would " 'find a way to check [him] out.' "[72] Nuala keeps this promise. Joining with him in the only physical intimacy still possible, Nuala acts as his companion and guide as he makes the journey to the other side. Blatchley dies not only in the company of but also aided by his "glimmering girl."

The phrase that so precisely captures Nuala is from William Butler Yeats's "Song of Wandering Aengus,"[73] in which the poet retells the story of Aengus (also spelled Óengus). Óengus is the hero of a group of ancient Irish stories known as the Ulster Cycle, which dates from a fifteenth-century manuscript but is presumed to be much older.[74] In the cycle, Óengus's courtship of a mystery woman begins with a dream of a beautiful young woman. Óengus tries to take her to bed with him, but when he does so, she vanishes. She returns in the evening, and continues to visit him for a year; he falls in love with her, but his unconsummated love sickens him, rendering him bedridden. He sends for a physician, who diagnoses lovesickness, and advises him to send his mother, Bóand, to hunt for the girl. A year of this yields no results; Óengus is as lovesick as ever. The aid of his father, the Dagdae or king of the fairies,[75] is enlisted; through the Dagdae's connections the girl is found, but for complex reasons she is not available for marriage. The elaborate mechanics of the courtship, a feature of other ancient Celtic myths as well, is an indicator of the great desirability of the woman being courted. Óengus is cured of his lovesickness only when he accepts that his lady has what her own father describes as " 'power greater than' " his own.[76] This power manifests itself in her taking the form of a bird one day a year, and human form on the days following. The metamorphosis of Óengus himself into a bird makes their union possible. Yeats's version leaves Aengus (Yeats's spelling) human, but metamorphosed into a prototype of the imaginative artist. Aengus, an old man in the poem, remembers a time long past when he created, either by magic or in his imagination, his ideal woman. Like the girl in the Óengus legend, she is a creature of his dream; when he awakens, she is gone. Unlike his mythic original, however, Yeats's Aengus never finds her. An old man in the poem, he still longs for the one woman with whom he could have achieved perfect human happiness. Unlike the character in the myth, Yeats's Aengus never becomes physically ill; but he is also never healed. He never finds the elusive beloved, indeed never even learns her name. The poem captures Aengus at the point of ultimate human longing.

Blatchley's story conflates both versions of the Aengus story, the myth's version and Yeats'. Sick in bed, Blatchley is visited, often at night, by a beautiful woman. She stands beside his bed, but does not join him there; then she disappears, to reappear regularly over a long period of time. The mythic Óengus is sick for a year; Blatchley is one of the longest-surviving patients in the ICU. In his illness, Óengus/Blatchley is helpless to find his beloved, much less to court her as she should be courted. With the help of others, Óengus can eventually find and marry his mystery woman. For Blatchley, a normal courtship is impossible; he is not only desperately sick but impotent. Even Óengus can only marry his love when they both are metamorphosed. Blatchley, too sick to change, ends his life in the state of perpetual longing captured in Yeats's version of the legend. Like Yeats's Aengus, he has created a dream woman, only to find her unattainable.

Blended with the story of Yeats's Aengus in Blatchley's mind as he dies is the traditional song "Carrickfergus."[77] This song too was recorded on the Morrison/Chieftains album *Irish Heartbeat*, to which Blatchley has been listening in the hospital. The bereft lover in the song is one who is "sick," whose "days are numbered" as are Blatchley's. In "Carrickfergus," with his beloved on the other side of a body of water, the singer is so lonely that he is often drunk and would rather be dead. His love-longing is expressed in images of the water journey: he "would swim over the deepest ocean, / The deepest ocean to be by your side." But (and these are the lines Blatchley remembers):

> "The sea is wide,
>   And I can't swim over,

And neither have I wings to fly.
I wish I could find me a handy boatman,
To ferry me over
To my love, and die."[78]

In this final scene, Blatchley conflates this song with Yeats's "Song of
Wandering Aengus." Nuala acts as the boatman for which the singer of
"Carrickfergus" longs, ferrying him over the water, as Charon does for the
spirits of the dead in Greek mythology. As in the ballad "*Siúil A Rúin*," in
which the lover helps the beloved "go quietly and peacefully" on a journey
that she cannot prevent his taking, Nuala uses her medical skills, as Brigit
had promised, to ease Blatchley's passage over the ocean separating life and
death. In the midst of a symbolic sexual act of sexual penetration, Nuala
allows him to die. Yeats is not so irrelevant as Blatchley and Brigit had
thought, as Blatchley dies with his "glimmering girl" beside him and Yeats's
phrase in his mind.

Blatchley cannot travel to Ireland except in his imagination. Thus he
cannot acquire the knowledge that he needs from the country itself, but
from Nuala, from Brigit, from the bits and pieces of Irish lore he remembers from the days before his illness, and from the songs he plays in his hospital room. But in his debilitated state, Blatchley is only an exaggeration of
the typical Irish-American as depicted in these novels. Because he is sick
unto death, Blatchley represents the ultimate in passivity: he is reduced to
pure observation and reflection. All the Irish-American characters in these
novels, though not physically limited as Blatchley is, do as he does, creating
their own imaginary country, which they must then correlate with the real
Ireland once they visit it, or with real Irish people, once they meet them.
While Blatchley never does get to visit Ireland, the ideal world he makes for
Nuala is a perfect metaphor for the re-creations of Ireland made, in their
various ways, by all the Irish-American characters in the fiction considered
here. Having taken their picture postcard, it is then their task, as it is
Blatchley's, to refine the image, to add depth and texture to it. They do this,
as he does, by learning to understand the Irish people they meet. Set against
an idealized background, some Irish people, even the country itself, are a
disappointment to the American characters, who have created them, as
Yeats's Aengus does, as "glimmering" images in their mind.

Chapter 4

Naming the Past:
Lisa Carey's *The Mermaids Singing*

Lisa Carey's *The Mermaids Singing* tells the story of three generations of Irish women: Clíona, Grace, and Gráinne. In an effort to secure a nursing education in Boston, Clíona emigrates from a small island off the west coast of Ireland called Inis Murúch, Island of the Mermaids. While employed as a domestic, she has a brief affair that produces her daughter, Grace. When Clíona returns to Ireland, she brings a reluctant Grace, then fifteen and in full adolescent rebellion. On Inis Murúch, Grace marries an island man, Seamus O'Flaherty, and they have a daughter, Gráinne. Unable to acclimate herself to the island way of life, Grace leaves Seamus and returns to Boston with Gráinne, there to take a succession of lovers. In her mid-thirties, Grace dies of breast cancer, and Clíona journeys from Ireland to claim her granddaughter and bring her back to what Gráinne has never been told exists: her father and her homeland. The story of the three women is narrated in three voices: Clíona's, Gráinne's, and a third-person narrator speaking from Grace's viewpoint. This fine first novel is an absorbing family saga focusing on a young girl's coming of age. On the plot's simplest level, the psychological, Gráinne must come to terms with grief; with sexuality; and with exile. But on a deeper level, Gráinne's story is a synthesis of key elements of the Celtic past, its mythology, history, and theology. In addition to all the other elements of her psychological journey, Gráinne must also reach back into that past and decide what she will accept, what she will reject. Central to this process is her increasing understanding of the power of names, especially the human connection affirmed by shared names. What Gráinne must learn to do is to name, in some cases rename, the past, thus incorporating it into her maturing self.

Names and Naming Customs

In many cultures, the naming of children allows parents an opportunity to make a statement about their image of their children and hopes for their futures. For Americans, child naming also gives parents an opportunity to affirm or deny their culture or cultures of origin. Parents can pay tribute to a mixed ethnic heritage by giving children first names that link them to their mothers' roots, as last names traditionally link them to their fathers'. In naming their children, first-generation emigrants in particular must make a decision: to reinforce their ties to the new country, or to the old. In addition, the practice of naming after someone honors the original bearer of the name, but also sends a message to the child that the parent considers the namesake worthy of emulation. If the namesake is linked to the traditional past, that fact encourages the child to consider the country of origin and its tradition worthy of his or her attention. All of this must then be accepted or rejected by the child, a process that is particularly complicated in the case of the emigrant's child. In *The Mermaids Singing*, ambivalence about names is a sign of each character's conflict about her ethnicity, as well as about her relationship to her mythological or historical namesake. In this family, bilingual movement back and forth between the Irish and English versions of names adds to the complexity (even confusion) concerning the naming issue.

Clíona's ambivalence about her own name sounds the theme early in the novel. Named after the Celtic goddess Clíodhna, Clíona "dropped the silent consonants,"[1] which she regards as superfluous in that they are difficult for Americans to pronounce. In this way she tries, with only moderate success (even with the simplification of spelling, her employer, Mrs. Willoughby, consistently mispronounces her name), to ease her assimilation in the United States. When she names her own child Grace, she confirms her identification with the United States by choosing a name impossible for an American to mispronounce. This action shows some ambivalence about her relationship to her native country: if she does indeed intend to return to Ireland, why be concerned about how Americans pronounce her daughter's name? Although she picks an American-sounding name for Grace, Clíona also embraces Irish tradition by naming her daughter as she herself was named, after two Irish heroines: Grania, a mythological figure whose name is the Celtic original of the Anglicized name Grace; and the pirate queen Grace O'Malley (both women's stories are discussed later in this chapter). Since Clíona never married Grace's father, Patrick Concannon, the child assumes Clíona's surname, becoming Grace O'Malley; thus Grace's name is identical to that of the English name of the pirate queen. When Grace names her own daughter Gráinne, the traditional Irish equivalent of her own name Grace, then drops the Irish "O" in her surname, she is, like her mother, making conflicting statements, simultaneously identifying herself with her child and sending a strong signal of her own ambivalence with regard to their shared heritage by giving her a Celtic first name and an Anglicized last name. This mixed message affects Gráinne Malley ever after.

Gráinne's ambivalence about her own name is consequent upon Grace's actions and inactions. As an American girl in Boston with no knowledge of her Irish past, Gráinne regards her first name as odd and is unhappy at the difficulty most Americans have in pronouncing it; her mother's final boyfriend Stephen is unusual in being able to pronounce her name correctly. Her last name, though easy to pronounce, is still anomalous. Had Gráinne been baptized into the Catholic faith in Ireland, which a child of two Catholics would ordinarily be, she would have been named Gráinne O'Flaherty, taking her father's surname. In the United States, however, people define themselves as they choose, and so she is known by her mother's Anglicized last name. Grace has refused to tell Gráinne that she has an Irish father, treating herself and her daughter as if they were a unity created without male intervention. So Gráinne is offended when, in church in Ireland, she is called Gráinne O'Flaherty; she cannot identify with a father about whom she knows nothing, and wants to be identified only with her mother. While her name connects her with the Irish past, the voice with which she speaks that name identifies her as an American: this contradiction is the heritage bequeathed to her by her mother. But Gráinne's ambivalent name also points to the possibility that Gráinne can ultimately adapt herself to life in Ireland. When Gráinne arrives, like any tourist she browses the ubiquitous racks of cards and other memorabilia bearing Irish names. In the United States, Gráinne was never able to find her name on the small personalized items that children love. But the postcards tell her that in Ireland, there are others like her; she belongs. At the point at which she examines the postcards, she resists that idea. It becomes the task of four people—Clíona, Seamus O'Flaherty, Liam MacNamara, and the parish priest Father Paddy—to show her that she is linked to the Irish past and is welcome in the Irish present. They do this through storytelling.

The theme of storytelling, as discussed earlier, is central to these Irish-American novels. Storytellers are "tradition-bearers,"[2] preserving and transmitting traditional stories. Often it is the function of a single character to do this (e.g., Nuala in *The World I Made For Her*). For each tradition-bearer, there must be at least one character by whom the tradition is received (e.g., Blatchley in that novel). In *The Mermaids Singing*, the tradition-bearing role is shared by four characters and the role of receiver is shared by two: Grace and Gráinne. In the case of Gráinne, the bearers' role becomes more complex, as they must convey the traditional narratives of the Irish mythical, historical, and theological past that her mother either withheld entirely or communicated unclearly.

One element of the novel that can be confusing is the similarity between the characters' names. Names and identities are meant to shift and conflate; but to understand how names work together, they must first be understood separately. To that end, the following conventions of spelling will be maintained. "Gráinne" is the third-generation adolescent character in the novel, "Grace" her mother. "Grania" is the heroine of Celtic myth, and "Granuaile" the sixteenth-century pirate queen also known as Grace O'Malley. "Clíona" is the first-generation character, the emigrant, mother of Grace and grandmother of Gráinne; and "Clíodhna" is her mythological namesake. The reader should note, however, that the use of variants of the same name, in Irish and English versions, is part of the novel's technique of back-and-forth allusiveness. Because the names are vehicles by which stories of the past are transmitted, each woman's feelings about her own name and about the name she has chosen for her daughter reflect her ambivalence about the Irish past.

Courtship and Elopement in Celtic Mythology

While Grace names her daughter after the pirate queen, another, more primitive Grania lies in the background: the Celtic mythological heroine of the Fenian cycle. As Lady Augusta Gregory tells the tale in *Irish Myths and Legends*,[3] Finn McCool, a great king in Ireland in his youth, is lonely in his old age and seeks a wife. Grania is suggested to him as a young girl whose father might agree to such a match. At first Grania consents to the arrangement made between her father and Finn's emissaries, but when she meets the old man, and when at the wedding feast she meets the younger and sexier Diarmuid, she reconsiders. Grania seizes the initiative by administering a sleeping potion to everyone but Diarmuid. Because he is bound in fealty to Finn, Diarmuid does not want to elope with her or worse, to have sex with her; but Grania lays upon him a *geis* or "magic oath,"[4] which makes it impossible for him to refuse. Diarmuid and Grania undertake a wandering life, with Finn in pursuit. Because of his loyalty to Finn, Diarmiud refuses for years to consummate his relationship with Grania, leaving Finn a sign of unbroken bread as symbol of Grania's continued virginity. This state of affairs is not acceptable to lusty Grania. According to Alwyn and Brinley Rees, when the couple are crossing a stream, the water splashes about

Grania's legs; Grania mocks Diarmuid's self-restraint by commenting that, although his "bravery is great in battles and contests, I think this bold splash is more daring than you are."[5] Lady Gregory's translation of the tale is more decorous, involving Grania's removing a knife that she had previously "struck" in Diarmuid's thigh; the metaphoric nature of both knife and thigh is indicated by the narrator's comment that this act was "the greatest shame that ever came upon her," and by the fact that thereafter Diarmuid leaves "broken bread" for Finn.[6] For a time, the lovers settle down and have children, but finally Diarmuid is grievously wounded by a boar, and can only be saved by a drop of water from the hands of Finn, who has the gift of healing. Vengeful Finn refuses, and Diarmuid dies.

The Grania story is an example of a tale type in early Irish literature, the elopement story, which can best be defined by contrast with its opposite, the courtship story. According to Lisa Bitel, the courtship story or, in Irish, *tochmarc*, represents male–female coupling as an orderly society wishes it to be: male-initiated, family-arranged, practical, leading to a "formal, legal relationships" involving "social alliance, property exchange, and procreation."[7] An elopement story or *aithed*, on the other hand, recounts a tale of love arranged by the individuals themselves, but at the instigation of the woman, and without concern for the needs of the social group. Blind to practicality, disorderly, and female-initiated, such "affective coupling" never ends peacefully but rather in a "devastating social conflagration."[8] Both story types serve as warnings to the young, as social approval or disapproval is implied by the divergent plot outcomes: "Whereas the lovers in *tochmarca* usually concluded a successful union, *aitheda* generally ended tragically for both men and women."[9] Successful courtship ending in marriage is applauded; elopement leads to ostracism, loss, and death.

Had Grania married Finn, their story would have been a *tochmarc*: Finn initiates the courtship and arranges the marriage with Grania's father. But by taking matters into her own hands, Grania makes her story into an *aithed*. Because their relationship is unsanctioned, Diarmuid and Grania must "flee fatal opposition to their covert union and live like animals, beyond the bounds of society in the forests, on unsettled islands, or abroad."[10] This kind of life is not considered romantic, but rather as deprivation of all that had once been held dear. In Lady Gregory's translation of the story of Grania and Diarmuid, Diarmuid eloquently laments the losses that he has endured because of Grania: " 'I lost my people by you, and my lord . . . lost my country and my kindred; my men that were used to serve me; I lost quietness and affection; I lost the men of Ireland and the Fianna entirely."[11] *Aitheda* involve loss, *tochmarca* involve gain: the socially sanctioned nature of the relationship means that neither lover need lose anything. On the contrary, men of the *tochmarca* typically move into a higher status, "changed from sons to husbands and fathers, from dependents or outcasts to stable householders."[12] The women fare well too: had she married Finn, Grania would have been a queen. Diarmuid's fate particularly is a warning to all young men to engage only in legitimate unions. At the end of the *aithed*, Diarmuid is dead, and Grania returns to Finn, where she was supposed to have been all along. Social order is restored after the elaborate and, for Diarmuid, fatal detour of elopement.

A sexual rebel herself, Grace nonetheless withholds the story of Grania from her daughter. It is consistent with Grace's character that she not pass along such traditions as limited women with regard to their sexual choices. The *aitheda* were meant for their original audiences as cautionary tales for both men and women, instructive models of how they were to behave in matters marital. In the *tochmarca*, a courted woman is seen as a "good" woman, passive, cooperative, submissive to being "traded" between two men. On the other hand, the eloping woman of the *aitheda* is a "bad" woman, because she does not accept social controls and male authority. An eloping woman, according to Muireann Ni Bhrolcháin, is a woman who "chooses her husband,"[13] that is, exercises self-determination. Lady Gregory, in the afterword to her play *Grania*, describes her heroine as just such a woman, one with "power of will . . . [who] twice took the shaping of her life into her own hands."[14] This is consistent with Gregory's translation of the tale, for in it Grania is praised for the quickness of her mind;[15] not for her, at least not until after the death of Diarmuid, when she chooses to return to Finn (and social acceptability), to accept a man chosen for her when her own choice might well be better. That this is still a controversial issue is evident in the comment of Richard Berresford Ellis, an analyst of Celtic mythology writing in the 1990s, who criticizes Grania for being "shallow . . . wilful, ruthless, sexually passionate and somewhat neurotic."[16] Because of the eloping woman's tendency to involve herself in unsanctioned sexual relationships, she exposes herself to just such judgments as Ellis's, especially since the modern Irish woman lives in a culture shaped by the sexual prohibitions of Catholicism. Clíona and Grace have problems stemming from expressing their sexuality in ways unsanctioned by the larger society; and by not telling her daughter this story, it appears that Grace wants to prevent Gráinne from having similar problems.

Despite Grace's firm belief that her mother Clíona was the kind of sexually repressed woman that Grace herself despises, Clíona bears a resemblance to her own namesake, the mythological Clíodhna of the Fair Hair, and to Grace's namesake Grania, in also being an eloping woman. In Lady Gregory's version, the object of Clíodhna's affection is Ciabhan of the Curling Hair, son of the King of Ulster and so handsome that "not a woman of their women, wed or unwed, but gave him her love." Because it is a convention of such stories that the eloping woman act precipitously, so Clíodhna gives her love to Ciabhan and immediately "agreed to go away with him on the morrow." So they do; but when Clíodhna falls asleep in the little boat in which they are eloping, "a great wave came up on the strand and swept her away."[17] When Clíona tells Clíodhna's story to her granddaughter Gráinne, Gráinne reacts by labeling the mythical Clíodhna " 'a loser'. "[18] Clíona remembers Grace's similar reaction to the story, which suggests why Grace did not think that this was a story worth transmitting. As Grace instinctively knows, *aitheda* heroines' attempts at self-determination end in disaster, and this is not a message Grace wants to transmit to her daughter as it was transmitted to her. But Grace misses an important point of her mother's tale, and with it the meaning of her mother's name: the story of Grace's own conception is an *aithed*. Clíona has engaged in an impulsive, unsanctioned relationship with Patrick Concannon, and while such liaisons lead to trouble, they also demonstrate the heroine's adventurousness and self-determination. In her later years, Clíona makes a proper marriage to Marcus. But in her youth, she was the same kind of sexual rebel that Grace is, and that Gráinne might become.

Carey does not use these stories of Grania and Clíodhna as simple analogues to the modern narrative action, but rather as a rich complex of allusion, which integrates the three women's stories with each other and with their namesakes in the mythic past. Once the reader is aware of the function of Celtic myth in the novel, it is clear that the relationships between the various couples can be seen as either courtships or as elopements, as Bitel defines these tale types. Clíona's relationship with Patrick Concannon might have, in other circumstances (in Ireland, for example), been a courtship. But in the United States, without the social sanctions that would condemn such a relationship or at least, had Patrick lived, mandate a marriage once Clíona became pregnant, the relationship follows a pattern more like that found in the elopement stories. Clíona chooses Patrick, engages in what to Irish Catholics of the time would constitute illicit sex, and produces a child unacceptable to either family. Her choice of Jacob is similarly outside the bounds of conventional Catholic morality in being directed neither toward marriage nor procreation but solely toward pleasure. But when Marcus proposes to Clíona, a proper, orderly courtship results in a proper, orderly marriage, providing Marcus with a mother for his children and a partner in his hotel, and providing Clíona with the opportunity to return to Ireland and with the financial security she needs. The trade-off, at least as Grace sees it, is the absence of passion. But in *aitheda*, passion leads to disaster; and passion is characteristic of youth, not maturity. Even Grania returns to Finn at last.

Grace, who does not live to be old, reenacts the pattern of the *aitheda* in her serial relationships with men, with mixed results. Her relationships before and after her marriage fall into the category of elopements—in one case, with the boat owner who takes her off Inis Murúch, a literal one—in being self-initiated and outside social boundaries. Her first love and the father of her lost child, Michael Willoughby, is an unsuitable attachment: they are both very young, rendering him incapable of initiating the kind of courtship that would lead to marriage; and they are divided by class barriers, as the Willoughby family obviously has more ambitious plans for its only son than marrying the servant's daughter. Grace's rebelliousness and imprudence in this case sets up a chain of events: her miscarriage alerts her mother to her sexual activity; the loss of the child places her in a vulnerable position at the same time as she is destabilized by her mother's decision to bring her back to Inis Murúch; and all of these circumstances render her receptive to the courtship initiated by Seamus O'Flaherty.

The courtship of Grace and Seamus would seem entirely suitable, the outcome a successful marriage, linking Grace to the island and the child to her extended family there. But Grace cannot be satisfied with a conventional life, even one with enough steamy sex to ward off the damp and chill of Inis Murúch. The reasons for the breakup of Seamus's and Grace's marriage range from the prosaic (Grace cannot live on Inis Murúch and Seamus cannot live anywhere else) to the mythic. Like the heroines of Celtic mythology, Grace desires many sexual partners, and takes the initiative in carrying out that desire. Seamus, whose body is perceived by both his wife and his daughter as being preternaturally hot, is identified with the sun god, Lugh, commemorated in the great fire festivals, especially Lughnasad, celebrated on August 1.[19] But because, as is discussed later, Grace is identified with the water creature, the mermaid, Seamus's fire is canceled out. The mermaid can only be captured for a time, even by the strongest man, even by a sun god; at last her own nature will reassert itself, and she must return to the sea.

Gráinne must decide if her relationships with men will follow the same pattern as her mother's. In her desire to identify herself with her mother, she places herself in sexual situations as her mother would; in fact, in the earliest stages of her grief for the loss of her mother, she even makes advances to her mother's last lover. Were Stephen to accept Gráinne's advances, Gráinne would resolve the problem of her own sexuality by in effect becoming her mother, Stephen's lover. But when Stephen appropriately rejects Gráinne in this role, she must find her own way of creating a sexual self. As the novel ends, she is still a virgin. Her relationship with the boy who calls himself Mark does not end in intercourse; the boy in the pub in Ireland calls her a tease for behaving seductively, then backing off; and, though Liam has been given a Christmas present of condoms by Seamus, the couple are content to defer having sex. On the psychological level of the novel, Gráinne's sexual restraint (compared to her mother and grandmother), together with

Seamus's gift of condoms, can signal the end of the cycle of unplanned pregnancies that disrupt the lives of these young women. As a reenactment of Irish myth, Gráinne is establishing a relationship with Liam that is more like a courtship in being suitable, family-oriented, leading to the integration into the larger kin group that the last chapter celebrates. But because Gráinne is a modern woman, the choice is hers, even if her father does sanction it. Before she can make that choice, she must weigh the significance to her life of another strong woman of the Irish past linked to her by her name: the pirate queen Grace O'Malley, in Irish Granuaile Ni Mhaille.

The "Notorious Woman": Grace O'Malley, the Pirate Queen

A contemporary of Shakespeare, Grace O'Malley (ca. 1530–1603) seems to have been created by him, similar as she is to his gender-bending heroines. Daughter of a seafaring clan active in legitimate trade as well as piracy, she was born at Clare Island Castle in County Mayo. She grew up with a love of the sea and a desire to emulate her seafaring father, Owen O'Malley. Like other favored daughters of powerful fathers, Granuaile redefined femininity. Like many such daughters too, she was educated more than was typical for women of her time, as is indicated by the fact that when in 1593 she met Queen Elizabeth, the two women conversed in Latin.[20] Most significantly, she chose her father's male-dominated career. Although she conformed to women's ways sufficiently to be married at sixteen to Donal O'Flaherty, *tainist* or heir to the chieftaincy of clan O'Flaherty and thus a good match, she did not allow marriage or childbirth to cause her to redefine her goals. She had three children, Margaret, Murrough, and Owen, but like a modern career woman she soon returned to work. When her husband died in a revenge killing, she became "*de facto* chieftain" of clan O'Flaherty, despite the fact that this was technically illegal. But law never stopped Granuaile: "what Gaelic law denied her as a woman she simply took for herself."[21] She attacked castles and defended her own; she could muster 200 soldiers and commanded as many as twenty ships.[22] She became a formidable enemy and a desirable ally. Typical of Granuaile's exploits is the story told in *The Mermaids Singing*, her abduction of the heir of the Lord of Howth Castle in County Dublin. When Granuaile was refused hospitality at the castle, she kidnapped the young boy and would not return him without a promise from the Lord of Howth that "the gates of Howth Castle would never again be closed and that an extra place would always be set at his table for anyone seeking hospitality." According to Chambers, this story is true, and to this day "an extra place is set at the table" of Howth castle, in case Granuaile should return.[23]

Such deviation as this from acceptable feminine behavior did not go unnoticed or uncriticized. In 1576, Sir Henry Sidney, Lord Deputy of Ireland, called Granuaile " 'a notorious woman in all the coasts of Ireland.' "[24] In 1578, Lord Justice Drury, a representative of the British government in Ireland, castigated her as " 'a woman that had impudently passed the part of womanhood.' "[25] Deviance in any area, at least for women, has historically invited accusations of deviance in sexual matters as well; thus, according to Chambers, "tradition maintains that [Granuaile's] sexual exploits were as notorious as those of the men she led."[26] But, again according to Chambers, the number of her historically verifiable relationships following the death of Donal O'Flaherty was much more modest than tradition suggests. Granuaile had a short affair with a younger man named Hugh de Lacy whom she, in a neat reversal of gender roles, had rescued as a castaway. De Lacy died, as Granuaile's husband did, at the hands of his enemies; Granuaile subsequently avenged de Lacy's death. At about the age of thirty-seven, Granuaile initiated a marriage proposal to Richard Bourke. Like many second marriages, this one had its practical side in that Bourke was both the owner of a "strategically situated castle" and at the same time willing to accept the one-year trial marriages then "in vogue among the Gaelic aristocracy."[27] The trial year was apparently a difficult one:

> Tradition . . . holds that when their marriage had reached the year's duration, and when Granuaile had installed herself and her followers in her husband's castle of Carraigahowley, she locked him out of his castle, and from the ramparts shouted down the words of divorce, "Richard Bourke, I dismiss you," thereby at one fell swoop acquiring herself a castle and ridding herself of a husband.[28]

Whatever discord led to Granuaile's flamboyant gesture, and despite the ease with which couples divorced at the time, she and Richard reconciled and remained married until his death in 1583. They produced a son, Tibbot-ne-Long or Toby of the Ships, who "was traditionally said to have been born on board his mother's ship."[29] This son is remembered to history as his mother's son, not his father's. Described in a sixteenth-century praise poem as " 'heir of Gráinn,' "[30] Toby joined forces with his surviving O'Flaherty half-brother Murrough following Granuaile's death, and both took a significant part in the political adventures and misadventures of their time. Two dynastic marriages punctuated by a brief love affair: these constitute Granuaile's known sexual history. The affair, the marriages, and her piratical career continuing throughout demonstrate Granuaile's outstanding characteristic: self-determination.

In naming her daughter after the "notorious woman," in choosing Granuaile's story as one of the few elements of the Celtic past that she transmits, Grace Malley sets before her daughter the task of becoming like this strong woman out of the Celtic past. Grace may not want Gráinne to own much of her own personal history, but she does want Gráinne to be shaped by this superwoman of Irish history. When Grace imagines herself leaving Ireland and her husband Seamus, she consciously models herself on the pirate queen, "a being independent from any race or family. Like Granuaile, who took her father's and husband's kingdoms and made them into her own."[31] Even as she is dying, Grace keeps that image in mind. Though exhausted by cancer, Grace still sets the extra place at the table, as if her cottage by the sea were Howth Castle, and as if Granuaile might well appear.

Gráinne's musings on her historical namesake show that she is conscious of her mother's plan for her. But she would not be proper heiress to the Celtic tradition of powerful women unless she were to shape the story of the pirate queen to her own life and circumstances, not merely imitate either her mother or Granuaile. Even as a child, Gráinne adapts the legend. Preparing a "pretend tea," the child Gráinne "laid one extra place, reverently . . . and left the chair empty." When questioned by her mother whether the seat was " 'for the pirate queen,' " Gráinne replies that it is not; it is for her absent father.[32] Later, in Ireland, when Gráinne refuses to be called O'Flaherty and wants to be called Malley, she stresses her identity with the pirate queen.

When, after Grace's death, Gráinne finds Granuaile's story on a postcard and learns that her namesake "commanded a respect and fear that no other woman in her time in Ireland had," she feels that the burden of that history is hers: she must live up to the name her mother gave her. At this point, newly bereaved, she is "uneasy" about this responsibility.[33] The issue is further confused because Clíona does not take the story of the pirate queen too seriously; she who gave her own daughter what she regarded as a "normal name" that would "help her fit in" wonders if Gráinne resents Grace for giving Gráinne so Irish a name.[34] What Clíona does not understand is that Grace has given her daughter a task as well as a name. Gráinne must learn, in the country of her namesake, the courage and independence of the two women named Grace O'Malley: her historical ancestress and her mother. At the same time, she must avoid the self-destructive impulses of the mythical Grania.

At the time of her mother's death, Gráinne is not ready to emulate the pirate queen. For one thing, unlike her mother, she has developed a fear of the water, whether as a swimmer or as a sailor. In a curragh with Liam, rowing toward Granuaile's castle, Gráinne "couldn't imagine being far out to sea in such a little boat."[35] When as a daring three-year-old she jumped out of the boat taking her away from Ireland, Grace rightly discouraged her from being in the water without her mother; now, forever without her mother, Gráinne must somehow find within herself the courage to go into the water alone: to live the rest of her life without her mother's physical presence. At this point, she is afraid that she cannot do this. As Liam tells her the story of Granuaile, giving birth to her son in the castle while simultaneously directing her soldiers' defense of that same castle, Gráinne's reaction is not admiration but fear that she cannot even emulate her dying mother, much less Granuaile. She has attempted to resemble her mother in destructive ways. First she has tried to seduce Stephen, which, if she were successful, would in effect make her into her mother, taking her mother's place in Stephen's life at least. Then, her anorexia is an attempt both to shape her body to resemble that of her cancer-ridden mother, and to retreat to an earlier time in her life, even to die, thus avoiding the difficult task before her. Finally, her self-mutilating attack on her own hair in a paroxysm of grief at the realization that her mother had died is another way of attempting both to be like her mother, bald from chemotherapy; to be like "Bald Gráinne," Granuaile in one of her manifestations; and not to be like a woman at all. In Ireland, Gráinne is beginning to sense that becoming either like her mother or the pirate queen, much less both, will involve more than superficial external change, like losing hair or even flesh, and certainly more than merely having sex. She must somehow learn to pull together the disparate pieces of the tradition that has been offered to her by all the taletellers in her life. A key element of tradition she will need to consider is the folklore tradition surrounding a creature associated with her mother: the mermaid.

Creatures of the Sea: Mermaid Lore

The mermaid has a long history as an iconographic and literary symbol. In the visual arts, she is depicted as fish from the waist down, naked woman from the waist up; she holds a comb and a mirror, symbols of her vanity. In Homer's *Odyssey*, singing mermaids test the hero's mettle. Odysseus's sailors were lured by mermaids to their deaths beneath the sea. Odysseus wants to hear their enchanting song but not drown; he instructs his men to lash him to the mast, so that he might hear their song and live. In Homer's epic, the hero must not avoid hearing the mermaid's song, but he must master the situation. Christian allegory (apparently seeing men in general as more like Odysseus' sailors than like Odysseus himself) was not so optimistic about the ability of men to withstand the mermaid's allure. Thus in Christian iconography the mermaid "became a symbol of lust, vanity, sexual display, seduction and a sort of temptation which led to damnation. She still seduced and drowned sailors, sometimes devoured them as in classical mythology, but now she seduced specifically Christian souls . . . and destroyed them."[36] Christian doctrine is unambiguous: avoid the sin by avoiding the temptation. Carey takes her novel's title from T.S. Eliot's "Love Song of J. Alfred Prufrock," in which Prufrock, walking along the beach, imagines these sea creatures singing to each other, but not to him. Unlike Odysseus, Prufrock is no hero; and it is a measure of his weak nature that he cannot even imagine hearing the mermaid's song.

In pagan Celtic folklore, the mermaid is a complex figure. While still preternaturally alluring, she "is not always evil or maledictive, she can be neutral, is sometimes captured and frequently marries or mates with humans."[37] A typical example of mermaid folklore is the story "The Lady of Gollerus," about a mermaid who is temporarily captured by a certain Dick Fitzgerald who is able to steal her *cohuleen driuth* or enchanted cap without which she cannot dive beneath the sea to her normal abode. The mermaid marries Fitzgerald and they have a child, but one day, while he is away, she retrieves her magic cap and returns to the realm of her father, the King of the Sea, never to be seen again."[38] Here the message is different from either the Greek tale or the Christian allegory. In Celtic lore, the man who loves a mermaid must "capture" her and keep her with him by appropriating to himself what is most distinctive about her, her magic cap. This results in an ambiguous outcome. On the one hand, the mermaid and the human husband live together happily and productively for a period of time; they have a child or children who share the nature of both. But sooner or later, the mermaid will revert to her true nature, take back what rightfully belongs to her, and return to the sea. To a greater extent than in the Greek epic, the mermaid's man must master the situation, "capturing" and "stealing." Unlike Christian allegory, which counsels avoidance, Celtic folklore tells men not to avoid mating with a mermaid despite the risk. The unique element of Celtic mermaid lore is the inevitable triumph of the mermaid's own nature, despite all the man's efforts.

Imagery of the mermaid abounds, almost to excess, in *The Mermaids Singing*. The most obvious use of the mermaid symbolism in the novel is in regard to the sexual meaning of women's breasts. Clíona, making love to Patrick Concannon, compares her own breasts to the mermaid's, as her daughter Grace also does in the same situation with Michael Willoughby. But the mermaid's breasts, like the mermaid herself, have the kind of ambivalence that is characteristic of the Celtic mythological figures. Touching the breasts of the mermaid carving is a good-luck gesture, and, in the several scenes involving foreplay in the water, the allure of breasts is obvious. But Clíona's mother and Grace both die of breast cancer; Gráinne binds her breasts to simulate her mother's post-mastectomy figure; and

Gráinne's breasts vanish as her anorexia worsens. Thus the source of pleasure and nurturing is also the source of disease and death.

At the same time, the story of the mermaid is an important part of the characterization of Grace. Seamus tells Grace a mermaid story similar to "The Lady of Gollerus," that of a mermaid who fell in love with, married, and had children with his great-great-grandfather, but who, because "the pull of the sea was too great,"[39] ultimately returned to her natural environment. Seamus's tale contains both the pagan and the Christian meanings of the mermaid, as well as another meaning specific to the novel. In *The Mermaids Singing*, a mermaid is a woman with an urge to self-fashion, to follow what pulls her, without regard to social expectations. This means that, because Grace shares the mermaid's nature, Seamus's power to keep her on land (that is, living the traditional life of an island wife and mother) would compete with, and eventually be defeated by, the power of the sea (a self-constructed life). Gráinne comes to understand this aspect of her parents' relationship. When Grace is dying in the cottage by the sea, Gráinne copies William Butler Yeats's "The Mermaid,"[40] a poem that acquaints Gráinne with one element of the mermaid tradition: the fear that the unconventional woman, because she must follow her own nature, must inevitably break the heart of the man she loves.

When Gráinne returns to Ireland, history repeats itself as Liam tells her the story of the mermaids on the same trip on which Seamus told the tale to her mother, the trip to Granuaile's castle. Liam shows Gráinne mermaid carvings, and tells her the story of Irish families like his own who are said to have descended from mermaids. Liam's story is corroborated in folklore, according to which both his family, the MacNamaras, and Seamus's family, the O'Flahertys, are said to have descended from mermaids; the mermaid actually appears in the MacNamara family crest.[41] His story also provides Gráinne with an explanation of the failure of her parents' marriage. On the simplest plot level, Grace leaves Seamus because she can't adjust to "becoming an island wife,"[42] and he will not leave the island. Grace, as women do, married a man to change him, "because she hoarded a secret hope that someday things would reverse, and she would be able to take him away with her."[43] On the mythological level of the novel, the level at which Liam's story operates, Grace's reason for leaving is that she is a mermaid, whose natural instinct is to return to the sea. The clever man might keep her from the sea for a time, but not forever. The only way to keep the mermaid on land is to steal her magic cap, that is, deprive her of what makes her distinctly herself. Gráinne senses that the mermaid whose red cap had been stolen is " 'doomed.' "[44] Liam's story explains that, though the mermaid might love her husband, " 'the pull of the sea was too great and she had to go back eventually.' "[45] Through the myth, Gráinne is able to come to accept her parents' choices. As she becomes a mythmaker herself, Gráinne is able to express her new understanding of why her mother left her father: she *"left him because her love for him was not as strong as the pull of her own spirit."*[46]

Gráinne's task is now to decide how much of that mermaid spirit is in herself and what the sea means to her. Were she to marry Liam, two families, both mythically descended from mermaids, would be united. Would this be a good thing? Again the significance of names is crucial here. Gráinne's father, Seamus O'Flaherty, has a surname identical to that of the husband of Granuaile, the pirate queen; therefore Seamus's family descends from mermaids and at least one member, Donal, has had the experience of living with an unusual woman. Liam's family, the MacNamaras, the "sons of the sea," are similarly descended from mermaids. The suitability of Gráinne's eventual marriage to Liam is suggested by the combinations of names. Were she eventually to marry Liam and take his name, she would be the pirate queen married to the son of the sea: Gráinne O'Malley MacNamara. Both surnames, as well as her first name, link Gráinne to her Irish ancestry. Ironically, Gráinne seems well on her way to becoming the kind of woman her mother wanted to avoid becoming. She is incorporated into a large, and patrilineal, Irish family; she seems on her way to making a most suitable marriage; and she seems to be losing her rebellious edge and with it any desire to return to the United States. These questions are left unresolved as the novel ends, and rightly so: after all, Gráinne is only fifteen, and such questions are not answered in adolescence.

Issues that must be resolved sooner are connected with the imagery of the sea and the mermaid's place in it. At the end of the novel, Gráinne identifies her mother, not herself, with the Muirgen, the mermaid, she who is "born of the sea."[47] Gráinne has never been comfortable in water; she depended on her mother, the sea creature. Like incompletely assimilated emigrants, mermaids are half one thing, half another. Beings of the sea, their natural habitat reflects the "betweenness" of their split selves. Carey's point may be that a person with allegiances to two cultures must learn to live with, indeed to enjoy, a permanently divided self, never one thing or another; like the mermaid, Grace is happiest in the sea as it expresses her sense of her own relationship to her two countries. Gráinne may take a second alternative: to choose one country over another. Mermaids signify the divided psychological state of those who have emigrated to America from Ireland, and the ambivalence they experience because of their divided allegiance. The sea connects and divides. Inis Murúch, a tiny island off the coast of a small island country, contains what Grace, at least, defines as Irishness in its most concentrated form, and she longs to cross the sea to avoid it. But, ironically, when she does cross the sea she follows the pattern of many emigrants before her and hugs the Atlantic shore, settling in Boston, an American city with a history of Irish settlement and a large Irish-American community. There she escapes to the sea "and imagines another beach across the Atlantic, an Irish shore, the landscape a mirror reflection of this one."[48] And when it is time, "she finished dying in a cottage on Singing Beach,"[49] by the sea, at the closest point to Ireland.

Pagans and Christians

At Liam's father's wake, in response to a question about a funerary custom that Gráinne does not recognize as Catholic, Clíona tells Gráinne, " 'We Irish are devout Catholics, but we're fanatic pagans as well.' "[50] Gráinne's introduction to the pagan past has included the story of her mythic name-sake and the folklore surrounding the mermaid. Now she must consider what another aspect of her Irishness means: the Catholic church. In the United States, it is not necessary for Gráinne to come to terms with Catholicism; in her mother's lifetime the only contact she has had with the Catholic mass has been via television, which can easily be turned off. But the message of her mother's traditional Catholic funeral is reinforced when she returns to Ireland: she must recognize that Catholicism is part of her heritage not easily turned off. Each of the three women in the novel has a different relationship to the Catholic church. Clíona in her maturity is a conventional pious Catholic, but in her youth she violated Catholic sexual norms. The product of that rebellion, Grace, lives like a Celtic pagan but is buried like a Catholic, thus introducing her daughter to Catholic ritual. Ireland's pervasive Catholicism is an element of the past that Gráinne must either accept totally, reject totally, or incorporate into her developing sense of her own spiritual needs.

Gráinne's orientation to Catholicism begins with her mother's funeral, with its traditional yet, to Gráinne, unfamiliar trappings. Grace, who did not live a conventional Catholic life, plans a conventional Catholic funeral. Clearly this is to initiate Gráinne into a portion of her heritage. Complex psychological connections exist between Catholicism and Gráinne's anorexia. Gráinne first connects with religious ritual by way of food ritual. Immediately after meeting Gráinne at Grace's wake, Clíona makes tea for her in the Irish way, by rinsing the kettle with boiling water before adding the tea—in this case tea bags, not loose tea, as Grace, even in small things, chooses the American custom over the Irish, and so has no loose tea in her house. Clíona's tea-making seems at that point to Gráinne like "some sort of religious ritual, like the priest I'd once seen on Sunday cable, with white crackers, water, and wine, all laid out in preparation."[51] Gráinne's connection of food rituals with Catholicism will continue to develop in Ireland, and will help her overcome her anorexia.

Gráinne's first mass in Ireland is an even more emotionally charged experience. Her first reaction is negative: annoyance at the priest's asking the congregation to " 'think of Gráinne O'Flaherty, who has returned home to us all.' " She does not want to think of herself in any sense as a returned Yank, or even as the daughter of her father: "My name wasn't O'Flaherty. My mother and I had the last name Malley, without the O. Who did these people think I was, some kidnapped waif returned to civilization?" But her response to the ritual evolves beyond this initial negative reaction. Seeing the liturgy in reality, not on television, for the first time, Gráinne regards it as an unfamiliar tribal ritual. Her previous impression of the Catholic mass had been associated with food. The mass reminds her of "paintings of the Last Supper in the Museum of Fine Arts in Boston," which in turn reminds her not of the historical event being reenacted by the mass but of her mother's fondness for giving dinner parties.[52] Gráinne now associates the crucified Jesus with her bleeding, suffering, wasted mother, who had once given great dinner parties, and at the same time her anorexic self, suffering in sympathy.

Later she reflects on the meaning of what she has just seen. Because Liam has been raised in the church, she wants to ask him, "What does it mean . . . *This is my body, it will be given up for you?*" She relates Jesus' suffering body to her mother's, especially the "marooned blood clots" symptomatic of her mother's illness.[53] Gráinne does not have the theological vocabulary to comprehend Catholic beliefs with regard to Jesus' suffering; so at this point the mass and all it represents to Catholics can only baffle her. Because at this crucial time in her life Gráinne is mainly mourning for her mother and integrating the significance of her death, the God-man is not a meaningful figure for her. Any religion Gráinne adopts will need a mother goddess at its center, and will need to accommodate the strong sexual drive that binds her to her mother and both to their grandmother's younger self.

The conversion of the Celts to Christianity changed men's perceptions of women and women of themselves. Celtic myth has its goddesses and warrior queens, powerful, sexually voracious women who chose their own men and conferred status on the men they chose rather than taking their own status from stronger men. For such women, no sense of sin was attached to their sexual behavior. With the conversion of the Irish to Christianity in the fifth century, sexual restrictions were imposed, particularly on women. The Christian ideal of womanhood is Mary, Jesus' mother, and the doctrine that she was perpetually virginal defined sexual inexperience as the highest

virtue. In addition, the social concept of legitimacy as derived from an iden-
tifiable father made the monogamy of a mother of paramount importance
in linking a child to his or her father's lineage and thence to the larger social
group. Finally, the authority structure of Christianity, especially the brand
of Catholicism practiced by the Irish, is patriarchal; an all-male hierarchy
attempts to impose its will on those beneath them. All of this means that,
for Gráinne, to accept religious orthodoxy is to reject much of what her
mother taught her, by word and by example.

For many young people, the church's uncompromising position on the
issue of sexuality is a sticking point. In developing her clerical characters,
Carey alludes to the well-known sexual puritanism of the Catholic clergy,
but also offers a contrasting view. When Grace goes to confession and con-
fesses to involvement in the death of Mrs. Willoughby, the priest assumes,
and correctly so, that this event was a " 'tragic accident.' " But then he questions her on her sex habits. The priest also assumes, and correctly so again,
that a young person is likely to commit the sins of youth. Because she comes
to confession without a strict religious upbringing, therefore without any
vocabulary of faith, when the priest asks her if she has " 'respect for the body
God gave' " her, Grace regards this as a question about her health. When it
is clear that she does not understand his question, the priest drops the
euphemistic language and asks her if she is a virgin. When she says that she
is not, the priest's language shows that he sees sex as something she " 'let' "
a boy or boys " 'do . . . to' " her; he clearly has no notion that even a young
woman like Grace can be active in pursuit of her own pleasure, much less
that her sexuality is an element of her character, which she cannot abandon
without negating her very self. A key requirement of confession is that the
penitent must define the confessed behavior as sinful and have the intention
of abandoning the sin—neither of which conditions apply in Grace's case.
The priest is theologically orthodox when he tells Grace that " 'any relations
with a man are a sin unless you are married in the eyes of God. I cannot
grant you absolution, unless you cease such behavior.' " Grace notices, ironically, that "the comforting tone he'd had for her murder confession was
gone."[54] This type of cleric, the insensitive priest who encounters a wavering
Catholic at a critical time, is a stock figure of Irish Catholic fiction.

Lisa Carey offsets this stereotype with another Irish priest, Father Paddy.
He also encounters Gráinne at a crucial moment; but, despite his stage-Irish
name, Father Paddy is no generic-brand bearer of Catholic tradition. By the
time she encounters him in the church, Gráinne has started to become comfortable with the liturgy and with the church building itself, if not with the
theology that both signify. One day she takes refuge in the church from one
of Ireland's sudden rainstorms. Her feelings for the structure are connected
with her newly developing sense of family: "The benches all had plaques on

them, dedicated to dead people. The last names were familiar: MacNamara, O'Malley, O'Flaherty. It was strange to think I was related in some way to almost all of them."[55] She who had been raised to think that she and her mother were alone in the world now knows that she has family members, that they are Irish, with O's before their names, and Catholic. She and Clíona have been attending mass in this parish church regularly, and the soothing sameness of the ritual, along with its connection to the secular food rituals of her own past (mass reminds her of "helping my mother set the dinner table"[56]) have a healing effect on Gráinne. At this point, she has her conversation with Father Paddy.

Father Paddy is the opposite of the judgmental priest encountered by Grace. His answers to Gráinne's questions about the stained-glass windows depicting the Seven Deadly Sins clarify for Gráinne some of her mother's witticisms: urging Gráinne from bed in the morning, Grace would "yell: 'Sloth is one of the Deadly Sins!' I thought she'd made it up." Though Grace "didn't even believe in sins, or religion at all," she spoke with the language of faith; but Gráinne had not recognized it as such until now. But Father Paddy guides Gráinne gently away from thinking about religion in terms of deadly sin and the flames of Hell.[57] Unlike Grace's clumsy confessor, Father Paddy does not question Gráinne, but responds to her questions, and with answers that do not depend on a language which Gráinne cannot speak. Father Paddy's gentle manner is partly an acknowledgment of the fact that he is not hearing Gráinne's confession, but rather engaging in conversation with her (a crucial theological distinction); and partly a recognition of change in the church from the time of Grace's encounter with a priest to Gráinne's.

For one thing, unlike Grace's confessor, Father Paddy also does not imply that he has all the answers. When Gráinne tackles the toughest of all theological questions, that addressed by the Book of Job—how to explain the presence of suffering in a world created by a good and loving God— Father Paddy answers simply but not simplistically, with the sense not to be judgmental about Gráinne's beloved mother. When Gráinne expresses disbelief, he accepts that: " 'I don't think you're supposed to know what you believe in at fifteen.' "[58] The only profession of faith that Gráinne can make at this point cannot, she thinks, be made to Father Paddy: "I believe in my mother, I wanted to say, but I kept quiet. I believed in who I was when I was with her. But now I'm not sure of anything."[59] Father Paddy invites Gráinne to visit him if she is " 'needing to talk,' " with an assurance that he can be " 'a good listener,' "[60] as he has shown himself to be. Gráinne's primary task now is to heal herself, and the place of the Catholic church in that process is by no means clear. Gráinne doesn't think that she will go to see Father Paddy; "He could answer questions about windows and prayers but he couldn't tell me what I needed to know. Like who I was and why I was here,"[61] here in the world as well as in Ireland. Leaving the church and heading outdoors into the warm sun of the capricious Irish day, Gráinne senses that answering these questions will involve some sort of homecoming, Gráinne must "*come home*,"[62] not only by acclimating to Inis Murúch but also by synthesizing what she has come to know of her religious past, in a way that will carry her forward into a future without her mother's physical presence. Gráinne must form her own synthesis of the pagan and Christian elements of the Irish past, which will allow her to place at its center the goddess that she desperately needs to replace her lost mother. The final chapter suggests that she is able to do this.

Gráinne's Synthesis: Food, Family, and the Mother-Goddess

On one level of the plot, Gráinne's story ends like a fairy tale: it seems clear that, unlike her mother, Gráinne will be happy living on the island and loving an island man. It is also clear, from the gift of condoms that Seamus makes to Liam, that Gráinne's sexual maturation will not involve guilt (her father has symbolically accepted the eventual end of her virginity), nor will she, like her mother and grandmother, have her life's choices narrowed by an early, unintended pregnancy. Although considering what might be the correct sexual choice(s) for one such as Gráinne is an interesting issue, Gráinne's sexual maturation is not the most important element of her coming of age. Gráinne is beginning to heal herself by integrating her lost mother into herself and by accepting the love of the living. On yet another level, Gráinne seems ready to accept a divided self, part American and part Irish. Gráinne is learning to be her own kind of mermaid, comfortable, metaphorically, with the water in between Ireland and America. On the plot's most abstract level, Gráinne is forming her own theology, composed of the elements she needs from the pagan and Christian religions of Ireland.

As Father Paddy wisely observes, it is difficult to make an act of faith at fifteen. But what Gráinne does know is that she believes in her mother. Therefore the only religion possible for Gráinne must have a woman at its center, which eliminates orthodox Irish Catholicism. Gráinne cannot find comfort in the image of Jesus in kitschy Irish domestic art. But a different kind of Jesus can be imagined to embody some of what she loved in her mother: the blood sacrifice, the communal meal, the continuing connection to the dead, the promised reunion with them. At first Gráinne connects only the suffering Jesus to her mother's painful dying; but she must move beyond this, to more positive images. When Gráinne recreates in her mind the "myth" of her own life,[63] she fuses Jesus' Last Supper with her own family's food traditions, and both with the story of Granuaile. One of Gráinne's most pleasant childhood memories is setting the table with her mother; the painting of the Last Supper and the Catholic liturgy remind her of this private ritual. Her father too had continued the tradition by laying the table with a third, empty place awaiting the return of the pirate queen as at Howth Castle. The chair now stands empty for the lost mother. The returning Jesus is imagined within this personal myth as a fusion of two women: Grace (as eloped wife and mermaid), and Granuaile the pirate queen. The third place at the table is set for the one who will complete the family. Family itself is a " 'place at the table' "; and while Gráinne may not accept all the theological symbolism of the mass, she can accept that symbolism in what is now becoming her home. At home with family, Gráinne can take the physical and spiritual nourishment she needs, and so end her self-starvation.

At Christmas dinner, Gráinne begins to understand why her mother allowed her to be brought back to Ireland. At the key holiday of Christianity, Gráinne, who thought that her mother was her only family, is surrounded by family. For the first time, she is "able to look into faces and see my own features, to be told that my love of poetry comes from my great-grandfather, my swimming from my father, my tendency to brood from the O'Malley side."[64] Grace's opposing desire, to escape the family, the island, and Ireland, shaped Gráinne's early life. But on this first Christmas in Ireland, Gráinne understands that Grace wanted her daughter to come home and to rejoin the family, even if she herself could not. The communal meal is the family's celebration of its own unity: the family traits, physical and spiritual, that link one to another. Gráinne now realizes that all these people are linked to her. She has even accepted the family's Irishness, adding (without comment, perhaps without consciousness) the "O" prefix that her mother had rejected.

The final chapter echoes these themes: the importance of family, the communal meal, the return of the lost beloved. Gráinne is able to enjoy the ritual surrounding the preparation of the communal meal, and to incorporate her memories of her mother into it, remembering her mother with affection, not pain. As the chapter opens, Gráinne sets the table for the meal of a huge Irish family: "eleven adults and fourteen children." She is careful to set the extra place at the table for the missing Grace/Granuaile/mermaid. She imagines that, when the meal is done, her mother comes to her, and eats from the place setting that Gráinne has set for her; she imagines a natural mother–daughter conversation in which her mother "will laugh music, tease me, offer advice." She imagines her mother's approval of the elements of her developing self that differentiate her from Grace: her still-unconsummated sex life; her comfort within her "cheery mob of a family"; her lack of desire to return to the United States, "a place where people don't speak in tunes."[65] What Gráinne imagines here is the young adult's hope for the uncondi- tional acceptance by an ideal mother, even if the daughter has deviated from her mother's life plan for her.

In this dreamlike sequence, Gráinne imagines herself finally at peace with the loss of her mother, "no longer afraid of her dying." Although she has lost her mother's physical presence, and although she cannot believe in an orthodox version of the hereafter, she imagines an afterlife for Grace as avatar of the pagan past. This enables Gráinne herself to become a teller of tales:

> Perhaps one of my little cousins will come downstairs for a glass of water or a secret snack, and see the retreating shadow of a woman, hear the gulp of water and the far-off moan of wind.
>
> "Who was that lady?" the little girl will say, and I will settle her in my lap.
>
> *She is the pirate queen, Granuaile, who barges in, hungry and battle-worn, leaving her sword to glint by the fire.*
>
> *She is the sea-woman, Muirgen, who transforms from the ocean at night, to steal one last look at her sleeping human children.*
>
> "She," I will say, "was my mother."[66]

This lyrical expression of grief, loss, and acceptance represents Gráinne's synthesis, formulated not only in Ireland but also in Irish terms. She has developed for herself a theology with her mother at its center, Grace raised to the pantheon of Celtic deities, Grace imagined as a conflation of a ideal human mother, Jesus sharing the Last Supper with his disciples, Granuaile the pirate queen, and the mermaid mother Muirgen. Afterlife for such a person as Grace would be such as Gráinne imagines: accepting the daugh- ter's life, visiting the daughter where she lives, being a continuing part of the life of the only human being with whom she admitted connection. Having redefined Grace, Gráinne defines herself less in terms of being Irish or American, or as virgin or not, or as Catholic or not, than as the daughter of this particular mother.

Chapter 5

The Pain of Not Knowing:
Katharine Weber's *The Music Lesson*

Katherine Weber's *Music Lesson* is, for all its brevity, a complex work. It can be read on a number of levels: as a novel of international intrigue; as a midlife crisis story; as a psychological analysis of a woman suffering from grief and loss; as a study in art theory; as a philosophical discourse on the nature of truth. As a study of Irish and American relations, it explores the gaps in Patricia Dolan's understanding of Irish history and literature, gaps that, combined with her own self-deception, cause her to engage in a love affair, and then an art theft, with her purported cousin Mickey O'Driscoll. Patricia, an art historian and fifth-generation Irish-American, thinks at first that she understands Ireland, and therefore Mickey; on this basis she also believes that she has entered freely into a relationship with him, a relationship that she imagines as mutual. But as events unfold, it becomes clear that Patricia does not know Mickey at all. The novel's epigram is a quotation from James Joyce's *Portrait of the Artist as a Young Man*: "It pained him that he did not know well what politics meant and that he did not know where the universe ended."[1] The source of Stephen's pain is also a central theme of *The Music Lesson*: not knowing. If Patricia knew Irish history and literature as she does Dutch art, she would understand that Mickey is what William Shannon calls an "Irish type": the "hard man," the "violent rebel," a man whose life is dedicated to righting the political wrongs of Ireland, whatever the cost.[2] That she does not so recognize him leads her into actions that result in at least one other person's death, and possibly her own. While Patricia is confident that she knows the Irish past, which in turn makes her confident that she knows Mickey, the novel's events unfold in such a way as to call her knowledge into question.

The Dolans and the Irish Past

As has already been seen in Lisa Carey's *The Mermaids Singing*, the story-teller character is the bearer of tradition, and Patricia's father Pete plays this role in *The Music Lesson*. Much of what Patricia thinks she knows of the Irish past comes to her through him. Pete tells his daughter tales of ancient Celtic tradition, about "fairies, ring forts, Celtic gold turning up under farmers' ploughs, the way stone circles and standing stones sprout on the misty hills like toadstools," and about her namesake Patrick's expulsion of the snakes.[3] But in addition to this "playful, magical side of Ireland,"[4] Patricia also learns about the key actors and events in the 800-year effort to unite Ireland and rid it of foreign dominance. The stories of Brian Boru, the Battle of the Boyne, Michael Collins, the Black and Tans, the Easter Rising, and the Famine are in effect a survey course in Irish history from the eleventh to the twentieth centuries, as taught by Pete to his daughter.

As early as the eleventh century, Irishmen were fighting for Irish unity. Brian Boru, a king and the son of a king, fought the Uí Néill clan for the kingship of all Ireland. When he was killed at the Battle of Clontarf in 1014, Brian Boru was on the verge of uniting Ireland under one kingship.[5] But a disunited Ireland was to remain a battleground between opposing forces. In 1690, the armies of King James of England (supported by Irish Catholics) and Prince William of Orange (supported by Irish Protestants) clashed at the River Boyne.[6] William's victory, interpreted as a triumph for England and for the Protestant faith, is celebrated to this day in Ulster with parades by Protestants through Catholic districts on July 12. These "Orange Parades" have often been accompanied by sectarian ill-feeling, even violence (Tim Pat Coogan, with whom Pete would probably agree, calls the Orange Order an "instrument of savagery"[7]). It is to the Irish term for the annual recurrence of these parades that Patricia refers: "They have had their marching season and now we will have ours."[8] Patricia has been raised to scorn the "Orangemen marching in their silly sashes,"[9] but she sees only silliness, not "savagery," in their marches.

Pete's history course as Patricia remembers it leaps forward 155 years to the Great Hunger, the potato famine of 1845–49. Exacerbated by British mismanagement, this natural disaster had a devastating effect on the population of Ireland. Though population was not counted accurately either before or immediately after the Famine, historians generally agree that at least 1 million died of hunger and attendant diseases in Ireland and another million emigrated, many of these to die also either on "famine ships" or shortly after arriving in Canada or the United States.[10] When during his "basic Pete Dolan rant on the subject of Charles Edward Trevelyan and the obscenity of the so-called Relief Commission, which presided over the genocide we call 'the potato famine,' "[11] Patricia's father castigates those responsible for the ineffective rescue efforts, he is not expressing an idiosyncratic opinion. Many modern historians also believe that the British were at best indifferent to the loss of Irish life during the Famine, at worst pleased to allow this seemingly natural solution to what they saw as an overpopulation problem, which, to them, multiplied the general troublesomeness of the Irish.[12] It was Trevelyan who uttered the famous comment blaming Ireland's hunger not on the Famine itself but on the " 'moral evil of the selfish, perverse and turbulent character of the people.' "[13] And it was on Trevelyan's watch that "huge quantities of food were exported from Ireland to England throughout the period when the people of Ireland were dying of starvation."[14] Thus Pete's "basic . . . rant" is the expression of a commonly shared opinion, in Patricia's words, that "the terrible famine . . . was utilized by the British to rid the Irish landscape of my ancestors."[15]

Patricia's history lesson continues into the twentieth century. The Easter Rising of 1916 was an attempt on the part of a revolutionary group, the Irish Republican Brotherhood (IRB), to declare Ireland's independence from England. After "carnage and devastation," particularly in Dublin,[16] the uprising failed, and its leaders were executed. This organization was a forerunner of today's Irish Republican Army (IRA);[17] Mickey O'Driscoll's group, the Irish Republican Liberation Organization (IRLO), is a fictional splinter group of the IRA; thus Mickey's group is a direct descendent of the organization formed by men who are still widely regarded as martyrs to the cause of Irish independence. One IRB participant who escaped execution in the wake of the Easter Rising was Michael Collins, who continued to provide leadership for the IRB. As Patricia knows from Pete's lectures, Collins became one of the signatories of the 1921 agreement between Ireland and Britain establishing partition between Northern Ireland and the Irish Republic in the south; the political division established by this treaty exists, and remains problematic, to this day. The partition of Ireland established by the treaty conflicted with the great goal of the Easter Rising, the goal for which Brian Boru had fought and died 900 years earlier: a single Ireland governed only by the Irish. When Michael Collins signed this treaty, he knew, according to Tim Pat Coogan, that he was "signing his own death warrant" for his part in negotiating this less-than-perfect arrangement.[18] Collins was killed in an ambush in 1922 (and, in the novel, it is in belated retaliation for his alleged part in the Collins assassination for which, according to Annie Dunne, "original IRA" member Denis O'Driscoll was murdered).[19] The post-treaty violence continued with the involvement of the Black and Tans, an auxiliary force sent by the British to support the police during Republican military actions. The Black and Tans were generally believed to have committed many atrocities against the Irish;[20] their violence, and the fact that they were perceived as an army of occupation, fueled the deep divisions already existing between the south and the north, the Republican and the pro-British factions in Ireland.

What Patricia learns from Pete's stories is "that part of being Irish is having a deep relationship with history writ large and small. We rarely forgive, and we never forget."[21] What she should also have learned is the capacity for violence inherent in the Republican movement, especially in its secret paramilitary groups like the one to which her lover belongs. From its earliest days, the effort to unite all of Ireland under one political leadership has been accompanied by violence. Thus, despite her protestations to the contrary, Patricia is naive in thinking that this long history could culminate in a genteel and bloodless art theft. Each of the stories told by Pete to Patricia involves the violence attendant upon the centuries-old conflict between Ireland and England, the same conflict to which Mickey is committed and to which Patricia commits herself. So it is ironic that, though she prides herself on her knowledge of Irish history, she does not situate Mickey and his movement in the context of that history. Thus she underestimates both the movement's and Mickey's capacity for violence.

The family histories of her father's family, the Dolans, and her mother's family, the Kellys, are typical of their time and consequent upon the larger historical events related to her by her father. Both families emigrated during the Famine period, the Dolans at its height in 1848, and the Kellys shortly after its end, in 1851. The Dolans in particular epitomize the Irish Famine experience, coming as they do from West Cork, near Skibbereen, an area so hard hit by the Famine that its sufferings were immortalized in an emigrant ballad, "Revenge for Skibbereen."[22] Both Michael Dolan and his son Vincent's future father-in-law Joseph O'Driscoll sailed from Queenstown (now Cobh) on a Famine ship, landing in Canada as did many such vessels. It is through Maureen, daughter of this Joseph O'Driscoll, who married Michael's son Vincent Dolan, that Mickey claims a relationship to Patricia. Michael's grandson and Vincent's son, Paddy, moves south to Boston, where he, like many other Irishmen, "became a policeman—truly a Paddy on the beat."[23] Paddy's son Pete follows his father's calling and rises to become a detective in the Boston Police Department. Though he is a fourth-generation Irish-American, Pete does not move to the suburbs as did many like him; instead, Pete lives in "Southie," South Boston, an Irish enclave, and frequents an Irish pub there, Foley's, where, if Mickey is to be believed, Pete maintains contacts with the organization of which Mickey is a member, the IRLO.

Because of her mother's early death, Patricia knows less of her mother's family, the Kellys; but what she does know shows that they too followed a typical Irish pattern. Emigrating from Mallow, in Cork, in 1851, the family eventually winds up in Queens, a borough of New York City, where Patricia's Kelly grandfather finds work as a fireman. Like Paddy and Pete and so many other Irish after him, he found his niche in one of the financially secure but physically dangerous uniformed civil service positions. Appropriately, the Dolan and Kelly clans join when Pete Dolan meets Louise Kelly at a St. Patrick's Day party. While this is a proper Irish-American marriage, members of both families also formed what were then considered unsuitable alliances: Paddy Dolan married an English nurse, to the chagrin of the Dolans; and Patricia's Kelly grandfather married "a Gross from Bridgeport, Connecticut, possibly Jewish."[24] As multiethnic Americans often do, Patricia edits out parts of her heritage, in this case its English and Jewish components: a fifth-generation American, she considers herself exclusively Irish. Even so, it is the Gross family's trust fund that enables Patricia to finish her education in art history, moving her into a more rarefied intellectual atmosphere and away from the passions of Southie and Foley's. In her studies and in her work at the Frick Museum, she encounters only one mild instance of prejudice against the Irish; she has no personal experience to fuel the intense hatred that drives Mickey.

While Patricia seems to know a great deal about her family's connection to Ireland and its Troubles, she does not address the implications of the behavior of her father and her grandfather with respect to that connection. In some ways these two men are stock characters: two Boston cops, one even named Paddy. But raising a motherless child as they do, with a strong sense of her heritage, suggests that they are involved in Irish politics themselves. Paddy, for example, pays the ten-year-old Patricia to memorize the last words of James Connolly, Irish patriot executed by the British for his part in the Easter Rising of 1916: "I do know that I believe with all my heart that the British government has no right in Ireland, never had any right in Ireland, and never can have any right in Ireland. The presence of the British government in Ireland is a usurpation and a crime."[25] Pete teaches her Irish lore and legend, Irish history and politics. So influenced is she by the men in this political household that in the ninth grade Patricia declares that "everyone knew that the two most evil men in history were Adolf Hitler and Lloyd George."[26] David Lloyd George was the prime minister of England who negotiated, with Michael Collins and other representatives of the Irish Republican movement, the 1921 treaty that partitioned Ireland. When the history teacher, obviously noticing the discrepancy between Hitler's slaughter of 6 million Jews and Lloyd George's lesser offense, laughs at Patricia, she learns that the opinions with which she was imbued at home are not shared by the general run of humankind. What she might have inferred, but does not, is that Paddy and Pete might associate with others who translate such beliefs into action. What she thinks she has learned about Irish history from them is enough to make her feel not only that she is slightly better informed but also that she is more authentically Irish than the average Irish-American. Lulled into a sense of complacency by her own presumption of superior knowledge, she is ill-prepared for meeting Mickey O'Driscoll.

At least at first, Mickey's appeal is both stereotypical and political. To Patricia, he seems an exemplar of "the outlaw," a romantic figure that Maureen Waters calls "one of the great archetypes of Irish literature."[27] This outlaw character seems to step out of Ireland's stormy past into Patricia's troubled present. Like his analogues in Irish history, "daring Robin Hood figures who harassed landlords and English settlers,"[28] Mickey is conflated in Patricia's mind with the cause of Irish freedom itself. When she first meets him, she is pleased with herself (Pete's star student) that she can identify Mickey's hometown, Rosscarbery in County Cork, as the birthplace of the Irish revolutionary Jeremiah O'Donovan Rossa and of Michael Collins. While this contributes to the smug sense of unity with the Irish people that she brings with her to the west of Ireland, she does not identify Mickey with "hard men" like O'Donovan Rossa and Collins. As her love affair with Mickey develops, her commitment to his cause develops in parallel—but not without some vacillation on her part. On January 21, her diary records her feeling that she is not so much committed to Irish freedom as she is in love with Mickey. But by January 25, she is convinced that she is indeed so committed: she sees herself as "the true fruit of the Dolan tree in my hatred of the British in Ireland and my belief that I am taking part in an action that will help move us closer to a solution."[29] Note Patricia's "us": her cause is Ireland's; she identifies completely with a group of people she has in reality only just met and knows very slightly.

To identify with the Irish, Patricia needs to dissociate herself not only from the British but also from other Americans as well. Patricia, a first-time visitor to Ireland, takes care to distinguish herself from mere "tourists." Her contempt for the tourist is akin to her art historian's distaste for the "public," which, in her view, merely "glances at the art and then stampedes to the gift shop."[30] Just as her education in art history sets her apart from the average museum visitor, so, she thinks, her superior knowledge of Ireland's history means that she is not actually a tourist at all, only playing the part of one. As she takes up residence in a cottage in the west country in January, which is decidedly not the tourist season, she is smugly certain that, because of her political mission, she is above and beyond the typical "amiable American tourist," whom she sees as "possessing neither curiosity nor a sense of history." No such "cultural amnesia" for her. Not for her an allegiance only to the United States, a country based on newness, its citizens living in the present, with no sense of the past except as belonging to "a faraway place across an ocean." She scorns her hypothetical tourist's incomprehension of "the way history is still playing itself out today in the six counties of the North."[31] She looks for evidence that she is at home in her new environment; she is self-congratulatory when Mary Carew praises her tea-making skills as "unusual . . . for a Yank," and at one point even thinks she might want to live in Ireland.[32] All this assures her that she is indeed in touch with Irish reality.

But what is Irish reality? Whether Mickey is what he appears to be is related to the larger question of whether anything in Ireland is. Nora O'Driscoll's story of a wooden settle is itself one of the novel's central images, embodying appearance and reality, Irish style:

> There's a wooden settle in the room Nora O'Driscoll calls the kitchen . . . The settle is like a church pew, but the bottom is a hinged box and opens into a bed, of sorts. When I opened it, I was surprised to find a stained and narrow old blue-and-white striped mattress, so it has been used for sleeping in recent times.
>
> Apparently, people used to hide in these settle beds. Though it seems obvious enough, Nora has told me with great drama that the Black and Tans didn't know that they opened, and when they raided a farmhouse in pursuit of someone, if there was an old granny peeling potatoes in the corner on the settle, who would expect to find a fugitive or two beneath her?[33]

The closed wooden settle, the granny sitting upon it, even the potatoes, form an image of traditional Irish life: rural, primitive, innocent. But when the settle is opened, an entirely different reality appears beneath. Even the old granny is a soldier in the battle for a free Ireland.

When Patricia is leaving, or thinks she is leaving, Ireland, she describes it as the "land of eloquent storytellers who cannot distinguish truth from fiction."[34] Ironically, Patricia, who came to Ireland believing herself more Irish than the usual run of Irish-American tourists, prepares to leave it knowing less about the reality of her experience there than she thought she knew when she arrived. The vehicle of this unlearning is, paradoxically, language.

Language and Silence

When Patricia first meets Mickey, one of her early reactions to him is a common one among Irish-Americans meeting the Irish: she is charmed by the way he speaks. Because she and Mickey share a common language, Patricia assumes that the only "linguistic differences" between them[35] are those of accent and vocabulary: harmless, funny, easily sorted out.

But when she gets to Ireland, she begins to feel that she does not understand the way the Irish use language. She senses a difference between the way she speaks and the way they speak, but she cannot pinpoint exactly wherein that difference lies, or what it means. Because Patricia conflates Mickey with the stock figure of the comic Irishman, she underestimates his commitment to the IRLO and its violent agenda. Finally, preoccupied with the details of dialect, she is distracted from the more radical division between speech and its converse, silence. What she does not ask Mickey, but should have; what Mickey does not say, as opposed to what he says: these are the vehicles not only of misunderstanding but also of deliberate deception.

To Irish-Americans, the sound of Irish speech is often perceived as delightful in and of itself without regard to what is being said. In Ireland as in America, accents serve as geographical and class markers. To American ears, the distinctions between different Irish accents cannot be as readily perceived as can the speech differences between, for example, a Brooklynite and a Texan. Patricia therefore cannot evaluate Mickey's accent as to region or social class, as another Irish person might be able to do; if she could, that ability might help her evaluate the truth of his claim to kinship. But, upon meeting Mickey in New York, she focuses not on his accent or on the content of his speech, but rather on the different meaning of words in Irish English and American English. At first this linguistic difference is a cause of humorous interchanges between them, as they play with words, enjoying "all the little moments between us in those New York days when our conversations had constantly smacked into hair slides or barrettes, face flannels or washcloths, kerbs or sidewalks, strands or beaches, queues or lines."[36] Since nothing significant follows from these verbal differences, Patricia is reassured that, on a more fundamental level, she and Mickey are speaking the same language. Patricia enjoys this humorous miscommunication with Mickey. At least partly because of their wordplay, Patricia casts Mickey in her mind as a particular Irish comic type, the "rogue." While this role seems to conflict with that of the "outlaw," the man who "lived on the fringes of the community,"[37] the danger associated with Mickey is offset by the fact that he is funny, and that he is physically attractive. Since people often tend to trust those who look like them, Patricia is rendered complacent by Mickey's Irish good looks: his family resemblance, so strong that they "could have been brother and sister";[38] his blue eyes so like her father's; his "deceptive baby face."[39] Not only an American but a New Yorker, Patricia is not even conscious of how the diversity of her adopted city has conditioned her to see Mickey as more like her than he really is. For all these reasons, any miscommunications between them appear to Patricia as not only harmless but aphrodisiac.

But when she gets to Ireland (and is dealing with people to whom she is not sexually attracted), she senses that a common language may not in fact lead to clear communication. She begins to suspect that there may be some truth to another stereotypical notion, the Irishman's "blarney." P.W. Joyce defines blarney as "smooth, plausible, cajoling talk. From Blarney Castle, near Cork, in which there is a certain stone hard to reach, with this virtue, that if a person kisses it, he will be endowed with the gift of *blarney*."[40] The Irish in general are famed for their "highly cultivated pleasure in the spoken word";[41] but there is a more complicated dimension to Irish speech habits. In his history of the IRA, Tim Pat Coogan notes that the "urge to conceal and at the same time express oneself is a very Irish characteristic."[42] Because of their history of oppression by a foreign power, and a subject population's consequent need for secrecy, some of the verbal fluency of the Irish was channeled into copious, facile speech that entertains without revealing. One of Seamus Heaney's poems, titled after an old Ulster saying, sums up this manner of speaking: "Whatever You Say Say Nothing."[43]

In her first encounter in Ireland, with the shopkeeper Kieran O'Mahoney, she finds O'Mahoney's Irish English musical and appealing, but hard to interpret, because what he says may or may not coincide with what he means. Ironically, Patricia suspects that she is not able to "read" O'Mahoney, but is in Ireland precisely because of her assumption that she can "read" Mickey. Patricia's misgivings with respect to O'Mahoney suggest that language can be a vehicle of mis- or noncommunication. Similarly, Patricia senses a discrepancy between the superficially pleasant appearance of the shopkeeper Annie Dunne, from whom she buys scones, and the shopkeeper's "energy for sly, presumptive interrogation."[44] Like Kieran O'Mahoney, like the settle on which the old granny sits to conceal the fugitive beneath, Annie Dunne might not be what she seems to be: "she affects friendliness, but there's something really sinister about her; she might not mind baking me some special thumbtack scones just for the hell of it."[45] In both townspeople, Patricia senses an artificiality of speech, which conceals as much as it reveals; but she does not connect this ability to the more sinister form of blarney practiced by Mickey.

The humor of Mickey's language, the mutual comedy of conflicting vocabulary, obscure the much more fundamental contrast between speech and silence. The way Mickey uses speech is conditioned by his IRLO training. Mickey has come to Patricia in the first place for information, for professional expertise; therefore he encourages her to talk, and Patricia does so, eagerly. But this sharing of information is not reciprocal. When Patricia asks a question that Mickey does not want to answer, he "would go silent."[46] While Patricia thinks of herself as being one with Mickey and with his cause, Mickey's silence shows her that she is not. Additional evidence that

Mickey considers her an outsider is the way he talks to his IRLO colleagues, in "carefully coded language that didn't even sound as if it carried any meaning at all,"[47] and by his habit of running bath water to conceal his conversation with them from her. These precautions should tell her that she is not really part of the conspiracy.

She also has not been trained to communicate as carefully as Mickey does. Compared to the Irish, who seem friendly because they speak fluently and melodiously, Americans like Patricia can be more self-revelatory, much more likely than the Irish to share personal information. For all their fluency in speech and the high value placed on eloquence, the Irish are at the same time a more private people than are many Americans. Long speeches like that of O'Mahoney, melodious and enchanting as only Irish speech can be to the ear of an Irish-American, can ultimately communicate nothing at all. Patricia, in contrast, communicates reflexively if not compulsively, and without the control that Mickey exerts over his own speech. Untrained in deceptive speech, when she does attempt to deceive, as she does with her unnecessary pseudo-explanation of the arrival of the Samsonite suitcase containing the painting, she does so clumsily, giving more information than she needs to. When, against orders to "keep [her] distance from other people,"[48] she befriends Mary Carew, it is because she reacts to Mary with the friendliness of the American tourist that she has denied herself to be. The mistakes that she makes, mistakes that result in Mary's murder, are due to a characteristically American eagerness to confide, a trait that cannot be suppressed simply because she is temporarily involved in an international conspiracy.

Differences in the use of language between Patricia and Mickey go further, into a difference as stark as possible, that between speech and silence. Patricia comes to see that "part of the understanding has been . . . that I would not ask any questions at all. In the beginning, whenever I would blurt out an irresistible question, Mickey would go silent."[49] In choosing not to ask questions, Patricia is acting as if not knowing absolves her from moral responsibility. On January 28 and 29, she reflects on her own culpable ignorance of what she should know: the circumstances surrounding the theft of the Vermeer. As if in answer to any diary-reader's obvious question—how was the theft accomplished?—she says she "didn't ask,"[50] she "prefer[s] to imagine that it was clever and clean," requiring no "violent confrontation."[51] Patricia's term "violent confrontation" is the kind of euphemism for murder that she will later despise in Mickey. Like her decision not to ask, not to know, the term is also a symptom of moral evasiveness. In the epigram from Joyce's *Portrait of the Artist as a Young Man*, Stephen feels "pain" at not knowing;[52] Patricia should feel pain but instead expresses a "preference" for not knowing. This preference does not obviate her moral responsibility, which is precisely to know about the foreseeable

consequences of her own actions. At first she is "terrified" at Mickey's report
that the art theft " 'went off a bomb,' "[53] because of the violence implied in
the word "bomb." When she learns that this is merely one of their "linguistic differences,"[54] and that Mickey means only that the theft went well, she
is overly reassured, considering the fact that she does not indeed know, and
does not want to know, how the theft "went off." Mickey does know, but he
will not say.

At first Patricia cooperates with Mickey's silence, seeing it as part of their
"understanding."[55] Only gradually does she begin to suspect that Mickey is,
on the one hand, withholding more information than he is sharing, and, on
the other hand, sharing information that might not be true: the great
"information specialist" may also be a great "disinformation specialist."[56]
The honesty that Patricia expects in a love relationship is not forthcoming
from Mickey, because his loyalty to the IRLO supercedes his loyalty to her.
So, when Mickey reveals (or invents) Pete's role in the plot, and that of
Patricia's childhood friend Jimmy Leary, Patricia does not know what is
truth and what is fiction, and how to adjust her own sense of reality accordingly. Between Mickey and Patricia, a common language is no longer a
vehicle of truth-telling.

This latter is most obvious when Mickey admits to the murder of Mary
Carew. When earlier, in their first days together, Mickey and Patricia joked
about flats and apartments, police and *gardai*, "linguistic differences" were
funny and sexy. By the end of the novel, such differences are sinister, as they
come to signify a radical difference in their respective views of the world.
Patricia is shocked when Mickey describes, with only a mild trace of regret,
Mary's murder as " 'wet work.' "[57] Yet she herself has earlier used her own
euphemism, "violent confrontation," to describe the Vermeer theft.[58] As
Tim Pat Coogan points out in his book on the IRA, language such as
Mickey's is a "component of the 'justification factor' " that enables members to engage in violence with something like a clear conscience. If the
organization is an army, its members are soldiers; and in a just war, loss of
life is justified also. The language with which such killing is described is
adjusted in such a way as to minimize its emotional impact; thus "an opponent is not murdered. He is 'hit,' 'done,' 'knocked off,' or 'executed.' " To
Coogan, this "dialectic" (while of course not exclusive to the IRA) "means
that all action can be rationalized in de-personalized language." If a military
action results in civilian casualties, this is "defended by pointing out that
'civilians die in war. It's a regrettable inevitability.' "[59] These would be the
assumptions behind Mickey's attitude to the " 'wet work' " done on Mary
Carew. Patricia's shock at Mickey's casual acceptance of what she thinks of
as murder shows that she knows nothing about the mentality of warfare in
general or the IRLO in particular.

Mickey's trivialization of the horror of Mary's death is followed rapidly by the revelation that the cottage, scene of their erotic interludes, was what Patricia calls " 'bugged.' " To Patricia, this use of her own speech against her is a betrayal of love and trust; to Mickey, it is a " 'routine security precaution.' "[60] Now their linguistic styles have shifted, with Patricia using the blunt description and Mickey the more elaborate euphemism. The fact that Mickey assumes that "security precautions" are needed in the cottage they share negates Patricia's definition of their relationship. To Patricia, Mickey is the great love of her life; to Mickey, his relationship with Patricia has been a "great run," and he has been "very fond" of her.[61] In the act of sex, Patricia thinks that she receives unmistakable physical proof that Mickey loves her. But she comes to realize that in this case sexual knowledge is no knowledge at all. At this point, she learns through the language that he uses to discuss love that, for him, love is impossible: "If I had a life that let me love anyone a'tall, I would love you."[62] The conditional phrasing with which Mickey expresses his love for her—his version of blarney—evades the question. What is the truth of Mickey? Is he like the old granny and her settle, appearing authentic but concealing a contrasting reality? Earlier Patricia suspected that Mickey was not real, that he was "an atavistic fantasy of [her] own devising."[63] Patricia had fantasized a man who could replace the love she lost with the death of her child and the breakup of her marriage. To Patricia, such love is an ultimate value. To Mickey, only the organization matters.

Whether this organization is called the IRLO, as Mickey calls it, or the IRA, to which it is an obvious parallel, does not matter; this particular play with language has little to do with truth. What is more important is that Mickey's organization has common goals with the IRA, and that Patricia, priding herself as she does on her knowledge of Irish affairs as she is, should have known more about such organizations than she does.

Mickey as Culture Hero I: The Irish Republican Army

In the outlines of his life story, the fictional Mickey O'Driscoll is the kind of person who, according to Tim Pat Coogan's definitive study of the IRA, would join such an organization. Like the prototypical IRA volunteer, Mickey, fifteen years old, joins the Provos, a division of the fictional IRLO as well as the real IRA,[64] "as he always knew he would do, from the time he was a little boy."[65] Shaped from childhood by Ireland's Troubles, Mickey is educated in politics by his father and his father's friends at the pub, "where he would gather with some of the men in the village to watch the news of the day's bombings and shootings in the North and drink pints and talk politics." By age five, Mickey is already "nourished on . . . hatred, on . . . obsessions with secrets and retribution."[66] He is recruited into the IRLO by his friend Eamonn O'Doherty, whose "section" was "made up of lads just like Mickey—passionate boys, raw patriots eager to give up their lives for a free and united Ireland, and eager for weapons more sophisticated than 'beggars' bullets'—rocks."[67] Mickey himself is initiated into the culture of violence by transporting, making, and planting bombs made of gelignite, a typical substance used by IRA bomb-makers.[68] When at seventeen his friend Eamonn O'Doherty is killed by a British sniper, Mickey is fully initiated into this radical movement. But the "innocent face" that so appeals to Patricia has prevented him from being arrested for or even suspected of IRLO activities.[69]

According to Tim Pat Coogan, new recruits for the IRA are often much like Mickey. One of the recruits Coogan profiles, Seán Ó Broin, could be a rough draft for the fictional Mickey. Seán Ó Broin was sixteen, raised in a political household to believe that he " 'would have been shirking a duty not to' " join the IRA.[70] Typical of adolescent boys in his restlessness and rebelliousness, Ó Broin was attracted to the " 'element of excitement in it. Raids, arrests, secret parades, arms classes and the occasional public parade, which were a challenge to authority, helped to make it attractive.' "[71] Again like many young people, Ó Broin was affiliative and idealistic, and the IRA met these needs too: in Ó Broin's words, " 'You felt you were part of something and had a sense of identity with the high ideals of the past.' "[72] Many other recruits were like Seán Ó Broin. Young, influenced by a respected mentor, "confused, well-meaning, idealistic, uneducated,"[73] they defined themselves as the "army" of the legitimate government of Ireland, and their actions as justified even by religious standards, as the actions of an army waging a just war.[74] As Coogan explains it, the IRA's point of view on the use of force has an ideological basis. Especially in Northern Ireland, "the system is regarded as so evil that any evil may legitimately used to destroy it. This and the sense of historical continuity of keeping faith with the patriots who died in this and earlier struggles makes up [sic] the 'justification factor.' "[75] At the same time, the element of violence, however controversial, is seen as essential; it guarantees that attention will be paid, and that new recruits will appear. "The guns, the excitement and the secrecy attract new members thirsting for adventure. The guns go off and the authorities act. Take away the guns and the excitement, and how do you offer a credible possibility of achieving the IRA's objectives and so attract new members?"[76] Violence has a momentum of its own. By 1979, according to Coogan, the issue of "justifiable" force had become a moot point: the only useful distinction became that between "effective or ineffective force, and effective force was decided upon, whatever the cost."[77]

Mickey's story of his early training, as well as the history of the IRA itself, should alert Patricia to the likelihood of violence; with a linguistic evasiveness of her own, she says she "gathers" he carried and is "fairly certain" he planted and assembled "bomb-making equipment."[78] Sexually besotted, she chooses not to explore the implications of that information, while all the time reassuring herself that she did indeed know what she was doing. But she chooses to ignore the violence characteristic of such organizations as the IRLO. Her naïveté about such an organization as the IRLO is shown by her incredulity that the possible murder of Denis O'Driscoll, the man whose cottage she is occupying, might have been arranged as retribution for his part in the assassination of Michael Collins in 1922; despite her own earlier observation that the Irish "rarely forgive, and . . . never forget,"[79] she is skeptical that an old cause could still generate such passion. In fact Denis O'Driscoll's death is one of the few clues as to the time period in which the novel is set. If he was eighty-nine when he died, and if he was suspected of complicity in the plot to assassinate Michael Collins, and if it is assumed that he was fifteen or sixteen (close to Mickey's age when he joined the IRLO) when he would have participated, that would mean that the novel takes place in about 1996. That would give the postcards in his cottage, sent to him by a Sister Ann on her pilgrimage to the shrine at Knock in 1989, time to "curl" under the bowl on O'Driscoll's mantle.[80] This would also account, at least in part, for Patricia's incredulity that revenge might still be taken on the old man for a crime committed about seventy-four years ago. But, given her supposed knowledge of all things Irish, she should not be surprised that the movement is still active and that IRLO contacts are everywhere: the Telecom Eireann man, the mussel-picking woman, are both affiliated with the organization, and her father in Boston may be as well.

At first she thinks being involved with IRLO as a "lark," a "fantasy," a "game," an "adventure"; later she suspects that she has been a "pawn in a dangerous game" that she "didn't understand at all."[81] The death of Mary triggers her realization that she has been a "naive idiot."[82] Her love for Mickey is replaced by a realization that he is "evil incarnate," worse than the Troubles he is seeking to end.[83] Thus she denies the only justification for violence, that it is righting an even greater wrong.[84] At this point Patricia compares Mickey to James Fenimore Cooper's Leatherstocking, an American hero, as described by D.H. Lawrence: "*hard, isolate, stoic, and a killer.*"[85] Had Patricia been a student of Irish history and literature instead of American literature and European art theory and criticism, she would have recognized Mickey earlier for what he was, an heir to the Irish literary tradition that defines the hero by his capacity for violence, his willingness to kill and to die.

Mickey as Culture Hero II:
The Cúchulainn Legend

Patricia says that her "mind is far more attuned to the visual world";[86] unfortunately so, since what she needs to know is the epic tradition involving the Irish hero, and how that tradition came to be shaped to political ends. If she knew more about Irish literature, for example, she would know that the great literary culture hero for the Republican movement was Cúchulainn, the central figure of the Ulster cycle and of its epic, the *Táin Bó Cuailnge*. The Cúchulainn figure is connected to Irish Republicanism through Patrick Pearse, composer and signer of the "Declaration of the Republic" that proclaimed the Easter Rising of 1916, and executed by the British for his role therein.

The Ulster Cycle, generally believed to date to the first century BC, is a series of stories concerning the people of Ulster, and especially their superhero, the warrior Cúchulainn. Born under miraculous circumstances (his mother's complicated reproductive history reads like a conflation of several birth-of-the-hero stories), the infant Cúchulainn is given to King Conchubar to be raised as suits his future dignity. As a young boy, he shows great promise, and all agree that he has the makings of a great warrior. He stands out among the members of the "boy-troop," his contemporaries, in his ability to fight off many invaders simultaneously. Tales of his early exploits feature superhuman strength and preternatural war-fury, imagined as a kind of physical transfiguration upon the battlefield:

> "The Warp-Spasm overtook him: it seemed each hair was hammered into his head, so sharply they shot upright. You would swear a fire-speck tipped each hair. He squeezed one eye narrower than the eye of a needle; he opened the other wider than the mouth of a goblet. He bared his jaws to the ear; he peeled back his lips to the eye-teeth till his gullet showed. The hero-halo rose up from the crown of his head."[87]

This "Warp-Spasm" not only makes him fearsome in battle but also apparently renders him irresistible to women. When the seer Scáthach hears of it, and his accomplishments while under its influence, she sends her daughter to investigate, and not only permits but also encourages her to go to bed with the hero. In this pagan society devoid of the prohibitions against sexuality characteristic of Irish Christianity, success in battle and in bed were related; and women were enthusiastic participants in the latter. But Cúchulainn's behavior is not affected by his personal relationships with either women or men; he is capable of violence against lovers, friends, and even his own son. When his wife Emer tries to dissuade him from killing Connla, the only son of his earlier wife Aife, Cúchulainn sets his priorities: " 'No matter who he is, wife . . . I must kill him for the honor of Ulster.' " Mortally wounded, the child asks that his father " 'point me out the famous men' " present, that he might " 'salute them' " before he dies: " 'He put his arms round the neck of each man in turn, and saluted his father, and then died.' "[88] Despite this pathos, the child's death is seen as necessary "for the honour of Ulster."

Thus, generalizing from the *Táin*, the characteristics of the Irish epic hero include loyalty to a nationalistic concept; indifference to personal safety; indifference to personal relationships; capacity for violence; and sexual appeal. All these character traits connect the Irish mythic hero to the political revolutionary. According to Declan Kiberd, "the hypermasculinity of the heroic figures of the Ulster Cycle was a major part of their attractiveness" to the generation involved in the 1916 Easter Rising. Rather than perceive themselves as a subjugated people, Irish nationalists, reading the ancient texts of Irish poetry, could "see themselves as the lawful descendants of dispossessed noblemen," first among them the hero of the *Táin*. Seeing Cúchulainn as a "role model" for Irish revolutionaries involved making a strong "connection between violence and poetry, a bloody crossroads indeed."[89] And since the epic was written in the ancient Irish language, reading the text in the original would advance the linguistic component of the nationalist agenda.

Mickey as Culture Hero III: Pearse, Cúchulainn, and the Irish Republican Army

The nexus between the ancient sagas and revolutionary violence in modern Irish history was Patrick Pearse. Schoolmaster, poet, revolutionary, finally martyr, Pearse embodied all that was idealistic about the 1916 Easter Rising. As a young adolescent, Pearse began to study Irish and to read the legendary Celtic tales. This early interest was to define his life, as he became not only a passionate advocate of the Irish language but also a believer in the power of the ancient stories as guides to present behavior.[90] When he founded his school, St. Enda's, Pearse attempted to apply what he saw as the values contained in the earliest Irish literature to shaping the political beliefs of his students. In the school's prospectus—but, significantly, only in the Irish-language version—was this goal: "to inculcate in them [the students] the desire to spend their lives working hard and zealously for the fatherland and, if it should ever be necessary, to die for it."[91]

When the school opened, it contained works of original art, one of which was a panel showing the boy Cúchulainn taking arms, framed in his most famous words: "I care not though I were to live but one day and one night provided my fame and my deeds live after me."[92] Thus, in his role as educator, Pearse was already "making the connection between poetry and violence."[93] He reinforced this belief with his students (most of whom, and eventually all of whom, were boys) by causing them to imagine themselves as the "boy-troops" of the Cúchulainn sagas. The final school play for the year in which St. Enda's opened was one based on "The Boy-Deeds of Cúchulainn" from the *Táin*.[94] This pageant was so successful that it was repeated the following year; and Pearse also reinforced the lesson by addressing the student body on the topic of Cúchulainn as hero.[95]

Pearse's literary and political theories shaped his educational mission. He came to believe that Ireland could only be redeemed by some form of violent "catharsis," and that this must involve "sacrificing the young"; his own first original play involved the death of a boy-child while leading troops to victory in battle.[96] While his biographer Ruth Edwards believes that "he was not training revolutionaries," but rather inculcating a "sense of service" in his students and a "belief that they should be ready for self-sacrifice,"[97] the line she draws is a fine one. If Pearse intended to teach by example, his own life is evidence of his revolutionary principles, for which he died at thirty-seven. Pearse links the epic hero Cúchulainn with the 1916 Easter Rising; and Pearse's organization, the IRB, was the ancestor of the IRA (of which Mickey's organization, the IRLO, is a splinter group). Thus the hero Cúchulainn is a literary ancestor of Mickey O'Driscoll. According to Tim Pat Coogan, Pearse has been and continues to be "the most important influence on all sections of Republican thought," not just Mickey's fictional organization, an influence traceable to his emphasis on the study of an Irish hero, which in his day was itself a revolutionary gesture.[98]

In his dedication of his youth to the cause of Irish self-determination, in his willingness to kill and to die for his country, Mickey O'Driscoll would have been an ideal graduate of Pearse's St. Enda's. Where Mickey would be less than ideal to Pearse (who, if his biographer Ruth Edwards is right, was a celibate homosexual[99]) is in his use of his own sexuality to further the nationalist cause. While Pearse, a Catholic, was shaped by the church's well-known aversion to sexual expression, Mickey is more like the pagan hero Cúchulainn. Like Cúchulainn, Mickey is enormously attractive; but this sexual allure conceals a fundamental indifference to, even hatred of, women. One episode in the *Táin* illustrates these characteristics of the pagan Celtic hero. Cúchulainn is at war against Queen Medb and King Ailill of Connacht for the Brown Bull of Cuailnge when a "young woman of noble figure" comes to him. Having heard stories of his prowess, she offers him her wealth as well as herself. But Cúchulainn is too preoccupied with battle to take her up on her offer. She offers to help him; he scornfully rejects her help. She persists, offering to come to him in various shape-shifted forms. To each suggestion, Cúchulainn replies with the threat of violence. If she comes as an eel, he will " 'catch and crack your eel's ribs' "; if as a wolf, he will " 'hurl a sling-stone at you and burst the eye in your head' "; if as a heifer, he will " 'hurl a stone . . . and shatter your leg.' "[100] Cúchulainn's behavior is mirrored in Mickey's attitude toward Patricia in the cottage after she learns of Mary's murder, when he deliberately injures her hand.

If Patricia knew her Irish literature as well as she knows her Dutch paintings, she would recognize the Cúchulainn parallel: women's sexual allure can hinder great achievements; women must be kept in their place, with violence if necessary. Although she never realizes it, this similarity between Mickey and the Celtic war-hero puts Patricia's survival in doubt.

Patricia as "Legitimate Target"

If the struggle to free Ireland of British dominance is indeed a war, then a "legitimate target" in that war[101] might be defined as anyone or anything that, if attacked, could lead to the desired result. Patricia is brought into the IRLO conspiracy when she accepts the idea that Vermeer's painting is a legitimate target. If "Betty Windsor" does not deserve to own this beautiful object, if the queen cannot appreciate it and indeed does not even seem to notice that it is gone, if she is like the many museum-goers at the Frick who are unable to distinguish a genuine painting from a reproduction, then, Patricia reasons, why not translate the Vermeer into funds for the IRLO? Seen this way, the theft of a painting appears to be a "lark."[102] But Patricia's reluctance to ask questions is a way of protecting herself against the knowledge that people—the anonymous guards protecting the painting; Mary Carew; Patricia herself—might also be considered legitimate targets.

When Patricia and Mickey plan the theft of the Vermeer, they try to "pinpoint the weakest security moment"[103] in the painting's journey between museums. Since Mickey knows about Patricia from his intelligence sources (one of which might be her father), he knows that Patricia is at a "weak security moment" of her own. She has recently suffered the death of her child, the breakup of her marriage, the end of an affair. In addition, at forty-one she feels herself to be in the waning years of her youth and sexual attractiveness. Alone in New York, working at a job that fills only some of her time and engages her mind but not her emotions, Patricia is vulnerable. As the painting is to her, she is to Mickey: a legitimate target. Mickey uses his sexuality to transform Patricia into a member of his intelligence network, then into a coconspirator. Patricia's overwhelming attraction to Mickey is clearly a result of her being in transition between her old life as wife and mother, and a yet-to-be-formed new life. She finds in Mickey not only a lover but also a focus for her energy and intelligence.

But beyond even the midlife-love-affair motif, which has become trite in the contemporary novel, beyond even the political ramifications of Patricia and Mickey's affair, the novel engages the reader in philosophical issues. The portions of the novel in which Patricia reflects on the art theory of Walter Benjamin deal with factors affecting the truth, value, and beauty of the work of art. Patricia meditates upon a variety of conundrums. What makes the original work of art more valuable than even the best reproduction? What impact does mass reproduction have on the viewer's appreciation of the original? Can an unseen work properly be said to be beautiful, or does the concept of beauty require a human viewer? In its final resting place, is the Vermeer still beautiful? Some of these theoretical issues also apply to Mickey. It is as if on one level Mickey himself is a work of art, and Patricia his viewer/critic/evaluator. But is Mickey merely an artificer/artifact, either of Patricia's own contriving or of his own? If he is, could any aspect of her relationship with him be valuable, true or beautiful? While women have long been suspected of faking eroticism, it would seem self-evident that men cannot. But Mickey might be such a consummate artist of the erotic that he can conjure sexual impulses at will. Is Mickey an original, or merely a good reproduction? The final substitution of a Frick gift shop copy for a Vermeer original highlights the difficulty of discerning the genuine from the artificial.

This ambiguity permeates the novel's conclusion. Since the story is related throughout as Patricia's diary, the reader cannot know Patricia's fate after she has stopped writing. Patricia seems confident that she will survive; but her confidence in Mickey has already been shown to be misplaced. Even when she learns that Mary Carew has been murdered and that the cottage has been bugged all along, even when she comes to think of Mickey as "evil incarnate,"[104] Patricia does not extend the "legitimate target" theory to herself. Her part in the art theft complete, why would the IRLO leave Patricia alive to tell the tale? She knows who stole the painting and who killed Mary; she can identify three IRLO members. As the novel ends, Patricia knows that Mickey is evil; but she still believes that he would not kill her or allow his IRLO associates to do so. Perhaps Mickey believes that the threat of retaliation against Pete will suffice to silence his daughter. But perhaps Mickey's apparently helpful suggestion that Patricia return to New York on a Panamanian freighter rather than on an Aer Lingus airplane as she had planned is a way of disposing of her. After all, as Mickey says, " 'most of the Panamanian ships don't ask a lot of questions.' "[105] Airline passenger lists are public information, but not so those of Panamanian freighters; a two-week trip on a boat on which her presence is unrecorded would allow for Patricia's convenient disappearance. Mickey could well know the instinctive appeal a sea voyage to America, especially from Cobh, departure point for many Famine emigrants, would have for Patricia. She frames this new travel plan in terms of retracing her ancestors' path across the sea: "I will sail from this land, as Michael Dolan sailed, heading for the New World, hoping for a better life."[106] The ease with which the journey begins—Billy Houlihan just happens to pick her up on the road to the village—does not arouse her suspicions. Still under Mickey's influence, she accepts his plans for her. The fact that Patricia ends her diary with hope for the future does not mean that she will have a future. What better place than an anonymous freighter for "wet work"?

Unlike Stephen Dedalus, whose lament for his lack of knowledge constitutes the novel's epigram, Patricia knows more than she did about the meaning of politics; like him, she does not know what her place in the universe might be. Stephen inscribed his notebook by situating himself at the center of the cosmos:

Stephen Dedalus
Class of Elements
Conglowes Wood College
Sallins
County Kildare
Ireland
Europe
The World
The Universe[107]

Patricia situates the Vermeer painting in the same way: "in the graveyard in Clonakilty, in County Cork, in the Republic of Ireland, in the world, in the universe."[108] But though the painting is secure in the center of its world, Patricia is not. She has come only a little closer to knowing what is true and real. If Mickey is the artist/artificer, then Patricia's trusting him to allow her to arrive safely home is as naive a belief as she has ever harbored. Not only is her life again without direction or focus but her physical survival is also far from certain. Patricia ends her trip to Ireland with mixed feelings of resignation, regret, and hope. No longer intending to return, she says she will "miss this land of eloquent storytellers who cannot distinguish truth from fiction."[109] If Patricia is right about the Irish here, then she can rightly regard herself as truly Irish: she is herself an eloquent storyteller; and she too cannot distinguish truth from fiction. Though her life depends on it, she cannot know if Mickey is on any level genuine or all artifice, or if he is, as she has suspected, "just some atavistic fantasy of [her] own devising."[110] The novel ends without providing the closure of Patricia's safe arrival in New York, thus transferring the pain of not knowing to the reader.

Chapter 6

Bringing Paddies Over:
Alice McDermott's *Charming Billy*

Alice McDermott's novel *Charming Billy* begins with the luncheon following the burial of Billy Lynch, an alcoholic who to everyone's sorrow but no one's surprise has drunk himself to death. At this luncheon, the mourners—an Irish-American equivalent of the Greek chorus—try to "redeem Billy's life"[1] by explaining his death. One theory, Dan Lynch's, is that Billy drinks to heal a grievous wound: the loss of his "Irish girl,"[2] Eva. Billy meets Eva on Long Island while she is working as a summer nanny for a wealthy Irish-American family. Just discharged from the service after World War II, psychologically as well as physically on " 'hiatus,' "[3] Billy pins his hopes for the future upon Eva. When Eva returns to Ireland, Billy makes it his life's goal to bring her back over to the United States and marry her. His cousin Dennis, who is having an affair with Eva's sister Mary, tries to help Billy by convincing his own stepfather, a shoe store owner named Holtzman, to lend Billy the five hundred dollars he needs to pay Eva's return passage. When Dennis learns from Mary that Eva has married another and used Billy's money to open " 'a gas station on the convent road outside Clonmel,' "[4] Dennis invents the story that Eva has died of pneumonia. Thus—so goes Dan Lynch's theory—Billy drinks in response to tragic loss; though Billy eventually marries Maeve, that marriage is "only a faint consolation, a futile attempt to mend an irreparably broken heart."[5] But, according to another theory advanced primarily by Billy's sister Rosemary, Billy's drinking antedated his failed love for Eva: " 'He always drank . . . We all knew.' "[6] In life, alcoholism may have many causes; in the novel, only two are suggested: disease of the body and disease of the spirit.

The reader's understanding of which disease killed Billy is complicated by the novel's choric narrative technique. Those who loved Billy tell their own versions of his tale to each other and to the narrator; but Billy takes his own story to his grave. The central narrative consciousness is the adult daughter of Billy's cousin Dennis, home for Billy's funeral. This narrative mode is well suited to the nature of its subject in being recursive and selective. The taletellers, each of whom were to some degree participants in Billy's story, remember only the details that justify either their own interpretation of the story, or their own behavior at the time when the events took place. A generation younger than the principal characters in Billy's story, unborn at the time of the key events, the narrator must rely on the selective memories and self-exonerating theories of other members of Billy's generation, primarily those of her father Dennis. These fragments of Billy's tale tell as much about those who remember Billy as they do about Billy himself. Dennis in particular must see Billy's life in a way that validates his own role in it, as teller of the single most important tale, the one that shaped Billy's life ever after.

The choric narrative technique places the reader alongside Dennis's daughter, who simultaneously is a listener to and a teller of Billy's story. Hence, when theories about Billy are postulated, the reader's ability to judge is comparable to Dennis's daughter's. Comments such as "Billy thinks" or "Billy believes" are the reader's interpretation of the narrator's retelling of the characters' interpretations; and but for the problem of infelicitous style, should probably read, "according to the various theories of the various observers of Billy's life, Billy seems likely to have thought or believed." As becomes apparent, Billy does not see Eva clearly; but neither do these observers, or the narrator, or the readers who rely on these characters' often contradictory perceptions, see Billy clearly. On the most obvious level, those who espouse Dan Lynch's theory make Billy into an American Romeo who outlives his Irish Juliet, and drinks to kill the pain of loss. At another level, the observers see Billy mainly through the cracked lens of their Irish-American-Catholic cultural conditioning. The novel, then, is about Billy, but also about what these others think of Billy, and how those thoughts of him are shaped, as was Billy's life, by an understanding of their mutual Irish heritage, which turns out to be both fragmentary and distorted. Though those who loved him do not see it, Billy's tragedy is caused by his (and their) inability to perceive Eva in anything other than terms derived from his (and their) incomplete understanding of Ireland and the Irish.

An American of Irish heritage, Billy is not therefore Irish; by understanding himself he does not therefore understand Ireland, the Irish past, the Irish present, or any Irish person; but he thinks he does, and so do the other Irish-Americans who, together, tell his story. All of them understand the emigrant past and the Irish present only in the most oversimplified terms. All operate under the assumption that the Irish are simple, innocent, primitive people whose greatest desire in life is to be "brought over." It is important that only Eva and her sister Mary are Irish, and that the Americans identify them specifically by their Irishness: Eva is always "the Irish girl," her sister "Irish Mary." The members of Billy's generation are second-generation Americans of Irish descent, connected to Ireland mainly through the family's emigrant hero Uncle Daniel. None of them has been to Ireland, nor do they really know any Irish people; so their vision of Eva is shaped by oversimplified concepts. When Billy first sees Eva, he is swimming off a Long Island beach and his glasses are with his clothes, on the beach; thus his perceptions of Eva are blurred. But the other characters see unclearly too, through the distorted lens of cultural assumptions formed by recurrent but imperfectly comprehended bits and scraps of the Irish past: the legendary Daniel; the emigrant ballad "Danny Boy"; two poems by William Butler Yeats; and the tradition of sending letters containing money "home" to Ireland. All of these interlaced fragments of tradition, incomplete and outdated as they may be, shape Billy's response to Eva, and the mourners' response to Billy.

Uncle Daniel and his "Paddies"

A key to understanding both Billy's response to "the Irish girl" and Dennis's to Irish Mary is the example set by Daniel, Dennis's father and Billy's uncle. Daniel is well known in the Irish-American community as importer of "Paddies," an "endless string of penniless Irish immigrants."[7] In subsidizing other emigrants, Daniel is an example of a larger phenomenon. As Kerby Miller explains, "even when entire families were eager to emigrate, financial exigencies usually demanded that only one member—usually the son most likely to succeed—be sent abroad initially, burdened with the obligation to earn enough money to finance the journeys and prepare a home for his parents and siblings."[8] Daniel is larger than life, however, in the extent of his commitment to the "chain of remittances"[9] that financed so many Irish journeys: " 'He brought his six brothers and a sister over here and God knows how many other friends and relations. All on a motorman's salary. . . . He was a saint.' "[10] Going far beyond the emigrant's duty to family, Uncle Daniel reaffirms his ties to Ireland and wins the admiration of all by sending money over to import ever more Paddies. When the emigrants arrive, Daniel provides temporary accommodations for them until they are self-supporting. In this too, he operates within the best Irish emigrant tradition; according to Kerby Miller, "the continued willingness of most Irish emigrants to remit money and assist new arrivals" was a major factor in the success of Irish emigration.[11] In the context of the emigrant tradition, then, Daniel is a hero.

But in the context of American family life, Daniel is less successful. His need to play the rescuer is at least one element of his relationship with Sheila, who, eighteen years old, tiny, orphaned, and exploited, needs a home and a husband. At forty-four, Daniel seems to be that man. Young and naive, Sheila does not see that Daniel's need to rescue ever more Paddies will compete with her need for financial security. Daniel became "Holy Father to a tenement's worth of Irish immigrants but kept his wife and son mostly impoverished and never—what with one wetback mick after another being reeled in from the other side and slapped down on their couch—alone in their own home."[12] Thus it is with some relief that, following Daniel's death, Sheila marries the affluent but frugal Holtzman, owner of a shoe store and of the two houses that she obviously has always wanted, and of which Daniel's addiction to Paddies deprived her. Holtzman, being German, is no link in the Irish-American emigrant chain; this frees up enough money to provide Sheila with the security that eluded her in her first marriage.

Despite his inadequacies as a provider, Daniel remains the model of Irish manhood to his son and to his nephew Billy; but his example has different consequences for each of them. One of Daniel's several roles is as a storyteller. The stories he tells to his passengers on the trolley car feature a composite Irishman, a character named Paddy, "sometimes . . . a brother and sometimes . . . a cousin and sometimes an uncle or a friend," but always a greenhorn, getting into trouble and needing to be rescued by a savvy Yank.[13] On the surface, these stories seem harmless. Everyone enjoys charming, funny Daniel. But the storytelling both perpetuates a negative Irish stereotype and provides Daniel with a self-protective response to it. According to the stereotype prevalent in the late nineteenth and early twentieth centuries, the Irish male, generically named "Pat," is "always drunk, eternally fighting, lazy, and shiftless"; though "affable," Pat is "feckless"; he "drank and brawled . . . his simianlike face indicated his degraded level of both civilization and intelligence."[14] Daniel's stories stress the Irishman's affability, but the price of this humor is the perpetuation of a stereotype that had long placed the Irish at the bottom of the American social ladder.[15] As William V. Shannon observes, the Irish do enjoy a "national capacity for satire and self-burlesque,"[16] which is obvious in Daniel. But mockery of the Irish in Daniel's Paddy stories has a darker side. As Shannon notes, "Unable to be king, the Irishman frequently settled for court jester [which] too often has signified a fatal lack of self-confidence that tends to settling for something less than the highest success."[17] Daniel's failure as provider and his modest career is linked to his relationship with his fictitious Paddies as well as his real ones. In his greenhorn stories, Daniel condescends to the native Irish, distancing himself from them in order to bolster his own self-image as a sophisticated New Yorker. In the narrator's image, the emigrant chain becomes a fishing line, with Daniel the fisherman and the "mick" the fish; the relationship is that of superior to inferior. Therefore, he passes along a diminished image of the Irish people to his son and nephew, with different consequences for each of them.

Having experienced the negative side of the emigrant chain (the poverty, the lack of privacy), Daniel's son Dennis inherits no desire to sponsor more Paddies. But what he does inherit is a certain contempt for the emigrant, a contempt that resurfaces in his relationship with "Irish Mary." Mary wants to marry Dennis, but Dennis has an affair with her without intending to marry her. Given the time period and the characters' upbringing, Dennis's behavior is exploitative. As Janet A. Nolan points out, at that time both Irish and Irish-American sexual mores were rigid.[18] When Dennis and Billy were growing up at home "before the war, all the girls they'd known had seemed to be another cousin's schoolmate or the daughter of an aunt's best friend";[19] so Dennis and Billy leave for the war as virgins and come back the same way. Compared to the neighborhood girls, however, Mary is not connected by blood or friendship; since, ironically, the Irish-American community does not encompass Irish Mary, no one will know of Dennis's affair with her, no accountability will be demanded of him. Although Dennis thinks that he would have married Mary if she became pregnant, when he finds that she has not, even though he made "promises" to her "at moments when the girl had every right to believe him,"[20] he breaks off the relationship. Dennis certainly behaves as if he does not regard Mary as a significant person.

In his family life, she becomes a convenient comic symbol. Often the narrator heard her father say, "when my mother had run up a big bill at Gertz or A&S, or had forgotten to buy dessert or had dismissed him with a wave of her hand, I should have married Irish Mary."[21] To the family, Irish Mary stands for the simpler life that he might have enjoyed if married to someone whose only distinguishing characteristic was her Irishness. The insensitivity involved in Dennis's use of Mary as a figure of fun becomes clearer later in the novel, when it emerges that Mary never did marry after Dennis jilted her. As his father did with the Paddies, Dennis condescends to Mary. Dennis does not truly regret not marrying her; in fact, Eva's betrayal of Billy provides him with the perfect excuse for ridding himself of a woman he did not wish to marry. Dennis backs off from Mary to marry Claire Donavan, who, significantly, he thinks of as an individual, by her name, not as a stereotyped "American Claire." The contrast between these two women reinforces the habit of mind Dennis learned from his father: depicting the Irish as a lesser breed, functioning as comic relief rather than as serious characters in his life's story.

More significantly for Billy, Dennis models himself on his father in two other ways: when he borrows money from Holtzman to help Billy bring Eva over and when he tells stories. Whatever Eva's inadequacies as the heroine of Billy's dream, her responsibility for Billy's drinking and his consequent early death is clouded by Dennis's actions. Influenced—though not to the point of considering committing his own earnings to the cause—by the example of his father's beneficence to Paddies, Dennis accelerates Billy's relationship with Eva by asking his stepfather to lend Billy the passage money. This step, which Dennis takes because it is what Dennis thinks Billy " 'really needs,' "[22] is one that Billy would not have taken on his own. Putting the check in Billy's hands is for Dennis the equivalent of acting like his father Daniel. Even as he does so, Dennis knows that his own motives are not, and his father's were not, entirely pure. Dennis "understood for the first time why it was that his father had bankrupted himself and estranged his wife and filled their tiny apartment with far-flung relatives from the other side: simply to know this power, this expansiveness."[23] Dennis too enjoys reeling in a "wetback mick."[24]

Dennis's borrowing the passage money on Billy's behalf moves the Billy/Eva relationship to a point at which Billy is further committed and Eva has to make the decision to come or not. Had Billy been required to wait until he earned the passage money himself, as Holtzman, correctly, prefers, time might have given Billy a different perspective on the relationship. But the apparent miracle of money descending from heaven—perhaps an allusion to the "streets paved with gold" illusion[25]—speeds up events. Speed in the relationship of this would-be Irish-American Romeo to his Irish Juliet is reinforced by Billy's wiring the money to Eva, not sending it in the traditional letter or in the form of a prepaid ticket. Without Dennis's intervention (or interference), these events would have played themselves out more slowly, and perhaps in a different way.

Then, Dennis's story that Eva is dead of pneumonia fictionalizes Eva even more than Billy has done on his own. Dennis had been ready to tell Billy the truth, "but his courage failed him. His thoughts, to be frank, going more and more to the other people he would have to tell once he'd given Billy the news"—his mother, Holtzman, "the fellows in the office . . . the rest of the family . . . the neighborhood."[26] Rather than expand the audience to which a true story would have to be told, Dennis opts for fiction. Thus he assigns Billy a part that will become permanent, the part of chief mourner at Eva's mock wake:

> Better the women gather around Billy in real mourning, sit up with him all night if they liked, moaning about fate and loss and the inevitability of death, than have them turn their gummy sympathy, their studied silence on him every time there's a mention of love and marriage. A gas station on the convent road. Better he be brokenhearted than trailed all the rest of his life by a sense of his own foolishness.[27]

Realizing even then that he was "creating" a "world . . . that even now he saw he would not be able to sustain,"[28] Dennis tells his story. With Dennis's lie added to his own self-deception, Billy really cannot see Eva clearly; now, she is a character in a story right out of the emigrant ballad tradition, the dead love buried beneath the soil of Ireland. Billy "lived thirty years with a mistaken belief"[29] because Dennis is, like his father, a storyteller.

Uncle Daniel's influence on Billy is a more complicated matter. Billy makes a major life decision affecting at least thirty years of his life on the basis of the assumption, inherited from Uncle Daniel, that not just some but all Irish people want to be brought over. Like his uncle, American Billy sees himself as rescuer of Paddies; and he assumes that Irish Eva will play her assigned part in the emigrant story by allowing herself to be rescued. It never occurs to Billy that Eva might not be the simple, trusting Paddy girl that his fantasies of Irishness suggest; her brand of casual self-absorption does not fit the image of the Irish that he has constructed in his mind from the bits and pieces of lore connecting Ireland to "the world of Irish Catholic Queens New York."[30] One of these fragments of the Irish past is the best-known emigrant ballad ever written.

"Danny Boy" and the Emigrant Ballad

At Uncle Daniel's funeral, an episode takes place that is burned into everyone's memory, not just Billy's. As Daniel's coffin is lowered into the earth, Billy Sheehy's dad, "all unrehearsed,"[31] sings "Danny Boy." This impromptu performance is a highly emotional moment for the mourners: "It nearly killed everybody, it was such a moment."[32] No other emigrant ballad is as well known among Irish-Americans as this one; none better embodies the " 'sunshine and shadow' motif" of Thomas Moore's *Irish Melodies*.[33] The coincidence of names makes "Danny Boy" appropriate to the fictional situation of Uncle Daniel's burial; but more importantly, the ballad contains in brief the major themes recurring in other emigrant ballads.

Though Irish emigration is unique in including at least as many women as men,[34] the Irish emigrants in the ballads are usually imagined as male and as, like Danny, boys: unmarried young men. In both fact and fiction, mostly young people emigrated; in Edward Laxton's *Famine Ships*, the passenger lists[35] include a disproportionately large number of young people. In the first place, the extreme danger of a trip that could be survived only by the strongest discouraged older people. In addition, as Arnold Schrier points out, "old people were cautioned to stay away from a country in which the pace of life and work would be too much for them."[36] As song lyrics tend to do in any case, the ballads drew dramatic and sentimental pictures based on extreme contrasts of age between those who left and those who stayed behind. No matter how young the emigrants in the ballads are, their parents are aged; this heightens the pathos of the emigrant's departure. It is common in the ballads for the emigrant to idealize these virtuous peasant forebears, symbol of a pastoral childhood so different from life in New York or Boston. The ballad emigrant hopes to bring his parents over if they lived; and, if they did not, to visit their graves. It is the latter situation that the ballad "Danny Boy" dramatizes.

In this saddest possible emigrant situation, this "almost sacred" Irish song so revered that it was once imagined to have been composed by fairies,[37] the voice is that of the emigrant's mother or father, the ambiguity of gender making the ballad suitable for both male and female performers. Because of the difficulty of the voyage in the mid- to late nineteenth century, the emigrant was imagined as leaving Ireland forever. Thus arose the custom of the American wake, a mournful farewell assembly in honor of the family member who would be in effect dead to Ireland.[38] The song is one that could be sung at such a wake, by a parent whose son is about to leave for America. While in other emigrant ballads the hope of bringing the parent over is often expressed, "Danny Boy" offers no such hope. The emigrant's parent imagines that the son will indeed return, but too late: the parent will be dead, yet still waiting patiently for the beloved Danny.

The parent's faith that Danny Boy will return to pray at the grave is connected in Billy's mind to his love for Eva, to the whole complex of concepts that Eva comes to represent to him. To Billy as to these other "*Natives of Queens,*"[39] both the parent in "Danny Boy" and Danny himself personify love and longing; unwavering faith; that which "will not change."[40] Billy extrapolates the transatlantic link of love and loyalty represented by Danny and his parent to himself and Eva. Because he and Eva share an Irish heritage, Billy assumes that they also share the emotions dramatized in the ballad. As William H.A. Williams points out, "sentimental" songs such as "Danny Boy" "helped establish the romantic image of Ireland and the Irish: to be Irish was to have experienced a great sense of loss";[41] Billy lives his life in commemoration of just such a loss. Every other Irish-American in the novel, including Dennis, also sees Ireland and the Irish through the lens of ballads like "Danny Boy." Therefore it is hard for Dennis to tell Billy that the loss Billy experienced has not been due to the ultimate tragedy of death but rather to a casual betrayal, and by a member of a people who to both of them stand for the very concept of loyalty. The idea of a loved one buried in Ireland both provides Dennis with the plot for his own version of the Paddy story and determines Billy's response to it.

Eva, the story's central character, is imagined by Dennis and accepted by Billy in the mold of the Irish girl in the Irish songs. Irish girls in the love songs that such Irish-American men as they would know are highly idealized versions of the "ideal sweetheart": a girl who was "of rural background, young, and marriageable. She asked for neither wealth nor position. She was simple but not stupid, naturally sensitive and naturally beautiful. However, she was also characterized by a passive, child-like innocence that seldom suggested the emotions of a mature woman. Above all, she was faithful. . . ."[42] Billy falls in love with his Eva without seeing her clearly; thus he has no other basis but the stereotype on which to judge her. Then, Dennis's story casts her as the heroine of still another category of Irish love songs: "Songs mourning the death of the beloved," which, says Williams, "seem to have been especially important."[43] From imagining a loved one dead in Ireland, it is only a short step to imagining visiting the grave. Both Dennis and Billy are second-generation Irish-Americans; their dead are buried in the Catholic cemeteries in Queens and the Bronx. But Dennis, under the influence of his father's stories and the song tradition, finds it more acceptable to imagine a false story, Eva dead in an Irish grave, as in "Danny Boy," than a true one, Eva alive in a gas station. For Billy, life comes to imitate Dennis's art; so Billy easily imagines Eva's grave in Ireland waiting for him to visit it. Indeed he writes to Eva's parents, urging them to keep the five hundred dollars he had sent Eva for her passage money " 'to pay the funeral expenses and to keep a fresh wreath on her grave.' "[44] Going over to Ireland to visit Eva's grave becomes a goal for Billy, substituting for his lost dream of bringing Eva over. But Dennis, who now must cover his lie, discourages Billy on the grounds that " 'it would be awkward, maudlin.' "[45] So it comes to pass that Billy defers his visit; by so doing, he "lived thirty years with a mistaken belief,"[46] seeing himself and being seen as the grieving Danny in the ballad.

When Billy finally does get to Ireland, his mind is filled with the images of the ballad sung at his uncle's burial. On his way to Clonmel, Billy

foresaw a grassy plot and a granite stone engraved with her name, and the dates, the last not merely marking the end of her life but the end of his youth and that glorious and astounding possibility that he had once inhabited. He foresaw his own pale fingers, which trembled anyway, tracing the carved numbers and words. He thought of "Danny Boy" (he was in Ireland, after all, and the clouds were low over the fields he was passing, they were casting their shadows on the green and melancholy hills all around him), even hummed it as he drove—"Ye'll come and find the place where I am lying / And kneel and say an Ave there for me"—which in turn brought him thoughts of Uncle Daniel, and of Billy Sheehy's dad singing out all unrehearsed at the side of his grave. A moment that might have killed them all. The pain of it no less than the beauty. In his own prayer he would say that he had not returned to the house on Long Island either, and never would: such was his sympathy and his outrage, both of them as keen as ever, regardless of the time gone by.[47]

Uncle Daniel, "Danny Boy," and Eva are all linked in Billy's mind as he imagines himself as a character out of song and story.

" 'Living Isn't Poetry' ": Two Lyrics by Yeats and a Nursery Rhyme

Eva's fate and his own role as mourner are connected for Billy to eastern Long Island, which Billy imagines in terms of the idealized setting of a poem by William Butler Yeats. Trying to " 'get to the bottom of things' " with Dan Lynch about Billy's drinking, Dennis (ironically, given his role in the fiction-making) argues that Billy " 'needed someone to tell him that living isn't poetry.' "[48] To Billy, living was poetry in the sense that he shaped his life around poetry. The poetry of William Butler Yeats, or at least the scraps of it that they can remember, is a major component of the Irish identity of these Americans. "The Lake Isle of Innisfree"[49] is a particularly influential poem for Billy, causing him to identify the south shore of Long Island as his personal Innisfree. In Yeats's poem, the speaker lives stressfully in the city, but imagines himself as living simply in the country. Like the emigrant ballads, Yeats's poem idealizes the rural peasant life.

For Billy, Irish-American Queens is the equivalent of Yeats's urban scene, and East Hampton of Innisfree. In some ways, Billy's identification is apt. Long Island, especially along its shorelines, is as Billy imagines it, a beautiful island. Queens, and its fellow New York borough Brooklyn, are geographically on Long Island, but to residents of Queens are identified with Manhattan, which they call "the city." Queens people like Dennis and Billy see Nassau and Suffolk counties as across a psychological divide. In Queens parlance, Nassau and Suffolk alone are termed "the Island," and when a

Queens or Brooklyn resident crosses the Nassau border, this is termed "going to the Island" and is imagined as a journey of some magnitude. To some of the "*Natives of Queens*" in the novel,[50] Suffolk seems still more rustic; Billy's mother's "vision of eastern Long Island, Billy said, was of wild black ducks and desolate potato fields and a mad, foaming sea. She'd never understand what he saw in it."[51] To others, "the Island" represented a better life; it does to Sheila, for whom Holtzman's Long Island house "was a toe-hold in the world of spacious lawns and famous artists and summer colonies."[52] Billy sees Long Island somewhat as Sheila does, with admiration. Sheila's concept added to that of Yeats provides Billy with his image of Long Island as rural paradise, a Queens native's version of Yeats's Innisfree.

But Billy goes one step further than Yeats in imagining Long Island as heaven itself. He imagines Eva, himself, and their future children in an "Eden . . . at the other end of the same island on which they had spent their lives."[53] At the end of an ideal life, he fantasizes being dead in a particularly pleasant Long Island house, a "great house on the hill"; this is Billy's "idea of heaven": " 'Prop me up on the porch with a pitcher of martinis and a plate of oysters on the hard shell and I'll be at peace for all eternity. Amen.' "[54] Billy is not alone in his fantasy; as the narrator observes of her father's generation, Long Island was "all they knew of heaven."[55] But Dan Lynch's book of Irish names that traces the name Eva to the Eve who lost Eden, is hardly necessary to these Irish-American Catholics who know that there is no paradise on this earth, much less on Long Island.

For Billy, loss of Eva must result in loss of the idyllic place as well. When married to Maeve, Billy purchases a house in Queens, in Bayside: a nice semi-suburban neighborhood, but hardly a bucolic paradise. This house, like Maeve herself, represents Billy's compromise of his ideal. Billy could have sought his version of Innisfree, Eden, or heaven on Long Island with Maeve as well as with Eva. But Billy's notion of proper mourning demands that he never admit to Eva's family, especially her sister Mary, "that he had married, bought a house, carried on."[56] As if to recompense Eva for all she lost by dying young, Billy refuses, from 1945 to 1975, to go back to East Hampton without her; thus he denies himself the peace that he might have found there.

In addition to "Innisfree," two other lyrics cited in the novel—the nursery rhyme "Billy Boy" from which the author takes the novel's title and Yeats's "Down by the Salley Gardens"[57] that Billy recites to Eva—are other components of Billy's fantasy that life is poetry. Both send a less hopeful message than "Innisfree," a message that Billy chooses to ignore: the foolishness of youthful love. "Billy Boy," like most folksongs, exists in several versions.[58] The American and Irish versions both consist of a dialogue between an unmarried young man (Billy is by definition a boy, which is also

Irish vernacular for an unmarried man of any age[59]) and an older person; the subject is Billy's search for a wife. The older person's role is to question the suitability of Billy's choice of a beloved, whom Billy describes and defends in response to these questions. In the American version, the nameless girl is appealing (the "joy" of Billy's life), enticing (she "bade [Billy] to come in"), attractive (she has a "dimple in her chin," "ringlets in her hair," and "a twinkle in her eye"), and housewifely ("she can bake a cherry pie"). But she is perhaps not ready to marry, as Billy himself observes, because of immaturity and inability to detach from her mother ("She's a young thing / And cannot leave her mother"). In the Irish version, the girl is named Nancy Gray, her physical charms are not mentioned, nor is her attachment to her mother; but the question of wifely suitability is again raised by the questioner and answered by Billy in the affirmative. In the Irish version, her inability to leave her mother is not mentioned. What is common to both ballads is that a "boy," with all the connotations of immaturity that the term carries, is in love with and wants to marry an even younger, more immature girl. The questioner's purpose is to caution Billy; but in such situations, the young never listen to words of caution. Yeats's poem "Down by the Salley Gardens" has all the rhythms, repetition, stanzaic patterns, and deceptive simplicity that we associate with the nursery rhyme or folksong, and was indeed set to music in Ireland.[60] The general outline of Billy's love for Eva is set forth in Yeats's poem. In it, a young man meets his true love in an attractive natural setting (like Billy and Eva on the beach). The girl in the poem is in no rush to commit herself to the young man, and tells him in effect to slow down. But he does not recognize her lack of commitment, so the love ends sadly for him. This lyric describes a boy's love, an immature love, which does not mature into a man's love any more than a Billy Boy ever becomes William or even Bill.

The nursery rhyme and Yeats's garden lyric combine with "The Lake Isle of Innisfree" in Billy's dream of a world inhabited by children and simple childlike adults. Billy meets Eva while she is caring for picturesque children in an idyllic environment; so he imagines their own children in a similar Eden. While Eva goes on to make her peace with reality and have children of her own, Billy remains stuck in the dream. His and Maeve's childlessness, signified in the pathetic image of Maeve's doll, is a mournful acknowledgment of Billy's refusal to grow up, to give up his ideal love for Eva, and to make a real life with Maeve. On Maeve's side, mothering Billy is an inadequate substitute for having a child of her own. As the title indicates, Billy is a perpetual boy, forever needing care. Like his drinking, his inability to abandon a youthful dream for an adult reality is a component of his overall failure to become a grown man instead of a charming boy.

"American Letters" and Deviant Eva

Billy's behavior, as well as his observers' understanding of it, is clearly shaped by Uncle Daniel, the emigrant ballad, and the poems of Yeats. Of these three influences, both the character of Daniel and the ballad tradition point to another major theme in the novel: writing letters, especially letters containing money. Billy's propensity for writing letters is well known, says Bridie "from the old neighborhood."[61] Letter-writing is not just another element of Billy's charm, but a connection between Billy and the emigrant tradition of the American letter.

The American letter, usually containing either American money or passage money or both, was an important component of the emigrant chain, serving as a source of information as well as financial aid from America to Ireland. Such letters "encouraged departures through either the promises they conveyed concerning American opportunities or the prepaid passage tickets they often contained."[62] Once the emigrant arrived in the new country, he or she was expected in turn to save money to be sent home in more American letters; this money, according to Kerby Miller, stimulated further emigration by proving that America was indeed the land of plenty.[63] The money was sent either in the form of support of those left behind (American money) or in the form of either cash or prepaid tickets to bring another emigrant over (passage money or passage); American money was meant to be spent in Ireland, most often to pay rent or "local shopkeepers' bills."[64] But passage money was different, and it is this difference that explains Eva's deviation from traditional norms.

Uncle Daniel's story serves as a reminder that "the system of 'one-bringing-another' of which the Irish came to be the practitioners par excellence"[65] depended upon the passage money's being used only for passage and not confused with American money. Sometimes this use was assured by the passage money being sent in the form of a prepaid ticket, or at least encouraged by the cash remittance's being "specifically designated by the sender to be used for someone's passage."[66] But the two kinds of remittances were sharply distinguished:

> "Passage money" was never looked upon truly as "American money" because it never contributed in any way to the welfare of those at home. Except in very extreme cases of want or poverty, the people at home felt themselves under a moral obligation to use it only for passage. More often than not it was expected that the person who went to America on this passage money would either pay it back to the sender after he found employment or else send home an equal amount to bring out another member of the family.[67]

When Eva doesn't come to America; when she doesn't refund the money or "bring out" somebody else; when instead she uses the passage money as American money, Eva violates a long-standing emigrant tradition. While in fact sometimes American money "was used to purchase a small business in the local town into which a member of the family was installed," and sometimes it was used "to build up a dowry" for a female relative,[68] these uses were assumed to be with the consent of the sender of the money. But by the beginning of the twentieth century, a certain cynicism had crept in; Kerby Miller quotes an elderly County Mayo man's comment that " 'american letters is no use in ireland without money in them' " [sic].[69] Investing in a gas station on the road to Clonmel so that she and Tom could get married would surely not be a purpose to which Billy would consent; but Eva uses the money as if there were no obligations attached to it. According to Eva's friend Bessie, whom Billy meets in Clonmel, Eva has suffered from a " 'guilty conscience' " about doing so ever since,[70] as well she should; she has violated a respected tradition.

Eva's behavior is all the more corrupt in that she could not possibly imagine Billy as a rich Yankee like her employer, father of the many children for whom she and Mary served as nannies. How much Eva did know about Billy's finances is unclear; but Eva is surely too hardheaded to be operating under the influence of the "streets paved with gold" stereotype. She could not have assumed that Billy could recoup the money easily; she knows that the money comes from years of work at Holtzman's shoe store. While this knowledge makes her feel guilty, it does not make her change her behavior. Though she means to pay back the money, according to Bessie, other contingencies intervene: " 'there'd be another fuel crisis or Tom would get laid up or one of the children. And then she made up her mind to have this shop.' "[71] Billy is no match for such reflex selfishness. On one level, Billy's mistake is to wire funds to Eva instead of sending a prepaid passage ticket: by the latter method he could have guaranteed that the funds be used for transportation or refunded to him. Billy never thinks that he needs to do this; he trusts Eva. However, his trust is based not on Eva's own character but on his own beliefs about the Irish, mainly derived from Uncle Daniel.

The recipient of the American letter, the loved one left behind in Ireland, is assumed in the emigrant chain tradition to be weak and helpless, dependent upon the more competent, more affluent American. The central assumption is that the Irishman or Irishwoman wants to be brought over, and depends on American money to make that possible. As Daniel does with his Paddies, the sender of the American letter assumes himself to be superior, both financially and culturally; he offers a chance at what he assumes to be a better life; the recipient is imagined as an inferior, a sweet primitive from a land populated by those "content to lead simple lives."[72]

The stereotypical Paddy waits patiently for the money, is eternally grateful to his benefactor thereafter, even allows himself to be patronized in return for the patronage.

But Eva is no Paddy. The emigrant chain concept assumes that the recipient of American money both needs and wants to be rescued from Ireland and brought over to America. Shaped as he is by the sentimentality of the emigrant tradition, Billy assumes what Eva never promises. In the imaginative recreation of the conversation between Billy and Eva about Eva's return to Ireland, she never says that she will come back to the United States. Her intention is to visit, not to emigrate. It is mentioned several times in the course of the novel that Billy sees Eva through clouded vision: the first time he sees her, Billy is in the water and his "glasses were in his pants pocket on the sand," so he sees Eva as if she were surrounded by "an aura of royal-blue light" or is herself "a blur of colored light"; seen from a distance and without his glasses, she seems surrounded by "the illusion of an aura, a halo." This causes him to perceive her as "a mirage that perhaps only wild hope and great imagination could form into a solid woman."[73] But even Billy's distorted perception of Eva does not include a clear commitment on her part to come back to America. The reason he thinks she will is found in the ballad tradition and the emigrant chain tradition, not in Eva herself. This outdated equation between "Irish" and "emigrant" is more of a factor than his lack of glasses in Billy's distorted perception of Eva.

While in the throes of new love, few see clearly; but Eva's prompt departure means that Billy could not learn much more about her than he already knew. Thus he must rely on his partial knowledge of Irish people in general and Irish women in particular. While Irish men were negatively depicted in the anti-Irish propaganda, as discussed earlier, Irish women generally escaped similar condemnation: "the generalized image of the Irish woman, the stereotype of Bridget or Norah, carried with it fewer negative implications than did that of 'Paddy.' Although the stage character and the cartoon strip portrayal depicted Irish women and men as lacking in intelligence, manners, and common sense, Bridget was generally lovable despite these failings."[74] Billy's response to Eva is unconsciously shaped by the Bridget and Nora stereotype too. He cannot believe that she is not sweet, innocent, and loyal—is she not an "Irish girl"?

At first both Eva and her sister Mary seem to reinforce that stereotype in that they work as nannies for a rich Irish-American family. Historically, Irish women in the nineteenth century, almost alone among immigrant groups, not only did not avoid but actively sought domestic employment.[75] Circa 1884, the *London Times* described Irish women as coming to America specifically " 'in search of service and husbands.' "[76] Billy sees Eva in the context of these comforting and familiar images. She comes to the

United States to her sister (the emigrant chain operating again) and works as a nanny; she meets an American who is marriageable, though not rich. While Eva mentions her parents in Ireland, she never suggests to Billy that she has a potential husband there too. Billy does not even consider that possibility, since Irish women supposedly emigrated to America precisely to find husbands. Operating on the basis of unarticulated assumptions, Billy sees her as the stereotypical Bridget or Nora, and himself as Uncle Daniel. In his one discussion with Eva about the possibility of her emigrating to marry him, he cites Uncle Daniel as the pattern for how these things should go. She expresses reluctance, citing family obligations in Ireland as well as the cost of the trip. Billy, modeling himself on his Uncle Daniel, assures her that he would not only send for her, but send for her parents too, " 'and your sisters and the next-door neighbors if you want me to,' " including, only slightly facetiously given Uncle Daniel's example, the pastor, the milkman, the baker, and assorted nuns and cousins.[77] Never does it occur to him that she means it; she will not return, no matter how many Paddies he imports to keep her company. It never occurs to Billy that Eva is nothing like the French girl he met at the switching station during the war, " 'still here,' " still faithfully waiting for her true love.[78]

Eva is too ordinary to be the source of all evil as her name suggests, but neither is she the sweet Irish girl Billy imagines her to be. An atmosphere of ambiguity surrounds Eva. Even her appearance is described inconsistently, as at the funeral luncheon the mourners fit her to the part in which they have cast her in their trans-Atlantic drama. Rosemary says that Eva was " 'very pretty . . . like Susan Hayward,' " but Kate describes her in more moderate terms: " 'nice hair . . . big brown eyes . . . She was not very tall, even a little chubby . . . She did have a nice voice, you know. . . .' "[79] Given the passage of time, it is not surprising that the living Eva does not match the romance heroine of Billy's imagination. Billy's meeting Eva as a dumpy middle-aged housewife and mother means that, both literally and metaphorically, he has his glasses on now. Now he must overcome "half a lifetime of mistaken belief"; now he must reconcile himself not only to the fact "that she had lived" but also to "how she had lived."[80] Eva has violated all the rules of postcard Irishness. Her town is "not nearly as quaint" as Billy had imagined it; it features, bad enough, a Kentucky Fried Chicken, but worse, "a shabby sense of change, of the modern" that "had little to do with the backward, quiet little city she had once described for him." The gas station she betrayed Billy to buy is makeshift and artificial, featuring non-traditional materials, "false stucco . . . linoleum . . . Formica . . . plastic . . . something hasty and false about the place." Worst of all is her husband Tom, a generic native "in the ubiquitous Irish cap and a filthy pair of mechanic's overalls."[81] Eva's fall from grace includes her failure to meet the standards of picturesqueness that Irish-American pilgrims to Ireland feel they have a right to expect.

The sheer tackiness of Eva's life would be comical were it not for Billy's disillusionment and its devastating consequences. Far from requiring any rescue that Billy could provide, Eva wanted this life in Ireland. Far from sharing Billy's dream of an Innisfree on the Long Island shore, Eva chose this gas station in Clonmel. Now Billy must reconcile himself to the fact that the story of his life is not " 'something out of *Romeo and Juliet*' " at all. This realization leaves him with a "soaking sense of foolishness"—and a serious craving for a drink.[82]

Billy's Theology of Alcoholism

In life, alcoholism may have many causes, but the text offers only two for Billy's: physical disease on the one hand, and profound, life-shattering disappointment on the other. Rosemary espouses the theory of alcoholism as a predetermined biological disorder unaffected by life's successes and failures: " 'Billy would have had the disease whether he married the Irish girl or Maeve, whether he had kids or not. It wouldn't have been such a different life, believe me. Every alcoholic's life is pretty much the same.' " Dan Lynch, on the other hand, attributes Billy's alcoholism to a " 'sadness [he] can't get rid of.' " To Dan, people like Billy are " 'loyal to their own feelings . . . loyal to the first plans they made,' " perhaps " 'too loyal.' " To Dan, though Billy may have " 'made way too much of the Irish girl,' " to say that " 'it was a disease that blindsided him' " is to deny him " 'credit for feeling, for having a hand in his own fate.' "[83] Dennis comes to believe that both Rosemary and Dan are right about Billy, and to take some responsibility for his own hand in Billy's fate. Billy is a victim of Dennis's lie; but the effect of the lie on Billy is a function of Billy's preexisting characteristics: his sense of loyalty, however misguided; his religious faith, however ill-conceived; and his tendency to alcoholism. Billy's trip to Ireland demonstrates what is for him a complicated relationship between personal loyalty, his own brand of Catholicism, and alcoholism.

The way Billy tries to stop drinking is a particularly Irish Catholic way of going about it: he travels to Ireland, defining the trip in religious terms as a " 'pilgrimage' " with two related goals: "to take the pledge" and to visit Eva's grave.[84] The notion of "taking the pledge," especially in Ireland, alludes to the stereotypical link between the Irish and alcohol, but more specifically to the Catholic Total Abstinence Societies founded by Father Theobald Mathew in the 1830s.[85] Directing his message to "those Irishmen whose hard drinking has made this national trait proverbial in America,"[86] Father Mathew "joined with Protestant ministers and merchants to preach a nationwide crusade for total abstinence," which was successful in that millions "took the pledge."[87] According to Dan Lynch, Billy's choice was based on his belief that " 'AA was a Protestant thing,' " while the pledge was " 'the Catholic take on AA.' "[88] This Catholic version of Alcoholics Anonymous influences Billy's decision to take the pledge in Ireland, ironically with an equally bibulous priest as his traveling companion. Since Billy grew up at a time when the Catholic church maintained its own organizations parallel to secular ones, Billy would naturally seek out the Catholic version, without regard to relative effectiveness. Both pledging to stop drinking and drinking itself are related to Billy's second pilgrimage goal: to visit Eva's grave. Playing the part of the returned emigrant in "Danny Boy" is Billy's way of putting the causes of his drinking, as well as the drinking itself, to rest. When he finds Eva alive, Billy resumes drinking.

In love, Billy Lynch is an absolutist; when drunk, he is a theological absolutist as well; and, ironically, Billy's theology keeps him drinking. Deep in his cups, Billy meditates upon the value of Christ's crucifixion. If such a sacrifice is of value, it is because death is absolutely " 'terrible' "; if one who has lost his love can " 'reconcile' " himself, can " 'go on,' " that recovery mocks the crucifixion of Christ. If it is possible for the living to recover from the cosmic horror that is the death of a loved one, then " 'what do we need the Redemption for?' "[89] Because " 'death is terrible, a terrible injustice,' " mourning must be terrible too. To those who say, as Dennis does, that " 'life goes on,' " Billy replies with an everlasting refusal: " 'I won't let it.' "[90] To Billy, recovery diminishes the first commitment. Like Dan Lynch, Billy believes that a drinker's drinking is no disease but his unique response to tragedy, a key element of his self-definition, a way of " 'having a hand in his own fate.' "[91] Recovery, then, would not be a positive step, but a denial both of the seriousness of the precipitating event and of the drinker's uniqueness. Billy even takes the matter to a theological plane by interpreting recovery after a loss as a negation of the value of Christ's redemptive sacrifice. If a mere human could recover from the death of a loved one, was the death of Christ the cosmic necessity that Billy had been taught it was? If Billy could get over Eva, Christ's death would be in vain. This is the theology of a man not only superficially educated but also drunk; yet for him, it establishes the connection he feels between drinking, faith, and romance. Billy justifies his drinking as fidelity to a central value of the romance tradition: endless love as absolute, as irrevocable. Were Isolde to pull herself together and replace Tristan, were Heloise to shrug her shoulders and remarry after Abelard's castration, were anyone to recover either in the alcoholic or the romantic sense, the absolute uniqueness of the first commitment would be negated. Thus Billy's fierce refusal to " 'go back out to the Island' ":[92] earthly beauty is meaningless in the face of death's destruction. It is as if Billy is living his life in twentieth-century Queens, New York, according to the norms of medieval romance.

But Dennis, following his wife Claire's death and Billy's, comes to believe that there must be "some relief . . . some compensation" for those left alive, even, to the narrator's mind, "penance . . . compensation for an old and well-intentioned lie."[93] If Billy's theology stresses suffering and death, Dennis's theology stresses repentance and renewal. For all his faults—and they are many—Dennis is able to forgive himself and go on. Though he hurt Irish Mary, he makes a good marriage with Claire and maintains his commitment to her until her death, which is all the commitment that Catholic marriage vows require. Though his lie contributes to Billy's drinking, Dennis deals with the consequences; a central activity of Dennis's life is rescuing Billy. This culminates, as logically it would, in his being the one to identify Billy's body. Later, his marriage to Maeve sustains both their ties to their shared past, which irrevocably includes Billy and Claire. In psychological terms, Dennis is adaptable; in theological terms, Dennis acts as if he believes that God's forgiveness is possible. Whether Billy's theology or Dennis's theology is the correct one is left for the reader to decide: but the final image of Dennis and Maeve in East Hampton affirms the psychological value of self-forgiveness. Though for Dennis Long Island is no Innisfree and Maeve is no romance heroine, he is happy enough; he is not, as Billy is, in bondage to an ideal.

Eva as Religion

Eva assumes such overwhelming proportions as the central fact of Billy's life not because of who she really is but because of what she stands for, or what the mourners think she stands for: the nexus of his, and their, inchoate beliefs about their ill-understood Irish heritage. To Billy, Eva is his link to the Irish past, as to his mourners, a group of second- and third-generation Irish-Americans, Billy is. Once the emigrant generation (represented by Uncle Daniel) makes the great journey, none of them except Billy ever go to Ireland; Billy's generation stays put in Queens. By bringing Eva over, by marrying Eva, Billy seems also to seek a stronger link between Ireland and America than his own vague Irishness supplies. His failure to achieve this, and the mourners' disagreement about why he failed, stresses the discontinuity between the two cultures and the misunderstandings resulting therefrom.

All of them think of Eva primarily as "the Irish girl," but Billy needs to know more, and it is part of his failure that he does not.

Eva's role in Billy's life is to represent his vaguely understood ideals. In the absence of a father, Billy idolizes his Uncle Daniel and wants to continue the emigrant tradition to which Daniel dedicated his life. Billy wants to write American letters, to bring a Paddy over, to recreate Innisfree on Long Island. Dennis's lie gives Billy the option of imagining himself in yet another Irish context, as the returning emigrant in "Danny Boy" standing mournfully at the grave of a loved one. After a lifetime devoted to an imaginary Eva, Billy learns that the real Eva does not match his version of the Irish, especially Irish women. Billy's boyishness leaves him inadequate to deal with the belated knowledge of Eva's betrayal. Her presumed death was tragic, but the realization of a thirty-year-long deception is worse, so Billy's pilgrimage to Ireland fails: he returns to America the worse for the journey, to drink and to die.

Perhaps the reason the relentlessly ordinary Eva grows to such giant proportions in Billy's life is that she provides a focus for Billy's religious impulses, an absolute in which he can believe. These Irish-Americans are mainly cultural Catholics; the church is to them more an element of their Irishness than a theology. For Billy, Eva is like the churches and synagogues that he loves to visit, monuments that "stand and say, 'This will not change.' "[94] When he believes that she is alive and will be coming to him, his letter-writing, a Sunday-night ritual, becomes a form of worship; his work to repay Holtzman fills up one evening and all day Saturday; in short, loving Eva both structures and intensifies Billy's life. When he believes that Eva is dead, despite his mother's facile but realistic assumption that he can and will get over it, Billy chooses a life centered on mourning. His image of Eva, and of himself as bereaved, function as churches did in his childhood, standing as monuments to "the need for faith, for that which was steadfast and true."[95] Like the French girl's being " 'still here' " for her lover, Billy's "unwavering faith" will be a testimony to the possibility of permanence in a changing world: "This will not change. I am still here."[96] Therefore he wants "no comfort"[97] for the loss of his love. He could have made his marriage to Maeve the symbol of unchanging permanence, but he chooses the loss of Eva as the rock upon which he builds his faith. When he could have built his life on the living, he chose to build it on the dead, and on a hope for a future in which, when, drunk, he "turned his eyes to heaven . . . heaven was there and Eva was in it."[98] Billy's faith, though destructive to him, gives hope to others; according to Dennis, Billy's refusal to understand that " 'living isn't poetry' " made others keep alive the belief that living indeed *was* poetry: " 'every one of us thought that as long as Billy believed it was . . . then maybe it could still be true.' " For Dennis, who by the time of Billy's death has known the truth about Eva for over thirty years, the story was somehow sacred, "another sweet romance to preserve."[99] Thus the story of Billy and Eva becomes, for his mourners, a story of respected values: permanence, undying love, promises kept.

The wake over, the novel ends with a wedding: the marriage of Dennis and Maeve, in a church recently renamed after its patron saint was discovered not to have existed. The little detail, as Charles Fanning points out, of this obscure and debunked saint "leads to a last, emphatic affirmation of the wonder and the necessity of storytelling."[100] Like the medieval romance, the *vitae* or saints' lives of the early church were not based on what moderns consider historical fact. Instead, the purpose of such a story was to present virtues worth emulating. The more wondrous the tale, the better it would serve to impress the saint's virtues in the mind of the listener. By the end of her attempt to understand Billy's story, the narrator comes to see it as like the *vitae* with which she and her fellow Catholics are familiar, stories in which "what was actual . . . what was imagined . . . what was believed"[101] merge and conflate in such a way as to make the distinctions between them insignificant. Such stories celebrate the values inherent in the life of their central characters. Actual events, imagination, and belief inform all the versions of Billy's story, even the ones that contradict each other. Billy's story is spun out of mourners' platitudes at a funeral luncheon, and eulogy is no more a factual medium than the saints' lives were. Were the mourners to say, at that time and in the presence of his widow, that Billy's life was a farce built on a lie? That he was an ordinary drunk? That his romantic obsession with a girl as ordinary as himself was just an excuse for his drinking? Such talk would not be at all proper at an Irish wake.

Chapter 7

The Rage of the Dying Animal: Mary Gordon's *The Other Side*

On August 14, 1985, eighty-eight-year-old Vincent MacNamara reluctantly returns from a nursing home to the house he has shared with his wife Ellen, who is demented and dying at ninety, to keep his promise to her that he would let her die at home. Mary Gordon's *The Other Side* tells the story of the events leading up to this single day in the life of a family. On such a day as this, the whole family is expected to assemble; on such a day, all the flaws in this Irish Catholic version of the " 'house of Atreus' "[1] are exposed. The MacNamara family's history is narrated in a series of flashbacks from multiple viewpoints, explaining how each of the MacNamaras came to be what they are on this day. In his essay on recent New York Irish writing, Charles Fanning describes Gordon as portraying Irishness in this novel as "a genetic defect and a cultural curse, an unqualified burden to be escaped and overcome."[2] The negativity to which Fanning is responding is surely present in *The Other Side*, but it is mainly as part of the characterization of Ellen MacNamara; and it is counterbalanced by the characterization of Vincent, whose position with respect to his own past and to that of the Irish people is more subtle. While Ellen and Vincent are in many ways typical of their emigrant generation, Ellen diverges from type in her unremitting anger. Whether as a young girl considering emigration or as a dying old woman, Ellen rages against experiences shared by many of her peers. Both Ellen and Vincent participate, and with some success, in the great historical events in the joint history of Ireland and America in their lifetime; but while Vincent derives satisfaction from his own role in these, Ellen cannot.

When Ellen comes to America, her anger at the country from which she feels herself exiled extends to everything Irish. Her work, typical of emigrants like herself; the songs and stories that link the emigrants of her generation to Ireland; and, above all, the Catholic church: all are anathema to her. Conversely, whatever she can construe as the antithesis of Irishness and/or Catholicism attracts her fervent loyalty. Ellen's rage against Ireland is such that she cannot see that, like other emigrants, she has contributed to the remarkable progress of the Irish-American community in the twentieth century: their successful emigration; their incorporation into the American workforce; their economic and educational progress, for themselves and still more for subsequent generations of their family. While this vastly complex novel is not the story of a happy family, the "house of Atreus" metaphor is, as Cam and Dan, who use it, well know, exaggerated. *The Other Side* is the story of a family founded by two people with contrasting views on their joint heritage: Ellen is angry, and Vincent is forgiving. Since anger is by nature more overt, more demonstrative, than forgiveness, Ellen influences the family more than does Vincent, and the consequence of this is the transmission of Ellen's own conflicts down through the generations.

Bees in Church: Ellen as Exile

Ellen and Vincent must be understood first in terms of their reasons for leaving Ireland, and the impact of those reasons on the memories that they transmit to their children and grandchildren. In *Emigrants and Exiles: Ireland and the Irish Exodus to North America*, Kerby A. Miller examines the two possible self-definitions named in his title: one who leaves Ireland for any reason can be termed an emigrant; but when the leaving can be blamed on some outside force, that emigrant can imagine him or herself as an exile.[3] Kevin Kenny, in *The American Irish: A History*, analyzes the same phenomenon in terms of what he calls the "push factor" and the "pull factor":[4] that which pushes the emigrant out of the old country, as opposed to that which pulls the emigrant to the new country. Fusing the two sets of concepts, one who leaves Ireland because he or she is attracted to the opportunities offered in another country is, in Miller's term, an emigrant; in Kenny's term, such a person is "pulled" to the new country. This is a more accurate description of Vincent than it is of Ellen. Ellen is an example of the other alternative in that she feels herself "pushed" out, "exiled" from Ireland. Ellen, growing up in the early twentieth century as the favored only child of a prosperous publican, is not really " 'driven from' " Ireland or leaving because she " '*had to*' " as were the Famine emigrants upon whose letters and memoirs Miller bases his definitions,[5] but, influenced by the traditional perception of the Irish as exiles, she imagines herself in these terms. To do so, she creates a demon to substitute for England, for hunger, for all the suffering from which her forebears fled. For Ellen, that demon is represented by Ireland in general, and her father in particular.

Ellen's memories of her childhood are not such as were immortalized in the emigrant ballads. As a child and young girl, Ellen is witness to her mother's tragedy: a beautiful young woman, cursed by her body's inability to bring to term any child other than Ellen herself, suffers repeated miscarriages and stillbirths, and finally retreats into madness. Her mother's blood, spilled in futile attempts to bear the children she and her husband desperately want, comes to symbolize for Ellen the "oozing beds of ancient ill will" in Ireland itself.[6] The horror of Ellen's mother life is the more intense when seen against the background of the ballad tradition, in which Irish mothers are idealized. Ellen's motherhood, particularly with regard to her daughters, is poisoned at the source by her own mother's fate; when Ellen is herself a mother, when her daughters become mothers in their turn, the figure of the mad Irish mother haunts this family's history.

But it rapidly becomes clear that Ellen's "anger at the Irish countryside"[7] is a displacement of her fury at her father for what she sees as his role in her mother's tragedy. At the beginning of the twentieth century, Tom Costelloe cannot divorce his wife even if he wants to; divorce did not become legal in Ireland until 1995. Although he does not abandon his wife—he builds an isolated country house and hires a caretaker, Anna Foley, to care for her— he does go on with his life, moving to town with his mistress, Marin Monahan. Influenced by Anna Foley, Ellen comes to regard her father's sexuality as the cause of her mother's madness (she cannot imagine her mother as a willing participant in the act that doomed her). The father and Marin become to Ellen sign and symbol of corruption, of the "simple filth" of desire, which she believes destroyed her mother. Even on her deathbed, she longs for "vengeance" for this ancient crime.[8] As a young girl, she is determined to escape the place in which this terrible event occurred. Her mother's tragedy and her father's response to it could have happened anywhere; but because the destruction of her childhood Eden took place in Ireland, to her it took place because of Ireland. Thus Ellen must not only leave, she must leave irrevocably. She sends herself into exile as a criminal, a thief of her father's money to pay her passage; and, for the rest of her life, she demonizes Ireland as a place to which no one would want to return, and demonizes her father as a man who would send his only child to prison if she did return.

When Ellen is asked why she emigrated, she does not, however, tell her mother's story, of which she is so ashamed that she will conceal it as long as possible even from her husband. Instead, she tells the story of the bees in the parish church. The Catholic church in the town of Tulla, in County Clare, is infested by bees. The parishioners react by not reacting: " 'Bees, then,' they were saying, and that was the end of it."[9] The priest, the worshippers, everyone but Ellen will say no more about the problem. Eventually the bees swarm elsewhere, the cleaning woman removes all traces of their presence, and all seems well: "The priest stood in the pulpit and thanked God that through this tribulation no one had been stung, especially the children, and he offered three Hail Marys of Thanksgiving to the Blessed Mother, patroness of Ireland, who sheltered all in her motherly embrace."[10] But all is not well for Ellen: " 'Twas then I packed my bags,' she always ended the story. 'And I booked my passage . . . I knew 'twas not the place for me.' "[11]

Ellen's story of the bees in church illustrates an aspect of Irish Catholicism that Ellen finds intolerable. The priest's words drape the mantle of Catholicism over peasant fatalism. To the priest and to his congregation, the bees represent suffering that must be endured, in the Catholic expression "offered up" to God for one's sins or the sins of others. When the swarm vanishes, the priest credits this relief to supernatural intervention. Ellen cannot accept any of this. Her personal history disinclines her to have faith in a sheltering, embracing supernatural mother, when her natural mother "sat in the darkness gibbering."[12] Any improvement in her life, she realizes, can come only from her own efforts, and can occur only in a place where taking action is rewarded. The passivity of these parishioners drives Ellen from Ireland: " 'Twas then I packed my bags . . . and I booked my passage.' "[13] In choosing to explain her decision to emigrate by means of this bee story, by thinking about it and telling it repeatedly, Ellen reinforces the connection in her mind between fatalism and religion, fueling her hostility toward the Irish brand of Catholicism.

Ellen's hostility is not resolved merely by repudiating the Catholic church; she makes no distinction between the religion and Irish life in general. Ellen misses no opportunity to criticize the land of "pigs and dirt and begging relatives."[14] Rejecting Ireland means protecting her children from contact with any element of Irish culture that crossed the Atlantic. Her absolutism on this subject disrupts her relationship with her husband and even more so with her daughter Theresa. Ellen particularly scorns the emigrant ballads, with their nostalgia for Erin's green shores. When Vincent plays his gramophone recordings of tenor John McCormack singing "Kathleen Mavourneen" and "Molly Bawn," Ellen's mockery of McCormack's singing enrages Vincent more than her mockery of the Catholic church, and he reacts with uncharacteristic violence: "He broke the records, smashing them on the floor when she mocked him. She'd not done it again, but he'd never had the heart to replace the records, they'd never again had John McCormack in the house."[15] More damaging than this is Ellen's behavior toward Theresa. Against Ellen's wishes, Vincent buys a piano and encourages Theresa to take lessons and to play for him the very music that Ellen hates.

Theresa's music helps Vincent reconnect with the emotions he experienced upon emigrating, emotions that are still present to him years later as he recuperates at Maryhurst: "He loved the sad words of the songs Theresa sang for him and the music that went deep. It brought back everything, the greens of the woods around the river, the river itself, his leaving his mother forever. Once Theresa agreed to learn for his sake a song called 'The Old Bog Road.' There was a part in it about a mother dying that he lets himself cry over now."[16] This particular ballad would have emotional resonances for Vincent, as Ellen should realize. In the ballad, the emigrant, a laborer in New York, has come to America for "gold beyond the seas." But he feels lonely and unloved in the big city; he has missed his mother's funeral; and his sweetheart in Ireland has died.[17] Instead of sympathizing with the sense of loss expressed in the ballad, Ellen reacts with the same rage that she will feel on her deathbed, rage directed not only against Vincent for listening to the songs, but also against Theresa for playing them. Anger substitutes for the other powerful emotions with which she is still struggling, the grief and loss expressed in the ballad.

If even playing Irish music is anathema in the MacNamara household, visiting Ireland is unthinkable. Because Ellen has convinced herself that she cannot return, she discourages her family from doing so. She "mocked the rich first-generation greenhorns who took their families back home. To see what? she would say. The cattle shitting in the streets, right up to your door, the children with their teeth rotted out of their heads, the beautiful thatched cottages swept only once a year, the tinkers carrying their filthy babies in their filthy blankets?"[18] Ellen's perceptions are undercut, however, by Vincent's experiences. Her self-image as exile is based on the belief that her father would have her arrested and jailed for the theft of his money. But when Vincent goes back to retrieve Ellen's mother, he finds that Ellen's father is no such monster of vengefulness as Ellen depicts him; he had long since forgiven his daughter, perhaps never even blamed her; he has accepted responsibility for his wife's care; and he has even kept Ellen, not his mistress, as his heir. By not returning to Ireland, Ellen deprives herself of revisiting her home in the psychological sense: revisiting Ireland, the Catholic church, and even her father, as an adult. At the age of ninety, she still views her heritage as did the adolescent who emigrated so long ago.

The Sacrificial Lamb: Vincent as Emigrant

While Vincent's youth in Ireland is harsh too, his reaction to it and his motives for leaving are more rational than Ellen's; thus he does not feel compelled to reject all things Irish, he can take comfort in his religion and in his heritage, and he can go home again. This makes him, in Miller's terms, an emigrant rather than an exile. Vincent leaves to escape his fate as the landless younger brother of a man who hates him. While the primogenitive system of landholding served to keep larger land parcels intact, it also led to rivalry and hatred between brothers, as dramatized by the episode involving Vincent's lamb. As if to warn Vincent of the bleakness of his fate were he to remain in Ireland, his older brother kills a lamb that the two boys had raised as a pet, a lamb of which Vincent was fond. Even as an old man, Vincent is "frightened by the memory of that hate"[19] acted out on a surrogate, but really directed toward Vincent himself. This childhood trauma gives Vincent a sense of his own weakness and a reason to leave.

Vincent's decision to emigrate is impeded by two factors: the Catholic church and his family situation. Albeit painfully, Vincent deals with both. The conflicting attitude of the Irish clergy with regard to emigration is embodied in two characters, Father Sullivan and Father Lavery. Through these two priests, Vincent becomes aware of opposing viewpoints held by clerical authority figures; thus his perception of the church is altered sufficiently to help him make a decision on the union issue years later. Father Sullivan represents those members of the Irish clergy who focused on the dangers of emigration, its threat to traditional ways of life. His (probably apocryphal) sermon anecdote, the story of a young woman who had lost her virtue in America but regained it in Ireland, is reminiscent of the emigrant ballad "Noreen Bawn."[20] In the ballad, a young emigrant woman returns to Ireland dressed prosperously, in fine clothes, but with a rash of illness marking her face. Unlike the prodigal daughter of the priest's story, Noreen Bawn returns to Ireland too late to avert her fate; she dies of the moral corruption that threatened youthful emigrants alone in a strange land.

Although Vincent doubts the authenticity of the priest's tale, too pat and too similar to the ballad version, his respect for authority makes him question his own judgment rather than Father Sullivan's. Even at eighty-eight Vincent thinks about how "the words of Father Sullivan still make him afraid . . . He can hear in his skull once again the words, the hard words, the important words 'apostasy,' 'damnation,' 'treachery,' 'the bone and sinew of the Irish nation brutally cut out.' He'd sat in the church in Cork, trying the words out on himself: 'traitor,' 'apostate,' 'lucre-loving materialist.' He feared to say them to himself: what if they fit?"[21] At the time, to help assuage his guilt, Vincent takes the matter in confession to another priest, Father Lavery. " 'Vincent,' the priest had told him in the darkness of the sacrament, 'if I were a young man I'd be on the boat beside you.' "[22] Because of Father Lavery, Vincent's view of the church is never as monolithic as Ellen's is. This is why Vincent can join the union when many of the clergy were preaching against it, and without feeling that he must reject the church totally, as Ellen does, in order to do so. Vincent learns a useful lesson: authority, even within the church, does not always speak with a single voice. Resolving this issue, however, is only one step toward Vincent's decision.

At eighty-eight, Vincent still remembers how he "lost his home," and always regards that loss as the "biggest thing that ever happened to him."[23] To leave Ireland he must leave his mother, to whom he is greatly attached and who is pregnant with a child he fears he will never see, and in fact never does. The community's grief and loss at the departure of one of its members was ritualized at that time by means of the custom of the American wake. As Kerby Miller explains the custom, the American wake evolved in Ireland as a ritual response to the loss of its people through emigration. Like a real wake except for the living presence of the person being mourned, the American wake gathered the community to bid farewell to one who would soon be lost to them. Before advances in communication and transportation rendered it obsolete, the American wake acknowledged that emigration was "death's equivalent, a final breaking of earthly ties,"[24] all the more poignant in that the person waked was likely to be young.[25] In addition to the realistic factor, that the difficulties of the trip rendered return unlikely, the symbolic equation of all westward travel, and therefore the trip to America, with death was "rooted deep in Irish folklore . . . in voyage tales which symbolized death or banishment and in popular beliefs which equated going west with earthly dissolution."[26]

Like a real wake, the ritual took all night (hence the term "wake," keeping watch over a corpse), thus acknowledging the passage of the living person into "the realm . . . of the dead."[27] Like a real wake, the American wake took place in the home, and involved the same kind of "seemingly incongruous mixture of sorrow and hilarity, with prayers for the dead and the mournful keening of old women alternating with drinking, dancing, and mirthful games."[28] Emigrant ballads, stressing the emigrant's regret at leaving his homeland and the community's longing for his return, would be sung. As Grace Neville points out, archival accounts of American wakes do not mention "prayers or priests" at the actual wake,[29] which is consistent with the wake's being primarily a pagan custom. In the morning, visits would be paid, among them to the parish priest.[30] Finally, the ritual would conclude with the convoy, or the accompanying of the emigrant as far as possible by a smaller number of people, usually the closest members of his family, as if to let the emigrant go in stages.[31] The emotional tone throughout was grief and abandonment on the part of the family, grief and guilt on the part of the emigrant. Often emigrants would, as Vincent did, attempt to "relieve the tensions . . . by making elaborate promises to return or send remittances,"[32] thus reinforcing ties to the community.[33] No matter what the emigrant promised, however, everyone knew that he was dead to his old life.

Ellen escapes the grueling emotional experience of the American wake by leaving secretly; but Vincent is exposed to the full force of his family's, and particularly his mother's, grief. Even though he had been living in the city of Cork and needed to board ship at Queenstown (now Cobh), an inefficient journey as Queenstown is only a few miles from Cork, he feels the ritual need "to go home so he could leave from home" to acknowledge not only his own but also the community's need to mourn. But the ritual displeases him, especially "the family's cavorting and their loudness" when he "wanted to sit, holding his mother's hand."[34] The contrast between Vincent's mood and that of the other participants at the wake is not surprising. While the American wake was a community affair, many of those who attended would not in fact grieve for the emigrant as members of his family would; those might well "cavort," as for them the wake was only a party, a " 'bottle drink' " or a " 'spree.' "[35] In the morning, Vincent pays final visits, including one to the parish priest. His mother insists that he take a packet of shamrock seed for planting in America; this souvenir is typical of the items pressed upon the departing one, inscribed with cautions like " 'forget not the land of your birth.' "[36] Vincent's brief worry that he will not pass U.S. Customs with this bit of the homeland in his baggage is an indicator of the "pull" of his destination; he does not want to be held back by any archaic "home custom."[37] His parents accompany him on the convoy to Queenstown.

It is on arrival at the port city that Vincent's conflict—pulled toward America, but also regretful and guilty at leaving Ireland—becomes most evident. The rituals of departure—the farewell visits, the American wake, the souvenir shamrock seeds, the convoy—seem designed to increase the emigrant's guilt, drawing him back toward the country he has already determined to leave; and so it is with Vincent. His mother's presence on the convoy suits the nature of the ritual (Neville says that "women, especially mothers . . . seem to have functioned as lightning conductors for emotions such as grief on these occasions"[38]), but his own response to her, or lack of it, increases his guilt. Vincent has traveled little; not surprisingly, his attention is diverted from his mother by his interest in Saint Colman's Cathedral, then under construction. Vincent's attraction to the way things work will shape his career in New York, and will culminate in a job as model-maker for a scaffolding company; but he does not know this at the time. Because the construction of the cathedral distracted him from his mother in these last moments of their life together, he is never able to forgive himself. Only much later in life, in the nursing home, will Vincent finally allow himself to experience these feelings of guilt and loss, and the vehicle of this emotional release will be the emigrant ballads that Theresa plays, over Ellen's objections, in the house in Queens Village.

But at the time of his departure, the lure of "advancement" is strong in Vincent. Although he continues to fear that what he means by "advancement" might be what Father Sullivan describes as the "materialism" that kills the spirit,[39] he had already been fascinated by the city of Cork and is ready for even greater ventures. In Cork, Vincent begins to think in a new language, the language of business, which seems to him at once similar to yet incompatible with the language of faith. Thinking of the Capwell Carriage Works, the firm for which he worked in Cork, Vincent remembers how "he'd felt it was an honor to be part of such an organization. He was linked up with serious words again, like the words from the pulpit, 'conversant' and 'satisfactory' now, instead of 'eternal damnation' or 'apostasy' or 'sins against the Holy Ghost.' "[40] As he learns to think in this new language, Vincent seeks even greater opportunity. Beyond Cork lies New York. While Vincent never does abandon the church, never loses the vocabulary of faith, he becomes, in effect, bilingual, able to speak the language of American capitalism and eventually to work within the system to his advantage. At the time when Vincent emigrates, 1913, this can only happen on the other side.

Women at Work: Ellen as Domestic and Factory Worker

As Vincent is leaving Ireland, so is Ellen; but the job opportunities in New York do not pull her as much as they do him. Both enter the labor force, as did so many of their peers, close to the bottom. For Ellen, as for Clíona in *The Mermaids Singing*, this means domestic service. According to Daniel Sutherland, in the nineteenth century there was a "social stigma" on domestic service, at least partly because of its association with slavery; thus its ranks tended to be filled not by the American-born but rather by "the most scorned groups of foreigners, the Irish and the Chinese."[41] Because, like Ellen, most servants lived in, employers imagined that they had a right, even a responsibility, to supervise them, and to call upon domestic staff on what would be time off in the outside world. Such beliefs and practices persisted into the second decade of the twentieth century, when Ellen takes a job as lady's maid to Claire Fitzpatrick, but with a difference. Because of the physical difficulty of domestic work at a time before mechanization, the lack of privacy, the low job status, and the awkwardness of the relationship between servant and employer,[42] by the early twentieth century servants were in high demand and short supply. Nevertheless, employers' behavior, especially that of the woman of the household, did not change to compensate for the servant shortage. So it is that Claire Fitzpatrick loses her lady's maid.

The woman of such a house as Claire Fitzpatrick's had long been a symbol of her husband's affluence; her leisure, her conspicuous consumption, reflected credit on him. The role of servants was to do the physical work of the house, that the lady might do her own work, which was, primarily, living a life appropriate to her husband's social status; and, secondarily, acting as "regulator and manager" of the home.[43] This latter role included supervising servants but not doing any work that might have been done by them, for to do so would risk compromising all-important "class distinctions."[44] This is all the more important for someone like Claire Fitzpatrick. By the early twentieth century, at least some of the Irish, like the fathers of Claire and James Fitzpatrick, were rich enough to provide a leisured life for their offspring, a necessary component of which was employing servants themselves. Therefore Claire, an Irish-American, employs an Irish-born lady's maid. The similarities between employer and employee have consequences in that Claire Fitzpatrick is particularly concerned to maintain distinctions.

At one time, Ellen's being Irish would have precluded her from being considered for the type of work she does for the Fitzpatricks. When most employers were white Anglo-Saxon Protestants and most servants were not, anti-Catholic prejudice as well as discomfort with unfamiliar Irish ways and modes of speech caused the Irish to be shunned.[45] But by 1900, Irish women predominated in domestic service, constituting 41 percent of female domestic workers.[46] The image of the Irish servant had evolved also: "The stereotype of dirty, ignorant Paddy and Bridget was often overshadowed by that of the genial fun-loving lad or lass who attracted sympathy and won hearts wherever they went."[47] Influenced by the more positive stereotype, as well she might be considering her own Irish roots, Claire Fitzpatrick expects angry Ellen to be a "fun-loving" Irish lass. Ellen obliges by telling a story of a stereotypical Irish family bearing no resemblance to her own: "When Mrs. Fitzpatrick questioned her about her past she made up what she knew the woman wished to hear: the small farm, the countless brothers, cheerful sisters, stoical hardworking father, and her sainted mother, who slaved for the family but was never too busy for a laugh."[48] A complex interaction is occurring here. On Ellen's part, the storytelling is a means of withholding her true identity from a person who, she feels, has no right to know it. It gives Ellen satisfaction that Mrs. Fitzpatrick, though herself Irish-American, cannot detect Ellen's deception, cannot understand that Ellen is all the while inwardly raging against her employer. At the same time as she is showing her own ignorance of Irish ways and lack of understanding of Ellen herself, Claire Fitzpatrick is carefully preserving her own status by maintaining social distance, treating Ellen not as a fellow Irishwoman but condescending to her as to an inferior.

As a lady's maid, Ellen is a middle-rank servant, outranked by the house-keeper, butler, and chef, but herself outranking lower servants who did more arduous and dirty physical labor.[49] The lady's maid's work was in the same category of personal service that included a man's valet or a child's nurse; she is a "body servant,"[50] literally in service of the body of her employer. Ellen has nothing but contempt for this work. What Ellen resents in her job is exactly what the lady's maid does: readying a lady's body for public presentation. Other Irish emigrants might have felt as Ellen's friend Delia does, that such a job was " 'lovely.' "[51] Historians of the Irish in the workforce point out that jobs in domestic service readied the Irish for the next step on the social ladder, as women like Ellen "learned the touch of fine silver and porcelain and furniture, the feel of good linen and real lace. They also learned, from their mistresses, good manners. These were advantages that these girls would do their best to see that their children would have in the next generation."[52] But Ellen herself sees nothing good in the home of the Fitzpatricks.

Ellen's fury is directed against practices that were common at the time. For example, Ellen's room at the Fitzpatricks's house is typical in being "furnished with only the bare essentials," often unheated and poorly lit.[53] What bothers her even more is "the cast-off, the rag-endedness . . . and the sense that what was deficient could so easily be fixed. Nails for her clothes instead of hooks."[54] The door did not lock; lack of privacy was a common feature of servants' rooms of the period. While larger nineteenth- and early-twentieth-century houses were often designed to give the family privacy from its servants, with features like back entrances, servants' staircases, service areas located away from the family living quarters, and servants' quarters likewise spatially separated,[55] respect for privacy did not extend in both directions. It was common that, as was the case with Ellen, "a servant's solitude was at the mercy of whim."[56]

This situation, however, must be understood in a historical context. Alternative housing for new emigrants like Ellen was usually "squalid urban tenements,"[57] often in basements "completely without ventilation, drainage, or any form of plumbing."[58] Privacy would not be found there either, as often "families doubled or tripled up" in these substandard living quarters.[59] Compared to male emigrants, who often had to accept unhealthy and dangerous jobs like digging tunnels, women emigrants were better off as domestic servants. Such jobs were safer and more profitable than other forms of employment open to new emigrants. As Hasia Diner points out, "servants lived in a strikingly more healthful environment, residing in the best neighborhoods of the city, eating the same food—albeit as leftovers—as their employers."[60] Compared to their female peers who did factory work, their working and living conditions were better; and as for their salaries, considering that room, board, and often clothing were free, servants did well.[61]

Ellen's resentment focuses more on the attitudinal factors that operate in her relationship with Claire Fitzpatrick than on the work itself. First among these is Claire's use of her first name; but this too was common practice. In fact, one nineteenth-century Boston householder avoided the difficulty of memorizing the names of the many Irishwomen in his service by calling them all Bridget.[62] Compared to these women, Ellen is at least able to retain some small portion of her identity. When Claire Fitzpatrick instructs her with moral and religious platitudes, and asks Ellen to think of her as a mother, she is only doing what employers of the time were encouraged to do: taking responsibility for young people in the household who were deemed hardly more than children. Ellen resents this; but what irritates her even more is the sense that "the Fitzpatricks, in paying her, thought they had bought her life."[63] If they did think so, they were in good company.

Claims made on servants' time beyond what would be normal working hours in the world outside the household were common. As Ellen senses, employers did think they had purchased the whole lives of their servants. In the crucial event that triggers Ellen's resignation from her position in the Fitzpatrick household, Claire Fitzpatrick operates on the basis of an idea, outmoded even then, that the relationship between the lady and her maid was based on the assumption that "all of a servant's time belonged to the 'master,' " so that "servants, even when off duty, remained 'on call' for emergencies."[64] What constituted an emergency was, of course, up to the employer. In New York in 1903, Lillian Pettengill published an analysis of domestic life entitled *Toilers of the Home: The Record of a College Woman's Experience as a Domestic Servant*. In it, Pettengill reports an incident similar to the one that triggers Ellen's resignation: being asked to give up her afternoon off. Of her employer, Pettengill says, "Had she asked for the favour pleasantly, as one woman of another, I should have granted it. . . . But to be told as if I were a young child and she my guardian, that she chose not to give me what I had a right to demand, that it wasn't necessary that I have it, was insulting to my dignity as an adult."[65] Pettengill's language (she writes of a "favour," which, had she been treated as a peer, she might have "granted"; she mentions "rights," "dignity," and adult status) shows that she is radically unsuited to the life of a servant, with its built-in inequality. Similarly Ellen. To Ellen, her time off has a meaning, even if Claire Fitzpatrick cannot see it. To Ellen, her day off "*means [her] life*."[66]

Ellen's historical analogues resented the arbitrariness and the pose of ownership exhibited by domestic employers; many servants yearned to escape the control of such employers. Servants' lack of freedom, more than any other aspect of their lives, worsened the social stigma of service, and was the main reason given by factory, shop, and office workers for avoiding or abandoning service positions.[67] When Ellen complains at being asked to give up her free afternoon, she is a bad servant. The Irish were not good at being good servants, according to Stephen Birmingham: "the thorny Irish 'personality,' the Irish orneriness and stubbornness, and unwillingness to bow, scrape, and court favor" worked against them.[68] Brought up to relative affluence and with what passed in that time and place for a good education at the Presentation Sisters' convent school, Ellen cannot lower herself enough to be a domestic; yet, having ended her education at sixteen, she is too poorly educated to command a position in anything but one of the other low-level positions available to emigrant women: factory work.

As a needlewoman at Madame de Maintenant's factory, Ellen gains the ability to make her own living arrangements, to spend time after work and on breaks as she chooses, to "keep herself to herself," to associate with companions of her own choosing. "After work" (and, in factory work, unlike domestic work, there was an "after"), she "could take herself up once again, at no one's beck and call."[69] This new freedom has two consequences: her friendship with Bella Robbins and her private reading. Through both, she tries to compensate for the deficiencies of her education and open herself out to the world. But like domestics, women factory workers endured many hardships at the hands of employers. If domestic employers paid poorly, late, or not at all,[70] so did factory owners. The episode involving the protest of the woman whose sister died as a result of not having received her salary focuses Ellen's attention on the harsh working conditions endured by women in factory work. This leads to her unsuccessful efforts to unionize her shop, efforts that for a time make her feel content in her work: adversarial activities come naturally to an angry woman. However, unionizing women would remain a hopeless cause for many years. Ellen does not in any case spend enough time in the labor force to see any results of her efforts. Like many women of her time, Ellen interrupts her career outside the home to take care of children, her mother, and eventually her grandchildren.

Ellen's final attempt at working outside the home is as unsuccessful as the other two. When Vincent has a heart attack, she is offered a job staffing the change booths in the subway. This gives her an opportunity to join the Transport Workers Union (TWU), the union for which Vincent's labor organizing activity provides the groundwork. But Ellen refuses the job, and with it TWU membership, for Vincent's sake, "knowing it would be painful for him: her a part of it, him not."[71] She takes a job at the millinery where Bella works and joins the union there, but she never experiences the kind of job satisfaction that Vincent achieves. Some of this is due to the poor opportunities available to women at the time, especially women with Ellen's background and impractical education. Some of this is due to Ellen's innate discontentment. But while she is working at these unsatisfactory jobs, and while she interrupts her career, as women often do, to tend to her family, Vincent is deeply immersed in his own, much more satisfying, work world.

Men at Work: Vincent and the Transport Workers' Union

In Ireland, Vincent begins his working life at thirteen, as an apprentice mill-worker in Dromnia. From the start, he was enchanted by machines. To his father's relief, as Vincent will not inherit the land, Vincent makes machines his career, apprenticing himself at fifteen to ironworkers in Cork. This position does not meet Vincent's need for further training, so from there Vincent moves to the Cork firm of McArdle and Sons, Carriage Builders. There he finds a position of which he can be proud, and there he also meets Martin Ferris, with whom he emigrates in 1913. Like Ellen, Vincent arrives in New York with great anxiety, and like her he takes the first job that is offered: digging the subway tunnel that extends from Whitehall Street in Manhattan to Montague Street in Brooklyn. This job is typical of the kind of unskilled, entry-level position then available to emigrants; but with Vincent's training, he is not a typical rural emigrant. Unlike Ellen, he is able to move up a career ladder, becoming a signal repairman for the Interborough Rapid Transit subway line, the IRT. Vincent loves this job. In his old age, he reads the 1924 edition of the IRT operating manual as if it were sacred scripture; he loves its language, stately and authoritative, and its rules for maintaining and restoring order in the subterranean cosmos. Working for the IRT gives Vincent job satisfaction on many levels. He has colleagues who respect him and are worthy of his respect, and work that is absorbing, challenging, and fulfilling. As his granddaughter Sheilah interviews him for an oral history project, she clearly expects to hear complaints about the treatment of the Irish emigrant in the workforce; but Vincent cannot give her that. He loved his job: " 'It felt great being there. . . . Every day you felt great.' "[72] Yet, as the death of Vincent's assistant Dan Clark shows, these were dangerous jobs, lacking the good pay and job security that the unions sought. So when Vincent is asked to join the TWU in 1933, he has a great deal to lose: a job he loves, the respect of his colleagues, a steady salary in the midst of the Great Depression.

As if that were not enough, joining the union also presents him with a moral conflict similar to the one he experienced when he decided to emigrate: the opposition of vocal factions within the Catholic church. The church's opposition to labor unions has a history dating back to the rise of Freemasonry in the eighteenth century. In 1738, Pope Clement XII condemned Freemasonry, which in turn led to a blanket condemnation of all secret societies anything like the Freemasons, especially those that required oaths or incorporated rituals;[73] in other words, the church disapproved of any organizations which demanded the same kind of loyalty that the church itself did. Making matters worse, from about the 1870s on, the church associated such groups with the burgeoning socialist and communist movements.[74] Not all of these groups actually had ties to Freemasonry; but, since all new church pronouncements must be textually consistent with all prior church pronouncements, a key issue for churchmen in the late nineteenth and early twentieth century was which groups fell under Clement XII's 1738 prohibition of Freemasonry, and which did not.[75] The crucial forbidden elements were the "oath of absolute secrecy," the "promise of blind obedience," and the "ritualistic cult."[76] These, or any hint of socialism, or any propensity to violence or coercion, would place an organization beyond the pale for Catholics.

Another reason why some church spokesmen disapproved of the unions was the connection between organized labor and radical Irish groups. Secret societies flourished in Ireland. The Molly Maguires, a nineteenth-century secret society dedicated to agrarian reform in Ireland, by violent means if necessary, was condemned by the clergy for the same reasons as the Freemasons were—because of their "requirement that members swear a secret oath of fidelity to a secular authority outside the orbit of both church and state."[77] Organizations like the Ancient Order of Hibernians, which began its history as a secret organization, as well as the various labor unions, were conflated by some churchmen with the Mollies, thus forbidden.[78] Secret political societies like the *Clan na Gael* and the IRA were so prevalent in Ireland that it was inevitable that some of their members should emigrate and work in the New York transit industry; Vincent's friend and fellow emigrant Martin Ferris is one of these, "mad IRA."[79] Even those Irish who did not belong to secret organizations, then, were at least familiar with, and potentially receptive to, the idea of such organizations.[80] Because there were so many Irish, not even including American-born Irish, working in transit, and because almost all of them were Catholic, the TWU really needed the Irish, and wanted them as members, no matter what the church said.[81]

The church's response to the rise of the unions operated on many levels. Efforts to determine which organizations were opposed to Catholic teaching also came at a point in the history of the American church when Catholic institutions parallel to secular ones were developing in a variety of areas (schools, hospitals, social and fraternal organizations). One of these was a labor organization, the Catholic Workmen's Benevolent Union, founded in 1887.[82] The existence of Catholic workingmen's organizations gave credence to the church's claim that there was no valid reason for a Catholic to belong to a competing, and possibly Communist-influenced, secular organization.[83] In response to Communist activity both within and without organized labor, Catholic anti-Communist groups sprang up. The Brooklyn Diocese, which encompassed the borough of Queens in which Ellen and Vincent live, was at that time "deeply hostile" to the labor movement.[84] Some parish priests preached against the union; the diocesan newspaper, the *Brooklyn Tablet*, printed a letter "attacking TWU leaders as communists."[85] This strand of opinion did considerable damage to the unionization effort, as "among the Irish, the Church tended to both reflect and reinforce the fatalism and deference to authority that formed one side of their culture,"[86] the attitude that shaped the response of the parishioners of Tulla to the bees in church. Some clerical responses to the perceived threat of Communist influences in the unions provided cures worse than the illness: such was the case with Father Charles E. Coughlin, whom Ellen particularly despises. Coughlin's radio broadcast and his newspaper, *Social Justice*, combined anti-Communist material with "anti-Semitism" and "proto-Fascism."[87] Thus in the 1930s Vincent is caught in a situation similar to the one he encountered in Ireland with regard to emigration: he wants to do something that many Catholic voices prohibit.

Ellen, predictably, takes the most anticlerical position possible, supporting the union even when joining it places Vincent at risk of losing his job. This was a real possibility, as heavy unemployment and continued immigration supplied many companies with a "classic reserve army of labor, sometimes literally at the door"; these "extras" were "a living reminder to those with steady jobs of the ease with which they could be replaced."[88] Most women in Ellen's position were not pleased that their husbands were exposing themselves to this threat.[89] But Ellen's Marxist background resulting from her relationship with Bella's family—Vincent thinks that, were it not for his own disapproval, Ellen would actually join the Communist Party—has radicalized her sufficiently to see the value even in so risky a venture as joining a union. Then, she invites the union meeting into her home, thus avoiding the abandonment and boredom of the wife who is left out of events. Most of all, Ellen is energized, not discouraged, by the church's hostility to the stance she has taken. One of the high points of her life is ejecting the parish priest from her house when, chiding her for her union work, he calls her " 'no better than the satanic Communists of Russia.' "[90] She lectures Vincent on the insidious influence of the clergy: " 'They've threatened every Irishman who has a union card with eternal damnation. They've held the labor unions back for fifty years.' "[91]

But Ellen has always seen the church as more monolithic than it really is. She does not seem to know that other elements of the Catholic church were pro-union, critical of the Coughlinites and their allies among the parish clergy; Coughlin's own archbishop, for example, eventually silenced him.[92] Media attention to the religious right in our own time can obscure the fact that, today as in the 1930s, there is such an entity as the religious left, and leftist Catholics tended to support the union movement.[93] Catholics on both sides of the issue could find support in two papal encyclicals on labor: Leo XII's *Rerum Novarum* (1891) and Pius XI's *Quadrigesimo Anno* (1931). Both popes denounced socialism on the one hand, but also denounced the excesses of capitalism on the other. "Their solution was a call for a system of 'social justice' that recognized the rights of workers to a living wage and the obligation of capital to act in accordance with the dictates of the common good," a balancing act that Freeman terms a "noble quest for the impossible."[94] Enough disagreement existed that a potential member of the TWU who was Catholic, like Vincent, could take his choice between two opposing clerical viewpoints, pro-union and anti-union.

Then, too, Ellen is not the only Irish person who disdains, or at least discounts, the opinions of the clergy. Irish-American anticlericalism, fueled by the church's hostility toward the Republican movement in Ireland,[95] encouraged some to defy those clerics who would forbid them to join unions. Irish Catholic transit workers of the 1930s would have heard of the church's role in key episodes of Irish history, like the affair of Irish political leader Charles Stewart Parnell. Parnell's political program for Ireland included reform of land ownership as well as "Home Rule," political independence from England. But in 1889, Parnell's long-term liaison with a married woman became public, which in turn provoked condemnation from the Roman Catholic clergy, often from the pulpit. Parnell's political destruction, followed by his death in 1891, was widely regarded as not only a setback for the causes of land reform and Home Rule but also the fault of the Catholic clergy.[96] Incidents like this (and there were many others) caused many Catholics in Ireland to believe that the clergy should restrict themselves to theological matters only and leave the practical business of life to laymen.[97] Because many Irish Catholics believed, as did Stephen Dedalus's father in *Portrait*, that the clergy should "*cease turning the house of God into a pollingbooth*,"[98] laymen tended to separate themselves from the views of the clergy on many social and political issues.[99] This was even more the case in the United States, with its tradition of separation of church and state. American union leaders who were Catholic, as well as rank-and-file members, were likely to make up their own minds about the union. In fact the role of the Irish in the formation of the labor unions provided the larger society with evidence that, on this issue at least, the Irish in America were not mere "lemmings led by local parish priests," but rather capable of "strategic, independent action that was neither endorsed nor condoned by the Catholic Church hierarchy."[100] Thus the early union organizers were effective not only in improving working conditions for themselves, but in beginning to break down the stereotypical view of the Irish as, in the words of Stephen Dedalus's father at Christmas dinner, a " 'priestridden Godforsaken race.' "[101]

At eighty-eight, Vincent looks back at these heady union days as the most exciting of his long life. His heart attack keeps him in the hospital and away from the strike that he had so carefully planned, and forces him out of the career he loved. His wife, not he, becomes the union member; and she comes to lose respect for the non-union work he does as a model maker for a scaffold builder. This work, reminiscent of the scaffolding on the cathedral in Queenstown that absorbed him in his last hours in Ireland, is "good work" for him; "he liked it. But the pride he's had when he worked for the subways, like you were a part of something great, that had been lost."[102] Yet what Vincent does take from his working life, as Ellen does not, is the satisfaction of having taken part in a significant "event in history."[103] Ellen's work outside the home does not give her the same satisfaction.

The "Net of Kinship": Theresa and Sheilah, Cam and Dan

Vincent's work moves his family into the middle class by enabling them to take the definitive step: buying a house, in Queens Village, which, as its name indicates, is in the New York City borough of Queens. Some historians debate whether, because their strong desire for security closed off riskier but higher-paying options than the uniformed services, civil service, and union jobs, the Irish took the next step up the socioeconomic ladder too slowly.[104] But, slowly or not, take it they did, with consequences for the next few generations of families like the MacNamaras. As a group, the family is as successful as many other emigrant families in incorporating themselves into the new country. The American dream works for many of them. Educational opportunities make it possible for several family members to have jobs better than Ellen's and Vincent's, culminating in two of their grandchildren, Cam and Dan, becoming lawyers. Vincent, but not Ellen, is able to derive satisfaction from this collective achievement. Ellen's and Vincent's respective attitudes affect others in the family. One of the novel's central metaphors is the "net of kinship,"[105] the family imagined as an entity that connects, but also ensnares. Ellen's and Vincent's descendants are affected in various ways by the tensions between them. Four of them—Theresa, Sheilah, Cam, and Dan—are trapped in negative ways of dealing with the two key points of disagreement in their grandparents' marriage: Irish identity and the Catholic faith.

Theresa and her daughter Sheilah seem to divide up the two—religion and ethnicity—between them. Theresa embraces Catholicism, and in its most exhibitionistic form, the more enthusiastically for her mother's contempt of it. Charismatic Catholicism appeals to Theresa particularly for its public and communal character; a merely private form of religious expression would not satisfy Theresa's "interest . . . in punishment,"[106] an interest with roots in her childhood conflicts with her mother. The prayer group gives Theresa a sense of identity and self-importance, as well as a firm belief in her own infallibility. Religious practices structure her days and weeks: daily mass, Bible study, "lunchtime prayer meetings"[107] for just such a variety of right-wing causes as would most enrage her mother; and faith healing. This last is particularly important to Theresa. The prayer group prays for Ellen, which inflates Theresa's ego in proportion as it would infuriate Ellen. But Theresa herself deliberately withholds what she sees as her own gift of healing from her mother. Theresa feels that indeed Ellen should not be healed: "She says in her mind: This is the will of the Lord. She does not touch her mother. Deliberately, she folds her hands."[108] For Theresa, religion is an instrument of revenge against her mother for wrongs real and imagined.

Ironically, given the importance of religion in her own life, Theresa is insensitive to its role in her daughter Sheilah's life. In Catholic families, a son or daughter with a religious vocation would usually be considered a credit to the family. But July 11, 1965, the day on which Sheilah announces her intention to enter the religious life, her anticipated "great moment," is a great disappointment. Her mother's less-than-enthusiastic reaction enrages Sheilah. Later, Sheilah overhears a conversation between her parents on her decision to enter the convent: "Her mother's voice, bored at even this much attention to the subject, says: 'Cut your losses.' . . . Turning back to her reading: giving the subject no more time."[109] This (perhaps studied) indifference on Theresa's part denies Sheilah her star turn as the family's arch-Catholic, thus preserving that role for Theresa herself. Sheilah enters the religious life, but without the fanfare she expected. Her life as a nun ends when, as Sister Raymond Theresa, she has an affair with Father Steve Gallagher. During the 1960s, while still members of their respective religious orders, they were fellow participants in various left-wing political demonstrations, which led to their affair, which led to their appearance on the front page of newspapers "with their hair wet from the shower, in front of the Thunderbird Motel."[110] Despite their sexual unorthodoxy, Sheilah and her husband do not break with the church but, as canon law permits, after applying for and receiving release from their vows through proper ecclesiastical channels, they marry, have a child, and remain Catholic.

Although her life seems different on the surface from her mother Theresa's, Sheilah exhibits the same defining character trait as does Theresa: hyper-focusing on one aspect of life. This she does by becoming a devotee of Irish activities, and with such intensity that they structure her life in the same way as the rituals of charismatic Catholicism do for her mother. While Theresa defines herself mainly in terms of an idiosyncratic brand of Catholicism, Sheilah chooses Irish identity as her life's focus. "She travels regularly to Manhattan for meetings of a society dedicated to the preservation of Irish culture; with her son, Diarmid, and her husband she takes weekly classes in the Irish language and in Irish dance. In these circles of earnestness, she is respected and looked up to. But in her family she is seen by the kindly as pathetic, by the less kind as a joke."[111] The Irish culture group gives her the same sense of self-importance that her mother gets from the prayer group; and it is only within the context of the group that Sheilah can see her own, her husband's, and her son's lives as meaningful. Of Ellen and Vincent's descendants, Sheilah is the only one who consciously and purposefully attempts to integrate elements of Irish heritage into her daily life. The family sees these as clumsy, artificial, and superficial, examples of pseudo-Hibernicism. Sheilah cannot beat her mother at her religious game even by becoming a nun. Having failed at that, Sheilah becomes more conspicuously Irish than the rest of the family, as both a way of competing with her mother and as a substitute, obvious to everyone but her, for the vocations to the religious life that she and her husband abandoned.

While Cam's and Dan's professional lives are testimony to the upward mobility of Irish Catholics, their sexual conflicts are almost stereotypical renderings of the difficulty of living within Irish Catholicism's rigid boundaries. Cam's and Dan's situation is far more intricate than Theresa's and Sheilah's. Cam and Dan are each caught in an uncomfortable position in that their behavior violates the standards they have been taught to uphold; they do not consciously believe in those standards enough to stop the errant behavior; but they still operate on the basis of the very assumptions that their behavior flouts. Their problems begin when, for reasons directly connected to their religious upbringing, both of them marry unwisely. As a student at Bryn Mawr in 1959, Cam is influenced by the church's campaign to discourage what it called "mixed" marriages, marriages outside the Catholic tribe. To prevent such marriages, the church encouraged people like Cam and her fellow Catholic students in nonsectarian universities to form a smaller (protective, defensive) society within the larger world of the campus. Cam therefore assumes that she must choose a husband from among the small number of Catholic men on a nonsectarian campus; thus it comes to pass that Cam, in shock over her mother's cancer diagnosis, marries Bob Ulichni. Both their marriage and its ultimate failure are linked to their Catholicism. When Cam and Bob encounter sexual and infertility problems, they consult Larry Riordan, who is their doctor largely because Catholics of the time were also advised to stay within the tribe in choosing professional advisors, to have a Catholic doctor, a Catholic lawyer. Larry Riordan errs in attributing Cam's pain to psychological causes, mainly the aftereffects of a strict Catholic upbringing on both Cam's part and Bob's. His misguided solution, that Bob be more sexually assertive with Cam, so damages the couple's relationship that they do not seek further infertility treatment. All of this leads to the life that they are leading on August 14, 1985. Cam, Bob, and Cam's mother Magdalene still live together, but Bob Ulichni has not had sex with Cam or with anyone else since 1969, and Cam has a lover.

Cam's relationship with Ira Silverman grows out of the same religious and ethnic stereotypes that doomed her marriage to Bob: " 'The Irish,' they say. 'The Jews.' "[112] Ira had always wanted " 'an Irish girl,' " and Cam, believing that Jews are a " 'superior culture' " while the Irish are " 'a bunch of third-raters or self-destructors,' "[113] seems to want anyone who is neither Irish nor Catholic. As in *The Mermaids Singing*, the Catholic woman's Jewish lover provides the ultimate in sexual satisfaction. In Cam's view, Irish people are not even " 'interested in pleasure,' "[114] so she needs Ira as an antidote. Ironically, however, Cam herself can only conduct her pleasurable relationship with Ira in secret. Though not what Catholics call "practicing," she cannot bring herself to leave her failed marriage for twice-divorced Ira. She is still enough of a Catholic not to want anyone in the family, especially Vincent, to know about her affair, not to be in public anything that a Catholic woman has been taught not to be. Cam blames her own position in the family for this. Believing that she is "the one responsible for three generations of family life," it follows for her that she cannot be "publicly adulterous."[115] Underlying Cam's rationalizations are the norms of Catholicism that she is violating but also cannot reject. Like Dan, she has been taught that sin must be punished; since regularizing an illicit relationship rewards the sinner, she cannot do it. Although neither Cam nor Dan use the language of religion, although neither labels his or her sexual behavior as specifically sinful and the behavior consequent upon it as punishment, both are in fact following an ancient Catholic tradition: doing penance.

Dan too is rushed into marriage, in his case by the church's strong condemnation of premarital sex; like Cam, Dan marries unwisely. Despite his professed lack of respect for Ireland and Irish customs, his marriage stumbles for a peculiarly Irish reason. Valerie, herself an Irish Catholic, asks Dan for a commitment: "She said: Promise me we won't live anywhere near either of our families. The Irish genius for the local made her feel choked, balked, and trapped. Dan promised."[116] When Dan breaks his promise, the marriage is weakened, and finally collapses because of Dan's affair with his secretary, Sharon Breen. He and Sharon, both Irish, both Catholic, both racked with guilt, live in a state of self-inflicted punishment ever after. They cannot, as many moderns do, learn to move on with their lives in a new marriage. Because they cannot marry in the church, they do not marry at all; further, because their relationship caused the breakup of two marriages, they cannot reward themselves for that sin by marrying. When Dan raises the subject of marriage, Sharon refuses: "She took him from his wife, and she insists they both remember."[117] Though both Dan and Sharon are adulterers and Dan is a divorce lawyer, like Cam they live as if they believe in the Catholic doctrine of the indissolubility of marriage, as if they believe, as does Rita Breen, the absurd mother of Sharon's ex-husband, that sinners must not " 'get away scot-free.' "[118]

Dan's lifestyle, illicit by Catholic norms, is unsatisfactory by any norms. He is only slightly more successful in coming to terms with his Irish heritage than in coming to terms with his indelible Catholicism. On a vacation trip to Ireland, Cam and Dan's daughter Darci go mainly as tourists, and so they enjoy the trip. Dan, however, tries to understand the country, which he sees through the distorted lens of his grandparents' conflicting memories. The country that was "cattle shitting in the streets" to his grandmother was green grass, good milk, "the lovely bread, the songs, the smell of the peat fire" to his grandfather.[119] Ellen's viewpoint, as always, is more memorable because more vivid, more dramatic. At one point, Ellen devises, for Dan's benefit, a mock emigrant ballad: " 'My carefree youth / The cowshit and the toothless mother / And the starving tinkers out to steal me blind.' "[120] When Dan visits Ireland, he is predisposed to see that for which Ellen has conditioned him to look. Therefore Dan feels that "the country was a sign: they could never be happy, any of them, coming from people like the Irish. Unhappiness was bred into the bone."[121] While much in Ireland discourages Dan, he also comes to see that his grandparents' opposing viewpoints might be connected with the fact that Ellen was raised in the town, Vincent in the country. Vincent's influence causes Dan to see rural Ireland more positively, as the locus of "real life," as "miraculous"; in their different ways, Dan thinks, his grandparents might have "both been right."[122] Traveling, as Irish-American tourists do, to the native villages of the emigrant forebears, Dan comes to some understanding and acceptance, but no happiness: "they were his people, the Irish, and he pitied and admired them."[123] Dan carries

Ellen and Vincent in his emotional baggage, and typically, Ellen is the heavier burden.

Theresa, Sheilah, Cam, and Dan, then, all seek ways to deal with the conflicting ways in which their heritage was transmitted to them by Ellen and Vincent. In their behavior, much of it self-dramatizing, all four demonstrate a continuing need to live in the state of intense emotion that their grandmother's anger imposed on the family. The two satirical references to the Greek drama in the novel, in which Cam and Dan describe the MacNamara family as the "House of Atreus," allude to the hyperintense emotion within the family which is characteristic of this art form. Ellen has maintained the highest possible pitch of anger for seventy-four years, and transmitted it down the generations; the lives of these four family members have been most affected.

Sin and Forgiveness

In her essay on anger in *Deadly Sins*, Mary Gordon notes that, though the natural course of emotions is to dissipate over time, anger is different, because the angry person deliberately maintains anger, recommits to it over a long period of time, even begins "to worship it, to devote oneself to its preservation, like any great work of art."[124] This is true of Ellen who, on her deathbed, thinking of her mother's tragic fate years earlier, "renews her vow. That she will not forgive."[125] Such anger as Ellen's is consistent with Gordon's image of anger's momentum: "it rolls and rolls like a flaming boulder down a hill, gathering mass and speed."[126] The opposite of anger, Gordon says, is forgiveness. When the forgiving person refuses to recommit to anger, he or she allows it to fade naturally as other emotions do. Pride-filled people are particularly unlikely to forgive, to let anger die, because to do so would be "to give up the exhilaration of one's own unassailable rightness."[127] Unlike Ellen, Vincent can forgive (himself and others) and can live without "unassailable rightness." So he is happier. Vincent's ability to forgive can also be understood in a nontheological sense of flexibility, adaptability, as when one speaks of a "forgiving" substance that bends instead of breaking. Vincent's forgiving nature allows him to adapt, although not without pain, to situations common to many: the loss of his birth family through emigration; the loss of his son to war; the various disappointments inherent in marriage and family life; the coming of old age. Conversely, Vincent can also enjoy his own accomplishments and his family's, a quality that allows him to experience the pleasure in his work life that Ellen cannot. With regard to his religion, Vincent can tolerate—he can even enjoy—living with a woman who mocks his faith without allowing either faith or marriage to be destroyed. Finally, in great old age, he can leave a place he has come to love, and return home to keep a commitment that has long since lost any meaning it once had for him.

On August 14, 1985, as Vincent returns, Ellen's anger is the one thing keeping her alive. Whether this is good or not depends on whether one defines Ellen's life on that day as worthwhile. Would it not be better for one such as Ellen to let go, to let herself go to "the other side"? Any Catholic, Irish or not, would notice that, though Ellen is dying, though a nominally Catholic family has assembled, no priest has been called to administer the last rites. The purpose of the last rites of the Catholic church is to ease the passage by giving peace to the dying person and a sense that spiritual powers accompany him or her upon the great and final journey. According to historian Lawrence J. McCaffrey, for most of the first generation of emigrants attempting to make their way in an unfamiliar world, the Catholic church "bridged the chasm between rural Ireland and urban America, providing psychological and spiritual comfort in a strange and hostile environment."[128] By severing herself from the church, Ellen has always deprived herself of that comfort. Rejecting not only Ireland but all things Irish, including Catholicism, Ellen strands herself on one side of an even more formidable chasm, that between life and death, without the bridge that religion could have provided.

Whether Gordon's novel is seen to castigate or celebrate Irish-American Catholicism depends on whether the reader looks primarily at Ellen or at Vincent. While Mary Gordon is not given to ringing affirmations, the novel ends with a suggestion, albeit an ambiguous one, that the traditions out of which the MacNamara family has emerged have dignity and value. Like the MacNamaras, readers of *The Other Side* have often paid more attention to Ellen than to Vincent, as she is noisier, showier, more dramatic than Vincent. But if Vincent shares the role of central character with Ellen, then the novel ends affirmatively. In great old age, Vincent acts courageously and unselfishly, doing what he can to ease Ellen's passage, keeping a commitment made long ago. Even if Ellen does not know that Vincent has come home, other family members, with their history of broken promises, need to know that at least one promise has been kept. Since Vincent is as much a product of his country and his church as Ellen is, his actions can be read as testimony to the value of both.

Conclusion

The Journey

All Irish writing, whether it be literature or songs, is based on going away and coming back.

—Van Morrison

Next time I want to come back Irish.

—Beth, in Wendy Rawlings, "Come Back Irish"

Whether it be Æneas's or Odysseus's or Gulliver's, Stephen Dedalus's and Leopold Bloom's around Dublin or Alice's through the looking glass, the journey is one of the most common motifs in literature. Some of life's journeys may be meaningless, but seldom is this true of the journeys in literature. Fictional journeys involve the mind and spirit as well as the body; the character who makes the journey will often undergo some transformation of which the spatial motion is a metaphor. When a character comes full circle and returns to the place of origin, therefore making two journeys, one away, one back again, the result is often a better, or at least different, understanding of both places, and of him or herself.

In Irish writing, as Van Morrison points out,[1] the traveler's departure and return are central. What reader of *Angela's Ashes* can forget the McCourt family's trips, individually and jointly, back and forth across the Atlantic, each one marking a turning point in the life of the family? And, as we have seen, Irish songwriters have both celebrated and lamented journeys across the sea for over 150 years. In these works of Irish-American fiction, however, the journey theme is complicated by the fact that the character who leaves Ireland and the character who goes back are rarely the same character. In the emigrant ballads, the emigrant dreams of going home, rich and successful, to see his old parents again and marry the faithful Mary. But for the characters in these novels, there are no parents or beloveds waiting in Ireland. For them, the trip to Ireland is not repatriation because Ireland is not their home; America is. The journey is about the metaphorical space between the two countries and cultures. Somewhere in that space, the past lives; the traveler must come to terms with that past, and decide which elements thereof have meaning for the present.

The emigrants' motives for leaving Ireland affects the image of Ireland that they transmit to future generations, which will in turn affect whether, under what circumstances, and with what feelings these descendants return to Ireland. Despite the nostalgia of the emigrant ballads, nineteenth-century emigrants rarely returned. For these people, "the *idea* of returning," so prominent in song lyric, is "part of the cultural baggage";[2] but, compared to other ethnic groups of the same period, their actual return rate was low.[3] Especially during and immediately after the Famine, the sea journey was so difficult that many did not survive it, so those who did were loath to attempt the return trip. Until the advent of easy air travel and the increased economic success enabling Irish-Americans to afford it, few emigrants returned even to visit; and until the Irish economic boom at the end of the twentieth century, repatriation was little more than a ballad theme.

In these novels, the nature of the emigrant's journey is a key factor. In general, the more easily and often a trip can be made, the less its significance. Nineteenth-century emigrants' journeys were imagined, and historically usually were, unique and irrevocable; so are the journeys made by those who perceive themselves as exiles. While the exile is a dramatic, even tragic figure, in Irish literature, the returning Yank is often a satiric or comic one. Either he has become successful and wants to show off, or he has failed and returns in disgrace. Either way, he returns more a Yank than an Irishman, and does not fit into Irish society anymore. With the exception of Clíona and to some extent Gráinne in *The Mermaids Singing*, and Vincent in *The Other Side* who consciously rejects the role, this primarily Irish literary type does not figure prominently in these American novels; but other types of returnees do. Usually the returnees are descendents of the emigrants; they return for a specific amount of time or a specific purpose, but have no intentions of staying, and so they can be called either visitors or tourists. Visitors come to accomplish specific tasks or to see specific people, family members in particular; tourists come to see places or to attend specific events. Visits to family in Ireland would logically diminish in generations subsequent to the one that emigrated, as the older people in both Ireland and America die. But tourism to Ireland increases annually, fueled by ever-growing interest in things Irish on the part of Irish-Americans and others.[4]

A new possibility, of more recent origins, is that described by Dennis Clark: "Perhaps the ultimate in Irish and American trans-Atlantic journeying was reached when it became possible to live on both sides of the ocean in alternation so swift that the dual residence seemed almost simultaneous."[5] The novelist and short-story writer Colum McCann casts some light upon this transcontinental lifestyle. In an interview with radio host Leonard Lopate, McCann rejects the term "exile" to describe himself; instead, he calls himself a "commuter," one who travels "back and forth" so often between New York and Dublin that he essentially lives in both places.[6] The listener can tell from McCann's good-humored, casual tone of voice that he refuses the self-dramatization inherent in claiming the exile identity. For the commuter, there is no need, as there was in previous emigrant generations, to choose between cultures, no need to assimilate to one country or reject the other. At the beginning of the twenty-first century, a commuter lifestyle is not uncommon; it depends on personal ties on two continents, on ease of travel, and above all on affluence. The Irish themselves have traveled a great distance from the days of the American wake to a commuter situation like McCann's.

These distinctions between emigrant, exile, returning Yank, visitor, tourist, and commuter enable the reader to evaluate the significance of the various journeys from America to Ireland taken by characters in these novels. Much depends on who takes the journey; why they take it; how often; what it means to them; their response to the country and its people when they either return to or visit Ireland for the first time; and what they learn from the experience. If the returning character is not the original emigrant, what does the journey mean to him or to her? Since American characters never left Ireland, they cannot really return; what then do they imagine themselves to be doing? If they are exploring the meaning of their own Irish heritage, the physical act of crossing the ocean is a key event in these novels. Journeys that are unique hold greater significance than frequent over-the-pond trips. For the infrequent traveler, the Atlantic is no pond but a giant hyphen, a metaphor for simultaneous connection and division. In their own way, the characters who make the journey from America to Ireland serve as links between the two cultures as much as, if in a different way than, those who traveled the other way.

The World I Made for Her depicts the journey from America to Ireland as James Blatchley's personal metaphor for, first the earthly paradise, then the afterlife. Despairing of his ability to recover from his illness, he imagines his death as a trip across the sea to his own version of the Emerald Isle. The idea of Ireland gives him a geographical locus for his hope of immortality; imagining death as a journey to this perfect place eases his passage. Yet the fact that he never considered making the trip while he was physically able to do so casts the relationship of Irish-Americans to Ireland in a different light. If for Irish-Americans like Blatchley, the United States is reality, then Ireland is, and perhaps should remain, a dream. Dreams are kept alive by protecting them from reality; thus the vision of Ireland can only be kept pure by not going there at all. If the importance of a journey is inversely correlated with the frequency with which it is taken, then in this novel the most significant journey is one that is never taken.

In *The Mermaids Singing*, the back-and-forth motion of the characters across the Atlantic is crucial to the identity of three generations of women. Clíona emigrates for the usual reasons at the time: economic success and personal freedom. But she does not find either in America, and goes home—and to her, Ireland is home—for marriage and security. When Clíona repatriates, she fits easily into a preestablished social role: the returning Yank. But her daughter Grace sees herself as an American in exile. Though she marries there, she cannot acclimate as an Irish wife, and repatriates herself to Boston, where she can live as she chooses. Seamus, her husband, follows his wife and child to America, but secretly, as a visitor, to determine whether he could emigrate himself; he learns in Boston that his Irish identity is so strong that he cannot live anywhere else but on Inis Murúch. Unable to imagine any compromise between his way and Grace's, he resigns himself to a life with an ocean between him and his wife and child. When Gráinne involuntarily returns to Ireland, she scorns the repatriate role and the people who cast her in it. But Gráinne's psychological task is indeed to repatriate in the Latinate sense of the term: to find her father again, and further, to accept that Ireland itself and her family there can at least partially replace her lost mother. For each character, the trip across the ocean is a metaphor for a difficult process of self-examination, of evaluating one's own identity and placing it somewhere on the continuum between America and Ireland.

The Famine emigrant generation is in Patricia Dolan's distant past. In *The Music Lesson*, her memories of her father's stories cause her to identify with the Irish people without actually knowing any. When she meets Mickey, Patricia accepts his cover story that he is a commuter, in the United States only temporarily for work, like many other New Irish. But Mickey is a specialized kind of commuter: an international terrorist. He poses as a Paddy, a greenhorn in the big city; but in reality he is a sophisticated, well-trained operative, and it is the American who is the innocent. Patricia has been raised on Irish history and mythology, yet had hitherto no desire to visit Ireland even as a tourist. For her, the journey to Ireland means coming to terms with the Irish past, and deciding what action, if any, needs to be taken in the present to right the wrongs of that past. She also learns, perhaps fatally, that the face of evil can be an Irish face. The novel ends on an ambiguous note—it is not certain that Patricia survives the journey home to

New York—suggesting that modern Americans engage in Ireland's ancient troubles at their peril.

Billy Lynch's doom is sealed when he misinterprets Eva's return to Ireland, and then follows her there. Eva comes to Long Island as a visitor, and never intends to be an emigrant. Billy's error is to think of her in terms of the patterns of Irish emigration in the past, as being like Uncle Daniel's Paddies, avid to be brought over. But by the mid-twentieth century, Irish people no longer feel themselves as pushed out of Ireland or as pulled to America as they once did. It is clear to everyone but Billy that Eva intended all along to go back and make her life in Ireland. Eva's return is not repatriation for her, nor is it a rejection of American culture; it is merely the end of a visit, after which she resumes her ordinary life in Ireland. Billy's own journey to Ireland is planned as a one-time event of transcendent significance, its dual purpose to visit Eva's grave, and to take the pledge to stop drinking. He travels with the highest expectations, and with a nostalgic view of Ireland derived from the emigrant ballad "Danny Boy." By imagining himself, like Danny of the ballad, standing beside Eva's grave, Billy casts himself as the male lead in a highly emotional drama. His meeting Eva there, at the tacky gas station that she owns with her husband, leads to his fatal disillusionment with the country and its people. The banality of Eva's life, and of Eva herself, is too much for him to bear.

Vincent and Ellen, the founding parents of an American family in *The Other Side*, imagine their departure from Ireland in different ways. Because Vincent defines himself as an emigrant, not an exile, he can go home, and is the one member of the emigrant generation in these fictions who does so. To preserve Ellen's privacy, he avoids playing the role of the returning Yank before his surviving family; instead, he travels as a visitor, performs his specific task, and leaves. But even he finds the experience emotionally turbulent in that it causes him to revisit and revise his own and his wife's memories of the place. The next two generations of the MacNamara family go as tourists: Cam, Dan, and Dan's daughters Darci and Staci. Their reactions are mixed. Cam and Darci have a pleasant experience that seems to have no emotional resonances; they might as well have been visiting France or Italy. As tourists, they enjoy, albeit in a patronizing fashion, the ways in which the visible aspects of Irish culture differ from American. The fact that Staci's reaction is not mentioned suggests that some Irish-Americans will have no response at all to what is to others a journey of the profoundest significance. Dan, on the other hand, is saddened, coming to see not only the Irish in Ireland but those in America as well, himself included, as profoundly damaged people. Dan finds Ireland depressing, especially its towns, as his grandmother Ellen led him to believe; yet on the other hand he can also see the physical beauty of the countryside through his grandfather

Vincent's eyes. Dan's journey helps him to understand his grandparents and their influence on his life. It also gives him a handy scapegoat—Ireland itself—on which to blame his joyless life.

All the characters who travel to Ireland do so in response to a deep psychological need. The theme of departure and return, central to Irish writing across the genres, is crucial also in these American fictions. In the emigrant ballads of the nineteenth century, a key motif is the return of the emigrant in triumph, never again to leave his native shores. While for generations from the Famine to the advent of efficient air travel, this happened very little in fact, it remained nevertheless what Dennis Clark calls "a tantalizing dream."[7] This dream was passed down through the American generations. Estimates of the number of Americans of Irish descent in the United States alone run to 40 million.[8] The fact that even a tiny percentage of these make the journey to Ireland as tourists every year makes for a huge volume; by some estimates, more people visit Ireland each year than live there. In these novels, however, most of the characters who actually go find the experience unnerving. Some find that the country does not measure up to their dreams of it: Grace, Patricia, Billy, and Dan are disillusioned with Ireland. Gráinne, after an initial negative reaction, begins a psychological process of assimilation that will be joyous and painful at the same time. The one Irish-American who unambiguously maintains his illusions is Blatchley, who visits the country only in his mind.

In these fictions, an assumption of the Irish-American characters is that a journey to Ireland will in some way validate them as Irish. They travel because they believe that the country of Ireland is indeed the locus and focus of Irishness, a geographical point at which all forms of Irishness converge and from which not only the Irish people but also the quality of Irishness emanates. That idea is by no means universal in Ireland itself. For example, in Mary Robinson's inaugural speech as president of Ireland in 1990, she emphasized the centrality of the country to Irish identity worldwide, and defined her own role accordingly. But Robinson also defined Irishness as extending far beyond the borders of the country that elected her, and imagined her own role as representing all Irish people, not just the ones living in Ireland. As symbol of this larger international role, she instituted the custom of leaving a candle burning at all times in the window of the presidential palace, Áras an Uactaráin, the purpose of which is to signal Ireland's welcome home to the diaspora Irish. Whether this is a genuine and moving symbol to the Irish people, or a mere sentimental tourist attraction, is much in the eye of the beholder. The larger question of what constitutes true Irishness is a vexed one among the Irish in Ireland, much less the Irish elsewhere. As Jennifer Jeffers points out, questions like "Who is Irish? Who has the right to speak on the behalf of Ireland?" are addressed in fiction written in Ireland at the same time as the American novels considered in this book. The debate over who is "really" or "more" Irish, according to Jeffers, pits the usual suspects against each other: Catholics and Protestants, Northerners and Southerners, Irish speakers and English speakers, urban dwellers and rural dwellers; even generations and genders are divided on the question.[9] If the Irish are so divided, how can Irish-Americans not be?

These novels, while taking their own individual approaches to the issue, postulate at least some connection between the country of Ireland and the quality of Irishness. But that is only one way of addressing the question. Other fiction takes off in a different direction, disconnecting Irishness from the geographical place. Because there are so many more people of Irish descent outside of Ireland than inside, it has become, according to Breda Gray, "difficult to locate Irishness either culturally or geographically."[10] Irishness by some definitions is no longer tied to a single country; some would even deny the right to define Irishness to those who happen to have been born there.

Recent fiction suggests new ways of thinking about Irish identity. Wendy Rawlings's short story "Come Back Irish" explores, perhaps satirizes, the idea of becoming Irish by dint of conscious effort. Beth, a Jewish girl from Long Island, falls in love not only with an Irish man but also with "brogues, Emerald Isle kitsch, the shillelagh-and-tea-cloth brand of Irishness."[11] Although Beth does not mention it, clearly she could marry Eamon and subsume her identity in his by taking his Irish surname; the trip to Ireland to meet his family seems the traditional first move in that direction. Beth is also taking Irish lessons on her own, studying the Irish language, toting a copy of *Speak Irish Now* on the plane to Dublin. But in "the real Ireland, beyond the litter of claddagh rings and Erin go bragh, the high-stepping of Riverdance on videocassette," Beth finds herself disillusioned. Not only does her boyfriend, in his natural habitat, seem different from the "Hibernian hybrid" she loved in Manhattan, but Ireland itself is other than she expected. Although she mocks her own Jewish heritage, hates the sound of her American voice, and wishes for a reincarnation in which she could "come back Irish," it is clear by the end of the story that she is in fact a "species apart" from Eamon and his family.[12] The problem is the country itself, in which her fantasy of Irishness cannot be sustained.

Another fictional possibility is Irishness by proclamation. In Gish Jen's short story "Who's Irish?" the narrator, a Chinese woman, and an Irish-American woman are linked by their mutual grandchild, a three-year-old whose "skin is a brown surprise" to the Irish side of her family. The child's temperament, however, is equally surprising to her Chinese grandmother, who sees the child's "nice Chinese side swallowed up by her wild Shea side." The narrator's habit of thinking in Chinese/Irish dichotomies is called into question by the events of the story. The Chinese grandmother is forced to leave her daughter and son-in-law's home because of a disagreement over disciplining "wild" Sophie Shea. Although the Chinese grandmother had considered herself "fierce," and although the Chinese traditionally reverence the old, the narrator's daughter dismisses her from their home. When her son-in-law's mother, Bess Shea, offers the narrator a new home, the Chinese woman admires the Irish woman's ability to enforce her will in the family, to make her "talk just stick." One of Bess's authoritative proclamations is that her Chinese counterpart is to be considered "honorary Irish." While the narrator is skeptical ("Me? Who's Irish?"), the shared grandchild and Bess's strength have caused the narrator to doubt her assumptions about the impermeability of ethnic boundaries. It is as if "the voice of Bess" is so powerful that it can even confer Irishness upon a Chinese person.[13]

In life as in fiction, the issue of "Who's Irish?" has no simple answer. If the "Top One Hundred" Irish-Americans, as proclaimed by *Irish America* magazine, is any indicator, the parameters of Irishness are becoming increasingly flexible. In addition to the unsurprising names on the roster for the year 2001 (Frank McCourt, Ted Kennedy), the list also includes a few whose Irish ties are less obvious (Christina Aguilera, Colin Powell).[14] A *New York Times* article in honor of St. Patrick's Day of 2003 points to the many famous African-Americans (Eddie Murphy, Toni Morrison, Shaquille O'Neal) who bear Irish surnames. As the article notes, the reasons for this are not immediately clear. The names of Southern slaveholders were often shared by their slaves, whether biological ties existed or not; but few Irish were rich enough to own slaves in the antebellum South. Interracial relationships in the United States, which would account for the Irish names, were more frequent when the Irish had not yet, in Noel Ignatiev's ingenious phrase, "become white," thus distancing themselves socially from their African-American neighbors. Some black Americans might also trace their roots to the West Indian island of Montserrat, which bears Irish place names and thus must have been settled by Irish people. With all of these ties between the Irish and African-American people, why would one not wish, as the article does, happy St. Patrick's Day to Shaquille O'Neal? In Mr. O'Neal's case, the reason is that he does not consider himself Irish, nor, the article suggests, do most other African-Americans with "green" surnames.[15]

All of these phenomena ask, as Gish Jen's story does, who is Irish? What qualities determine Irishness? And are any of these qualities necessarily connected to a small island off the western coast of Europe? Or is Irishness, like beauty, in the eye of the beholder? In *The Whereabouts of Eneas McNulty*, the main character muses on being American: "It is a matter of hailing oneself as such, he supposes, in his own mind."[16] Perhaps the same is (or is becoming) true of being Irish: many people can "hail themselves" as such. The characters in these five novels, unlike Beth in Rawlings's fiction or the narrator in Jen's, do have a historical and genetic connection with both Ireland and America, and so can ask themselves if they are Irish, or American, or both. Perhaps other, newer fictions like that of Rawlings and Jen will work with the situation that often obtains in real life; as generations pass and interethnic relationships multiply, probably national origins will no longer be as clear or perhaps seem as important. But for the Irish-Americans in these novels, "going back to the beginning"[17] means experiencing the poles of their identity, the Irish and the American, and examining as well the simultaneous separation and connection: the space between the two.

Notes

Preface   Connections and Separations

1. McCourt, *Angela's Ashes*, 121.
2. P.W. Joyce, *English as We Speak It*, 304.
3. Ibid., 257.
4. Todd, *Green English*, 90.
5. Quoted in Gent, "Irish Arts Center," 72.
6. Ibid.
7. McCafferty, "Whatever You Say," 161.
8. Miller, *Emigrants and Exiles*, 346.
9. Quoted in Woodham-Smith, *Great Hunger*, 162.
10. Hayden, introduction to *Irish Hunger*, 12.
11. Quoted in Miller, *Emigrants and Exiles*, 306.
12. John Waters, "Troubled People," 103.
13. Lacey, "People Lost and Forgot," 85.
14. Ramsay, "Need to Feed," 141.
15. Miller, *Emigrants and Exiles*, 364.
16. Ibid., 571.
17. Diner, "Overview," 89–91.
18. Miller, *Emigrants and Exiles*, 382.
19. Miller, "Assimilation," 88.
20. Miller, *Emigrants and Exiles*, 368.
21. Kenny, *American Irish*, 105, 185.
22. Miller, *Emigrants and Exiles*, 429.
23. Schefer-Hughes, *Saints, Scholars, and Schizophrenics*, 3.
24. Ibid., 97.
25. Ibid., 81.
26. Quoted in Coogan, *IRA*, 15.
27. Townshend, *Ireland: The 20th Century*, 80.
28. Moran, *World*, 18.
29. Miller, *Emigrants and Exiles*, 273–74.
30. Bayor and Meagher, introduction to *New York Irish*, 5.
31. Miller, *Emigrants and Exiles*, 406–09, 415, 490; see also Diner, *Erin's Daughters*, 1–29; and Nolan, *Ourselves Alone*, 26–37.

32. Almeida, *Irish Immigrants*, 80.
33. Quoted in ibid.
34. Carey, *Mermaids Singing*, 28, 247, 272.
35. Moran, *World*, 146–47.
36. Almeida, *Irish Immigrants*, 61–82.
37. Truss, *Eats, Shoots, & Leaves*, 158.

Introduction   Irish Types, American Patterns

1. Quoted in Maureen Waters, *Comic Irishman*, 41.
2. Quinn, *Dictionary*, 309; see also Donovan, "Good Old Pat," on the decline of this character.
3. Quinn, *Dictionary*, 309.
4. Fanning, *Irish Voice in America*, 343.
5. James Joyce, *Portrait*, 45.
6. McCaffrey, "Forging Forward," 218; cf. McCaffrey, *Textures*, 3, 72.
7. Weber, *Music Lesson*, 34.
8. Shannon, *American Irish*, 23.
9. Fanning, *Irish Voice in America*, 329.
10. See Miller, *Emigrants and Exiles*, 405, on how and why this pattern developed.
11. Kenny, *American Irish*, 183.
12. Ibid., 229.
13. See Diner "Overview," and Ignatiev, *How the Irish Became White*, 107–21.
14. Diner, "Overview," 96.
15. Kenny, *American Irish*, 185–86.
16. Ibid., 185.
17. Ibid., 188, 190.
18. Ibid., 228.
19. Erie, *Rainbow's End*, 8.
20. Ibid., 242.
21. McCaffrey, *Textures*, 36–37.
22. Kenny, *American Irish*, 213.
23. McCaffrey, *Textures*, 37.
24. McCaffrey, "Forging Forward," 222; cf. McCaffrey, *Textures*, 4.
25. McCaffrey, "Forging Forward," 222.
26. Bayor and Meagher, introduction to *New York Irish*, 5.
27. McDermott, *Charming Billy*, 93.
28. Kenny, *American Irish*, 228.
29. Shannon, *American Irish*, 12.
30. Diner, "Overview," 95.
31. Kenny, *American Irish*, 186; cf. McCaffrey, *Textures*, 32.
32. McCaffrey, *Textures*, 74.

33. Shannon, *American Irish*, 23.
34. McDermott, *Charming Billy*, 154.
35. Moran, *World*, 56.
36. Ibid., 177.
37. Gordon, *Other Side*, 382.
38. McCaffrey, *Textures*, 57.
39. Ibid.
40. Stivers, *Hair of the Dog*, 126, 129.
41. Ibid., 130.
42. Kenny, *American Irish*, 246.
43. Ibid., 227, 236; McCaffrey, *Textures*, 8.
44. Kenny, *American Irish*, 259.
45. Ibid.
46. Geldof, *Is That It?*, 344.
47. Miller, *Emigrants and Exiles*, 271.

Chapter 1　What Americans Know and How They Know It: Song

1. Kiely, "Homes on the Mountain," 673.
2. Ibid., 677.
3. Ibid., 676.
4. Ibid., 681.
5. Moore, *Complete Poetical Works*, I, 171.
6. Kiely, "Homes on the Mountain," 674.
7. Sawyers, *Celtic Music*, 159.
8. Welch, *Irish Poetry*, 21.
9. Heaney, introduction to *Centenary Selection*, ed. Hammond, 9.
10. Williams, *Irishman's Dream*; see especially 19–31.
11. Ibid., 23.
12. Ibid., 27–28.
13. Ibid., 23, 25–27, 225; see Hammond, *Centenary Selection*, 40, and Moore, *Complete Poetical Works*, I, 172.
14. Williams, *Irishman's Dream*, 27.
15. Ibid., 28.
16. Moore, *Complete Poetical Works*, I, 172.
17. Ibid., 199.
18. Ibid.
19. Ibid., 175, 185.
20. Ibid., 216.
21. Sawyers, *Celtic Music*, 145–49.
22. Ibid., 229.
23. Wright, *Irish Emigrant Ballads*, 120, 350.
24. Ibid., 118.

25. Wright, *Irish Emigrant Ballads*, 614.
26. Ibid., 40.
27. Ibid., 131, 141, 350, 183, 124.
28. Ibid., 131, 143.
29. Ibid., 40, 117, 129, 153, 178, 406.
30. Ibid., 155, 40, 178.
31. Ibid., 178, 183, 117.
32. Ibid., 45, 120, 183, 350.
33. Ibid., 169, 178, 621.
34. Ibid., 40, 163, 168.
35. Ibid., 45, 170, 402.
36. Ibid., 353, 123, 138, 349, 364.
37. Ibid., 123.
38. Ibid., 183.
39. Ibid., 40.
40. Ibid., 104.
41. Ibid., 117, 138.
42. Ibid., 40, 47.
43. Miller, *Emigrants and Exiles*, 560–68.
44. Wright, *Irish Emigrant Ballads*, 118, 117, 35, 45; cf. 161, 164, 168, and many others.
45. Ibid., 180.
46. Ibid., 140, 160, 175, 180.
47. Ibid., 180, 163.
48. Ibid., 200.
49. Ibid., 45.
50. Ibid., 40, 129, 160, 175, 200.
51. Ibid., 130; italics in Wright edition.
52. Miller, *Emigrants and Exiles*, 566–67.
53. Wright, *Irish Emigrant Ballads*, 124, 130, 159, 170–72.
54. Ibid., 159, 45, 168.
55. Ibid., 138, 170, 175, 104.
56. Ibid., 35.
57. Ibid., 283–300.
58. Ibid., 132.
59. Ibid., 158.
60. Ibid., 104, 138, 170, 181, and Miller, *Emigrants and Exiles*, 134.
61. Wright, *Irish Emigrant Ballads*, 169, 140, 181.
62. Ibid., 160, 175.
63. Ibid., 525.
64. Ibid., 129.
65. Ibid., 153.
66. Ibid., 130, 169, 138.
67. Ibid., 130, 614.
68. Ibid., 104, 160, 190, 614, and others.
69. Ibid., 505.

70. Ibid., 159.
71. Miller, *Emigrants and Exiles*, 425; Schrier, *Ireland and American Emigration*, 111–13.
72. Wright, *Irish Emigrant Ballads*, 140, 153.
73. Ibid., 178; cf. 201.
74. Ibid., 159; cf. 427.
75. Ibid., 506.
76. Ibid., 158, 164.
77. Ibid., 129, 352, 132.
78. Ibid., 40, 117, 132.
79. Ibid., 129.
80. Ibid., 164, 203.
81. Ibid., 168, 120.
82. Sawyers, *Celtic Music*, 234.
83. Miller, *Emigrants and Exiles*, 565.
84. Ibid.
85. Ibid., xiv.
86. Miller, *Emigrants and Exiles*, 560–61.
87. Dezell, *Coming into Clover*, 2, 115.
88. Sawyers, *Celtic Music*, 245, and Williams, *Irishman's Dream*, 215.
89. Dezell, *Coming into Clover*, 101.
90. Williams, *Irishman's Dream*, 26.
91. Lyrics to both "Mother Machree" and "I'll Take You Home Again, Kathleen" can be found at websites cited in the Videography/Discography/Song Lyrics section of the Bibliography.
92. Williams, *Irishman's Dream*, 1, 18.
93. Ibid., 22–24.
94. Ibid., 33, 6.
95. Ibid., 6; italics are Williams's.
96. Ibid., 25.
97. Ibid., 27.
98. Ibid., 45.
99. Ibid., 38–48.
100. Dezell, *Coming into Clover*, 2.
101. Lysaght, *Banshee*, 64.

Chapter 2   What Americans Know and How They Know It: Story

1. Binchy, "Writers on Writing."
2. Ennis, introduction to Peig Sayers, *An Old Woman's Reflections*, vii.
3. Lysagh, *Banshee*, 64; see also MacLennan, *Lore of Annie Bhán*, 11.
4. Dezell, *Coming into Clover*, 2.
5. Harvey, *Contemporary Irish Traditional Narrative*, 20–32.

6. Harvey, *Contemporary Irish Traditional Narrative*, 7.
7. Ibid., 8; see also MacLennan, *Lore of Annie Bhán*, 14.
8. Harvey, *Contemporary Irish Traditional Narrative*, 7.
9. Ibid., 13.
10. Ibid., 12–13.
11. Ibid., 12, 48.
12. Zimmerman, *Irish Storyteller*, 432.
13. Harvey, *Contemporary Irish Traditional Narrative*, 12.
14. Ibid., 5; see also 4–6.
15. Ibid., 6, 12, 47.
16. Ibid., 6, 12.
17. Ibid., 9–11.
18. Ibid., 5.
19. Zimmerman, *Irish Storyteller*, 439.
20. Harvey, *Contemporary Irish Traditional Narrative*, 5.
21. White, *Remembering Ahanagran*, 51; cf. Zimmerman, *Irish Storyteller*, 358.
22. Ibid.
23. Quoted in Thomson, *Island Home*, 58.
24. Harvey, *Contemporary Irish Traditional Narrative*, 5–6.
25. Zimmerman, *Irish Storyteller*, 450.
26. MacLennan, *Lore of Annie Bhán*, 12.
27. White, *Remembering Ahanagran*, 49.
28. Ibid., 21.
29. Zimmerman, *Irish Storyteller*, 446.
30. MacLennan, *Lore of Annie Bhán*, 12.
31. Zimmerman, *Irish Storyteller*, 420.
32. Ibid., 433.
33. Harvey, *Contemporary Irish Traditional Narrative*, 20.
34. Ibid., 37.
35. Weber, *Music Lesson*, 47.
36. Ibid.
37. Zimmerman, *Irish Storyteller*, 10.
38. Ibid., 12.
39. Barry, *Whereabouts of Eneas McNulty*, 38.
40. White, *Remembering Ahanagran*, 6.
41. Ibid., 188.
42. Ibid., 50.

Chapter 3   "Picture Postcard Ireland": Thomas Moran's *The World I Made for Her*

1. Moran, *World*, 189.
2. Ibid., 17–18.
3. Ibid., 18.

4. Diner, *Erin's Daughters*, 70–71, 95; Coffey and Golway, *Irish in America*, 147.
5. Moran, *World*, 218.
6. Ibid., 47.
7. *Táin*, translated by Kinsella, 53.
8. Bowen, "Great-Bladdered Medb," 20.
9. Ibid., 19–20; see also Green, *Celtic Myths*, 70–74, 79–81.
10. Bowen, "Great-Bladdered Medb," 19.
11. Welch, *Oxford Concise Companion*, 234; cf. Green, *Dictionary*, 147, and Bowen, "Great-Bladdered Medb," 21.
12. Bowen, "Great-Bladdered Medb," 21, 24.
13. *Medline Plus Drug Information*, "Fentanyl (Systemic)."
14. Bowen, "Great-Bladdered Medb," 24.
15. Williams, *Irishman's Dream*, 23, 221.
16. In Pierce, *Irish Writing in the Twentieth Century*, 45.
17. In Murphy and MacKillop, *Irish Literature*, 114–16.
18. Welch, *Irish Poetry*, 103.
19. Kenny, *American Irish*, 246.
20. Williams, *Irishman's Dream*, 230.
21. Moran, *World*, 38.
22. Ibid., 39.
23. Yeats, *Collected Poems*, 39.
24. Dirk, "*Quiet Man* (1952)."
25. Williams, *Irishman's Dream*, 36.
26. Dezell, *Coming into Clover*, 2.
27. Williams, *Irishman's Dream*, 47.
28. Moran, *World*, 38, 39.
29. Almeida, *Irish Immigrants*, 58–59.
30. Moran, *World*, 3.
31. Ibid., 39.
32. Ibid., 1.
33. Ibid., 70.
34. Ibid., 121.
35. Ibid.
36. Ibid., 38–39.
37. Quoted in Townshend, *Ireland: The 20th Century*, 155.
38. Ibid.
39. Gray, "Unmasking Irishness," 211.
40. Ibid., 210–11.
41. Ibid., 214; italics are Gray's.
42. Moran, *World*, 154–55.
43. Ibid., 90.
44. Ibid., 111–13.
45. Ibid., 143–44.
46. See discussion of American money in chapter 6 in this book.
47. See Coffey and Golway, *Irish in America*, 147.
48. Moran, *World*, 146–47.
49. Ibid., 247.

50. Moran, *World*, 245–46.
51. Almeida, *Irish Immigrants*, 27.
52. Ibid., 126, 4–5.
53. Ibid., 80, 86.
54. Gray, "Unmasking Irishness," 218.
55. Ibid., 229.
56. Almeida, *Irish Immigrants*, 82.
57. Ibid., 140.
58. Dezell, *Coming into Clover*, 2.
59. Wallis and Wilson, *Rough Guide to Irish Music*, 68; Sawyers, *Celtic Music*, 276.
60. Sawyers, *Celtic Music*, 261, 275.
61. Ibid., 261, 275.
62. For lyric, see citation in Videography/Discography/Song Lyrics; see also Murphy and MacKillop, *Irish Literature*, 72–73.
63. Moran, *World*, 207–09.
64. Yeats, *Collected Poems*, 59–60.
65. Moran, *World*, 156.
66. Ibid., 207–09.
67. Ibid., 208.
69. See album notes to Van Morrison and the Chieftain's *Irish Heartbeat* for full lyric.
69. Moran, *World*, 209.
70. Keohane, "Traditionalism and Homelessness," 287.
71. For lyrics to "Siúil A Rúin," see citation in Videography/Discography/Song Lyric section of bibliography; for lyrics to "Tá Mo Chleamhnas Déanta," see album notes to Van Morrison and the Chieftains's *Irish Heartbeat*.
72. Moran, *World*, 52.
73. Yeats, *Collected Poems*, 59.
74. "Dream of Óengus," translated by Gantz, 107.
75. Dillon, *Early Irish Literature*, 50.
76. "Dream of Óengus," translated by Gantz, 111.
77. See album notes to *Irish Heartbeat* for full lyrics.
78. Moran, *World*, 272.

Chapter 4   Naming the Past:
Lisa Carey's *The Mermaids Singing*

1. Carey, *Mermaids Singing*, 7.
2. Lysaght, *Banshee*, 64.
3. Gregory, *Irish Myths and Legends*, 321–70.
4. Green, *Dictionary*, 108.
5. Quoted in Rees, *Celtic Heritage*, 282.
6. Gregory, *Irish Myths and Legends*, 354.
7. Bitel, *Land of Women*, 41.

8. Ibid., 41.
9. Ibid., 45.
10. Ibid., 51.
11. Gregory, *Irish Myths and Legends*, 353.
12. Bitel, *Land of Women*, 63.
13. Ní Bhrolcháin, "Women in Early Irish Myths and Sagas," 530.
14. Gregory, "Grania," 216.
15. Gregory, *Irish Myths and Legends*, 323.
16. Ellis, *Celtic Women*, 49; Ellis, *Dictionary of Celtic Mythology*, 140.
17. Gregory, *Irish Myths and Legends*, 129–31.
18. Carey, *Mermaids Singing*, 329.
19. Green, *Celtic Myths*, 46.
20. Chambers, *Granuaile*, 52.
21. Ibid., 64, 59.
22. Ibid., 68, 23.
23. Ibid., 71, 73.
24. Quoted in ibid., 11.
25. Quoted in ibid., 87.
26. Ibid., 68.
27. Ibid., 70, 77, 79–80.
28. Ibid., 80.
29. Ibid., 81.
30. Quoted in ibid., 82.
31. Carey, *Mermaids Singing*, 226.
32. Ibid., 27.
33. Ibid., 73.
34. Ibid., 8.
35. Ibid., 139.
36. Higgins, *Irish Mermaids*, 13.
37. Ibid., 23; cf. *Ireland On-Line*, "Galway's Medieval Mermaids."
38. Higgins, *Irish Mermaids*, 24–25.
39. Carey, *Mermaids Singing*, 195–96.
40. Ibid., 187–88.
41. Higgins, *Irish Mermaids*, 23, 32–34.
42. Carey, *Mermaids Singing*, 241.
43. Ibid., 242.
44. Ibid., 210.
45. Ibid., 142.
46. Ibid., 316; italics are Carey's.
47. Higgins, *Irish Mermaids*, 22.
48. Carey, *Mermaids Singing*, 2.
49. Ibid., 35.
50. Ibid., 278.
51. Ibid., 19.
52. Ibid., 131–33.
53. Ibid., 143.

54. Carey, *Mermaids Singing*, 155–57.
55. Ibid., 255.
56. Ibid., 256.
57. Ibid., 257.
58. Ibid., 260.
59. Ibid.
60. Ibid.
61. Ibid.
62. Ibid.; italics are Carey's.
63. Ibid., 314–20.
64. Ibid., 234.
65. Ibid., 338–39.
66. Ibid.; italics are Carey's.

Chapter 5   The Pain of Not Knowing: Katharine Weber's *The Music Lesson*

1. James Joyce, *Portrait*, 28.
2. Shannon, *American Irish*, 18, 23.
3. Weber, *Music Lesson*, 21.
4. Ibid.
5. Ó Corráin, "Prehistoric and Early Christian Ireland," 38–41.
6. Canny, "Early Modern Ireland," 150–53.
7. Coogan, *IRA*, 6.
8. Weber, *Music Lesson*, 29.
9. Ibid., 124.
10. Coogan, *IRA*, 5; see also Woodham-Smith, *Great Hunger*, 411–13; Mulcrone, "Famine and Collective Memory," 219; and Ó Gráda, *Black '47 and Beyond*, 41, 85, 105.
11. Weber, *Music Lesson*, 37.
12. See, e.g., the comments on Trevelyan and the Relief Commission in Woodham-Smith's *Great Hunger*, and Ó Gráda, *Black '47 and Beyond*, 78, 82.
13. Quoted in Mulcrone, "Famine and Collective Memory," 219.
14. Woodham-Smith, *Great Hunger*, 75.
15. Weber, *Music Lesson*, 21.
16. Fitzpatrick, "Ireland Since 1870," 239.
17. Coogan, *IRA*, 19.
18. Ibid., 20–21.
19. Weber, *Music Lesson*, 52–53.
20. Fitzpatrick, "Ireland Since 1870," 250.
21. Weber, *Music Lesson*, 21.
22. Miller, " 'Revenge for Skibbereen,' " 180–85; cf. Woodham-Smith, *Great Hunger*, 161–64, and Ó Gráda, *Black '47 and Beyond*, 68. Several versions of

the ballad Miller discusses can be found in Wright, *Irish Emigrant Ballads*, 52–64.

23. Weber, *Music Lesson*, 23.
24. Ibid., 33.
25. Ibid., 36.
26. Ibid., 29.
27. Maureen Waters, *Comic Irishman*, 28.
28. Ibid., 29.
29. Weber, *Music Lesson*, 69.
30. Ibid., 103.
31. Ibid., 8–9.
32. Ibid., 128, 50.
33. Ibid., 46–47.
34. Ibid., 176.
35. Ibid., 116.
36. Ibid., 132.
37. Maureen Waters, *Comic Irishman*, 5.
38. Weber, *Music Lesson*, 15.
39. Ibid., 13.
40. P.W. Joyce, *English as We Speak It*, 216.
41. Maureen Waters, *Comic Irishman*, 3.
42. Coogan, *IRA*, 35.
43. Heaney, *Opened Ground*, 123.
44. Weber, *Music Lesson*, 5.
45. Ibid.
46. Ibid., 115.
47. Ibid., 108.
48. Ibid., 75.
49. Ibid., 115.
50. Ibid., 104.
51. Ibid., 115–16.
52. James Joyce, *Portrait*, 28.
53. Weber, *Music Lesson*, 116.
54. Ibid.
55. Ibid., 115.
56. Ibid., 119.
57. Ibid., 147.
58. Ibid., 115.
59. Coogan, *IRA*, 291.
60. Weber, *Music Lesson*, 147–48.
61. Ibid., 149.
62. Ibid., 161–62.
63. Ibid., 36.
64. Coogan, *IRA*, 508.
65. Weber, *Music Lesson*, 105.

66. Weber, *Music Lesson*, 105–06.
67. Ibid., 106.
68. See Coogan, *IRA*, 94.
69. Weber, *Music Lesson*, 107.
70. Coogan, *IRA*, 165.
71. Ibid., 165–66.
72. Ibid., 166.
73. Ibid., 99, 290.
74. Ibid., xiii; 99; n. 168
75. Ibid., 290.
76. Ibid., 29.
77. Ibid., 223.
78. Weber, *Music Lesson*, 106–07.
79. Ibid., 21.
80. Ibid., 46.
81. Ibid., 117–18.
82. Ibid., 145.
83. Ibid., 158.
84. Ibid., 290.
85. Ibid., 161; italics are Weber's.
86. Ibid., 7.
87. *Táin*, translated by Kinsella, 77.
88. Ibid., 44–45.
89. Kiberd, "Irish Literature and Irish History," 287–88.
90. Edwards, *Patrick Pearse*, 14–15. The story can be found in *The Táin*, translated by Kinsella, 76–92.
91. Quoted in ibid., 116.
92. Quoted in ibid., 117.
93. Kiberd, "Irish Literature and Irish History," 288.
94. Edwards, *Patrick Pearse*, 119, 123.
95. Ibid., 131, 133.
96. Ibid., 142.
97. Ibid.
98. Coogan, *IRA*, 171, 181.
99. Edwards, *Patrick Pearse*, 52–54, 126–28.
100. *Táin*, translated by Kinsella, 132–33.
101. Coogan, *IRA*, 461.
102. Weber, *Music Lesson*, 117.
103. Ibid., 115.
104. Ibid., 158.
105. Ibid., 161.
106. Ibid., 177.
107. James Joyce, *Portrait*, 27.
108. Weber, *Music Lesson*, 178.
109. Ibid., 176.
110. Ibid., 36.

Chapter 6   Bringing Paddies Over:
Alice McDermott's *Charming Billy*

1. McDermott, *Charming Billy*, 5.
2. Ibid.
3. Ibid., 63.
4. Ibid., 26.
5. Ibid., 12.
6. Ibid., 12–13; cf. 67.
7. Ibid., 104.
8. Miller, *Emigrants and Exiles*, 271.
9. Ibid., 273.
10. McDermott, *Charming Billy*, 22.
11. Miller, *Emigrants and Exiles*, 520.
12. McDermott, *Charming Billy*, 39; cf. 108.
13. Ibid., 104–05.
14. Diner, *Erin's Daughters*, 66, 67, 117.
15. See Donovan, "Good Old Pat," and Dodge, "Irish Comic Stereotype."
16. Shannon, *American Irish*, 24.
17. Ibid.
18. Nolan, *Ourselves Alone*, 35.
19. McDermott, *Charming Billy*, 70.
20. Ibid., 119.
21. Ibid., 209.
22. Ibid., 123.
23. Ibid., 125.
24. Ibid., 39.
25. Miller, *Emigrants and Exiles*, 134.
26. McDermott, *Charming Billy*, 29–30.
27. Ibid., 31.
28. Ibid., 32.
29. Ibid., 34.
30. Ibid., 32.
31. Ibid., 214.
32. Ibid., 138.
33. Williams, *Irishman's Dream*, 27, 225.
34. Diner, *Erin's Daughters*, 30–31.
35. Laxton, *Famine Ships*, 15–17.
36. Schrier, *Ireland and American Emigration*, 25.
37. "Danny Boy: In Sunshine or in Shadow."
38. Miller, *Emigrants*, 560; this tradition is discussed further, in chapter 7 on Gordon's *Other Side*.
39. McDermott, *Charming Billy*, 51; italics are McDermott's.
40. Ibid., 115.

41. Williams, *Irishman's Dream*, 48.
42. Ibid., 39.
43. Ibid.
44. McDermott, *Charming Billy*, 10.
45. Ibid.
46. Ibid., 34.
47. Ibid., 213–14.
48. Ibid., 194.
49. Yeats, *Collected Poems*, 39.
50. McDermott, *Charming Billy*, 52; italics are McDermott's.
51. Ibid., 29.
52. Ibid., 37.
53. Ibid., 68.
54. Ibid., 114, 66.
55. Ibid., 227.
56. Ibid., 214.
57. Yeats, *Collected Poems*, 20.
58. See Videography/Discography/Song Lyrics for three versions.
59. Diner, *Erin's Daughters*, 11.
60. Loesberg, *Folksongs and Ballads*, 66.
61. McDermott, *Charming Billy*, 6.
62. Miller, *Emigrants and Exiles*, 425.
63. Ibid., 134.
64. Schrier, *Ireland and American Emigration*, 111–13, 115.
65. Ibid., 112.
66. Ibid.
67. Ibid.
68. Ibid., 117.
69. Quoted in Miller, *Emigrants and Exiles*, 485.
70. McDermott, *Charming Billy*, 219.
71. Ibid.
72. Miller, *Emigrants and Exiles*, 463.
73. McDermott, *Charming Billy*, 69, 74, 75, 73.
74. Diner, *Erin's Daughters*, 72.
75. Ibid., 74–94; Nolan, *Ourselves Alone*, 67, 79.
76. Quoted in Schrier, *Ireland and American Emigration*, 78.
77. McDermott, *Charming Billy*, 84–85.
78. Ibid., 68.
79. Ibid., 17.
80. Ibid, 221.
81. Ibid., 215–17.
82. Ibid., 222–23.
83. Ibid., 19–21, 23.
84. Ibid., 15, 4.
85. Diner, *Erin's Daughters*, 64; see also Shannon, *American Irish*, 21–22.
86. Shannon, *American Irish*, 21.

87. Miller, *Emigrants and Exiles*, 76, 241.
88. McDermott, *Charming Billy*, 14–15.
89. Ibid., 204.
90. Ibid., 206.
91. Ibid., 23.
92. Ibid., 204.
93. Ibid., 242.
94. Ibid., 113.
95. Ibid.
96. Ibid., 115.
97. Ibid., 131.
98. Ibid., 187.
99. Ibid., 194.
100. Fanning, *Irish Voice in America*, 391.
101. McDermott, *Charming Billy*, 243.

Chapter 7   The Rage of the Dying Animal: Mary Gordon's *The Other Side*

1. Gordon, *Other Side*, 185, 323.
2. Fanning, "Heart's Speech," 510.
3. Miller, *Emigrants and Exiles*, 4–5.
4. Kenny, *American Irish*, 134.
5. Miller, *Emigrants and Exiles*, 4–7.
6. Gordon, *Other Side*, 6.
7. Ibid., 41.
8. Ibid., 6.
9. Ibid., 85.
10. Ibid., 86.
11. Ibid.
12. Ibid., 87.
13. Ibid., 86.
14. Ibid.
15. Ibid., 249–50.
16. Ibid., 251.
17. Wright, *Irish Emigrant Ballads*, 610–13.
18. Gordon, *Other Side*, 159.
19. Ibid., 225.
20. Wright, *Irish Emigrant Ballads*, 626.
21. Gordon, *Other Side*, 229.
22. Ibid.
23. Ibid., 223.
24. Miller, *Emigrants and Exiles*, 557.
25. Neville, "*Rites de Passage*," 118.

26. Miller, *Emigrants and Exiles*, 557; cf. Neville, "*Rîtes de Passage*," 118.
27. Neville, "*Rîtes de Passage*," 121.
28. Miller, *Emigrants and Exiles*, 557; see also Neville, "*Rîtes de Passage*."
29. Neville, "*Rîtes de Passage*," 121.
30. Ibid., 120, 125.
31. Ibid., 126.
32. Miller, *Emigrants and Exiles*, 56.
33. See ibid., 557–68, and Neville's "*Rîtes de Passage*" for a fuller description of the American wake.
34. Gordon, *Other Side*, 242.
35. Neville, "*Rîtes de Passage*," 121, 119.
36. Gordon, *Other Side*, 243; cf. Neville, "*Rîtes de Passage*," 128.
37. Gordon, *Other Side*, 243.
38. Neville, "*Rîtes de Passage*," 125.
39. Gordon, *Other Side*, 235.
40. Ibid., 236.
41. Sutherland, *Americans and Their Servants*, 3–5.
42. Ibid., 10.
43. Ibid., 11.
44. Ibid., 27.
45. Ibid., 38–39; see also Dudden, *Serving Women*, 67–69.
46. Katzman, *Seven Days a Week*, 66.
47. Sutherland, *Americans and Their Servants*, 40.
48. Gordon, *Other Side*, 112.
49. Sutherland, *Americans and Their Servants*, 83.
50. Ibid.
51. Gordon, *Other Side*, 109.
52. Birmingham, *Real Lace*, 44.
53. Sutherland, *Americans and Their Servants*, 115–16.
54. Gordon, *Other Side*, 116.
55. Sutherland, *Americans and Their Servants*, 53.
56. Ibid., 117.
57. Ibid.
58. Birmingham, *Real Lace*, 42.
59. Ibid.
60. Diner, *Erin's Daughters*, 90.
61. Sutherland, *Americans and Their Servants*, 109.
62. Coffey and Golway, *Irish in America*, 138.
63. Gordon, *Other Side*, 117.
64. Sutherland, *Americans and Their Servants*, 99; cf. Miller, "Assimilation," 96.
65. Quoted in Katzman, *Seven Days a Week*, 36.
66. Gordon, *Other Side*, 118; italics are Gordon's.
67. Sutherland, *Americans and Their Servants*, 101.
68. Birmingham, *Real Lace*, 45.
69. Gordon, *Other Side*, 123, 122.
70. Sutherland, *Americans and Their Servants*, 110–11.

71. Gordon, *Other Side*, 302.
72. Ibid., 290.
73. Browne, *Catholic Church and Knights*, 7–11, 25–26.
74. Ibid., 13.
75. Ibid., 12–16.
76. Ibid., 98.
77. Kenny, *Molly Maguires*, 160.
78. Ibid., 161; see also Ignatiev, *How the Irish Became White*, 92–93.
79. Gordon, *Other Side*, 297.
80. See Freeman, *In Transit*, 34.
81. Ibid., vii, 27; see also Kenny, *American Irish*, 188–89.
82. Browne, *Catholic Church and Knights*, 118.
83. Ibid., 357.
84. Freeman, *In Transit*, 105.
85. Ibid.
86. Ibid., 104.
87. Ibid., 139; cf. Kenny, *American Irish,* 207–08.
88. Freeman, *In Transit*, 25–26.
89. Ibid., 123.
90. Gordon, *Other Side*, 168.
91. Ibid., 148.
92. Kenny, *American Irish*, 208.
93. Freeman, *In Transit*, 105.
94. Ibid., 104; cf. Kenny, *American Irish*, 168–69.
95. Freeman, *In Transit*, 106.
96. See Townshend, *Ireland: The 20th Century*, 25–34, and the famous Christmas dinner argument about Parnell in James Joyce's *Portrait*, 39–46.
97. Freeman, *In Transit*, 106.
98. James Joyce, *Portrait*, 39; italics are Joyce's.
99. Freeman, *In Transit*, 33.
100. Almeida, *Irish Immigrants*, 18–19.
101. James Joyce, *Portrait*, 45.
102. Gordon, *Other Side*, 302.
103. Ibid., 301.
104. Erie, *Rainbow's End*, 61; see also Bayor and Meagher, introduction to *New York Irish*, 5; and McCaffrey, "Forging Forward," 222.
105. Gordon, *Other Side*, 8.
106. Ibid., 9.
107. Ibid., 184.
108. Ibid.
109. Ibid., 361–62.
110. Ibid., 200.
111. Ibid., 34.
112. Ibid., 59.
113. Ibid.
114. Ibid.

115. Gordon, *Other Side*, 64.
116. Ibid., 23.
117. Ibid., 197.
118. Ibid., 192.
119. Ibid., 159–60.
120. Ibid., 160.
121. Ibid.
122. Ibid., 162.
123. Ibid., 163.
124. Gordon, "Anger," 30.
125. Gordon, *Other Side*, 63.
126. Gordon, "Anger," 37.
127. Ibid., 38.
128. McCaffrey, "Forging Forward," 218.

Conclusion   The Journey

1. " 'Danny Boy': In Sunshine or in Shadow."
2. Williams, *Irishman's Dream*, 227.
3. Clark, *Irish Relations*, 76–78; Miller, *Emigrants and Exiles*, 426, 428.
4. Ibid., 82–83.
5. Ibid., 84.
6. McCann interview. I am indebted to my student Richard Barkey for calling my attention to this interview.
7. Clark, *Irish Relations*, 77.
8. Neville, "*Rîtes de Passage*," 117.
9. Jeffers, *Irish Novel*, 1–6.
10. Gray, "Unmasking Irishness," 209.
11. Rawlings, "Come Back Irish," 2.
12. Ibid., 3, 7–9.
13. Jen, "Who's Irish?" 6, 3, 16.
14. "Top One Hundred."
15. Jamison, "How Green Was My Surname."
16. Barry, *Whereabouts of Eneas McNulty*, 38.
17. Brian Heron, quoted in Gent, "Irish Arts Center," 72.

Bibliography

Primary Sources

Barry, Sebastian. *The Whereabouts of Eneas McNulty*. New York: Penguin Books, 1998.

Carey, Lisa. *The Mermaids Singing*. New York: Avon, 1998.

Gantz, Jeffrey, trans. "Dream of Óengus." In *Early Irish Myths and Sagas*, translated by Jeffrey Gantz, 108–112. London: Penguin Books, 1981.

Gordon, Mary. *The Other Side*. New York: Penguin Books, 1989.

Gregory, Isabella Augusta (Lady). "Grania." In *Selected Plays*, 177–216. London: Putnam, 1962.

———, trans. *Irish Myths and Legends*. 1910. Reprint, Philadelphia: Running Press, 1998.

Hammond, David, ed. *A Centenary Selection of Moore's Melodies*. Introduction by Seamus Heaney. Skerries: Gilbert Dalton, 1979.

Heaney, Seamus. *Opened Ground: Selected Poems, 1966–1996*. New York: Farrar, Straus and Giroux, 1998.

Jen, Gish. *Who's Irish?: Stories*. New York: Knopf, 1998.

Joyce, James. *A Portrait of the Artist as a Young Man*. 1914–15. Reprint edited by R.B. Kershner. Boston: Bedford/St. Martin's, 1993.

Kiely, Benedict. "Homes on the Mountain." In *The Penguin Book of Irish Fiction*, edited and introduction by Colm Tóibín, 673–681. London: Viking Penguin, 1999.

Kinsella, Thomas, trans. *The Táin: From the Irish Epic Táin Bó Cuailnge*. Oxford: Oxford University Press, 1970.

McCourt, Frank. *Angela's Ashes*. New York: Simon and Schuster, 1996.

McDermott, Alice. *Charming Billy*. New York: Dell, 1998.

Moore, Thomas. *Complete Poetical Works*. Vol. I. New York: Crowell, 1895.

Moran, Thomas. *The World I Made for Her*. New York: Riverhead, 1998.

Rawlings, Wendy. *Come Back Irish*. Columbus: Ohio State University Press, 2001.

Sayers, Peig. *An Old Woman's Reflections*. Translated and introduction by Seamus Ennis. London: Oxford University Press, 1962.

Weber, Katherine. *The Music Lesson*. New York: Picador USA, 1999.

Wright, Robert L. ed., *Irish Emigrant Ballads and Songs*. Bowling Green, OH: Bowling Green University Press, 1975.

Yeats, William Butler. *The Collected Poems of W. B. Yeats*. Revised 2nd ed. Edited by Richard J. Finneran. New York: Scribner Paperback Poetry, 1996.

Secondary Sources

Almeida, Linda Dowling. *Irish Immigrants in New York City, 1945–1995*. Bloomington: Indiana University Press, 2001.

Bayor, Ronald H., and Timothy J. Meagher, eds. *The New York Irish*. Baltimore, MD: Johns Hopkins University Press, 1996.

Binchy, Maeve. "Writers on Writing: For the Irish, Long-Windedness Serves as a Literary Virtue." *New York Times*, November 4, 2002, sec. E.

Birmingham, Stephen. *Real Lace: America's Irish Rich*. New York: Harper and Row, 1973.

Bitel, Lisa. *Land of Women: Tales of Sex and Gender from Early Ireland*. Ithaca, NY: Cornell University Press. 1996.

Bowen, Charles. "Great-Bladdered Medb: Mythology and Invention in the *Táin Bó Cuailnge*." *Éire-Ireland* 10 (1975): 14–34.

Browne, Henry J. *The Catholic Church and the Knights of Labor*. Washington, DC: Catholic University of America Press, 1949.

Canny, Nicholas. "Early Modern Ireland, c. 1500–1700." In Foster, *Oxford Illustrated History*, 104–60.

Chambers, Anne. *Granuaile: The Life and Times of Grace O'Malley, c. 1530–1603*. 1979. Revised edition. Dublin: Wolfhound, 1998.

Clark, Dennis. *The Irish Relations: Trials of an Immigrant Tradition*. Rutherford, NJ: Fairleigh Dickenson University Press, 1982.

Coffey, Michael, and Terry Golway. *The Irish in America*. Edited by Michael Coffey. New York: Hyperion, 1997.

Coogan, Tim Pat. *The IRA: A History*. Niwot, CO: Roberts Rinehart, 1994.

Dezell, Maureen. *Irish America Coming into Clover: The Evolution of a People and a Culture*. New York: Doubleday, 2000.

Dillon, Miles. *Early Irish Literature*. 1948. Reprint, Dublin: Four Courts, 1994.

Diner, Hasia. *Erin's Daughters in America: Irish Immigrant Women in the Nineteenth Century*. Baltimore, MD: Johns Hopkins University Press, 1983.

———. "Overview: 'The Most Irish City in the Union,' The Era of the Great Migration, 1844–1877." In Bayor and Meagher, *New York Irish*, 87–106.

Dirks, Tom. "*Quiet Man* (1952)." <http://www.filmsite.org/quie.html> (July 30, 2002).

Dodge, Robert K. "The Irish Comic Stereotype in the Almanacs of the Early Republic." *Éire-Ireland: A Journal of Irish Studies* 19, no. 3 (1984): 111–120.

Donovan, Kathleen. "Good Old Pat: An Irish-American Stereotype in Decline." *Éire-Ireland: A Journal of Irish Studies* 15, no. 3 (1980): 6–14.

Dudden, Faye E. *Serving Women: Household Service in Nineteenth-Century America*. Middletown, CT: Wesleyan University Press, 1983.

Edwards, Ruth Dudley. *Patrick Pearse: The Triumph of Failure*. New York: Taplinger, 1978.

Ellis, Peter Berresford. *A Dictionary of Celtic Mythology*. Santa Barbara, CA: ABC-Clio, 1987.

———. *Celtic Women: Women in Celtic Society and Literature*. Grand Rapids, MI: Eerdmans, 1995.

Erie, Steven P. *Rainbow's End: Irish-Americans and the Dilemmas of Urban Machine Politics, 1840–1985*. Berkeley: University of California Press, 1988.

Fanning, Charles. "The Heart's Speech No Longer Stifled: New York Irish Writing Since the 1960s." In Bayor and Meagher, *New York Irish*, 508–31.

———. *The Irish Voice in America: 250 Years of Irish-American Fiction*. 2nd ed. Lexington: University of Kentucky Press, 2000.

Fitzpatrick, David. "Ireland Since 1870." In Foster, *Oxford Illustrated History*, 213–74.

Foster, R.F., ed. *The Oxford Illustrated History of Ireland*. New York: Oxford University Press, 1989.

Freeman, Joshua. *In Transit: The Transport Workers Union in New York City, 1933–1966*. New York: Oxford University Press, 1989.

Geldof, Bob. *Is That It? The Autobiography*. New York: Weidenfeld and Nicolson, 1986.

Gent, George. "Irish Arts Center—A Proud Beginning." *New York Times*, December 7, 1972, sec. A.

Gordon, Mary. "Anger." In *Deadly Sins*, 24–39. New York: Quill / William Morrow, 1993.

Gray, Breda. "Unmasking Irishness: Irish Women, the Irish Nation, and the Irish Diaspora." In MacLaughlin, *Location and Dislocation*, 209–35.

Green, Miranda Jane. *Dictionary of Celtic Myth and Legend*. London: Thames and Hudson, 1992.

———. *Celtic Myths*. Austin: University of Texas Press, 1993.

Gribben, Arthur, ed. *The Great Famine and the Irish Diaspora in America*. Amherst: University of Massachusetts Press, 1999.

Harvey, Clodagh Brennan. *Contemporary Irish Traditional Narrative: The English Language Tradition*. University of California Publications: Folklore and Mythology Studies 35. Berkeley: University of California Press, 1992.

Hayden, Tom, ed. *Irish Hunger: Personal Reflections on the Legacy of the Famine*. Introduction by Tom Hayden. Boulder, CO: Roberts Rinehart, 1997.

Higgins, Jim. *Irish Mermaids: Sirens, Temptresses and their Symbolism in Art, Architecture and Folklore*. Galway: Crow's Rock, 1995.

Ignatiev, Noel. *How the Irish Became White*. New York: Routledge, 1995.

Ireland On-Line. "Galway's Medieval Mermaids." <http://cgi-bin.iol.ie/resource/ga/archive/1995/Nov30/old.html> (February 15, 2005).

Jamison, S. Lee. "How Green Was My Surname: Via Ireland, a Chapter in the Story of Black America." *New York Times*, March 17, 2003, sec. B.

Jeffers, Jennifer M. *The Irish Novel at the End of the Twentieth Century: Gender, Bodies, and Power*. New York: Palgrave, 2002.

Joyce, P.W. *English as We Speak It in Ireland*. 1910. Introduction by Terence Dolan. Dublin: Wolfhound, 1991.

Katzman, David M. *Seven Days a Week: Women and Domestic Service in Industrializing America*. New York: Oxford University Press, 1978.

Kenny, Kevin. *Making Sense of the Molly Maguires*. New York: Oxford University Press, 1998.

———. *The American Irish: A History*. Harlow, UK: Longman, 2000.

Keohane, Kieran. "Traditionalism and Homelessness in Contemporary Irish Music." In MacLaughlin, *Location and Dislocation*, 274–303.

Kiberd, Declan. "Irish Literature and Irish History." In Foster, *Oxford Illustrated History*, 275–338.

Lacey, Brian. "The People Lost and Forgot." In Hayden, *Irish Hunger*, 79–92.

Laxton, Edward. *The Famine Ships: The Irish Exodus to America 1846–51*. London: Bloomsbury, 1997.

Lysaght, Patricia. *A Pocket Book of the Banshee*. Dublin: O'Brien, 1998.

MacLaughlin, Jim, ed. *Location and Dislocation in Contemporary Irish Society: Emigration and Irish Identities*. Cork: Cork University Press, 1997.

MacLennan, Gordon W. *The Lore of Annie Bhán [Seanchas Annie Bhán]*. Edited and translated by Alan Harrison and Máiri Elena Crook. Dublin: Seanchas Annie Bhán Publication Committee, 1997.

McCafferty, Nell. "Whatever You Say, Say Nothing." In Hayden, *Irish Hunger*, 160–164.

McCaffrey, Lawrence. *Textures of Irish America*. Syracuse: Syracuse University Press, 1992.

———. "Forging Forward and Looking Back." In Bayor and Meagher, *New York Irish*, 213–33.

McCann, Colum. Interview by Leonard Lopate. *The Leonard Lopate Show*. WNYC, January 22, 2003.

Medline Plus Drug Information. "Fentanyl (Systemic)." <http://www.nlm.nih.gov/medlineplus/druginfo/uspi/203780.html#SXX20> (February 15, 2005).

Miller, Kerby A. " 'Revenge for Skibbereen': Irish Emigration and the Meaning of the Great Famine." In Gribben, *Great Famine*, 180–95.

———. "Assimilation and Alienation: Irish Emigrants' Responses to Industrial America, 1871–1921." *The Irish in America: Emigration, Assimilation, and Impact*. Edited by P.J. Drudy, 87–112. Cambridge: Cambridge University Press, 1985.

———. *Emigrants and Exiles: Ireland and the Irish Exodus to North America*. New York: Oxford University Press, 1985.

Mulcrone, Mick. "The Famine and Collective Memory: The Role of the Irish-American Press in the Early Twentieth Century." In Gribben, *Great Famine*, 219–38.

Murphy, Maureen, and James MacKillop. *Irish Literature: A Reader*. Syracuse: Syracuse University Press, 1987.

Neville, Grace. "*Rîtes de Passage*: Rituals of Separation in Irish Oral Tradition." In *New Perspectives on the Irish Diaspora*, edited by Charles Fanning, 117–130. Carbondale: Southern Illinois University Press, 2000.

Ní Bhrolcháin, Muireann. "Women in Early Irish Myths and Sagas." *The Crane Bag* 4, no.1 (1980): 12–18.

Nolan, Janet A. *Ourselves Alone: Women's Emigration from Ireland, 1885–1920*. Lexington: University Press of Kentucky, 1989.

Ó Corráin, Donnchadh, "Prehistoric and Early Christian Ireland." In Foster, *Oxford Illustrated History*, 1–52.

Ó Gráda, Cormac. *Black '47 and Beyond: The Great Irish Famine in History, Economy, and Memory*. Princeton, NJ: Princeton University Press, 1999.

Pierce, David. *Irish Writing in the Twentieth Century: A Reader*. Cork: Cork University Press, 2000.

Quinn, Edward. *A Dictionary of Literary and Thematic Terms*. New York: Checkmark, 1999.

Ramsay, Carolyn. "The Need to Feed." In Hayden, *Irish Hunger*, 137–142.

Rees, Alwyn, and Brinley Rees. *Celtic Heritage: Ancient Tradition in Ireland and Wales*. London: Thames and Hudson, 1961.

Sawyers, June Skinner. *Celtic Music: A Complete Guide*. Cambridge, MA: Da Capo, 2000.

Schefer-Hughes, Nancy. *Saints, Scholars, and Schizophrenics: Mental Illness in Rural Ireland*. Berkeley: University of California Press, 1979.

Schrier, Arnold. *Ireland and the American Emigration, 1850–1900*. Chester Springs, PA: Dufour Editions, 1997.

Shannon, William V. *The American Irish*. New York: Macmillan, 1963.

Stivers, Richard. *The Hair of the Dog: Irish Drinking and American Stereotype*. University Park: Pennsylvania State University Press, 1976.

Sutherland, Daniel E. *Americans and Their Servants: Domestic Service in the United States from 1800 to 1920*. Baton Rouge: Louisiana State University Press, 1981.

Thomson, George. *Island Home: The Blasket Heritage*. Dingle: Brandon, 1998.

Todd, Loreto. *Green English: Ireland's Influence on the English Language*. Dublin: O'Brien, 1999.

"Top One Hundred." *Irish America*, April/May 2001, 28–84.

Townshend, Charles. *Ireland: The 20th Century*. London: Arnold; New York: Oxford University Press, 1999.

Truss, Lynne. *Eats, Shoots & Leaves: The Zero Tolerance Approach to Punctuation*. New York: Penguin/Gotham, 2003.

Wallis, Geoff, and Sue Wilson. *The Rough Guide to Irish Music*. London: Penguin Books, 2001.

Waters, John. "Troubled People." In Hayden, *Irish Hunger*, 100–112.

Waters, Maureen. *The Comic Irishman*. Albany: State University of New York Press, 1984.

Welch, Robert. *Irish Poetry from Moore to Yeats*. Totowa, NJ: Barnes and Noble, 1980.

———. *Oxford Concise Companion to Irish Literature*. Oxford: Oxford University Press, 1996.

White, Richard. *Remembering Ahanagran: Storytelling in a Family's Past*. New York: Hill and Wang, 1998.

Williams, William H.A. *'Twas Only an Irishman's Dream: The Image of Ireland and the Irish in American Popular Song Lyrics, 1800–1920*. Urbana: University of Illinois Press, 1996.

Woodham-Smith, Cecil. *The Great Hunger: Ireland 1845–1849*. 1962. Reprint, London: Penguin Books, 1991.

Zimmerman, Georges. *The Irish Storyteller*. Dublin: Four Courts, 2001.

Videography, Discography, Song Lyrics

"Billy Boy." In *Folk Music of England, Scotland, Ireland, Wales and America*. <http://www.contemplator.com/folk.html> (February 15, 2005).

Black 47. <http://www.black47.com/> (February 15, 2005).

———. *Fire of Freedom*. SBK Records, 1993.

"Danny Boy: In Sunshine or in Shadow." PBS Home Video DBSS-901.

"Down by the Salley Gardens." In *Folksongs and Ballads Popular in Ireland*, edited by John Loesburg, 66. Vol. 2. Cork: Ossian, 1980.

"I'll Take You Home Again Kathleen." <http://www.contemplator.com/tunebook/american/kathleen.htm> (February 15, 2005).

Morrison, Van, and The Chieftains. *Irish Heartbeat*. Exile Productions, 1998.

"Mother Machree." <http://ingeb.org/songs/theresai.html> (February 15, 2005).

Quiet Man, The. 1952. Dir. John Ford. Los Angeles: Republic Pictures Home Video, 1991.

"*Siúil A Rúin*." <http://www.ceolas.org/artists/Clannad/lyrics/Suiul.html> (February 15, 2005).

INDEX